Grimaldi knew their time was up

They had to reach the cover of the building. He wasn't concerned about his own life as much as Rajero's, and the spunky DEA agent didn't want to listen to anyone. He jumped to his feet, grabbed her and sprinted for the doors.

The Stony Man pilot waited for the sudden and thunderous blasts of the AR and subguns. Instead, his senses detected that the enemy's gunfire had changed directions. Grimaldi reached the front doors, dragging Rajero behind him. He started to push her through, then risked a glance over his shoulder. The gunners' concentration had been redirected to an all-too-familiar person, who was shooting at them from the passenger seat of a huge pickup.

Grimaldi could hardly believe his eyes as he watched Mack Bolan rain sudden and assured destruction upon the enemy.

D1005582

Don Pendleton's Mack Bolan®

Breached

Frontier Wars

BOOK II

A GOLD EAGLE BOOK FROM

WORLDWIDE®

TORONTO • NEW YORK • LONDON
AMSTERDAM • PARIS • SYDNEY • HAMBURG
STOCKHOLM • ATHENS • TOKYO • MILAN
MADRID • WARSAW • BUDAPEST • AUCKLAND

First edition September 2003

ISBN 0-373-61492-6

Special thanks and acknowledgment to
Jon Guenther for his contribution to this work.

BREACHED

Each man must for himself alone decide what is right and what is wrong, which course is patriotic and which isn't. You cannot shirk this and be a man. To decide against your conviction is to be an unqualified inexcusable traitor, both to yourself and to your country, let me label you as they may.

—Mark Twain

I will hold to my convictions until I take my last breath. But until that moment arrives, I will maintain the defense of America with the ferocity and vigilance she deserves, and will *never* betray her trust.

—Mack Bolan

To the members of the United States Border Patrol—
who protect our borders and allow Americans to
slumber with peace and security in that knowledge

CHAPTER ONE

Stony Man Farm, Virginia

Harold Brognola, chief of operations for Stony Man Farm, one of the most covert antiterrorist organizations in the world, was worried about his friend. Nobody had seen or heard from Mack Bolan, aka the Executioner, for the past two days. Stony Man's sources in local police agencies in the area where Bolan had last been seen had no leads. That was unusual, since it wasn't usually difficult for Stony Man to pinpoint the Executioner's usually thunderous activities.

Then again, it wasn't odd for Bolan to be incommunicado with Stony Man for weeks on end. But in the wake of the evidence, the circumstances for Bolan's silence *this* time were damning at best. The Stony Man chief had to shake thoughts from his mind that Bolan might be dead.

"Hal, you're going to pace a hole in the tile," Barbara Price said. There was an imploring tone in her voice. "Would you please sit down?"

"Can't," Brognola said. "I've been sitting so long my ass has gone numb. We've been inactive one day too long, as far as I'm concerned. I wish the Man would let me move on this."

"We don't have any evidence that something has happened to Striker," Price told him. "And we may not have it anytime soon."

"I'm open to suggestions."

"Able Team?"

Brognola shook his head. "Absolutely not. Striker would never forgive me if I went against his wishes."

"Yes, he would."

"Okay, maybe he would," the big Fed conceded, "but I'm not willing to take that chance."

"What about reaching out to local agencies?"

"Too risky, both to Striker and his mission. What we need to do is start pressing the FBI in Florida and Las Vegas to get us more information on Kung Lok activities. At least that would give us something more to work with."

Price reached over to a nearby mound of paperwork and began to sift through the manila folders she'd set there earlier. Brognola knew that the Stony Man mission controller could have probably pulled ninety-five percent of the information from her head, but he realized she was trying to find things to keep her mind occupied just as much as he was. He smiled at her, shaking his head but understanding how she felt.

Price's relationship with the Executioner had always been somewhat of a strange one. He suspected there wasn't any deep, passionate love there—at least not in the romantic sense like Bolan had shared with April Rose. There were few women besides April for whom Brognola could remember the Executioner had special feelings. Val Querente was one of them; Barb Price was another.

For Price to talk about her relationship with Mack Bolan was a sort of taboo. She'd never shared the personal details with anyone, not even Aaron Kurtzman. Not that Brognola cared to know them. Her personal life, and the life of the warrior she was intimate with, was none of his business as long as it didn't interfere with the smooth operation of Stony Man. It never had. As a matter of fact, it had strengthened it in some ways. Whenever Bolan visited the Farm, he left renewed and invigorated, ready to do battle against anyone seeking to pervert the American way of life.

But now he was missing, and Brognola couldn't do a damn thing about it. The Stony Man chief had a considerable amount of latitude, but the President had been clear. Too many past missions had nearly been compromised because of personal vendettas and agendas. Every member of Phoenix Force and Able Team was a professional, and they all followed orders. But Brognola also knew every one of them would have dropped what he was doing and come to Bolan's aid if called upon to do so.

Brognola felt on the brink of making that call. "I wonder if I should go myself."

"And do what, Hal? We've got Phoenix in South America, and Able Team's spread all over the country right now. I don't think there's much more we can do until we hear from Striker."

Brognola nodded in understanding and then slumped into his chair. "What else were you able to pull from the information on the Kung Lok's meeting in West Palm Beach?"

Price shook her head, a puzzled expression on her face. "There wasn't anything out of the ordinary observed by the FBI agents. The meeting took place over the course of a single evening, and most of the attendees departed for China the following day."

"Who stayed behind?"

"Well, we know that Lau-Ming Shui immediately flew out to Las Vegas," she replied. "Dim Mai is still in country, as well as General Deng Jikwan. Although they apparently lost him at the airport, so his destination is as yet unknown. Airline employees are still being questioned."

Brognola didn't quite understand the secretive actions on the part of the Kung Lok triad. As the Executioner had told Kurtzman in his last contact with Stony Man, it wasn't as if the big hitters attending the meet had expected their presence would be a secret. However, they were free to move about the country without reporting their presence to anyone except the embassy of their country, and even that mandate wasn't strictly enforced.

Most of the politicians from Hong Kong and Beijing traveled under credentials that gave them diplomatic immunity. It wasn't unusual for them to enter and leave the United States on a moment's notice, and even less so to undertake trips that might only last the course of a day. While the constraints of diplomatic immunity didn't extend to Stony Man, the President could still override its efforts. He'd chosen to do so repeatedly in the interest of keeping diplomatic channels open and minimizing the potential for an incident that might embarrass the Oval Office. It was just that simple—and it might have cost the country one of its most valued champions.

"I'm going to alert Able Team," Brognola said. "I'll have to just risk the heat from the President. Deng Jikwan may be a recognized official of the Chinese military, but most if not all of the agencies in the intelligence community know he's little more than a thug in a uniform."

"I'll touch base with Carl immediately. Where do you want them to assemble?"

"Let's not get them too close to the action. Just call them here. We'll worry about where they should go from there when we've got more answers."

"You know, there's another option you haven't considered," Price pointed out.

"What's that?"

"We could touch base with Jack." Price smiled and winked. "He's still in Texas on vacation, and not all that far from Striker's last known location. We've sent him on fishing expeditions before, and he's always done a crack job."

Brognola thought it over a minute. He could remember where using Grimaldi in that capacity had paid off a time or two. The ace flier had a knack for fitting into the crowd with his regular-guy looks and unimposing attitude. And he *was* close to where most of the action had taken place. If he was needed to transport Able Team, they could always recall him and he could fly out of Fort Hood.

"Okay," the Stony Man chief finally said. "Let's give it a try. Who was that DEA agent Striker mentioned he was working with?"

"Her name is Lisa Rajero," Price replied. "She's a first-class narcotics officer. Clean record and a top-notch investigator. I did some digging in her personal file, and every supervisor for whom she's ever worked concurs that she's reliable. Rajero was apparently involved in the arrest of Ramon Sapèdas, a division chief for the U.S. Border Patrol office in El Paso."

"Tell Jack to start there," Brognola said. "This Rajero might just happen to know where Striker's keeping himself.''

"I'll get on it immediately."

As Price rose to leave, Brognola said, "This is all on the q.t. for now, Barb, but it's a priority. Understood?''

Price nodded and then left the War Room.

Brognola didn't move for a long time. He sat and pondered the fate of the Executioner. He didn't know how any of them would deal with it if they had finally seen the last of their friend and ally. Brognola couldn't think of the number of times where Mack Bolan had gone thankless for the missions he undertook.

The head Fed had experienced a bad feeling about the Executioner's mission from the start. The minute that it became clear to Stony Man that multiple organizations could be involved in a greater threat, he'd gone to the President and asked permission to intervene. But it was the bureaucracy and red tape that stood in his way; it always seemed to stand in his way when it counted most.

Somewhere out there, while the country slept, men were putting it on the line. They were fighting so America could rest; they endured horrific circumstances so America could enjoy its blessings; they were subjected to explosive violence so America could experience peace. Those things were what the men of Able Team and Phoenix Force were about. But most of all, it was what the Executioner had lived for.

And perhaps, Brognola thought, it was what he'd died for.

El Paso, Texas

AGENT LISA RAJERO WAS LIVID, and she was making sure that Charlie Metzger knew about it. Mostly it was because the U.S. Marshals Service had come in and immediately taken over her investigation when they had no right. Unfortunately, Rajero's supervisor couldn't do much about it, and whether she liked it or not the DEA had no jurisdiction over internal matters within the U.S. Border Patrol.

"That's bullshit, Charlie!" Rajero was getting a variety of looks from the staff within the El Paso Intelligence Center, but she didn't really care right at the moment. "He nearly confessed his affiliation with Carillo's attempt to smuggle truckloads of drugs into this country! Doesn't that count for something anymore?"

"Nearly has never counted in court, kid," Metzger said. "And it sure as hell won't cut it if he decides to recant anything he said."

"But I'm an eyewitness to the fact he was traveling with a known criminal *and* tried to kill me. And let's not forget his wife has agreed to testify against him."

"Come on, Lisa. You know damn good and well Sapèdas's old lady can't be compelled to testify against him, and as far as his trying to kill you or his being with Diaz, there are no witnesses. So it's your word against his."

"That's just great," Rajero spit. "I'm getting screwed here."

"Look, Lisa, he's probably looking to make a deal," Metzger counseled her. "Nothing more, nothing less, nothing personal."

"It seemed personal when the bastard tried to kill me."

Rajero could hear Metzger sigh. "The U.S. Marshals Service will have to make the decision about whether or not Sapèdas's information warrants consideration for his candidacy in the Witness Protection Program. He's a small fish in a big pond. I'm sorry, but there's nothing more I can do on this end.''

''Aren't you connected with someone here? I thought you were friends with a governor or senator or something.''

Rajero could hear Metzger snort through the phone. ''Not. I golf with a representative from the state legislature and our kids go to the same school, but that's about the extent of the relationship. I don't know *anybody* who could pull strings like that.''

''All right,'' Rajero said in a quieter tone, although she was still seething inside. ''I'm going to spend a couple of more days here if it's okay with you.''

''That's fine,'' he replied. ''Just don't get us into any trouble, Lisa.''

''Now, would I do a thing like that?'' she asked sweetly, glad for a bit of comic relief.

''Yes. That's why I told you not to do it.''

She sighed. ''Understood.''

''Hey, what about Belasko? Has there been any more word?''

''No. I've got to go now, boss. I'll see you soon.''

Rajero noticed her hand shaking as she dropped the phone into the cradle. She muttered, ''Damn.''

The makeshift office wasn't all that great—a fairly sparse cubicle with some high gray dividers, but no real privacy. She sat and put her head in her hands, trying to be quiet as tears came to her eyes. No, there hadn't been any word from Mike Belasko.

Rajero had it on good sources that Conrado Diaz, chief enforcer for Jose Carillo, was alive and well. The last time Rajero had seen Belasko, he'd single-handedly destroyed an armed force while simultaneously yanking her from certain death. Then he'd gone after Diaz. But

the hood was still alive, probably back in Mexico with
his boss by now, and no one had seen hide nor hair of
the elusive Belasko.

But she wasn't crying over him—not really. Belasko
could take care of himself. Frankly, he was either alive
or dead, and she wasn't going to make any assumptions
about it right now. The tears were coming from exhaus-
tion and frustration. She'd come to El Paso on a mission
to either put Ramon Sapèdas behind bars or clear him
of any wrongdoing. Now there were fellow law officers
sitting with the slug in another office and actually buying
his load of shit.

Sapèdas had insisted Rajero not be allowed anywhere
near him. She sensed most of the marshals and other
police officers present there at the EPIC didn't believe
she posed any threat to him. They knew Sapèdas was a
worm, but their arms were pinned by the same rules that
pinned hers. It just wasn't right that sworn officers of
the law could buck the system, benefit from the activities
of hardened criminals and then get protection for biting
the hand that fed them.

Still, she knew Metzger was right and she couldn't do
anything about it. At least she had the support of fellow
DEA agents there, albeit she hadn't really reached out
to any of them yet. They were more welcoming of her,
since the El Paso Intelligence Center was owned and
operated by the DEA.

The EPIC had been created in 1974 to deal with the
increased flow of drugs and illegal immigrants across the
U.S.-Mexican border. Since that time, it had grown from
seventeen employees from the INS, U.S. Customs Service and DEA to over three hundred analysts, agents and
administrative personnel from the Texas Department of

Public Safety and Air National Guard, as well as fifteen separate federal agencies.

The database on criminal activity related to drug pipelines and narcotics trafficking was one of the largest in the free world. The EPIC also served as a central clearinghouse for all drug-related information in every state, and this information was then forwarded to the headquarters office for drug enforcement in D.C.

In part, she hadn't left because they wouldn't let her leave. Eventually, the U.S. Marshals wanted to hear her side of the story. At least they had set her up in a hotel room, so she had someplace to go every night. She'd spent the past few days putting together information, making phone calls and gleaning further intelligence in preparation for her "debriefing." Or at least that's what the marshals were calling it.

"Agent Rajero?"

Rajero looked up and saw a very good-looking middle-aged man staring at her. He had blond hair, a bronzelike complexion and soft blue eyes. His patrician good looks and dress could have left anyone thinking the guy could have been anything from a businessman to a movie star.

Rajero knew she probably looked terrible, but she didn't really care at the moment.

"Yes?"

"My name is Liam Hoffner. I'm—"

Rajero stood immediately and offered her hand. "I know exactly who you are, Director Hoffner."

For a moment, the DEA agent was completely stunned. She couldn't believe that the center's director of operations was actually there talking to her. In some respects, Hoffner was a bit of a celebrity—the stories of exploits and many successful arrests throughout his career as a DEA officer were the stuff of legend among present-day agents. In his time, Hoffner had gone up against names in the Colombian, Mexican and Cuban drug cartels just as big as Manuel Noriega.

Hoffner smiled. "I guess you do. Would you like to come with me to my office? I'd like to talk to you."

Rajero looked in the direction of the interrogation room. "Well, I'm not supposed to go too far. The U.S. Marshals may want to talk to me at any time now."

"They'll know where to find you. My office is just down the hall."

"Of course," Rajero said with a nod.

She followed him to his office, surprised at her good fortune. This was actually a bright spot to her day. Hoffner was one of the good guys—that was for damn sure. He ran a tight ship. If she could get him on her side, she figured she might actually have a chance against the bureaucracy that had her stymied right now.

Hoffner's office was fancy and immaculate, but without being gaudy. The guy probably made pretty good money for a government employee. His experience and knowledge of drug activity was said to have surpassed even that of the EPIC central database. But that was obviously just more of his legend.

She took the seat he offered and he sat next to her, rather than hiding behind his desk. Rajero was impressed with his demeanor. She'd only known the guy for a couple of minutes, and she already liked him. There was something attractive about him. She noticed a wedding ring, and that put her back in the right frame of mind. He was obviously hands off. Probably had a gorgeous wife who could easily make him forget her name within a minute or two.

"How are you holding up?" he asked, flashing a pearl-white smile.

"Okay, I guess, sir."

"You can call me Liam," he said. "I try not to be too formal with the agents. Out there you should address me as Director Hoffner. In my office, things are a little safer."

"Thank you, sir." She chuckled and added, "Liam, I mean."

He nodded with a congenial expression. "You've had a rough couple of days."

"Yes, sir," she said quietly, forgetting to drop the honorific.

"Anything you'd like to talk about?"

"That could be opening a can of worms."

"I wouldn't have asked if I didn't want to know what you really thought, Agent Rajero."

The fact he'd used her official title told Rajero it wasn't really a request. This might have been a more relaxed atmosphere, but Hoffner was making it clear this was still official business all the way. He was probably probing for liabilities that might be linked to the DEA. Such as responsibility for the mess left at Sapèdas's residence. She was certain that someone by now had told him and the marshals of her affiliation with a guy who carried automatic weapons and grenade launchers, dressed in black fatigues and wreaked destruction on every evil thing in his path.

"I guess I just want to know why I'm being treated like a criminal while Sapèdas is the real hood."

"I wasn't aware anybody was treating you like a criminal." Hoffner crossed his arms. "Do I need to talk to some people?"

"Well, I guess that's not completely fair." Rajero felt

stupid having to recant her mini-temper tantrum. "What I don't understand is why instead of being involved in the investigation, I *am* the investigation."

"Well, Lisa, you have to admit there are nearly a dozen dead people within a one-block radius of the house you were leaving. Not to mention the bullet holes in your rental car, a high-ranking Border Patrol officer in custody and this mysterious commando who's running around blowing everything to hell and back."

"I don't know about that man."

"That's not what I hear," Hoffner countered in a quiet but firm tone of voice. "Not that I don't believe what you're telling me. But the marshals claim to have information that you were seen with him in Brownsville *and* Las Vegas. They're also convinced he rescued you from some Chinese gangsters who may have official ties to the Kung Lok triad."

Lisa couldn't believe her ears. Had they been following her? Had Charlie really set her up after all, and he was now sitting back and watching the show from a safe distance?

Hoffner rose, put his hands in his pockets and said, "Do you see what I'm getting at, Lisa? I'm not here to grill you, I'm just here to point out what *they*'re going to point out to you. I'd take a moment or two and really think about how you're going to answer them. Otherwise, things might not go as well as you would hope."

"Are you trying to hint they're thinking about charging me with a crime?"

Hoffner shook his head. "I never said that. I'm just telling you that it's not going to be easy. You're one of my own, Lisa. DEA looks out for its own. I'd be ready for anything."

"I understand, sir. Thank you."

Rajero rose and left his office. She wished Belasko were around. Not that it would have made a difference, but out of all the people she felt she could trust, he was one of them. The thing that saddened her most was that the people she ended up trusting—the people she called her friends—usually wound up dead.

Peter Willy had died at the hands of Kung Lok soldiers. Noreen Zahn had been brutalized, molested, humiliated and beaten until granted the mercy of death. A horrible death, but at least she was no longer suffering. Rajero wished she could say the same, but she couldn't. She was suffering—she was suffering terribly for all of the loss and pain. She was suffering from the horrors she'd endured.

The more Rajero thought about the pain, the more it angered her. And she knew that at some point she would have to return the favor. She'd get through this little inquest. If they wanted to witch hunt, they were certainly welcome to try. And then she'd deal out some suffering of her own. The Kung Lok still had to pay for murdering her friends.

And in that moment, more than ever before, Lisa Rajero wished Mike Belasko were there to comfort her.

CHAPTER TWO

Chihuahua, Mexico

Jose "Panchos" Carillo had been glad to see his friend and chief enforcer alive, but he was suspicious all the same.

According to Conrado Diaz, Ramon Sapèdas had been killed during the battle between the man called Mike Belasko and triad soldiers. Carillo had finally spoken with a connection in Las Vegas who picked up the information on a leak in the police department. The Chinese were trying to take over the drug and skin action in the American Southwest. Carillo's source didn't know who was in charge of the operation, but it was a place to start.

Diaz had also said the shipment they'd managed to get over the border from Mexicali into Calexico had been destroyed by Belasko. And they apparently still had something to worry about because Belasko was most likely alive. Diaz was begging for the chance to find the meddler and kill him once and for all.

Carillo was inclined to let Diaz take care of the problem, but Colonel Amado Nievas had made it plain he didn't feel the same way. Belasko hadn't been easy to kill in the past, and he could hardly believe it would be quite that simple now. Nievas had heard the reports from his commanders about how Belasko had taken out a couple dozen of his best troops, not to mention some of his officers. The guy had killed more than one-quarter of the force Nievas had brought to assist in Carillo's plans, and the Mexican drug lord appreciated the sacrifice. He wished some of his own men had been as loyal. Still, he knew that Nievas was having his doubts.

In addition to all of the little issues, Carillo had a bigger problem: recovering from the destruction of the trucks in Calexico. He'd put nearly all of his resources into those shipments, and Belasko had sent them up in smoke—that had been the entire source of his profits. There wasn't enough of the stuff left now to fit in a plastic bag.

No, it was definitely a bad situation.

And it was obvious Nievas suspected what was going on, because he took one look at Carillo and shook his head. He hadn't planned for *this* eventuality. Carillo had figured that if anybody got to one truck, even two of them, he would have still made more than enough to recuperate the losses. He'd never thought all four trucks would go down.

"You didn't have an alternate plan," Nievas observed, "did you?"

Carillo shook his head and replied, "Nobody could have foreseen this would happen."

Nievas sighed and climbed from his chair. Carillo stared into the distance. They were seated on the rear veranda of his mansion, which overlooked grounds colored with lush and verdant gardens. Multihued flowers, patterned like pastures of rainbows, glowed under the midday sun. Carillo had a staff of five groundskeepers who spent six days a week just keeping his property looking that beautiful. It was probably one of the only pure and fresh things Carillo could think he'd ever had in his life—something untouched by the impurity of his business dealings.

"I do not know what to tell you, Jose," Nievas said. "But I must report this to my superiors. They will not be happy. I may not even be welcome back in my country."

Carillo waved his hand at Nievas. "I would ask you hold off just a little longer, my friend. This isn't over just yet. I believe we can recover our losses another way."

"And that is?"

"To take back what belonged to us in the first place. We need to go after the source of this takeover by the triads. My connections in Vegas tell me that whoever slashed my operations also rendered a similar fate to Danny Tang. This is the way they treat their people. They're barbarians."

"So what," Nievas said with a shrug. "Why do you care what happened to this Tang? What does he have to do with us?"

"Maybe a lot," Carillo replied. "You see, the Chinese triads may be powerful, but they don't know the territory like I do. Tang ran most of the major prostitution action in Las Vegas. They killed a great resource. In one sense, we owe Belasko our thanks because he thinned their ranks."

"You think they are in a moment of weakness?"

"I believe it is a strong possibility," Carillo replied, "and I think we ought to consider this as an opportunity to strike back while they are vulnerable."

Nievas snorted. "You're not seriously thinking about taking on the Chinese triads, are you? Do you have any idea what kind of problems that would cause for me? The Chinese are allies to many of my countrymen. They have provided us weapons on more than one occasion. Colombia needs them, as much as we once needed the Russians.''

''Amado, do you honestly think that they didn't know this when they began their little campaign to try and push me out of business in the States? And even if they didn't, you can't honestly expect me to believe they don't know by now. I think this entire operation was planned from the very beginning. By now they have to know that we are allies.''

''Perhaps you're right,'' Nievas conceded.

Carillo felt some of his anxiety ebb. He knew Nievas had to be a man divided right now. On the one hand, the guy was faced with reporting failure to his superiors. On the other, he was probably loyal to his men and wanting to appease himself over guilt that their sacrifices were in vain. After all, Nievas had lost a good number of his crack force of troops to Belasko. Not to mention those lost at the hand of the Scarlet Dragons. To return home wounded and empty-handed wouldn't look good.

''I wouldn't ask for your help, my friend, but I no longer have the manpower to do this on my own. I need well-trained men and lots of them, and at present I have neither. You are the only one who can pull us from the embarrassment and turn it around for good. We cannot just walk away now.''

Nievas nodded sharply and his chest seemed to swell with pride. ''Yes, I'm forced to agree with you now. There is more at stake here than profit. There is our honor to consider.''

''Exactly.''

''My men are returning today from Mexicali. I will

begin drafting plans for reprisal against the triads." He looked hard at Carillo. "But this time we shall do it *my* way, Jose. No more of your little schemes. If I am to stay, then we must use tactical means to destroy our enemies. This is a war and we must fight it like a war. Is that agreeable to you?"

"Yes. Tell me how I can help."

"I don't have those answers yet." Nievas said. He spun on his heel and headed toward the house. "I need some time alone to contemplate. When I have a plan, we will talk. Until then, make sure no one disturbs me."

Carillo just nodded, and could hardly contain the smile that played on his lips as he watched his associate depart. He didn't want to make an open show of his relief. This would be the opportunity he needed to get back on his feet. Between that meddling Belasko and the Chinese triads, they had done some significant damage to him.

Once Nievas had departed, Carillo turned to Diaz and said, "Conrado, I'm sure that Belasko will try to come here."

"We will be ready for him."

"No, *I* will be ready for him."

"What are you talking about? You cannot stop this man on your own."

"You think too much of yourself, Conrado," Carillo said with a warning smile. He didn't normally tolerate such contention from his men. Had he not considered Diaz a friend, he would have had him whipped for even talking back. "I need you to do something for me. I need you to return to the United States and contact a friend. We're going to need some help with this one."

Carillo pulled a card from his shirt pocket and handed

it to Diaz. The enforcer studied the name a moment, and then asked, "What makes you think this guy will help us?"

Carillo smiled. "He owes me a favor."

Las Vegas, Nevada

LAU-MING SHUI, Western underboss of the Kung Lok triad, chuckled with delight as he spoke in whispers to the woman.

Shui didn't want anyone to overhear the conversation, particularly not his second in command, Ing Kaochu. He'd never been unfaithful to his wife, but his recent meeting with a former lover had rekindled some irrepressible feelings. However, it was his personal business, and he was enough of a gentleman to want to protect her reputation.

Nyenshi Fung. Shui had hardly stopped thinking about her since leaving West Palm Beach three days earlier. He wished she were free to come to him there, but he knew that was out of the question. That would have raised too many eyebrows and set Dim Mai against him, to be sure. This wasn't a good time to have the largest arms dealer in the Pacific as an enemy. He knew there was a war coming with the Mexicans, and he didn't want the Scarlet Dragons equipped well enough to handle any threat.

"We are leaving for Beijing tomorrow," Fung said quietly. "I will miss you."

"I will miss you, too. I don't suppose you would reconsider staying a few weeks?"

She chuckled. "It's sweet of you to offer, Lau-Ming, but I have to return with my husband. I am bound to obey and honor Dim, whether or not I agree with his decisions. It is what I swore to do, and I will keep my oath.''

"But you do it out of duty?'' Shui whispered tightly into the phone. "Not out of love? If you do not love him, then I see no honor in what you do.''

"I think you can honor someone without loving them,'' she replied softly. "And I do love him in so many ways.''

"I don't believe that.''

There was a long silence on the other end of the line, and Shui wondered for a moment or two if he'd committed a blunder. He wasn't really trying to call her a liar, but in essence that's what he had just done. Nonetheless, Shui knew that Fung didn't love Dim Mai—she had probably never loved him, as her family had arranged the marriage—but her sense of marital duty was a strong one.

Shui also realized that perhaps he was committing his own errors in judgment. In his heart, he was being unfaithful to his own spouse, who had been faithful and supportive of him. Not that there was any strong tie between them. At least that helped him to justify this newly found passion for the woman who had come so close to being his bride. Shui couldn't help the way he felt about her—it was just something he either couldn't or didn't want to control.

"I am sorry to sound this way,'' Shui said abruptly. "I know that my words probably make you uncomfortable, and leave you to feel that you must defend yourself. That is not my intention at all.''

"But if your words are not meant to sting, or to make me defensive, then what is your intention?'' she asked.

Shui felt a chill run up his spine because the tone in her voice was almost taunting him. No...perhaps not taunting, but maybe teasing. Whatever she was doing, Shui hoped she would not continue, or he might find himself unable to resist boarding the next flight back to West Palm Beach and openly professing his new affections.

Shui tried to shake himself of those thoughts. She would only prove a distraction from his real goal, albeit a lovely distraction, and he knew that there were important business matters on which he had to concentrate right now. Women like Fung were like delicate flowers, pleasant to the eyes while their fragrance and bright cheeriness lit up a room. Yet beneath their external folds of beauty were hidden bees that stung, and if not nurtured correctly they withered and died even in their seasons.

"I don't think I am required to dignify that question for you, Nyenshi. You know how I feel. I made it no secret when I was there with you last week."

"I know," she said. "Lau, I must go now. We will be leaving within the hour. Take care of yourself, and please be sure to let me know when you return to China so we may see each other again."

"I will."

"Goodbye, my dearest."

Shui held the phone and listened to the dial tone for nearly a minute after she hung up, then slammed it in the receiver. He hadn't even told her what he really wanted to tell her. He couldn't bring himself to ask her to stay indefinitely, and he had other things that needed his attention. Still, he was feeling empty without her and had been feeling that way since his arrival in Las Vegas. Not to mention the fact that he wasn't very comfortable in the hotel suite that Ing Kaochu had provided for him.

The leader of the Scarlet Dragons knocked on the door

of Shui's makeshift office and entered as if on cue. He was a tall, slim Chinese man with a long, thin mustache to match and dark eyes with greased hair. Kaochu was as cold and brutal as any within his army of trained killers, and he'd faithfully served as protector and second in command to Shui for many years.

There were splinter factions of the Scarlet Dragons all over America—they were all over the world, for that matter. Some were actually Chinese gangs that called themselves by the same name, but they had no real relationship to the official organization within the Kung Lok Chinese triad. The real Scarlet Dragons were a professional group of hardened men, trained in the arts of assassination, terrorism, war, espionage and a score of other subversive methodologies.

Every Scarlet Dragon was also evaluated for certain psychological and emotional traits that were vital to the job. They generally had to have verifiable affiliations with the Communist Party, be pure Chinese—although even Shui didn't understand what that meant since it would have been almost impossible to discern this in every candidate—and usually be devout Buddhists. Scarlet Dragons were trained to the highest standards.

In short, the Scarlet Dragons were a unique, invaluable tool of protection and enforcement within the Kung Lok, and their leader was the epitome of those within their ranks. Ing Kaochu had proved himself both a worthy ally and a servile subordinate, and Lau-Ming Shui knew that when the time came for his replacement, it would undoubtedly be the rather unassuming man who now stood before him.

"Good morning, sir. Did you sleep well?" Kaochu asked.

"Not as well as I would have hoped, Ing. When are

you planning to move me to private quarters in your house? This waiting in a hotel is silly, and I'm growing tired of it. I am about ready to return to Toronto.''

"We are moving this morning, at your discretion," Kaochu replied with a slight bow and a smile.

"Finally?"

"My sources believe that this Mike Belasko is dead, and the majority of the drug shipments that fool Carillo tried to pipeline through Mexicali were destroyed.''

"And Carillo's connection with the Border Patrol?"

"As far as we know, Ramon Sapèdas is dead. The only one left alive that we still must deal with is Lisa Rajero.''

"The DEA woman that escaped from you?"

Ing Kaochu nodded and bowed his head. Having lost her to Belasko was embarrassment enough, but to be reminded of the blunder by Lau-Ming Shui was downright shameful. Shui felt uneasy making Kaochu relive such things, primarily because he was grooming the young Dragon to take his place one day, and didn't want to do anything that would shake his resolve or break his confidence. Still, underlings had to be reminded of their failures now and again, lest they lose the concept of humility and decide that perhaps attrition and betrayal were better options.

"Regardless of my failures, Lau-Ming, I'm still loyal to you," Kaochu replied. "I hope you know that."

"Of course I know it," Shui said with a light laugh. "If I wasn't convinced of that, you would be dead.''

"I understand. But we have nothing to fear from this Rajero woman. I have already sent six of my best men to make sure she doesn't leave El Paso alive.''

"Why so many for just one woman?"

"Our intelligence says that she's being held for questioning at the El Paso Intelligence Center. She will most likely be under guard, so I wanted to insure the job got done.''

''Excellent thinking, Ing.''

Kaochu nodded then asked, ''What about Jose Carillo and the remainder of the FARC troops working under Nievas? Is this the moment that you wish me to finish what we've begun?''

''Yes. Carillo and Nievas are most likely hiding their heads in the sand, and they will not be prepared for another crippling blow so soon. It would probably be wise to take your people into Ciudad Juárez and kill them before they gain the courage and consider retaliating. I'm sure that both of them are strong enough men to realize this is as much a matter of their honor as it is a matter of business.''

''You actually think they would dare attack us here in America?'' Kaochu asked, the surprise in his voice evident. ''That would be a foolish gesture, not to mention nothing short of suicide. We have too great a foothold on Carillo's holdings now.''

''Don't become overconfident, Ing,'' Shui warned him. ''It could become your undoing. Remember that you were overconfident with Belasko. Our honor and reputation were sullied by the fact that a single one of Carillo's men could do what nearly forty of your own people could not. That doesn't look very good for the Scarlet Dragons or the Kung Lok. And it was a personal blow to *my* reputation. I am grateful Deng Jikwan and his people offered to help me at the time they did.''

Kaochu forced a nod. ''I understand your disappointment, Lau-Ming, and I assure you that nothing like that will ever happen again. The American took us by surprise. Had I known his skills were what they were, I would have approached him with subtle methods rather than trying to overcome him by sheer numbers.''

Shui waved his hand. "It is forgotten."

Kaochu bowed with genuine respect.

Shui decided to change the subject. "Now, what of this American ally I have taken upon myself. Will he burden our plans?''

"The video you acquired was blank."

"What?''

Ing Kaochu shook his head apologetically. "I'm sorry, but there was nothing on those tapes. We can only assume that the American knew you would try this and got to them before you did. Either that, or the cameras were disabled for this particular event. In any case, we now have no idea where he is.''

"I should have left my protection behind to conduct surveillance.''

"I don't think it would have done us any good. Those particular men I sent with you are not skilled spies. They are some of the finest protectors in the Dragons, but not much for these kinds of things. Had I known your intentions, I could have implemented a more cogent plan.''

"So we now have no idea of our mysterious benefactor's whereabouts?'' Shui asked, not without some disgust.

"I'm afraid that is correct.''

"Well, I suppose that is not your fault. I should have spoken with you about it immediately. I know that you're much better equipped and far better trained for these things. I am, after all, a businessman and diplomat. I should have entrusted this matter to you sooner, Ing. Forgive me.''

"There is nothing to forgive, master. Despite what has

transpired, I will continue to utilize every resource to find out who this man is.''

"Do you think he works for the American government, as he claimed?''

"I would not know."

"I'm asking for your opinion based on what you do know.''

Ing Kaochu sighed and went over to the casement window. He opened the blinds and opened the window to let in some fresh air. He studied the city landscape. The sun was now high, as it was late morning, and the bronze rays seemed to add a glow to Kaochu's skin. Kaochu finally turned to face his master and replied, "The fact that he bothered to tell you that he did, and to use this as a method of getting your attention, would lead me to conclude it is probably the truth. At least in part.''

"Otherwise, why would he bother to come up with such an elaborate lie,'' Shui hypothesized.

"Exactly. Where he might have exaggerated was in his actual position within the organization. He might not be as high within the ranks of the American government as he claims. Or it is another possibility that he is higher than he led you to believe.''

"He was not specific about this, but he left me with enough information to convince me he knew what he was talking about.''

Kaochu interjected, "But not enough to tell you anything of value. The problem I see with this man is that he did not truly explain why hastening our takeover and fueling a war against the Mexican elements was so vitally important.''

"He thinks that this country will do everything they can to avoid that. He also claims that such a war, while it might create some havoc over our business dealings, will most definitely serve us profitably."

"So he wants a part of the action," Kaochu reminded Shui.

"But not our part," Shui protested.

"Then why would it benefit us to work with him? The money remains ours, no matter what his involvement. We're still skimming profits from our dealings with Nievas's associates in the FARC before we give the money to Dim Mai, and we're using those funds to take over Carillo's business operations. We have no overhead, so I don't see profit affected. I think your original plan was perfect."

"But with the kind of money this man talked about, we could do much more. So much more than we can do now."

"This is ultimately your decision, not mine, Lau-Ming," Kaochu stated. "I will follow your orders to the letter, whatever they are, as will my Dragons. There is no task too great or small. We would die for you, and you have told me you know this."

Shui acknowledged Kaochu's words with a graceful nod.

"But before you continue taking advice from this man," the Dragon enforcer continued, "you should allow us the opportunity to find out who he is. And we cannot do that if we must fight a war with the Mexicans and Colombians. Thus, I see what he's doing serves only to keep us occupied, and too busy to investigate his own interests."

"I had never considered it quite in this light before." Shui took a few minutes to think furiously about what his most trusted aide and friend said to him. It hardly seemed possible, but he couldn't understand why this

American would have dredged up such a story just to keep them occupied. Perhaps the truth was that the man was totally loyal to the U.S. government and simply trying to find other ways of solving the internal problems. Maybe it was nothing more than a ploy to pit the two groups against one another. Maybe the idea was to keep the Americans from having to spend the time and resources necessary to fight a war on two fronts, when in fact the real problem could be solved simply by pitting one warring faction against the other.

It was all beginning to make sense to Shui. There were always spoils of war—it didn't matter which side won and which side lost, as long as the victor could claim whatever was left over. But there really wouldn't be a victor in a war between the Mexican-Colombian connection and the Chinese triads, because it was a war without end. That left Shui in quite a predicament, one he'd never considered until taking Kaochu's words to heart. If it really came down to a war between them, there would be no real victors. Yes, men like the one he'd met in Florida would collect the spoils, while Shui and the Kung Lok were left with nothing.

That would never do.

"I think you're right. We go no further with this until we know who exactly it is we're dealing with. Find this man, find out who he is and then get back to me."

"And what about Carillo and the Colombians? What if they decide to try and take back Las Vegas and the other areas we've acquired?"

"Then we'll deal with them as we have before." In an even tone he added, "The result of their impudence will be death."

CHAPTER THREE

Stony Man Farm, Virginia

When Aaron "the Bear" Kurtzman answered the phone, he would have expected a lot of people on the other end of the line—but not the one who replied to his gruff hello. The very thought that he was talking to Mack Bolan sent a chill down his spine that coursed through the rest of his body like an electrical charge. He was all at once thrilled and disbelieving.

"We thought you were dead," Kurtzman finally blurted out.

"So did I," Bolan told him.

Even through the receiver, Kurtzman could tell the Executioner was trying to keep things light.

"What happened?"

"Nothing. I've just been keeping my head down and trying to keep off the police. After what went down at Sapèdas's place, it's been a challenge. And I don't have a lot of time to discuss it right now."

"But you're okay?"

"Yeah. I didn't want to worry any of you too much, but I had to lay low. I used the time to gather additional intelligence, and I've made some contacts."

"Where are you?"

"Down in Juárez."

"Can you be more specific?"

"Not right now. There's no time. I just called to find out where things stand. What else have you learned since we talked last?"

"Well, I know that Able Team's on its way to the Farm right now."

"For me?"

"Yes. Sorry, Striker. I know it's not what you wanted, and you didn't want to involve them, but Hal was convinced something went bad and he called them in. It was just a precaution, so I'm sure once he knows you're okay he'll have them stand down."

"It's all right. I figured Hal might get tired of waiting. I won't hold it against him. Is he there?"

"No, he and Barb are looking into some information on our mysterious government link to the Kung Lok."

"Do we have any more intelligence on that connection?"

"We've figured whoever's behind contacting the Kung Lok, and turning them onto the fact that the Mexicans and Colombians are working together, *had* to have pulled their information from multiple sources."

"Makes sense," Bolan interjected. "No single agency outside of you guys is going to put that information together."

"Exactly. Which told us that our little mole needed access to the information. From that assumption, we started narrowing down multijurisdictional agencies with enough clout to yank and disseminate that kind of intel, then categorized them by geographical location, which pulled many of the CIA and DOJ offices out of the loop. We've still got a lot of territory to cover, but we're already off to a good start, and the list is getting smaller by the hour.''

"Keep at it. I'm sure I'll be in touch again soon, and I know you'll have something by then."

"Hey, are you sure you don't want us to send help?"

"I appreciate it, Bear, but my answer is still no. I'm okay. My next step is to put a battle plan against Carillo into action."

"Well, just so you know, Hal ordered Jack to El Paso. He's looking for you, and he was supposed to start with Lisa Rajero. Last word was that the U.S. Marshals Service was holding her for questioning at the El Paso Intelligence Center."

"Holding her for what?"

"No idea yet. That's part of what Jack was sent to find out."

"Get in touch with him and tell him to watch out."

"Why?"

"I think our mole could be close to Rajero. Possibly her boss. Get all of the information you can on a guy named Charles Metzger. He's lead agent for the Brownsville DEA office. Check him out, and good."

"We've already done it. The guy's clean as a whistle."

"Too clean?"

"Not so much that we suspect him of involvement with either the Kung Lok or Carillo. No secret bank accounts...nothing along those lines. But if you're right, and our mole is somebody on the inside of the Justice Department, it could be why we're having so much trouble getting interagency cooperation."

"Hal's credentials aren't doing any good?"

"Not really. And it doesn't help with the Man telling him to back off every time we start to get somewhere."

"All right," Bolan conceded. "Then I guess we keep looking. Look, I need to go. I'll be in touch."

"Take care, Striker."

"Right."

The connection was broken.

Kurtzman wasn't sure what was going on, but he knew he didn't like it. Mack Bolan keeping his head down? Something didn't sound right, but Kurtzman couldn't put his finger on it. Striker hadn't sounded as if he was under any sort of duress, or like he'd been drugged, so it was improbable he'd been captured by the enemy. Kurtzman had decided to run a trace, and the computer was still finalizing it.

Well, the fact the Executioner was still alive was good news all by itself. In either case, he would follow Bolan's instructions and notify Grimaldi ASAP. And he'd let Brognola know as soon as he returned, which would definitely cause the Stony Man chief to breathe easier. He also needed to update the members of Able Team, all of whom were scheduled to arrive within a few hours under the impression they were headed to Texas on a search-and-rescue mission.

The report came through on Kurtzman's computer screen. He double-checked the trace and it came up—this time in a red-highlighted field—verifying that what he'd seen was absolutely accurate. It seemed Mack Bolan *was* in Ciudad Juárez. And there was only one damn thing there that he could think would be enough to capture the interest of the Executioner. Mack Bolan was probably planning to go after Carillo and Nievas—and end this war once and for all.

Ciudad Juárez, Mexico

HIS FIRST TASTE of true consciousness had started as a drab, dull swirl of colors, like the mixing of red and black paint on an artist's palette. Then the dream world became reality—and so did the pain. Not to mention the concept he was still alive. Over the course of the day, he drifted into periods of fitful dozing, never really sleeping deeply, but always aware of his surroundings and further cognizant that he was drugged.

Finally he began to come out of his drug-induced stupor, and that's when the pain hit him even harder. It felt as if someone had beaten him with a sledgehammer. His mouth was dry and pasty, he felt dehydrated albeit his keepers—whoever they were—had continuously pumped him full of fluids.

Finally, at long last, when his world came into focus and remained that way, Mack Bolan got his first glimpse of the woman to whom he owed his life. She sat in a nearby chair, her dark eyes fixed on him intently. There wasn't necessarily any real care in her expression—more like something bordering on altruistic interest. Nonetheless, it was like having an angel look upon him, from where the Executioner laid, and there was no doubt as to the beauty behind that studious gaze.

She had raven hair, with barely discernible laugh wrinkles around her coal-black eyes. Her face was heart shaped, with a dark complexion. Her lips were red and glossy, and everything about her was very Spanish and very beautiful. She reminded Bolan of a famous actress, a name he couldn't recall in the haziness, but she was definitely not hard to look at.

He then smiled weakly at her before drifting off to sleep, and the next thing he remembered was waking up suddenly, and finding a wide face covered with white whiskers staring at him with interest. The man was older, perhaps in his late fifties or early sixties, with thick-rimmed glasses and a nose that was way too small for the face. The man stood from where he'd been leaning over the bed, and Bolan's next look was toward the chair. The dark-haired beauty was gone.

"Ah, I know who you're looking for," the man said with a cheery grin.

He wore a white lab coat—a doctor of some sort? The man reached behind himself, retrieved a needle filled with a light yellow liquid and turned to inject it into an IV bag. Bolan looked down to see the bag was connected to his arm by a long tube. He reached up and grabbed the doctor's wrist, gripping it tightly and preventing him from injecting the ominous-looking syringe into the rubber stopper on the bag.

"What is that?" The man tried to pull away, but the Executioner tightened his grip and repeated, "What is that?"

The doctor stopped struggling and looked down at Bolan. His face was reddened with anger at first, but then he appeared to go calm and his body relaxed. He moved his hands away from the IV bag, and Bolan decided to release the hold. He didn't really expect the doctor was planning to kill him, but he didn't know who the guy was and he wanted some answers before he let anyone do anything else to him.

"I see you're getting your strength back," the doctor replied, rubbing his wrist after Bolan freed it.

"I'm not going to ask a third time," Bolan said.

The doctor looked puzzled a minute, then looked at the syringe and held it up for Bolan to see. "Oh, this? This is a mixture of meperidine hydrochloride and heparin. It's designed to kill pain and prevent the formation of blood clots."

"No more painkillers," Bolan said. "I need to think straight."

"But you still need the heparin. If you don't continue on a regimen of it at least another day or two, you risk a cardiac embolism from clotting around your wounds."

"They got infected?"

The man nodded, capping the needle and putting the syringe back in his bag. "I told Catalina we really should have taken you to the hospital in Juárez, but she insisted on bringing you here and making me travel across the border every day."

"Catalina," Bolan murmured. "The woman who was sitting in that chair?"

The man nodded. "Catalina Milaña."

The Executioner was beginning to remember what had happened. He'd escaped the El Paso police on foot after losing Conrado Diaz. That night, he'd stayed in a hotel and made some phone calls. Eventually, he'd been put in touch with someone and was supposed to meet them at a small bar in Ciudad Juárez. He'd waited there for a while, drank two beers, and then had he passed out? He could remember strong hands lifting him off the ground and riding somewhere in a comfortable car. But it was only bits and pieces of images.

"And who are you?" he finally asked the man.

"My name is Dr. Guajardo," he said. "I'm Catalina's uncle. She's the one who called me after removing you from the bar where you collapsed. Someone called an ambulance, and they wanted to take you to a medical facility. She convinced them to bring you here to her home instead, and she paid quite a bit of money to make sure everyone kept their mouths shut about the incident."

"She's the one I was supposed to meet."

Guajardo nodded and laughed good-naturedly. "I had no idea who you were, but Catalina apparently did."

"You didn't call the police?"

"I wanted to, but she said no." He shook his head and added, "She can be quite persistent, my niece. Once her mind is made up, that's the end of it."

"Why didn't she just turn me into Mexican authorities?"

He shook his head. "I'm afraid you're going to have to ask her those questions, young man."

"Whatever her reasons, I owe you my life," Bolan said. "Thanks."

"Forget it," he replied with a casual wave.

Bolan gritted his teeth, fighting the dizziness as he attempted to move. The doctor attempted to caution him against it, but the Executioner ignored his protests. He finally managed to sit upright in the bed and steeled himself against the nausea. After some clarity returned, Bolan managed to swing his feet around and the doctor stepped forward to help him stand. Again the soldier fought the urge to collapse, every fiber of his iron resolve and superhuman will urging him to steady himself. The dizziness cleared, although the nausea remained, and Bolan knew that had more to do with the drugs than anything else.

"Take this out of my arm," he ordered the doctor.

"I really would caution you against all of this," Guajardo said. "You're still weak and at risk for infect—"

"I'm weak because of the drugs and fluids you've been pushing on me. In addition, I've had nothing to eat for almost forty-eight hours. Now, take this IV out of my arm before I decide to do it myself and make a mess."

Guajardo studied the cold, blue gaze a moment and

then shrugged. He turned to his bag, withdrew a pair of latex gloves and within a moment he had the tape off and the IV catheter withdrawn from Bolan's arm. He expertly sterilized the spot with a pad soaked in iodine, then cleaned it with alcohol and bandaged it.

Bolan's legs were still wobbly, and one foot was asleep. The tingling would wear off shortly—a side effect of having his left leg propped higher than the right. It had probably been done by the doctor, designed to encourage blood return to his upper body. He turned to look at the physician, who was watching him intently. He could see the man was concerned about his condition, but Bolan couldn't be off his feet any longer. It was time to get back into the game. His battle with the Kung Lok and the Carillo-Nievas alliance was far from over.

With Guajardo's assistance, Bolan got to the chair where the woman named Catalina had been seated. He asked for a phone and Guajardo brought him one without an argument. After all, he wasn't a prisoner as the doctor reasoned verbally, and Catalina had left no particular instructions about it one way or another. The physician left the room to give his patient some privacy. After the Executioner completed his call to Stony Man and Guajardo returned to the room, Bolan said, "I appreciate your help. Now, would you please get me some clothes and my weapons."

"Now hold on a minute, mister," the older man said, raising his hands, "you can't just go walking out of here."

"Watch me," the Executioner growled.

"I wouldn't advise that just yet, Mr. Belasko," a soft voice interrupted.

Bolan turned to see that the woman who had watched

over him through his feverish and shaky recovery stood in the doorway on the far side of the room. He hadn't even heard her enter, which bothered him just a little. His senses were more finely tuned than that, which told him the drugs were still having some effects. He knew he wasn't anywhere near up to par, but he couldn't risk the lives of these people any longer.

"I beg to differ, lady, but I can. And how do you know me?"

"I know many things, Mr. Belasko. I have been following your campaign against Amado Nievas and the Carillo crime family for some time now."

"I sensed somebody was watching me," Bolan replied lightly. He studied her a moment with interest, then added, "I just figured it was either someone sent by Carillo or the Kung Lok."

"Ah, yes, we know of the war between Carillo and the Kung Lok Chinese triad. It's a most interesting situation."

Catalina Milaña walked across the room and put her hand on her uncle's shoulder. "How is he?"

"He's doing okay," Guajardo replied, nodding at Bolan. "I don't think it's wise for him to leave yet, but he's insistent."

"How long do you think he should stay?"

"Perhaps another two or three days. I wouldn't think he should have to convalesce more than a week, but he has to give his body a rest so it can fight infection."

The Executioner knew it might have been just pride that he'd been lying in bed under the care of others because of a near fatal mistake, but it angered him all the same they were discussing him as if he were still unconscious. Moreover, he didn't like the fact they weren't willing to give him his clothes and guns so he could leave. It was time to start taking control of the situation while he still had any.

"Now both of you listen to me a minute," he snapped. "First, I'm not staying here any longer, so there's no point in discussing it. Second, I want my clothes and guns, and if you don't bring them now I'm going to get ugly. Third, the longer you keep me here, the more you endanger me and yourselves."

Milaña's eyes narrowed and she scowled. Bolan could see she was angered, but he couldn't get over how beautiful she was even when angry. There was something different about her, though. Unlike Rajero, whose rage and fury were driven by a spirited personality, Milaña's anger seemed rooted in something deeper. There was also a sorrow behind those dark, sparkling eyes, some scar the woman carried with her constantly but did a hell of a job covering.

"Uncle, would you please go get Mr. Belasko's clothes? He's free to leave when he pleases. If he dies, it's nothing to us. I will find some other way."

Once Guajardo had left the room, she turned on Bolan. "I'm sorry we bothered saving your life. We will not make the same mistake twice."

"Wait a minute," Bolan said, getting to his feet and tightly holding the blanket he'd draped around his waist. "Don't think I'm ungrateful. I owe you."

"Then perhaps you could sit down and at least allow me the courtesy to explain why I've gone to such lengths to keep you alive," Milaña replied. "Is that too much to ask of you?"

Bolan shook his head and then sat. He owed her that much—despite the fact he knew every second that ticked by was just more time wasted. He was giving the enemy every opportunity to regroup and try for another major action inside America. Bolan figured by this time Carillo had to know it was the Chinese that had taken over the drug scene in all of his territories. He hadn't destroyed all of Nievas's men in Mexicali, and they were probably planning how to utilize their remaining forces to launch a counteroffensive against the Chinese. Unfortunately, neither side wanted to start that kind of war on their own turf. That left Las Vegas as the middle ground where they would draw the lines of battle.

Bolan planned to draw his own lines.

"You do not know me, but I know well of you," Milaña began. "My people have been reporting on your activities since you destroyed Jose Carillo's shipment in Brownsville over a week ago."

"Okay, I'll bite. What's your interest in Carillo and Nievas?"

"My husband used to be a member of the revolutionaries Nievas leads."

"He was FARC?"

"Yes, until he decided he no longer wanted a part in murdering babies," she said quietly. "My husband planned to move me and our new son to Mexico where we would find peace. When Colonel Nievas found out, he ordered the execution of my husband and our child. Our sweet, innocent boy who was only a few weeks old." Her voice quavered and her lip trembled, but she bit back her pain and continued. "I was freed by a sympathizer and smuggled into Mexico. I have vowed vengeance ever since."

Bolan made a sweeping gesture of the room and said, "You seem to live pretty well for a Colombian refugee. Care to explain that?"

She inclined her head and smiled. "It is a fair question. My husband had saved considerable funds from his activities. He managed to send most of what he earned here. I supposed you could call them spoils of war. In either case, I invested in local businesses in Ciudad Juárez, and those investments turned out to be fruitful.''

"So now you're using the money to avenge your husband and son?''

"I want Colonel Amado Nievas dead, Mr. Belasko. And I want you to kill him.''

"I see," Bolan replied quietly.

"And if you do succeed in killing him, I can promise that you will never want for anything in your life again. Ever.''

The Executioner chuckled. "You've got me all wrong, miss. I'm sorry about your family. I know how you feel, believe me, but I'm not a mercenary. I follow my own agenda.''

"So you're refusing?''

"I'll handle Nievas and Carillo,'' Bolan replied quickly. "And the Kung Lok. But I'll do it my way and on my terms.''

"I've heard of your methods,'' Milaña said. "You're highly effective, to be sure. It makes no difference to me how you do this. I'm just telling you that I want it done.''

"And I'm telling you I'll do what I need to do out of duty.''

"Then you work for your government.''

"For my country, government or no government.''

Milaña looked at the floor a minute, sighed deeply, then walked to the window and looked through the spotless glass. Bolan guessed it looked out to the west and the sun was dipping beyond the horizon because the red-and-orange light glistened off her hair with stark brilliance. She was undoubtedly one of the most beautiful

women he'd ever seen. There was just something all at
once sensual and deep about her looks. She had class
and grace, and Bolan found it difficult to take his eyes
off of her.

"You have said you know how it feels to lose family," she said distantly. She turned to face him and
added, "And I believe you when you tell me this. However, I do not think you understand how important this
is. If Colonel Nievas isn't stopped now, he will return
to my country with more guns and more weapons. He
will destroy more towns and murder more children. I
cannot watch this happen, Mr. Belasko. I cannot allow
him to just walk away and do this while I know in my
heart that I had the power to stop him."

"We don't have the power to stop people like Nievas,
lady," Bolan said gently. "We cut off one of the heads
of the monster, and another head just takes its place. The
best we can do is step on their necks and hope there's
enough feet to hold them down."

"I feel you are a man of great honor and discern-
ment," Milaña said offhandedly.

Her comment took the Executioner by surprise. She
had that kind of effect. She kept him off balance, and
he knew that he wanted her in a way he'd not wanted
any woman in a while. She had to have sensed his at-
traction because she walked over to him and lightly ran
her hands up his chest to encircle his neck.

"I also believe," she whispered, "you are a man of
great passion."

Bolan could feel a chill go up his spine, but he gently
pushed her away and stood. "Don't get me wrong.
You're very beautiful. But I need to get out of here, and
I need your help to do it. I'll make sure that Nievas
doesn't escape from Mexico."

She smiled. "If you promise to do this, then I believe it. I will help you."

"Good," Bolan said. "Now, why don't you start by telling me what you know about Nievas and Carillo."

CHAPTER FOUR

El Paso, Texas

Jack Grimaldi was preparing to land the Gulfstream C-20 when Aaron Kurtzman called him with the news: Mack Bolan was alive! Grimaldi couldn't hold back a shout of victory when the words echoed in his ears. He and Kurtzman briefly discussed their mutual relief at the thought that Bolan was alive.

Finally the celebration died out, and they turned to the ace pilot's mission. Grimaldi was probably less than forty miles from Mack Bolan's location, if Kurtzman's trace was accurate, but still the big guy was adamant about not involving Stony Man.

"I can't go against his wishes, Jack," Kurtzman said simply. "Now, if Hal told me otherwise, that might be another story."

"Does Hal know he's alive yet?"

"Yeah, I just got off the phone with him."

"Okay. Does this change my priorities?"

"Not from what he told me. He wants you to proceed to the El Paso Intelligence Center and find Lisa Rajero. He also wants you to do some digging while you're there. It's our understanding that Rajero's being held there pending further investigation of the action that took place a few days ago. We think this is too much of a coincidence to pass up.''

''In what way?''

''We believe our traitor is somewhere in that place. As a matter of fact, Hal's positively convinced of it. But we're going to have to get to this Rajero, and we're definitely going to have to keep her out of the line of fire.''

The pilot nodded his understanding even though Kurtzman couldn't see him, advised he was about to land the plane and he'd be in touch, then signed off.

Grimaldi made some adjustments to his instrumentation before performing a picture-perfect landing. The private airstrip was established specifically for any organization attached to the Justice Department, and since Harold Brognola still held an official position with them, it wasn't hard to utilize those vast resources on short notice. Very similar to the favor Brognola called in to get Grimaldi into a military version of the Gulfstream Learjet.

The Stony Man ace taxied to the empty hangar designated by the tower controllers, then locked the place tight before proceeding to a waiting car. He dropped his gear in the back seat, then climbed behind the wheel and was soon on the interstate headed into the city.

Despite the news Bolan was alive, Grimaldi was still worried about his friend. The Executioner had done a lot for him—saved his life time and again. Sure, he'd probably returned the favor tenfold, but it wasn't really about trading favors. Mack Bolan had given Jack Grimaldi something else—something way more important than his life. He'd given the pilot a sense of purpose and belonging. At first, Grimaldi had really viewed himself as a freelancer for Stony Man, but now he was undoubtedly one of their most valuable members.

On a few occasions, the pilot had even been caught in the line of fire and gone above the call of duty to help the teams accomplish their missions. But he was especially close to Bolan, and nothing would ever change that. He wanted to forget Rajero and this whole crazy scheme, go off in search of Bolan and bring the Executioner back to the Farm where he could recover.

But that just wasn't in the soldier's plans, and Grimaldi had learned long ago that there were times when trusting the Executioner was much better than trying to figure out what the hell he was up to. That's because Bolan didn't think like the average person. He wasn't a spy or government agent, and he didn't think that way. He could be deceptive and knew how to blend in. But his success always stemmed from military tactics, and most of the Executioner's enemies weren't prepared for that.

So Jack Grimaldi knew that if Mack Bolan wanted Stony Man to keep back and let him do his thing, then there was probably a damn good reason for it. And that was enough for him.

Grimaldi arrived at the El Paso Intelligence Center a half hour later and was ushered to a fourth-story wing housing the DEA offices after flashing his forged credentials. He was posing as Jack Grimes, U.S. Marshal from Wonderland and new lead investigator into the inquisition of Ramon Sapèdas and the action at his estate. Grimaldi hoped he could play a convincing role until he located Rajero and found out what it was she knew that was so important.

Grimaldi quickly located the other marshals who were clustered in a hot, dank room in the middle of interro-

gating a short, dark-haired man. Grimaldi immediately
knew the men hadn't exposed their prisoner to the best
conditions. Grimaldi could only assume that this was
Sapèdas, who was currently suspended as chief of the
U.S. Border Patrol office in El Paso.

"I think this guy needs a break," Grimaldi snapped,
shoving a thumb in the direction of the prisoner.

A tall, swarthy-looking type in a corduroy jacket and
open-button shirt turned to look at Grimaldi with surprise. The look on the man's face made it immediately
evident to the pilot that this guy wasn't used to taking
orders from a Washington type. He already sensed the
trouble before the guy opened his mouth.

"And who the fuck are you?" the man growled.

"For starters, you can watch your mouth," the ace
flyer replied.

Grimaldi tried to keep from breaking into a smile. He
knew he was enjoying the role a little too much, but he
couldn't help himself. Still, he didn't want to alienate
the guy. These men could have three days' worth of
invaluable information, and if he threw his weight
around too much, it might raise questions back in Washington. Stony Man easily had that covered, but fielding
uncomfortable inquiries and listening to other DOJ organizations holler about jurisdiction wasn't something
Brognola wanted to contend with right at the moment.

"Why?"

"Because you're talking to a superior officer, for
one," Grimaldi replied sharply. He flipped open his
badge in perfunctory fashion and replied, "I'm Special
Agent Jack Grimes, Washington office."

"No shit?" one of the other agents chimed in. The
man looked at the leader Grimaldi had been talking to

and said, "I wonder what's got the top so interested in this case."

The guy just shook his head, then returned his attention to Grimaldi. "Nobody told me about anybody from Washington coming. And orders or no orders, this is my case."

"Take it easy, guy," Grimaldi replied smoothly. "I'm not the least bit interested in stealing your case. No interest in the glory, either. I'm here to ask that DEA chick a few questions, then I'll split. Fair enough?"

The leader of the group eyed Grimaldi another moment with suspicion, then finally nodded and turned to one of his subordinates. "Dittweiler, take Grimes here to Agent Rajero."

Dittweiler nodded and then gestured toward the door. He opened and moved through it first, Grimaldi following a step behind him. Just as Grimaldi was leaving the room, he turned back to the agent in charge and said, "By the way, who's at the top of this operation here?"

"Guy named Hoffner. Dittweiler will show you where his office is."

Grimaldi nodded by way of thanks, then closed the door on his way out and rushed to keep up with Dittweiler's short but quick steps. Dittweiler led the Stony Man pilot down a long hallway that opened onto a large room. The area was split into cubicles divided by gray panels, and the walls surrounding the work areas were rimmed with large offices. Dittweiler wound a path through the maze of cubicles until they reached a plain, unobtrusive work space on the far side of the room.

The Hispanic woman seated there was dark haired and pretty, and at first glance she reminded Grimaldi of a younger version of Toni Blancanales. She had chocolate-brown eyes that flashed with spirited resolve, and she held herself with an air of confidence and authority. It looked as if someone had recently beaten her about the head and face with a heavy piece of mining equipment, but the remnants of her ordeal appeared to be fading quickly.

"Agent Rajero," Dittweiler snapped in a rude tone, "this is Special Agent Grimes of the U.S. Marshals office. He's here as on special detail to ask you some questions, and we'd appreciate your cooperation."

"I'll do what I can to help," Rajero replied, smiling at Grimaldi politely. "Will I be able to leave soon?"

"That's not up to him," Dittweiler said. "You can leave when we've concluded our investigation. Would you like me to stay, Agent Grimes?"

"No, that'll be all. Thank you."

Dittweiler studied Grimaldi a second, the look in his eyes betraying he wanted to say something else, but the guy just turned and walked away.

Once he was gone, Grimaldi focused his attention on Rajero and studied her a moment. Finally, he said, "So you're Lisa Rajero."

"Yes," she answered with a suspicious mask. "Why?"

Grimaldi couldn't help but smile. "You're just as Sarge described you."

"Who?"

"Oh, you've probably never heard anybody call him that. I'm talking about Mike."

"Belasko?" she said. "Where is he? Is he all right?"

Grimaldi looked around the office and waved his hand to shush her. "Tone it down a little, will you, lady? I'm not actually even supposed to be here talking to you right now."

"How do you know Mike?" she asked more quietly.

"Is there somewhere we can talk privately?" Grimaldi said, ignoring her question for the moment. "Maybe someplace where there aren't so many ears."

"There's a restaurant across the street. I'm famished anyway, and I've been there before. Inexpensive, unobtrusive and the food's decent. But I have to stick around in case they need me. They've had me here nearly all week, just waiting." She scooped up her handbag and indicated for Grimaldi to follow her.

As they walked down the hall and headed for the elevators, Rajero asked excitedly, "How's Belasko. Is he okay?"

"He took a bullet in the back," Grimaldi replied truthfully, "but he's okay. I haven't seen him, but my people just let me know he was alive."

"Your 'people'?" Rajero nodded as the elevator doors closed and they rode to the first floor. "I knew it. I knew Mike worked for the government."

"He doesn't work for the government," Grimaldi said. "Not exactly. Listen, I'm going to shoot straight with you because Mike trusted you, and I know you did what you could to help him. We think you're in danger here."

"Who's we?"

Grimaldi shook his head. "You know better than that, miss. I can't get into it, but I can tell you my information is reliable. We believed you were onto something when you told Mike about your suspicions regarding Ramon Sapèdas. We still think you're right."

"Well, it's obvious my theory about his involvement with Jose Carillo was right on the money. But with my star witness gone, we only have the word of his wife. And she can't legally be compelled to testify against him in court. She wants to, but that head marshal is totally against it. Plus, you're not the first one to tell me I'm courting danger here today.''

Grimaldi could suddenly feel the hairs stand up on the back of his neck as they exited the elevator and walked toward the front entrance. ''What do you mean by that?''

''Well, the director of the intelligence center pulled me into his office this morning. He had some very interesting things to say. He knew about the Kung Lok triad, and he knew about Belasko's part in this thing. He seemed to think they might try to hang me as the bad guy here, right along with Sapèdas.''

''That's pretty thin,'' Grimaldi said. ''You captured Sapèdas and brought his criminal ties to light. How could anybody think you'd be in on it?''

''I'll admit that it sounds anything but credible,'' Rajero replied, ''but I have a feeling he could be right. Since they're looking at Belasko as a fugitive and vigilante right now, and there are witnesses to my association with him, they could still turn this around and pin me with obstruction of justice.''

''How?''

''If I refuse to cooperate and tell them I was in fact working with Belasko.''

''If you turn evidence against him, in other words,'' Grimaldi replied.

She nodded.

''Who was it that told you they might try to hang you with this if you didn't cooperate?''

''A guy named Liam Hoffner. Very famous DEA agent.''

''I know the name,'' Grimaldi said, nodding. It didn't make a damn bit of sense to him, somebody in Hoffner's position offering advice to Rajero.

In Liam Hoffner's world, Rajero was a nobody and

not a somebody. It didn't make sense he would take an interest in something so seemingly minor, and especially not if there was a possibility Rajero was dirty. Grimaldi knew she wasn't, but Hoffner didn't. So why would he have risked soiling his hands? Just because Rajero was part of the DEA? No, the Stony Man pilot didn't buy that. Not one damn bit.

"So he thought you should roll over on Mike?"

"Yes." Rajero stopped Grimaldi just as they were about to walk out and touched his arm lightly. "Which I couldn't do in million years, no matter how much they might threaten me. I owe Mike Belasko more than I could ever imagine repaying, and I'm not about to betray his trust. I wouldn't do it even if I knew where he was."

"I know he'd appreciate your loyalty. You're a rare bird, Rajero. I won't forget the way you're sticking up for him."

"Thanks."

Grimaldi pushed open the front doors and allowed Rajero to exit first. They started to descend the steps when the first shots rang. Three Asians in black combat fatigues and scarlet headbands with Chinese writing on them were firing Jatimatic machine pistols from a van parked in front of the EPIC.

Grimaldi threw Rajero to the ground as the 9 mm slugs burned the air where they had been standing just moments before. Grimaldi managed to get his weapon clear, but Rajero was still fumbling for hers. Several agents who happened to be ascending the steps into the center turned, drew their pistols and began immediately returning fire.

Bystanders on the street began to scream and run into one another in their panic to find cover.

One of the agents who started returning fire with the

Chinese gunners fell under the impact of a dozen 9 mm rounds. Some were deflected by the vest he wore, but a few cut through a major artery in his leg and the wound began to spurt bright red blood. Another shot caught the unlucky DEA agent in the jaw, ripping part of his face away. He dropped his weapon and tumbled down the concrete steps.

Grimaldi and Rajero were nearly overcome by the sudden and vicious attack. The Stony Man pilot realized the three men and one woman who had been ascending the steps were now risking their lives to repel the assault. He shouted instructions to Rajero to get back inside the building as he raised his 9 mm Browning Hi-Power and returned fire with rapid, successive shots. He managed to nail one of their attackers, the 125-grain SJHP round striking one of the gunners inside the van and slamming him against its back wall.

Rajero had ignored Grimaldi, finally withdrawing her .380-caliber pistol from an ankle holster hidden beneath the cuff of her jeans and firing a few shots of her own. Two more DEA agents toppled under the onslaught of autofire from the Jatimatics. The two Asians inside the van sustained their heavy fire as another pair piled from the rear doors and opened up with AK-74 assault rifles in support of their comrades.

A burst of 5.45 mm rounds blew out stone chips around the remaining male agent, and he rushed for a nearby makeshift wall that served as one side of a brick garden box. Just as he reached the rail, the agent was cut down under the heavy rifle fire of the Chinese reinforcements.

Grimaldi knew their time was up. They had to get to the cover of the building or all would be lost. He wasn't concerned about his own life as much as Rajero's, and the spunky agent didn't want to seem to listen to anyone. He jumped to his feet, grabbed his prize and sprinted for the doors into the EPIC. They would either make it inside alive or die just like the rest had.

The Stony Man pilot waited for the sudden and thunderous blast of autofire—he could almost anticipate the burning of hot lead as it entered their bodies. Instead, his senses detected that their firing had changed directions. Grimaldi reached the front doors, dragging Rajero behind him. He started to push her through, then turned to risk a glance in the direction of his enemy. Their concentration had been redirected on an all too familiar form who was shooting at them from the passenger seat of a huge four-door pickup truck.

Grimaldi could hardly believe his eyes as he watched Mack Bolan rain sudden and assured destruction upon the enemy!

THE FIRST THING Mack Bolan realized as they approached the El Paso Intelligence Center was somebody was in trouble. It only took another moment for him to ascertain that that somebody was Jack Grimaldi. The Executioner's keen sense of sight immediately spotted the ace pilot as he rose, pulled Lisa Rajero to her feet and then charged for the doors.

"Get me up there!" Bolan commanded Milaña.

The Colombian beauty may have had the looks of a goddess but she drove like a bat out of hell. Nonetheless, her swerving tactics and insane maneuvers did in fact get Bolan to where the action was in record time.

The soldier already had his Desert Eagle out and ready for action. Bolan sighted on the two men standing at the back of the van, careful to keep one eye on another pair who had exited the side of the vehicle in an obvious attempt to pursue Grimaldi and Rajero. He steadied his arm on the window frame of the truck, ignored the pain in his shoulder and back, and gritted his teeth against the shock he knew would course a direct path to his wounds as he squeezed off the first shots.

The impact wasn't as bad as Bolan had originally anticipated. And it damn sure couldn't have hurt as much as the 280-grain bullets that left the muzzle of the .44 Magnum at a velocity of 450 meters per second. The first two rounds blew out the nearest man's spine and continued through his body to tear gaping exit wounds out the front of his upper torso. Bolan hammered the second man with two additional rounds, blowing the guy's leg off at the knee and shattering his skull in turn.

Bolan went EVA even as Milaña brought the pickup to a screeching halt. He raised the Desert Eagle and shot the driver of the van before the guy could react. The soldier moved around the front of the vehicle even as the remaining two Scarlet Dragon gunmen turned their attention to see the new arrival.

The Executioner didn't give them time to think about how they should react. He raised the Desert Eagle and emptied the clip in their direction. He wasn't nearly as concerned with hitting the targets as keeping their attention off Grimaldi. One of the rounds Bolan fired smashed the skull of the closest Dragon, nearly decapitating the guy as his corpse hit the steps.

Grimaldi, the attention now away from him, realized the Executioner would soon be out of ammunition. Even as Bolan slipped behind the van to reload, the Stony Man pilot took careful aim and opened fire on the remaining gunman. The 9 mm rounds punched through the guy and dropped him to the steps. His body fell on that of his comrade before flipping over and rolling down the steps in grisly concert with his clattering machine pistol.

Grimaldi motioned to Rajero as Bolan rose and quickly checked the van for remaining opponents. It was empty, except for the bodies of the two who had never stood a chance against the crack marksmanship of the Stony Man warriors.

"You okay?" the Executioner asked, turning as Grimaldi and Rajero descended the steps quickly.

"Fine," Grimaldi said. "Just in the nick of time, Sarge."

Bolan quickly surveyed the scene and nodded. "Yeah."

Rajero stepped forward and threw her arms around Bolan in a very unceremonious fashion. "Damn you, Belasko!" she said into his shoulder. "I thought you were dead."

"Hardly," Bolan said, gently pushing her away.

Agents were rushing from the building, and Bolan gestured curtly toward the truck. "Get in. We need to make tracks out of here."

"Understood," Grimaldi replied.

The threesome quickly reached the truck and climbed in. Bolan didn't bother to make introductions. There would plenty of time for that later. The important thing at the moment was to get away from there as quickly as they could.

The Executioner didn't even want to imagine what would have happened if he hadn't convinced Milaña to drive him into El Paso so he could find Rajero. Something, some instinct, had told him that the Kung Lok would consider her a threat. As long as she was alive, she could identify Ing Kaochu as the murderer of several

DEA agents, not to mention Kaochu's direct ties to the Scarlet Dragons and Lau-Ming Shui.

Now that she was safe, Bolan knew he could concentrate on the job at hand. It was time to put an end to the Nievas-Carillo drug cartel. They were the more immediate threat. And when that was done, he'd wrap up his business with the Kung Lok triad, and find this traitor who was fueling a war between the two factions. The next forty-eight hours were going to be busy—real busy.

CHAPTER FIVE

"So what the hell happened to you, Belasko?" Rajero demanded.

"It's a long story and there's no time for ancient histories," Bolan said from the front seat of Milaña's pickup.

He nodded at Grimaldi and added, "Good to see you, ace."

"Same here, Sarge. I take it our friends back there were Kung Lok."

Bolan nodded. "I think Rajero was their target. She's the only logical choice."

"Maybe not," Rajero interjected.

Bolan raised his eyebrows and studied the beautiful DEA agent with surprise. "You have a better explanation."

She nodded. "Sapèdas. It's possible they were planning to either snatch him out of custody or assassinate him. I'm guessing kidnapping, since he's worth a hell of a lot more alive than dead to the Kung Lok. Remember, he's got a considerable amount of information on the Mexican-Colombian drug alliance, since he worked directly for Jose Carillo."

"Not to mention he's in a law-enforcement position," Grimaldi added. "She might be right, Sarge."

The Executioner gave it serious thought but quickly dismissed the idea. The very fact they attacked as soon as they saw Rajero told him the Kung Lok assassins weren't worried about drawing attention to themselves. An attempt to take Sapèdas would have been carefully planned to the last detail, and done in secret if possible. A gun battle on the streets wasn't exactly discreet.

"No," Bolan replied, "I don't buy that. I'm sure they wanted Rajero dead and they were probably told to make it happen at any cost."

"Unfortunately for them, the costs were high," Milaña cut in quietly.

Bolan realized he'd been ignoring her. "I want you two to meet Catalina Milaña. She's a Colombian national who got involved with all of this very early on, and her intelligence on Nievas is phenomenal. She's proved herself quite an ally."

Grimaldi nodded with a casual wave at the back seat, but Rajero only half smiled. Bolan could immediately tell there was a bit of jealousy chiseled into her suddenly frosty look. Well, the two women would have to work it out because he had no time for those games. He'd done nothing to encourage either of them, and he couldn't help their assumptions. Still, it wasn't the first time Bolan had been caught between two females pacing each other for control of unclaimed territory.

"You still haven't said what's on your agenda," Grimaldi piped up.

"Well, I'm going to need some wings before this is over. Did you come back to El Paso by chopper or jet?"

Grimaldi cleared his throat and said, "A good friend of mine loaned me a Gulfstream."

Bolan nodded. He knew exactly to which "friend" Grimaldi referred: Harold Brognola. The Stony Man chief was probably pacing like a caged animal right now. Bolan could almost picture his longtime friend chomping on a cigar, the worries of the entire world on his shoulders. It wasn't as if he didn't have good reason to worry; Brognola had a tremendous responsibility. Sure, he didn't face the bombs and bullets of field life, but he was responsible for the action of every member on the Stony Man team. In addition, he had to answer to one of the most powerful individuals on Earth, and still maintain some sort of official position in the U.S. Department of Justice.

That was the primary reason Mack Bolan had chosen to keep Stony Man out of this war very early on; at least in any official capacity. And looking at recent events, the Executioner was glad he'd trusted his instincts. There was now enough intelligence to support the theory an official within the U.S. government was involved. On the north side of the U.S.-Mexican border, there was a Chinese crime lord bent on owning all of the drug and porn action in the Southwest. On the south side, a Colombian military leader and Mexican kingpin were interested in only three things: control, destruction and the wealth that could be made from obtaining the first two.

The efforts of these powerful factions were finally coming to a close, and Mack Bolan knew it was time to stop them. They wanted to wage their war in the middle—in *his* country against *his* people—and that just wasn't going to happen. Not while there was still breath in his lungs and blood pumping through his body.

"What about me?" Rajero asked.

"I think you'd better get back to Brownsville and lay low. Get your people to hide you."

"But the U.S. Marshals Service won't allow me to leave—"

"I'll take care of that," Bolan said sharply. "As long as the Kung Lok knows you're alive, you pose a threat to them. Not just because of the information you possess, but also because of your knowledge of their operations in Las Vegas. You could bring the whole DEA down on them, and that would be bad for business."

"What makes you believe I'm a threat?" Rajero asked.

"Think about it from their point of view," Grimaldi replied. "What's the point of controlling the drugs and sex-for-hire here if you know the Feds are going to be on your back every second. Sarge is right. These people know exactly who you are, who you work for and where you're going. They'll come after you as long as you're alive, which means you endanger everyone you meet. You need to find a place to lay low."

"Lay low?" Rajero echoed hollowly. She shook her head furiously. "No. Absolutely not. I'm not hiding from these bastards one second. They killed my friends, and I'm going to do everything I can to cooperate with other agencies and bring them down. I'll go straight to Liam Hoffner if I have to, but I will see every one of them come to justice. Especially Ing Kaochu, for kidnapping federal agents and murdering Noreen Zahn."

"Suit yourself, but I can't allow you to do it around me, Lisa," Bolan said coolly. "I can't afford the distractions. If you choose to go after the Kung Lok, you do it on your own. I won't be able to interfere."

Rajero nodded slowly, although he could tell she wasn't happy about it. "I understand."

Grimaldi gave Milaña directions to the private airfield. She dropped them near the hangar. As Bolan and Grimaldi got out of the vehicle, Rajero took Bolan's place in the front seat.

The Executioner studied the two women and tried to present them with a reassuring smile, although he didn't feel reassured. "Okay, Lisa, she'll take you to the airport. You catch the next flight out to wherever you want to go, but be careful. I guarantee you the Chinese triads won't give up as long as you're breathing. Once you've dropped her off, you know what to do, Catalina. We're still on schedule, so don't be late."

Milaña nodded and Bolan tapped the side of the pickup truck with his fist lightly as a way of telling them to get going. Once Milaña and Rajero were gone, Grimaldi led Bolan to the plane. There was plenty of spare gear inside, packed with a standard complement of explosives and weaponry in the storage lockers courtesy of Stony Man. Bolan made a quick check and traded his two older Beretta 93-Rs for a freshly cleaned and well-oiled version of the same model.

Grimaldi immediately prepared to get under way. The jet had been fueled and serviced by the ground crew just as he'd requested before leaving for the El Paso Intelligence Center, so there was little more to do other than the standard preflight checks.

Bolan also retrieved an FNC from one of the storage lockers and ten box magazines that each contained thirty rounds of 5.56 mm NATO ammunition. The Belgian-made rifle had become a personal favorite of the Executioner in recent years. Manufactured by Fabrique Nationale, maker of the FAL battle rifle, the FNC had a cyclic rate of fire around 750 rounds per minute, and an effective range of approximately 350 meters. It was lightweight and usable in almost any environment without rusting, jamming or exhibiting any of the other faults experienced by weapons of similar design.

Bolan then moved to another crate, hoping he would

find the ultimate in personal weapons. Unfortunately, this particular plane wasn't carrying any of the Diehl DM-51 offensive-defensive grenades, but rather just standard M-26 frags. Well, he couldn't win every time. Still, he attached six of them to his black flak vest. Bolan sat in a rear chair and then set up the weapons and gear so they were ready on short notice.

Throughout his inspection of the weapons, he'd barely noticed that Grimaldi was airborne and ready for action. When he'd completed his work, the Executioner squeezed into the copilot's seat and donned a set of headphones so he could talk with the pilot.

"Where to?" Grimaldi asked.

Bolan reached into the pocket of the flannel shirt and retrieved the coordinates that would supposedly bring them directly over Jose Carillo's estate in Chihuahua. The Colombian beauty had provided the information, and her tenacity amazed Bolan. When it came to intelligence on Carillo, there was no question Milaña had done her homework.

Grimaldi studied the figures a moment and then adjusted his instrumentation. "This isn't far," he said. "We'll have barely reached cruising altitude before we're over the area."

"That's okay," Bolan replied. "As a matter of fact, I want you to come in as low as you can, but not so low we arouse suspicion. I'm sure Carillo's plenty used to DEA and Mexican police planes flying overhead. I'm not concerned about that. I want to get an idea of how his estate is laid out, and the best way to make an approach."

"What's our mission?"

"I don't know until I see the layout. I'm thinking about a night drop."

"I don't suppose role camouflage would be an option."

"Not my preference in this case, but I haven't ruled out the idea."

"Okay," Grimaldi said with a nod. "But you're still recuperating from a bullet in your back, and if it was me I wouldn't push it too far. You could wind up paralyzed or dead if you don't watch it. And maybe I'm sounding morbid, but if that happens this whole trip will be for nothing, Sarge."

"Understood and agreed," Bolan replied. "Don't sweat it, Jack. I'm not going to do anything to compromise my mission."

"You're going to bring Nievas and Carillo down in one shot?"

"That's the idea." A low whistle sounded in the cockpit. "What's that?"

Grimaldi made a slight adjustment and the whistling ceased. "We're over the coordinates you gave me."

"Acknowledged. Take us down and let's see what we're up against."

Ciudad Juárez, Mexico

CATALINA MILAÑA MADE SURE she wasn't late for her meeting. In fact, she was purposely early by twenty minutes so she could check things out.

Ciudad Juárez wasn't the kind of place for a lone woman, particularly in this part of town at this time of the evening. But it wasn't any matter of worry, even to someone as beautiful as the Colombian widow. First, this had been her home for many years now, and she wasn't about to be afraid in her own arena—she'd spent enough time being afraid in Colombia. Second, she could feel the comfortable weight of the 9 mm Walther P-5 pistol tucked at the small of her back, concealed by a light-weight leather jacket. Her dark hair cascaded across her shoulders, glittering in the lights of the dance club. This wasn't the nicest place—usually populated by the dregs of the city—but it was public. Not to mention it was populated with enough beautiful women that Milaña didn't stand out from the crowd. Sure, perhaps a glim-mer of something betrayed a grace and elegance greater than that possessed by other women in the club, but for the most part, she looked her role. It was important to remain inconspicuous.

Milaña didn't have to wait long before he appeared. She could feel a chill run down her spine as she watched the man search the room for her. His cold, hard eyes scanned the faces through the dark and smoky atmo-sphere until finally coming to rest on her. Something like wickedness appeared in his features. The dimples at the corners of his mouth would have been charming on most men, but they looked cruel on him.

It hadn't been that long since Milaña had last seen General Deng Jikwan, but that didn't make the meeting any less uncomfortable for her. She would have pre-ferred to deal directly with his superiors, but she knew that the Chinese warlord saw an advantage when he'd first learned of Milaña's unquenched hatred for Colonel Amado Nievas. She cared little for Jikwan's political views or aspirations. To a military thug like him, the interests of Red communism were the only important ones—and the representatives of the party who paid the most.

Jikwan was loyal to nobody but himself and his Chi-nese masters; there was no doubt about that. But he'd become even more loyal to Catalina Milaña. This was a fact she'd chosen to keep from Belasko for the time being. It was one thing to expect Belasko would make good on his promise to deal with Carillo and Nievas, but it was quite another for him to actually go through with it. Jikwan was Milaña's insurance policy in the event Belasko went back on his word. And for the time being, her relationship with Jikwan wasn't something Belasko needed to know about.

Jikwan finally closed the gap and gave her a quick and unsolicited kiss on the lips before taking a seat across from her. Milaña squirmed in her chair with the blatant assumption and audacity of his action. The guy was a killer and professional soldier through and through, and ultimately she knew he wanted her physically. Well, it was never going to happen as far she was concerned. Never.

"Don't do that again, General," she snapped quietly.

"Or?"

"Or I'll stick a knife in your back."

He studied her murderous glance a moment before smiling. "Of course you would. I just couldn't control myself. You are a most ravishing woman, Catalina. It is hard not to think about how much we could enjoy each other...to steal, perhaps, just a moment of pure lasciviousness. Of course, you aren't Chinese but that isn't your fault and I wouldn't imagine holding it against you."

"That is magnanimous of you, General. But I'm afraid it wouldn't happen even in your wildest dreams."

"Don't mock the virility of a Chinese man until you have tried it."

"Stop patronizing me, and say what you have come to say. Is Nievas going to return to Colombia?"

Jikwan signaled a server, ordered vodka, then sent her

away before returning his attention to Milaña. He grabbed a handful of salted peanuts from the basket on the table and shook his head. "My intelligence team doesn't believe he will leave. It is not in his best interests to return to his people empty-handed. They are expecting weapons, and Nievas is too proud not to deliver."

"You are certain of this?"

Jikwan's expression was frosty. "He is first a soldier, my dear. This I understand. He will do nothing short of killing his entire command to maintain his honor. That is what is really at stake for Colonel Nievas."

"Perhaps," Milaña replied challengingly, "but we're not talking about honor, General. We're talking about revenge."

"I know what you're talking about," Jikwan said, lowering his voice as the server brought his drink, but doing nothing to hide his expression of disgust. "I believe it is now *you* who are patronizing *me*. Let us not forget that I am the one who facilitated your meeting with this American, Belasko. Now that you've enlisted him to kill Nievas, I do not think he will disappoint us."

"I don't have a crystal ball, General. I know that you have your own aspirations and political agenda where these matters are concerned. I also believe that the death of Nievas alone will not help you to accomplish your plans. Jose Carillo must die, as well, in order for the Chinese empire to subvert the American government."

Jikwan nearly choked on his drink in reaction to her remark. He let out a bellowing laugh, and a few bystanders glanced at him as if he were insane. Milaña noted that some of the din of conversation died in the cantina, but the onlookers returned to their own business quickly enough. Minding your own business in such a place like Juárez was always a good idea.

Jikwan didn't appear to care about the attention he'd drawn in that moment. "Are you trying to insult my intelligence, Catalina? My government has not been an empire for a long time."

"It was a figure of speech," she replied.

"It was a foolish statement," Jikwan said quickly. "We are not an empire, neither are we a democracy. I know in my heart that China is not the great nation she once was, but that is all about to change. This little war my people have decided to start with the Mexicans and Colombians is of particular interest. It could prove advantageous to my people, both politically and militarily. Don't you realize the impact this will have? Don't you see what we stand to gain?"

"No. Why don't you enlighten me?"

Jikwan started to open his mouth but then seemed to think better of it. "This is neither the time nor the place to openly discuss these issues. Perhaps you would like to accompany me back to my hotel?"

"Not in this life," Milaña said as she rose from her chair.

"Where are you going?"

"That is not of your concern," she replied haughtily. "I will be in touch when I have more to report."

Jikwan shook his head. "You are playing a dangerous game, my dear. You would do well to be careful."

"I will manage just fine without your concern."

Milaña whirled and left the cantina, glad for the burst of fresh air that greeted her outside. It cooled the perspiration that had collected on her body as she dealt with Jikwan. The Chinese military leader made her nervous—she didn't like dealing with him and his kind. He was a pompous and overconfident lout. Jikwan thought he owned her, but that wasn't really the case. She knew better, and so did he. Catalina Milaña was her own woman, and she had no stake in his game. She surmised the possibilities for his superiors. A war between the Colombian-Mexican alliance and the Chinese triads was definitely to the advantage of the Chinese powers, just as Jikwan had said—and she knew why. War on American streets meant one thing to those like Jikwan: vulnerability. And any political or military body would use that for advantage if the opportunity arose.

Milaña thought of Belasko at that moment. He was a good man, but highly unrealistic in his ideals. If he really thought he could stop this, he was as crazy as Jikwan. Killing Nievas and Carillo wouldn't solve the problem of anarchy in his country. He was only destroying one side of the front. The Kung Lok would just move into those territories held by Carillo, and either other Mexican crime families would step in for a piece of the action or feuding would ensue between the different factions of the Chinese underworld. Other triads would try for a piece of the action, and the war would continue.

Nonetheless, Milaña couldn't concern herself with Belasko's problems. She had to continue to make the guy think she wanted what he did, and ultimately he would accomplish her goals. She respected him, but she was also using him. She knew it, and so did Jikwan, and once Belasko had taken care of Nievas, she knew that Jikwan would launch a strike of his own. Jikwan sought power. Belasko sought power. Carillo and Nievas sought power. That's what men did, because they knew with power came wealth and women.

This was why they ultimately fought and killed one another, and if that happened to serve her purpose, then Catalina Milaña could be satisfied with that.

CHAPTER SIX

Chihuahua, Mexico

The time to attack had come and the Executioner was ready.

Mack Bolan had enough intelligence from his reconnaissance mission with Grimaldi to launch an assault against Jose Carillo's stronghold. Despite the fact a week had passed since Bolan's last encounter with Carillo's enforcers, the soldier knew that Nievas's private army was still reeling from its battle with him in the Baja, and the Kung Lok in Las Vegas.

It seemed obvious—from the air, anyway—that the remaining FARC troops were preparing for an offensive. The time to hit them was now. Bolan knew it, and he also knew the overall success of his mission hinged upon it. So rather than have Grimaldi return to El Paso, Bolan ordered the pilot to put him down about a klick outside the stronghold that served as home to Jose Carillo.

As the Executioner checked his equipment once more, Grimaldi watched him with concern. "Are you sure about this, Sarge? Maybe you should get some backup."

Bolan shook his head and sighed. "No time, Jack. I told Hal I didn't want him bringing Stony Man into this, and I meant it. This is my fight."

"I hate to disagree with you, but this is everybody's fight."

"We're not going to argue about this, Jack," Bolan replied quietly.

Grimaldi said nothing, nodding instead. He understood the warning tone in Bolan's voice, and he knew just how far to push it. He didn't always agree with the Executioner's methods, but he believed in the soldier's War Everlasting, and he understood there were good reasons for every decision Bolan made. Actually, his old friend hadn't really told him why he didn't want Stony Man involved. He'd taken that position from the start, but Grimaldi didn't understand it.

Brognola probably understood it all too well. But for whatever reason, the head Fed had chosen not to disclose this to the rest of them, which wasn't surprising. Harold Brognola knew the Executioner better than anyone else. They were all familiar with Mack Bolan in their own unique ways, but Brognola knew him like nobody else did. It didn't mean the Stony Man chief wasn't sometimes frustrated by the decisions Bolan made—and this was definitely one of them—but he understood them.

"Will you need me for extraction?"

"Yeah. I'm betting most of the FARC troops are taking a break before their retaliation against the Kung Lok."

"So they're vulnerable," Grimaldi interjected. Now he understood why Bolan was so insistent on launching his assault immediately. He wanted to catch the enemy with their pants down, and now was the time. "But that doesn't mean Carillo won't have sentries posted."

"Agreed. He might even have patrols. But once I'm inside, there's no doubt things will go hard."

"You'll maintain radio contact?"

"Until I hit the target. I'll have to disconnect there, then reestablish contact when I'm ready for pullout."

"How long will you need?"

"I'm guessing twenty minutes, give or take. Give me a total of thirty on the long side. After that, don't wait for me and don't move in on your own, Jack. If you don't hear from me within thirty minutes of H-hour, it means I'm dead."

"All right. Good luck, Sarge."

Bolan nodded, shouldered his backpack, then turned from his friend and headed for Carillo's fortress. The foliage was green and lush, thick with vines and thicker with bugs, snakes and other wildlife, reminding Bolan of Vietnam. He was on his own again, his body loosening up in preparation for his thousand-yard trek through the verdant landscape of northern Chihuahua, fed by the waters of the Rio Grande.

Bolan planned to make his approach on the north side of Carillo's estate, where brightly colored gardens would provide ample cover once he made it past the external security. An eight-foot-high wall surrounded the estate and judging by the aerial shots he'd taken, the wall was about eight inches thick. Five feet inside the perimeter was an electronic security system, which the Executioner knew he'd trigger as soon as he advanced on the house itself. The soldier hadn't seen any military-style obstacles, such as concertina wire or ground marks indicative of mines. Carillo probably figured his security system was enough to deter any unwanted visitors.

What had Bolan most concerned was the sheer force of Nievas's army. The Executioner had been up against troops as highly specialized as the FARC were, but he'd nearly lost his life against this band in Mexicali. It seemed like ages ago—so much had happened in the past week.

The pain in his back had returned in full force. Bolan knew he probably could have survived without the extra gear in his small backpack, which would have taken some of the strain off the wound. Still, he didn't want to risk running out of ammunition or supplies in the middle of a firefight. He'd survived this long on the theory that a prepared warrior stayed alive long enough to learn from the mission.

The Executioner pushed the pain from his mind and pressed onward. Another complication was the recent involvement of Catalina Milaña. She was a gutsy woman, full of mystery...and pain. She was like him in a lot of respects, dealing with her own past and looking for vengeance. But Bolan's temper against his enemies had been seasoned by many years of combat. It had hardened his personality and steeled his resolve, but he surmised that wasn't the case for Milaña. She'd let her thirst for vengeance burn inside her, unable to release it in fury against Nievas and the FARC as Bolan had done when first learning of the Mafia's involvement in the deaths of his loved ones.

Not that she could have done anything about it at the time. Bolan couldn't blame her for her feelings, but that didn't mean he had to trust her—and he didn't. When people were angry enough, it clouded their judgment. That might be a luxury she could afford, but it was one the Executioner had learned to quell within his spirit. Anger and vengeance were okay, but not during the heat of battle. The thirst for blood could get a warrior killed very quickly.

While Amado Nievas was still alive, Milaña's thirst for revenge would go unquenched. And because of that,

Mack Bolan believed she posed a serious liability to his mission. She didn't really want the same thing he wanted—she wanted Nievas dead and his FARC army destroyed for personal reasons. The Executioner wanted the enemy neutralized because of the threat they posed to his country. He felt the same for anyone who dangled a corrupt and evil sphere of influence over America.

And if fate were with him, that sphere would be nonexistent before sunset.

MACK BOLAN HEARD the first signs of enemy activity much sooner than he'd expected. It took the form of a small squad of men on patrol probably fifty yards from the perimeter of Carillo's stronghold estate. Bolan crouched a moment, assessed the situation, then quickly climbed a nearby tree. He'd let them pass underneath before making his move.

None of his aerial reconnaissance had indicated patrols this far from the well-tended gardens that made up a majority of Carillo's property. Still, Bolan knew the jungle could conceal dangers undetectable even by the most advanced electronic surveillance equipment.

It seemed to the Executioner that these guys could use some pointers. They were stomping loudly through the thick underbrush, making entirely too much noise for him to believe they were concerned about stealth. It was odd behavior. According to intelligence gleaned by Stony Man's vast computer networks, there had been several attempts by various Mexican and U.S. law-enforcement groups over the years to penetrate the Carillo estate. All of them had failed. But those groups obviously hadn't possessed two things the Executioner did: surprise and ferocity.

The security team wasn't attired in the traditional uniforms of FARC troops, but instead wore civilian bush clothes and toted pistols, which were holstered at present since their owners were too busy hacking through the dense jungle growth with machetes. Only one carried some additional firepower, and Bolan noted the impressive addition as its carrier passed almost directly under his cover.

The drug soldier was toting a Beretta RS 200-P pump-action combat shotgun. While Bolan knew the weapon was no longer in production, replaced by the RS 202-P model, he realized it was formidable all the same. It chambered 12-gauge 2.75-inch shells with an effective range of 100 meters and had a magazine capacity of six rounds stored in an under-barrel tube when fully loaded. That meant this particular hardcase was the biggest threat, so he had to go down first.

Bolan waited until the guy was just past his scout point, then he jumped from the low-hanging branch. He landed with Beretta in hand, grunting against the impact as he went to a crouch. The shotgunner whirled, expecting his assailant to be upright. The assumption cost him his life, as the extra time it took him to align the shotgun on his target was all Bolan needed. The Executioner squeezed the Beretta's trigger, and the weapon chugged out three subsonic 9 mm rounds, catching the shotgunner in the chest. The impact threw him onto his back, his eyes open and glazing over with sudden death.

There was swearing and shouting in the thick foliage surrounding Bolan as he scooped up the shotgun and slung it across his shoulder, muzzle down. It might come in handy to have a little extra firepower. Bolan had counted a total of four in the group, which meant there was a trio of confused men now scrambling in his general direction, and they were probably nervous and trigger happy. While the reports from the Beretta weren't enough to have reached back to the sentries at Carillo's stronghold, they were definitely loud enough to attract the attention of the shotgunner's comrades.

The first one appeared in the shadow of a rubber tree, calling out to his companion.

Bolan snap-aimed as he thumbed the selector to single shot and squeezed off a round. The bullet took the hardman in the forehead, blowing off the top of his skull and taking part of his brains with it before his body staggered into the tree and collapsed to the ground.

The soldier whirled to the sound of a man screaming like a banshee. The guy burst through a small opening in the jungle growth and swung his machete downward. Bolan rolled away just in the nick of time, the machete whistling as it cleaved the air where his skull had been a moment before. The Executioner gritted his teeth in agony as white-hot lances of pain shot through his lower back. His assailant flailed at him in a backward slashing motion that was too low to avoid with a simple duck.

The Executioner stepped into his assailant and grabbed the man's wrist with his left hand as he drew his combat knife with the right. Bolan propelled the guy in a circular motion, matching the speed of the man's back swing and thereby using his own force against him. At the same moment, the soldier drove the blade of his knife straight into the guy's chest and buried it to the hilt. The guy's body went erect before falling backward and hitting the ground with a dull thud.

The Executioner dropped to one knee, the pain in his back now almost unbearable. Sweat poured down his face, and his clothes were soaked.

The soldier didn't find much respite, as his fourth opponent appeared wielding a large revolver. The man was a little taken aback at the sight of his two dead buddies, but he quickly moved past that and raised his pistol. Bolan had dropped his pistol in the fray with the machete-wielding man, so his only hope lay in the shotgun. He swung the muzzle of the RS 200-P into play and disengaged the safety as he dived to the right. His opponent managed to get off one shot, which whined past Bolan's ear as the Executioner returned fire. He pumped two shells into his enemy, the first blowing out the man's knee and the second punching a grapefruit-sized hole in his chest. The guy collapsed to the jungle floor and lay still.

Bolan swore as he wearily got to his feet. The pain was enough to make him pass out, but he fought the waves of blackening nausea and tried to coax a few deep breaths from his battle-worn body. He'd tried to take them all quietly, but that final encounter had spoiled his surprise. It was unlikely they were far enough out that nobody had heard those shots. A single shot from the pistol might have been masked by the trees, but the RS 200-P was definitely loud enough to draw attention.

Carillo and Nievas would certainly send out reinforcements, and that spelled big trouble for Bolan's mission. He had to get up and moving. He collected his weapons, lifted a radio from one of the dead patrollers, then continued toward Carillo's estate. There hadn't been enough shots for them to really pinpoint a direction, but they would probably have known the general direction of the patrol, so it wouldn't take them long to flood the area with troops.

Bolan monitored the radio as he walked, circling away from the site of his first encounter, then moving back in the general direction of the drug lord's encampment. Surprisingly, he didn't hear any activity over the radio.

Not so much as a message to check in. Bolan understood enough Spanish that he could avert any suspicions until close enough to the target, provided, of course, they didn't ask for a code word. He doubted it. They weren't expecting visitors, and especially not in the form of the Executioner. After all, if Milaña's intelligence was correct, they were assuming he was dead and no longer posed a threat to their plans. And they were probably confident enough in the fact that the Kung Lok didn't know the actual location of Carillo's stronghold.

Of course, to Bolan's way of thinking, this was a foolish assumption. There was no question in his mind that Lau Shui had enough resources to gain this information, and even enough of a private army to act on it once he did. Still, he didn't think this was what Shui really sought. The Chinese mobster was a businessman—he thought and acted like a businessman. He was looking for profit and a way to exploit the American people. He wanted money and control, not a war with the Mexican underworld.

Mack Bolan, on the other hand, was looking for exactly that. He'd declared war on Carillo's drug operations, and in so doing he'd declared war on Amado Nievas and his private army of FARC mercenaries. And he was at war with the Kung Lok triad. If he could have arranged a war between them, and done it off American soil, he would have. But there was now more than one front. Bolan was doing what every soldier dreaded and feared most—fighting a battle on two fronts. But he couldn't help that. He'd chosen the time and place to confront Carillo.

That time was now.

Bolan emerged from the tree line and encountered the wall enclosing Carillo's estate. He crouched in the shadows, checked his watch and confirmed he had perhaps ten minutes of sunlight left. Despite his run-in with that patrol, he was still on schedule.

He reached into the side pocket of his combat black-suit and withdrew one of the maps he'd drafted aboard the plane. Bolan did some quick math and estimated his position on the map. He knew the approximate locations of the guards and the intervals of their patrols. His guess was maybe six men were actually roving the exterior, or watching from close to the house. The warrior double-checked his weapons, secured the map, then drew the Beretta 93-R and moved to the wall.

He checked his watch and decided to give it another minute or two. The darker it got, the easier it would be to take out the opposition. Sundown was the time Grimaldi would expect his call anyway, and according to his information from Milaña, there was a camouflaged airstrip within the grounds. The Executioner could only hope fate was on their side this night, because Grimaldi would have a very narrow window of opportunity to get inside the camp, touch down and extract him before the enemy managed to damage the plane.

The Executioner drew a deep breath, then turned on his radio and keyed the small but sensitive throat microphone taped beneath the turtleneck of his blacksuit.

"Striker to Eagle One, you copy?" he whispered.

"Loud and clear, Striker," came the reply.

"I'm moving in. Twenty minutes, no more. You hear?"

"Understood."

"Out here."

Bolan clicked off the radio, then found a foothold on the wall and went over the top in one fluid motion and landed in a crouch, the Beretta ready. The first guard would be along shortly. He pressed himself against the wall, confident he hadn't triggered the electronic security net he knew Carillo had set up within the grounds. The place where he'd made his entry was actually thick with flowers and fruited bushes, and they wouldn't have set the electronic security at a sensitive level. Otherwise, everything from wind and small animals to the roving patrols would have set off alarms.

Bolan tensed his body as he heard the footfalls of the first guard. When the guy was even with the bushes, the soldier leaped out and took his opponent down hard and fast. He clamped a hand over the man's mouth and drove the blade of his knife through an opening at the base of the man's skull. The attack immediately cut off signals between body and brain. It was actually a quick and merciful way to take out opposition.

After quickly dragging the body into the bushes, Bolan waited in silence. The grounds were extensive, so it would be a few minutes before the next guard came along. Once he'd taken him out, it would be easy going. He was certain additional sentries were in the vicinity, but there was enough space between them that Bolan wasn't concerned. He only wanted to make sure he'd covered his flank before handling the main force.

While he waited, Bolan decided to shed his pack and retrieve his night-vision goggles. It was now dark enough that the NVDs would prove invaluable in his mission. As it was, the enemy probably wouldn't be prepared for his attack, and especially not at night. While most believed in attacking just before dawn, the Executioner liked to vary his tactics. Dawn was when average people were most tired and least alert, but there was no doubt in Bolan's mind that Nievas would have trained his men for this. An attack immediately after sundown, however, that was something quite different and most likely unexpected.

Bolan scanned the grounds, but there was no movement. An eerie feeling crept over the soldier. The place seemed too quiet, and he was beginning to experience a sense of foreboding, as if something just wasn't right. Well, only time would tell. At this stage of the game, he knew there was no calling it off. He was out of time, so all he could do was make his assault and hope fate was with him.

The sound of the second guard approaching demanded his attention, and Bolan crouched in anticipation. He waited until the guy was nearly on top of him, then jumped from his hiding spot and took him out in the same fashion he'd done the first. As soon as he'd hidden the body in the foliage, he traded the Beretta for his FNC rifle and set off across the expansive lawn. He tracked the gloom with his weapon but nobody appeared to challenge him, and Bolan began to get a refreshed sense that something was wrong.

Yeah, trouble was near. He managed to make it all the way to a corner of the house without firing a shot. Bolan removed the night-vision goggles and put them into his pack. He sat quietly, not moving a muscle as he let his eyes grow accustomed to the dark. Only a few lights were visible from the interior of the house, and the rest of the place was quiet. Too damn quiet, for Bolan's liking. He waited another minute and then crouch-walked along the low foundation wall that supported an elevated porch.

Suddenly, armed men in fatigues emerged from the blackness, rushing toward his position from every direction.

CHAPTER SEVEN

Mack Bolan dropped to cover behind the porch wall. He aimed at the nearest pair of aggressors and triggered the FNC rifle. The 5.56 mm NATO rounds stitched gruesome patterns in their chests, the impact knocking one guy off his feet, while the second fell forward and skidded to a halt on his chin. Both men were dead before they hit the ground.

Bolan was about to align his weapon sights on a new pair when a noise to the right caught his attention. Even in the darkness, the Executioner could make out the shape of the object well enough to know what it was. It seemed for the span of a heartbeat or two that an eerie silence had fallen on the battleground as the grenade struck the hard flagstone tiles of the porch, skidded to a halt and wobbled on its long end. Bolan didn't wait for an invitation. He rose and jumped over the wall, feeling the heat on his back even as the grenade exploded.

The Executioner rolled out of the jump and began to sweep his weapon back and forth, smashing the enemy troops with a burst of NATO slugs. The FNC chattered, smoke and flame shooting from the barrel as the bolt ratcheted through its cycle and the extractor spit brass. A pile of shells was developing at Bolan's feet as he quickly traded out magazines and sent a new volley in the enemy's direction to keep their heads down.

He finished off a second magazine, then moved away from the main force and jogged along the perimeter of the veranda-style porch. His violent response to their attack had caused them to fall back out of effective firing range and regroup, so now was the time to put some distance between them. The soldier had been expecting something like that, but not quite that way. It was almost as if they had been lying in wait for him, somehow managing to maintain cover along the perimeter of the wall and then converge when the time was right. But there were two things he didn't understand: why had they even allowed him inside the perimeter and why had they waited to attack until he was almost at the house? It seemed like a lot of trouble and loss for just one man. Not to mention the fact Bolan had pretty much figured it would go down this way once he was near the house.

The other puzzling factor was the absence of Nievas's men. His attackers here were definitely hired guns dressed in paramilitary fatigues. They didn't wear FARC uniforms and they didn't move like FARC troops. It had been too easy to repel their attack—Bolan could immediately tell his enemies weren't trained combatants. They could have seized their advantage of sheer numbers, and yet they hesitated.

Bolan found an easy way into the house just as security lights pierced the night. He closed and locked the porch door behind him, then crouched and put his back against the cool wall to one side of the door. He needed a breather and a moment to collect his thoughts. He was still experiencing some aftereffects of the drugs Guajardo had pumped into him, as well as the residue of his infection, since he was certain his fever had returned. He had to make sure he didn't have a repeat of passing out in the heat of battle. Carillo's men wouldn't be as accommodating as Milaña had.

The soldier stopped, trying to make out the shouts of the enemy leaders, but they were in Spanish and too faint to understand. Suddenly, he heard footfalls near the door and he tightened his grip on the handle, steeling himself for the inevitable. The porch door was covered with a thin lace curtain, but Bolan could see the forms of the troops silhouetted by the outside floodlights. The thin door rattled as they tried it twice.

The Executioner's attention was suddenly diverted from what was happening on the porch as the clatter of more booted feet resounded from behind a door across the room. Most likely they were conducting a room-to-room search. If he didn't act now, Bolan knew he'd be caught in a crossfire. He rose from his cover behind a heavy circular table, fired a quick burst at the door, then dived under the table for cover. As he expected, the door flew open a moment later as the soldiers outside forced open the porch door in response to his firing. Soldiers crashed into the room from both ends, and the darkness didn't allow for immediate identification of their enemy. The troops coming from the interior of the house opened fire first, assuming those making forced entry from the outside could only be the enemy.

Carillo's soldiers shot one another, both sides losing several troops before the leader of the interior squad called a cease fire. By that time, they were too late. As the lights came up in the room, Bolan tossed a primed grenade into their midst while upending the table for cover and firing on the remaining trio of gunners just inside the porch doorway. Bolan dropped the last man of the exterior team as the grenade exploded. The heavy

table protected him from the blast and shrapnel. The table deflected some of the superheated, razor-sharp metal
while others lodged in furniture. The blast alone was
enough to slice one member of the interior team to
shreds, while dismembering two others. The fourth soldier was blown into the hallway, and the impact against
a stairway banister broke his neck.

The Executioner jumped from cover and tossed another grenade underhand through the porch doorway. He
knew that would keep heads down while adding to the
confusion as he moved deeper into the house. He needed
to find Carillo and Nievas, the ultimate goal of this mission. And he only had seventeen minutes before Grimaldi touched down. That gave him about seven minutes
to find and destroy the Mexican drug lord and his Colombian partner. Then he'd have to break off.

Bolan continued through the house on his search-and-
destroy mission.

Las Vegas, Nevada

THERE WAS NO WAY Lisa Rajero was going to hide!

She wasn't going to run away like a sniveling little
coward, or bury her head in the sand and whimper when
the enemy posed a threat. Instead, she was going to remain the hard charger she'd always been, and deal with
the Kung Lok in her own way.

Rajero knew her anger with Mike Belasko was part
of this drive. For some strange reason, the guy had
treated her like an incompetent. Sure, she'd hit a few
bumps in the road and nearly died at the hands of the
Kung Lok, but she'd managed to survive and bring a
major criminal to justice. Her capture of Ramon Sapèdas
should have been enough proof of her innocence, but

she felt that more was needed. Perhaps her superiors and the investigators with the U.S. Marshals Service would be satisfied if she managed to arrest Ing Kaochu.

What bothered her most was the fact that she had proved herself to Belasko, and yet he'd called her...what was it? Oh yeah, a threat. What a joke! Rajero didn't know whom Belasko worked for and she didn't care anymore. Obviously, he'd used her for what he needed and now he was done with her. She understood he had his own mission, but that didn't mean she could drop *her* responsibilities, and it sure as hell didn't mean she was going to let the Kung Lok get away with murdering her friends. The deaths of Peter and Noreen wouldn't be in vain, nor would the murderers go unpunished.

Now, as she left the airport and drove to the local DEA office in downtown Las Vegas, she knew that it was only a matter of time before she would confront the Kung Lok. She reached up to her jacket pocket one more time and made sure her orders were still there. After her experience at the El Paso Intelligence Center and her subsequent report of the incident, Metzger had immediately made some phone calls and called in some favors. Within a few hours she was on a plane to Las Vegas, charged to lead a massive DEA-INS task force against the Kung Lok, seize any weapons or drugs they found and eject any aliens among them from the country once and for all.

She dreaded the thought of returning to the place where she'd been tortured and watched her friend die, but in some bizarre way she also found a shred of poetic justice in it. Rajero had never considered herself a vengeful person, but she would do whatever it took to take down the Kung Lok forever. She wanted justice for her friends, sure—she couldn't imagine any decent human being who wouldn't have wanted this. But she also wanted to make the streets safe for kids again. These were lofty ideals, and the kind her trainers had warned her against. Vigilance was okay as long as it wasn't misplaced in idealism and patriotism, and ran through the heart and mind unchecked. In other words, it was okay for her to feel that way but she was required to temper it with common sense and critical thinking.

Well, to hell with that. She would destroy the Kung Lok. She would bring them to their knees and worry about idealism and all of that other bullshit later.

Rajero arrived at the government office housed in a small, nondescript building on the Strip, and made her way to the third floor. The place was a beehive of activity. INS, BATF and DEA tactical agents in various modes of dress from fatigues to full body armor sat around drinking coffee and munching snacks. Given the hour, only the key office staff was still present. There wasn't even a lull in the buzz of conversations, and most took scant notice of Rajero as she crossed the room and entered the office of the local DEA commander. Perhaps none of them realized who was in charge yet.

Rajero closed the plate-glass door behind her and immediately drew the attention of the commander and the tactical squad leaders from the three respective agencies participating in the operation. The men studied her for a moment with surprise, and then the DEA commander spoke.

"Can I help you with something, miss?"

She held up her badge and her orders. "The name is Rajero, and I'm taking charge by order of Washington. Didn't they tell you I was coming?"

"No, ma'am," he said, glancing at the orders, then returning them to her. "What's this all about?"

"It's about the Kung Lok," Rajero snapped. "And it's about us kicking their ass out of here and all the way back to China if we have to."

The tactical officer from the BATF didn't appear impressed, and he didn't mind hiding the fact with a smirk. "Is that right?"

"That's right," Rajero said, fixing him with a hard stare and adding the best confident edge to her voice she could muster. "Now, I'm not here to lord it over everybody that I'm in charge. I'll leave special tactics to the individual officers, because that's your expertise and not mine. You can report most developments to the commander here. Still, I expect to be fully briefed on everything you're doing."

She looked expectantly at the commander. He extended his hand and said, "Haggis. Wesley Haggis."

She shook the guy's hand and then turned to the tactical officers. "Okay, you keep Haggis here briefed. He'll keep me briefed."

"Begging your pardon ma'am," the DEA tactical officer piped up, "but just exactly what is your specialty in this area?"

Rajero checked the guy's name tag: Capt. R. Cooper. "Well, Cooper, I know the Kung Lok Chinese triad better than all of you put together."

"Come again?" the BATF officer said.

"I've been in gun battles with them and was kidnapped at gunpoint," Rajero snapped challengingly. "If anybody in this room can say that, I'll let you call the shots. If not, then I'd suggest we quit standing around here like a bunch of stiff-legged dogs and get down to business."

There was a dead silence in the room.

"That's what I thought," Rajero said with a quick

nod. She went over to look at the map spread across Haggis's desk. It had blueprints of what looked like the block where Tang's house was located, as well as floor plans of the moderate but large suburban home itself. "Tell me what you have to this point."

Haggis began, "Well, we've only got one snitch that works that area, and she covers a lot of territory. But we do know there's been a lot of activity at the place lately, especially a few nights ago."

Rajero was sure she already knew the answer, but she asked anyway. "Which was?"

Haggis shrugged. "Well, you might call me crazy but a bunch of Las Vegas's finest shot it out with some kind of militant group."

"A large militant group," Cooper added, "that was armed with automatic weapons. Seems it all started when they attacked this residence."

"Which, incidentally," Haggis continued, "is the first time we heard about this lone commando who traded shots with them also. At first, the LVPD thought he was part of this group, but turns out he ended up saving a bunch of their asses."

"Took out a bunch of the bad guys, too, before he disappeared into God knows where," Cooper concluded.

Rajero only nodded with seeming interest, although she knew exactly which encounter they were talking about. As a matter of fact, she probably knew more about that than Haggis did. She indicated for him to continue.

"Police detectives are still trying to sort it. They've been snooping around us quite a bit, but so far we've managed to keep them in the dark."

"All of our agencies agreed they want the locals to keep their noses out of this," the BATF officer interjected. "Since automatic weapons and high explosives were used, it became a federal issue. Especially in light of some similar confrontations that took place right here on the Strip."

"And wherever there's this kind of trouble, we always get the same descriptions from witnesses," Haggis continued. "Something about this commando. A big guy, dressed in black and dishing out some serious whip-ass. But, we've never been able to catch this guy. We think he may be either a freelancer, or possibly working for the Kung Lok and eliminating competition."

"We think it's more likely he's working for the Chinese," Cooper added, "since witnesses have reported seeing him leave the Kung Lok's place more than once."

"Okay, so we know they're holed up there," Rajero cut in dismissively, trying to change the subject to something other than Belasko. "What about recent activity?"

"Been quiet," Haggis replied. "Hardly a peep out of those guys since the last incident. There's been literally no movement in or out of the place in almost a week. Frankly, we thought D.C. was about to forget the whole thing and turn it back to the local boys."

"Not much chance of that," Rajero replied icily. "The Kung Lok is an international crime gang, and that means the problems they cause fall under the jurisdiction of the federal government. Washington wants them out, and we now have the green light to move on them with everything at our disposal."

Cooper now fixed her with a concerned expression. "You don't think they'll go quietly."

"No," Rajero said, shaking her head. "As a matter of fact, I think we're in for the fight of our lives."

Chihuahua, Mexico

THE EXECUTIONER had scoured the house floor by floor and room by room until he finally found Carillo. The guy was hiding in his bedroom on the third floor, barricaded behind a bathroom door made of heavy oak. Bolan had made short work of the four-man squad protecting the drug lord, their bodies now scattered throughout the bedroom. The soldier had locked the bedroom door to the hallway, and destroyed the landing between the first and second floors with a grenade. That would buy him enough time to finish his business with Carillo. The Executioner didn't waste any time blowing a hole in the lock and kicking in the door.

Carillo was crouched in the tub, and he had a .38-caliber snub-nosed pistol pointed in Bolan's direction. Even from a distance, the soldier could tell the drug lord was trembling. His entire body shook almost uncontrollably. Even if he hadn't been shaking, Bolan knew fear when he saw it.

"I'll kill myself before I let you capture me," Carillo declared with a sneer.

Bolan squeezed the trigger of the FNC and blew the gun from Carillo's hand. The man screamed, retrieving his injured limb, his white silk shirt now covered with blood and wet bits of flesh.

"Where's Nievas?" Bolan stated quietly.

"I will never tell you anything, Belasko, so you might as well kill me now."

Bolan stepped forward, drew the Desert Eagle, aimed at Carillo's leg and squeezed the trigger. The heavy-caliber round blew out the drug lord's left knee, and he screamed in pain. This wasn't the soldier's preferred interrogation technique, but he didn't have time for games. It wouldn't be long before Carillo's men found another way to the third floor. Even now, Bolan could hear shouts on the patio immediately below the bathroom window. And if he could hear them, they could certainly hear the misery he was dealing out to their boss.

"Save yourself the agony, Carillo. Tell me where Nievas is."

"You are running out of time, Belasko," Carillo said through gritted teeth. "You might as well kill me now."

"No dice," Bolan said. "I'll leave a scum-sucking leech like you here to bleed to death before I show you that kind of mercy."

"Then do it."

"Answer my question, Carillo," Bolan said. He looked at his watch and added, "I figure I still have about five minutes to spare, and that can be a lifetime for someone in your position."

"What does it matter to you?" the drug lord asked, his face going flush now. "Nievas isn't here! He's gone to Las Vegas to defeat the yellow bastards who destroyed our plans. They betrayed him, and they ruined my chances of ruling a new empire! So fuck you and your heroics!"

Carillo began to laugh uncontrollably. The guy had finally snapped. Yeah, the concept he had finally lost his mind became clear to Bolan as he watched Carillo's slavering, pathetic form lying in that bathtub and slowly bleeding to death.

"Do you think I care anymore?" Carillo cried. "I have nothing left! Nothing! I knew you would come here, and that is why I volunteered to stay behind so Nievas could accomplish his mission! I've lost everything! If the Colombians don't kill me, the *federales* or my competitors will! So it's the least I could do to make sure that you are detained long enough until Nievas can accomplish his mission!" With those words Carillo slumped to one side, either unconscious or dead from blood loss.

Bolan could feel the rage welling in him. He tried to hold his anger in check, but this was a situation where he realized he had been outwitted. Carillo and Nievas may not have accomplished their plans, but they had done enough to put in motion the exact events the Executioner had hoped to avoid. They were going to start a war on American soil, and he would probably be too late to stop it.

A gas canister suddenly shattered a window on Bolan's right. The canister clattered to the bathroom floor and immediately began to flood the area with CS. Bolan left in a hurry, moving through the bedroom doorway and out into the hallway.

As he descended the stairs, he realized that his troubles were only beginning. Because he'd risked the precious minutes interrogating Carillo, he would now have to push the envelope to get out in time for his rendezvous with Grimaldi. Now it was time to really show the enemy he meant business.

Three of Carillo's soldiers appeared around the corner of the massive stairwell leading from the third to the second floor. Bolan triggered his FNC and flooded the area with high-velocity slugs. The soldiers, cramped in the confines of the stairwell, weren't expecting such a sudden and close-quarters encounter with their enemy. The rounds hammered into them, and they collapsed under the onslaught as the bullets ripped through vital organs. Two fell in the stairwell, and a third flipped over the banister.

Bolan could now hear footfalls thundering on the stairwell en masse. The soldier immediately realized there was no shortage of troops—they just weren't

FARC, and he couldn't understand that. Still, whether it made sense or not wasn't the main point right now. Getting out quickly and alive was the key. He hit the stairwell, nimbly dropped a foot between the two dead men, then vaulted the banister.

He dropped the eight yards to the first floor and hit the carpet rolling to lessen the impact on his legs. He got to his feet and continued toward the area where he'd made his entrance. More resistance met him in the hallway, blocking his path. Bolan dived for cover against a paper-thin wall, and the bullets whizzed over his head.

Bolan already had a grenade in hand with the pin extracted. He let the spoon fly, counted off three seconds, then tossed it. He reached six on his count before the screams and sounds of scrambling men were overcome by the high-explosive blast.

The Executioner was on his feet and moving before raining plaster, glass and flaming sheets of wallboard hit the floor. He nearly choked on the thick, acrid smoke that clogged the narrow hallways and he had to keep low in order to see the path ahead.

As he reached the patio where he'd originally made his entrance, he spotted only two of Carillo's troops. He dispatched them both with a short burst from the FNC, then yanked a fresh magazine from his gear and palmed it into the rifle as he headed for the grounds that would serve as Grimaldi's makeshift airfield. He keyed up the miniature microphone as he sprinted toward the rendezvous point. "Striker to Eagle One, you copy?"

"Loud and clear, Sarge. What's up?"

"Ready for extraction."

"Roger. Stand by for touchdown."

"Copy. Out." Bolan clicked off. He vaulted a wall and landed in a cluster of geraniums, then waited in the bushes for his ride. The plane touched down less than a minute later, and Grimaldi had to take nearly the entire length of the runway to bring the plane under control.

Bolan bound from the bushes and headed for the Gulf-stream C-20 as Grimaldi turned the plane to prepare for takeoff. The soldier boarded the jet, then tossed Grimaldi the high sign. Stony Man's ace pilot smiled at the Executioner from the cockpit before returning the gesture, then pushed forward on the throttle lever. The plane began to accelerate down the grassy runway.

Some of Carillo's troops emerged from various openings in the walled gardens and fanned across the field in an attempt to cut them off. Bolan donned the earphones that facilitated communications with the cockpit.

"Trouble, Sarge," Grimaldi said.

"Just focus on the ride, Jack," Bolan replied, "and I'll plow the road for you."

"Roger."

And the Executioner did just that, pointing his FNC out the open door and sweeping the area with autofire. Some fell under the Executioner's furious defense, but most just dived for cover in an attempt to avoid certain death. It seemed like an eternity, but only thirty seconds later the jet left the ground. Bolan closed the door, and the beeping and buzzing sounds emanating from the cockpit to alert Grimaldi the doors were still open suddenly ceased.

Bolan hurried into the cockpit, donned the copilot's headset and slapped Grimaldi on the shoulder with a cocksure grin.

"Good timing, Jack," Bolan commended him.

"Yes, we at Grimaldi Air pride ourselves on being punctual."

"How's the fuel situation?"

"We're okay. Why?"

"Enough to get to us to Las Vegas?"

"Easily," Grimaldi replied. He studied the Executioner suspiciously with a sideways glance. "What's up?"

"There's about to be big trouble. We need to get there before something disastrous goes down."

"How disastrous?"

"How about a full-scale war between Nievas's FARC troops and the Kung Lok's Scarlet Dragons?"

"You mean *in* Las Vegas?"

"Yeah," the Executioner replied with a grim nod.

"Consider us there," Grimaldi said, flipping a few switches before opening up full throttle.

CHAPTER EIGHT

El Paso, Texas

Ing Kaochu waited and watched.

He could sense the tension in the vehicle as he watched the El Paso Intelligence Center intently from across the street. His men were obviously nervous, and that made him nervous, but Kaochu had neither the time nor the inclination to put their fears to rest. He wasn't a nursemaid—these were professional soldiers and they needed to act like it. Still, Kaochu knew he couldn't be too hard on them. Six of their comrades had died on the steps of the EPIC less than twelve hours earlier at the hands of the American, Mike Belasko.

He was still alive! Kaochu couldn't believe that Belasko was alive, or that Ramon Sapèdas was still alive, for that matter. Kaochu somehow found it easier to accept Belasko wasn't dead than Sapèdas, which was odd to him. Not that it was a surprise—the DEA's decision to keep Sapèdas's confinement a secret was a shrewd one. Still, there were no secrets to the Scarlet Dragons. They had eyes and ears everywhere: government offices, bars and clubs, casinos, Chinese restaurants and legitimate, as well as illegitimate, businesses.

The Scarlet Dragons were scattered throughout every

major city in America, forming probably the single largest spy network in the U.S. For the most part, there were no secrets, and generally nothing happened in their areas of operation without Ing Kaochu knowing about it. The Dragons were a very large and complicated organization to manage, but Kaochu managed it without too much of a problem.

When he'd finally learned that Sapèdas was still alive, he'd also discovered Belasko was alive. Not only had Belasko destroyed the hit team sent to kill Sapèdas and Carillo's chief enforcer, Conrado Diaz, but he'd also eliminated the strike team sent here to eliminate the DEA woman, Rajero. That was when it had all come together, and it amused Kaochu in some respects that he'd originally come to kill Sapèdas, but was now tasked with snatching him from the custody of the U.S. Marshals and keeping him alive.

Ramon Sapèdas knew a lot of things about Carillo's operations along the border. Because of that, Shui told Kaochu he wanted them to grab up the Border Patrol chief and bring him straight to Toronto. Then they would have time to deal with the guy. Shui hoped that they could get Sapèdas to turn on his former master under the assumption the Kung Lok would protect him. Then, when they had used him up, it would be Kaochu's job to insure Sapèdas disappeared—forever.

Kaochu didn't like it, but he knew it was of no consequence. He and his men followed orders, and it didn't matter what they thought about them. He looked at his watch again. He was becoming impatient at this waiting game. He'd come by some information that had probably originated from the American government man whose identity was still a mystery to Kaochu. The caller told him that they were going to move Sapèdas to a safe-house on the East Coast, and Kaochu saw that as the best opportunity to grab him. As a matter of fact, there wouldn't be a better time. He knew that if they got Sapèdas out of the Kung Lok's immediate intelligence network, the authorities would have a fair amount of difficulty locating him, and even more difficulty getting past the security. His plan to do it now was the best idea, because after the incident in front of the EPIC early that morning, another hit that soon in the same place wouldn't be expected.

Kaochu turned to his associates and nodded. The four Dragons exited the vehicle and crossed the street and headed by pairs in separate directions. The plan was to skirt the building and make their entrance through a back alley, since that's where they planned to leave with Sapèdas, not to mention the front was still cordoned as a crime scene.

The quartet met four minutes later. Several transport vehicles were already waiting, their engines running, although they were unattended. Kaochu shook his head. The Americans were as sloppy as ever—they were so secure in themselves and their abilities that they'd almost come to believe they were invincible.

Kaochu retrieved the 9 mm Jatimatic machine pistol from beneath his jacket and put the weapon in battery. His men followed suit, and then the four turned and fired into the plate-glass doors, which shattered under the autofire. The gunners ducked to avoid the jagged edges of hanging glass, then pressed onward. They leapfrogged down the narrow hallway as an alarm rang loudly in their ears.

Their first encounter was with a couple of DEA agents they met rounding a corner in the corridor. The two men were looking wildly in every direction, but neither one had his weapon drawn. Kaochu raised the Jatimatic and opened fire, cutting them down before they had a chance to defend themselves. The Scarlet Dragons never stopped moving, realizing that moving targets were much more difficult to hit, not to mention that most of the staff were office and clerical people who had no clue how to handle storm tactics.

Three women rushing to find the nearest exit nearly ran into the Chinese soldiers. Kaochu and his men either shoved them aside or knocked them unconscious with punches. They weren't in the business to kill women— even American women. Kaochu considered it unprofessional to kill unnecessarily, although his predecessors had felt differently in operations like these. Still, Kaochu had killed many people. He got nothing from the task, and he didn't have anything to prove. It was just a messy way of conducting operations, so he avoided it and expected the same discipline from every one of his Dragons.

They reached the stairwell and advanced with more caution. Kaochu had memorized the layout of the EPIC, and he knew exactly where they were holding Sapèdas. The guy wasn't going to get away; that much was certain. Shui had made it abundantly clear that he wanted Sapèdas alive, if possible, but not at great cost. They had already lost too many of their men to Belasko, and they couldn't afford to lose more to the American police. So Kaochu had an additional order. If he couldn't take Sapèdas alive with acceptable losses, he was to destroy the man.

They reached the third floor, where Sapèdas was confined. The four Dragons exited the stairwell and fanned out, Kaochu in the lead. Several agents who had taken up cover positions in the hallway and were obviously waiting for their enemies opened fire. The hallway was filled with crisscrossing rounds of 9 mm as Kaochu's men hit the ground and returned fire. Only one of the agents actually had sufficient firepower to counter their attack and sprayed the area with fire from an MP-5. The rest were carrying standard-issue Glocks, and one of Kaochu's men fell under the defense.

The remaining Dragons returned fire, dropping two of the five agents instantly. It was becoming increasingly obvious to Kaochu that they might not make it out of there alive. They were running out of time. He'd known they were stepping into a hornet's nest, and his fears were quickly becoming a reality. Still, they had a chance if they could locate Sapèdas. They pressed onward with the attack.

CONRADO DIAZ ENTERED the office of Director Liam Hoffner and took a seat. He'd come to Hoffner as a special envoy, determined to carry out his mission as ordered by Carillo. Hoffner was Carillo's greatest secret—the ace in the hole that would ultimately restore the Carillo empire to its former glory. He'd known who Hoffner was, but he hadn't a clue the guy was on the boss's payroll.

So it had finally come to this. Here was Diaz, a Mexican criminal on the Top Ten Most Wanted list in his own country, as well as in the U.S., sitting in the office of a director of DEA without a care in the world. It seemed almost laughable that men like Hoffner could be bought so easily, but it didn't surprise him.

What did surprise him was when Hoffner reached into his desk, calmly withdrew a pistol and pointed it at Diaz's chest.

''What the fu—?''

"Don't bother wondering, Diaz," Hoffner said calmly. He flashed an almost charming smile and added, "I've been expecting you to show up for some time now. Ever since the shipment got hit in Mexicali, anyway. And you nearly got caught right along with Ramon."

"What the hell are you talking about?" Diaz asked. "You work for us."

"Did you actually think I would stoop low enough to work for your boss?"

"Jose Carillo was your friend, Hoffner," Diaz said, careful to keep his hands away from the weapon concealed beneath his jacket. He knew the guy would cap him if even so much as flinched.

"Carillo is no friend of mine. I've spent the better part of my career putting scum like you in prison. Your kind has killed many good friends. It just goes to prove what a fool Carillo really is, thinking I'd actually let him put me on the payroll."

"You've already taken money from him," Diaz said.

"Actually, I haven't taken a dime from Carillo. And I wouldn't have. All of that cash was turned over to the triad. So you can now see why *I'm* the one who's going to come out clean in all of this."

Diaz suddenly realized what was happening, and the whole thing came together in an instant of understanding. "It was you. *You're* the one who told the Chinese about the shipments out of Mexicali."

Hoffner grinned again. "And about your business dealings in Las Vegas and L.A. I don't know where they got their intelligence about the rest, but they offered me way more than you people ever could have."

"So it's about money."

"No, Diaz," Hoffner snapped, "it's about power.

Power Carillo could never offer me. Power and control like you could never understand. Who do you think it was that brought Sapèdas into this in the first place, huh? Who do you think it was that set up the weapons deals between the triad and the Colombians? All of the stuff that came through here went right back out again. Sapèdas made sure the guns got into the right hands, so we could sell them to the Colombians. *I* suggested Carillo hook up with Nievas, and *I* arranged an alliance with Kung Lok. And you wetbacks bought it, hook, line and sinker.''

''You won't get out of here alive, Hoffner, so it makes little difference,'' Diaz replied with a sneer.

Alarms suddenly resounded throughout the hallway outside Hoffner's office. The DEA man smiled with satisfaction, and a glint of anticipation appeared in his eyes. ''Ah, they're here at last. Just in time.''

''Who's here?''

''My salvation. So long, Diaz,'' Hoffner said as he squeezed the trigger.

ONLY ONE of Kaochu's men survived the battle against the U.S. Marshals, but it was a sweet victory. The pair advanced through the hallway, finally discovering the room where Sapèdas was located. The Border Patrol chief was manacled to his chair, but a single shot from the Jatimatic took care of that problem.

Kaochu hauled Sapèdas from the chair and tossed him in the direction of the door. One of the other gunners took hold of Sapèdas's collar and they exited the room. The area was still clear, although the Scarlet Dragon leader knew their fortune wouldn't hold out much longer. They had to get away from the area as quickly as possible with their prisoner intact, and it would prove much more difficult getting out than it had getting in.

They were halfway down the hallway when the elevator doors at the far end opened to reveal a tall, good-looking man in a three-piece suit. Kaochu started to raise his weapon, but the man threw up his hands to show he was unarmed.

"Stop!" the guy hollered. "Get over here!"

Kaochu stopped a moment and looked at his comrade before returning his attention to this mysterious new arrival. A moment elapsed before he realized the man matched the description of the American who had propositioned Lau Shui in Florida. He took a few hesitant steps and then stopped again.

"Quit fucking around and get over here! The only way out of here alive is to take me as a hostage. If you choose to kill me, you're done, and I don't think Lau-Ming can afford to lose you."

That was the only thing Ing Kaochu needed to hear. It didn't need a second invitation, and he directed his comrade to obey the man's directions. They stepped onto the elevator, and the guy turned a key in the elevator panel before pushing a button for the basement level.

Kaochu kept his weapon trained on the man. "Who are you?"

The guy cast a sideways glance at the Dragon leader. "I think you've already guessed that, Ing."

Kaochu had to admit that the use of his name came as a surprise. After a few seconds he said, "I would guess you're correct."

"My vehicle is in the basement. Most parking is across the street, but we do have an underground garage. I was wondering how long it would take you to get here."

"You knew we were coming?"

"I was hoping."

"I don't believe it," Sapèdas interjected. "You're working for the Chinese?"

"Shut up, Ramon," the man said quietly. "You're already skating on very thin ice with me, and I have no qualms about asking these men to silence you permanently if I feel it becomes necessary. You've already proved yourself a tremendous liability for me, so don't speak unless spoken to."

The way he talked to Sapèdas seemed almost conversational to Kaochu. The man was every bit as graceful and charming as Shui had described him. Kaochu didn't know his name, but he didn't care much at that point. If this guy was legitimate, then Kaochu knew their chances of getting out of that place alive had just increased a thousandfold.

"We may encounter resistance," the man continued. "If we do, don't panic. I'm in charge of this outfit here, and they won't risk killing me to get you. Just follow my instructions and we'll all come out of this in one piece. Understood?"

Kaochu nodded, and then said, "I will comply with your wishes for now. But if you do anything other than what I think you should, I will kill you where you stand."

"That would *not* make your master very happy," the man replied. "Because without me, Lau-Ming Shui will never control the American territories. So please be sure before you decide to pull the trigger that I am an enemy and not an ally. Otherwise, the only thing killing me will accomplish is your own death."

For some unexplainable reason, Ing Kaochu knew in that moment that he was hearing the truth.

Las Vegas, Nevada

"A WAR?" Harold Brognola's disbelieving voice echoed through the cellular phone. "In downtown Las Vegas? It's unthinkable. The risk to innocent bystanders alone could be disastrous."

"Yeah, but I got it right from Carillo, Hal, and I took him at his word. We have to assume this is the real thing."

"No chance he was bluffing?"

"Doubtful," Bolan replied. "He knew he was as good as dead, anyway. He was almost bragging about it. I think the guy flipped right there in front of me. I'm guessing he figured I couldn't get here in time to stop it."

"He could be right."

"Maybe, but I can't think about that right now."

"What's that?" Brognola replied, but the faintness in his voice told Bolan the Stony Man chief wasn't talking to him. The big Fed's booming tone came back in full volume as he said, "Bear just managed to pull some information from our computers. He says that a few hours ago the DEA secured a warrant to storm a house the DOJ believes occupied by several known members of the Kung Lok. Our intelligence has it one of the targets might be Lau-Ming Shui himself. They've organized a multidepartmental task force."

"That's probably Danny Tang's place. I've been there before. Any idea when they plan to hit it?"

"No, but we do know they put Lisa Rajero in charge."

Bolan sighed with frustration. "I told her to lay low when I pulled her and Jack out of El Paso."

"Doesn't sound like she took your advice."

"No, it doesn't."

Brognola paused again, directing his voice from the phone. The Executioner waited patiently for the head Fed. He couldn't quite make out what Kurtzman was saying in the background. They were obviously having a tense discussion about something, although it sounded as if they were stressed rather than arguing a point. Bolan was beginning to wonder if his original idea of keeping Able Team and Phoenix Force out of the game on this one had been such a good idea after all.

Finally, Brognola said, "We also just got a report that something major went down at the El Paso Intelligence Center. We don't know the details yet, but apparently there was more shooting, and quite a few government agents and staff members were killed."

"Damn! I wish I had been there to stop it."

"I know. I'm sorry, Striker."

"It's my fault, not yours. Let's get that cleared up now," Bolan said quickly. The Executioner gave it only another moment's thought before adding, "Look, I can't be in two places at once and this deal that might go down in Vegas is priority. If you feel it's time to utilize Able Team, then send them to El Paso to see what they can dig up."

"Understood. I know they'll be anxious to hear that. Ironman's restless."

"I don't doubt it."

"Um, what specifically are they supposed to be looking for?"

"There's been a lot of trouble at that place in the past twelve hours," Bolan replied. "I think you guys were on the money in your original suspicions about this mystery U.S. government man working with the Kung Lok."

"You think he's there, as well?"

"Maybe. But if not, it's a good bet somebody there knows whoever it is. If nothing else, at least Able Team can get involved. They're a tremendous asset, and doing little good idle."

"Agreed."

"I need to sign off. I'll wait until we get to Tang's before deciding the best course of action. I hope the locals don't know. I've already had one encounter with Las Vegas PD. I don't want a second."

"Understood. Watch yourself out there, Striker."

"Out here." Bolan disconnected the call and handed the cellular phone back to Grimaldi.

They had arrived in Las Vegas fifteen minutes earlier, and immediately headed for the Strip. Bolan had decided it was better to attempt to stop Rajero from executing their plan, rather than risk entering the fray after the fact. By that time, it might be too late. Still, the Executioner realized if he could at least keep allies out of the line of fire, then he stood a chance of confining a Kung Lok–FARC conflict to a relatively safe area of operations.

The only downside was if Nievas chose to hit them in individual locations. It was a wild scenario, but all too possible. It wouldn't make any sense for the FARC gunners to hit them just at Danny Tang's place. Retaking the major centers of control over the drug and sex action seemed the better course for Nievas; it posed less risk and allowed him to coordinate a multipronged attack.

That was the biggest problem for the soldier. He was trying to second-guess Nievas's plan when he didn't have any real intelligence with which to work. It could turn out to be a lose-lose situation for both the innocent, as well as the law, and the Executioner would probably wind up where he usually did—in the middle of the worst of it. Still, he couldn't base his actions on a whim, and his instinct told him he was doing the right thing.

While Rajero and her law-enforcement comrades-in-arms knew the risks, that didn't mean he would let them die unnecessarily. Rajero was a good agent and a hell of a lady, but she was rash at times. She might jump into this thing without enough forethought, and those kinds of tactics could end up getting her killed. Bolan, on the other hand, was an experienced combatant who knew how to fight fire with fire. He understood his enemy like nobody else, and he had reached a level of maturity in his skills that allowed him to predict the next logical step in nearly any battle plan.

Grimaldi nearly jumped the curb as he brought the government SUV to a screeching halt in front of the DEA offices. Bolan jumped from the vehicle before it had reached a complete stop, and ran for the doors. They were open, and security agents greeted him at the desk, coming to their feet and drawing their weapons. Bolan stopped short and raised his hands.

"Whoa, just take it easy."

"Who are you and what's your business here?" one of them demanded.

Bolan heard Grimaldi come through the door behind him. "Stay cool, Jack. Listen, I'm not here to cause trouble. I'm looking for Special Agent Lisa Rajero with the DEA."

"Concerning what?" the security agent asked, still not lowering his weapon.

"Concerning official government business, pal," Grimaldi answered.

"We know there's a raid planned," Bolan said calmly, "and if we don't get to the agent in charge, it's going to get ugly. So get her on the phone and do it now.''

The obvious leader of the pair studied Bolan's face a moment, then turned and nodded for his cohort to place the call while he kept Bolan and Grimaldi covered. The Executioner waited patiently. There was no point in getting these guys excitable by trying something stupid. They were just doing their job, and Bolan could tell by the way the younger man held his pistol he was well trained in dealing with crises. The Executioner knew good and well if he tried to circumvent the system, he'd wind up dead; dead men didn't pass on any information.

The guard on the phone looked up at Bolan. ''What's her name?''

''Rajero. Special Agent Lisa Rajero.''

The guard spoke into the phone quietly a moment, and then returned his attention to Bolan. ''All right, I've got her on the horn now. She wants to know who you are.''

The Executioner felt something inside of him relax. ''Tell her Belasko.''

The guard nodded, again spoke quietly into the phone, then nodded in understanding and hung up. He looked at his partner and said, ''It's okay, Jeff. She's on her way down right now.''

The guard nodded and holstered his weapon. Bolan and Grimaldi lowered their hands and waited. Bolan knew that every second ticking by was one second closer to disaster. He was already formulating a plan for how to deal with the various possibilities. Surprisingly, it now all hinged on Rajero. She had to call the shots as far as her team was concerned. Bolan knew he could turn the tables with a phone call, but this wasn't a time for politics. He'd have to get Rajero to trust him on this one.

She was already dressed in tactical gear, complete

with vest and body armor, as she stepped from the elevator. Four men accompanied her. Rajero had a momentary expression of surprise, but then the cool yet beautiful mask fell again as she drew near.

Bolan spoke first. "Lisa, you have to call this off."

Rajero didn't say anything at first. She put her hands on her hips and studied him with resolute skepticism. Bolan couldn't understand her reaction. She was acting as if he and Grimaldi were total strangers. Something wasn't right, and Bolan immediately felt the hairs stand on the back of his neck. That sixth sense was telling him this had been a mistake.

And he knew he was right when Rajero turned to the men and said, "These two men are under arrest. Take them into custody."

CHAPTER NINE

"You want to tell me what the hell you think you're doing?" Mack Bolan asked.

He and Grimaldi were now seated in the temporary office Rajero had commandeered for the duration of her assignment to oversee the Las Vegas task force.

The spunky DEA agent shook her head and sneered. "I'm trying to prevent myself from making the same mistake twice."

"What mistake is that?"

"Trusting you to take me seriously, and then letting you blow me off. You treated me as if I weren't important."

"Grow up, lady. The only mistake you're making is planning this raid on Tang's house." Bolan held up his cuffed hands. "And what's with these?"

"Those were the only way I could get your attention."

"He's trying to save you a lot of trouble, Lisa," Grimaldi said. "I'd listen to what he has to say before jumping to conclusions."

"Whatever he has to say still isn't going to change my mind," she replied, tossing back her shoulders and fixing Bolan with a haughty glance. "I was put in charge of this mission for a reason, boys. It's because I'm the only one in the DEA who's faced the Kung Lok and lived to tell about it."

"Look, I don't have time for this nonsense," Bolan said. "We're on the same team. Now, if you don't want to trust me, then don't, but don't let a lot of innocent people die because of it."

Rajero frowned. "What in blazes are you talking about?"

"Nievas and the FARC are planning to take back all of Carillo's holdings here in Las Vegas."

"How do you know that?"

"Carillo told me."

"And you believed him?"

Bolan sighed. "Call it a hunch. The point is I don't think Tang's house is the target."

"But why wouldn't it be? That's where our intelligence says that the leader of the Kung Lok is holed up. And we know Ing Kaochu is there. It's time for us to take our streets back from these crooks, and I plan to start with the one where they're hiding."

"Hitting Tang's place is hardly going to take back the streets of this town," Bolan replied. "I don't know what you're trying to accomplish, but this isn't what you think it is. This goes a lot farther than a few drug pushers, and hitting Tang's place won't accomplish a thing."

"You have a better idea?"

"You take these cuffs off me, I'll be happy to tell you what I think."

Rajero didn't hesitate to walk over and unhook both men. Grimaldi rubbed his wrists as Bolan immediately stood and walked to the desk. The map the tactical leaders had reviewed with Rajero was still spread across the desk. Bolan studied the blueprints for a moment, and almost instantly recognized the layout was that of Tang's house, then focused his attention on the area map. He scrutinized the map a few more minutes as Grimaldi and Rajero stood next to him and waited patiently. Finally, the Executioner shook his head and turned to Rajero.

"They have a map of the whole city here?"

She nodded and then turned and gestured with a finger for them to follow. The trio walked through the busy office, and the tactical officers briefing their individual groups were obviously miffed to see the two men they'd just hooked up now walking around as free as birds. Bolan noticed how they were watching him, but he played it cool. He knew they were well trained and well armed, so there was no point in making them nervous. Besides, he meant what he'd said to Rajero; they *were* all on the same team.

Rajero signaled for Haggis, Cooper and the other two tactical officers to accompany them. They fell into step behind the threesome. Rajero led them to some kind of briefing room where a large map of the city was spread across one wall. Bolan reached into a concealed pocket of his blacksuit and withdrew a small notepad. He flipped back a few pages until he found what he was searching for, then studied the map. Finally, he smiled and nodded to his companions with a grunt of satisfaction.

"All right, here's how I see it. I have some pretty reliable intelligence from Milaña on Nievas and how he operates. I'm betting he's going to try to hit as many places at once as he can."

"What makes you think that?" Rajero interjected.

Bolan looked at her and said, "Because I know his kind, and that's what I would do if I were in his position."

"You think he knows the Feds are all over the Kung Lok, Mike?" Grimaldi asked.

Bolan nodded. "I'm sure he's counting on that. He knows they don't have the manpower or time to sit on every place in Vegas. He might send a team to hit Tang's place, but it will be a small one and it will be strictly for the purpose of damage control. Tactically speaking, it makes the most sense for him to hit the larger areas where the Kung Lok did the most business."

"And just exactly what makes you an expert, mister?" Cooper asked.

Bolan returned his question with a frosty smile, and it was Rajero who had to intervene with a shocker. She jerked her thumb in Bolan's direction and said, "This, gentlemen, is your mysterious commando."

"You?" Haggis asked, staring at Bolan.

The Executioner nodded, and his audience began to murmur among themselves. The INS lead agent even shuffled his feet, not meeting the Executioner's icy gaze. Bolan had to give Rajero credit—her decision to break the news to them in this way had actually quelled any thought of territorial conflict in their minds. Rajero was one of the few women Bolan had ever met who could keep him on his toes. She'd managed to put this whole thing together in a matter of hours, in addition to the fact she had probably become closer to the Executioner than he'd let any woman become in a long time.

"Okay, so let's assume you're correct, and Nievas plans to hit several major Kung Lok operations at one time," Rajero said. "What do we do about it? We don't have nearly enough people here, and I don't think we could get enough here even if we tried. At least not in time to stop him."

Bolan looked at the city map and nodded. "I can't

argue with that. So I have a plan. You might have enough agents to hit any one given place at one time, but you may have enough to cover the most likely targets.''

''And you just happen to know which ones those will be?'' Haggis asked.

''Yes.''

''That's great,'' Cooper interjected. ''That's just great. So you spread us so thin we can only watch locations with two…maybe three men at most. How is that going to help us?''

''We can monitor all positions from the air. We'll communicate on a secured tactical frequency of Rajero's choosing. She can assign one of you to take a counter-reaction team and put them in one chopper, my pilot and I will go in another. First sign of trouble, the closest chopper can get to the site of the problem and hit the ground running.''

''What if they strike in more than two places simultaneously?'' the BATF leader asked.

''We'll cross that bridge when we come to it,'' Bolan replied, ''but I wouldn't sweat it, guy. At most, Nievas's force totals about fifty men. That isn't a lot in a city the size of Vegas. Carillo had a lot of small operations going.''

''So we're going to watch the bigger ones,'' Haggis interjected.

Bolan nodded.

Rajero said, ''That actually makes sense, Mike. Nievas probably figures if he hits the larger ones, the smaller gigs will either fall into line or pack up and split.''

''Now you're catching on.''

The INS tactical officer raised his hand.

''Lieutenant Miller,'' Rajero said. ''Question?''

"Yes, ma'am. I was just wondering who this Nievas guy is that we're talking about. I thought we were after a Chinese gang leader named Ing Kaochu."

Rajero immediately looked at Bolan, who answered, "The man we're talking about is Colonel Amado Nievas. He's a fugitive and member of the FARC, and extremely dangerous. Recently, Nievas formed an alliance with Jose Carillo, and the two planned to increase drug-smuggling operations throughout the Southwest."

"Wait a minute," Cooper said, "are we talking about *the* Jose Carillo?"

"The *former* Jose Carillo," Jack Grimaldi said.

"Carillo is dead, as are most of his men," Bolan added. "About a week ago, we learned that Nievas and Carillo were at war with the Kung Lok Chinese triad, which is how Ing Kaochu fits into the picture." Bolan decided not to elaborate; he didn't want to tell them about Lau-Ming Shui. It would have only fueled the fire, and he didn't really have a lick of proof that Shui was even in Las Vegas. Beside, Lau-Ming Shui was Bolan's personal mission. He would deal with the Kung Lok boss in his own time and on his own terms.

"So now Nievas is coming to Las Vegas to take back what he sees as rightfully his," Haggis said.

Bolan nodded.

"Well, what the hell are we waiting for?" Cooper asked them. "Let's get cracking. I'm anxious to get out there and whip this Nievas's ass."

"Slow down a bit, soldier," Bolan said calmly. "You don't just run out and start shooting the place up. There are civilians and innocent bystanders to consider. Not to mention the fact that you're going against well-trained guerrillas."

Cooper stood straighter and puffed out his chest some.

"You're talking to the leader of one of the finest tactical response units in the entire DOJ. We're award winners. The elite of the elite."

"And these are terrorists who consider themselves heroes and freedom fighters. They don't care who gets in the way, and they're trained to kill on sight. Most members in the FARC don't know the meaning of fear or retreat. They do what they're told, when they're told and they won't back off until either all of them or all of you are dead. Try to keep that in mind."

"We've faced worse," Cooper snapped.

Bolan shook his head and replied, "That's what you think."

Canadian airspace

WITH THE HELP of Liam Hoffner, Ing Kaochu managed to escape El Paso with Sapèdas alive and intact—barely. He still wasn't sure he completely trusted Hoffner, but a quick phone call to Lau-Ming Shui from the private jet alleviated some of his fears. Still, he planned to keep a very close eye on Hoffner.

They had traveled through U.S. airspace aboard one of Lau-Ming Shui's personal jets, and were approaching Toronto. Kaochu had insured their prisoner was put in the most uncomfortable of conditions. He had orders to keep Sapèdas alive; he didn't have to be nice to the guy. Moreover, Shui hadn't actually decided what he was going to do with the traitorous U.S. policeman, and until he did, Kaochu planned to make the guy as miserable as possible.

On the other hand, he had orders to treat Hoffner like gold. In some respects, Kaochu had accomplished both missions for his master. Not only had he retrieved Sapèdas alive, but he'd also managed to discover the identity of the Kung Lok's most recent benefactor. In some respects, there didn't appear to be anything special about Hoffner—he seemed like just another self-absorbed, cocky American. But Lau-Ming Shui had obviously seen some promise in Hoffner, because he would not have otherwise made any such alliance with an American—ever.

The cellular phone rang before Kaochu could say anything to their guest. He picked it up, and the crisp, sharp voice of his second in command, Yin Kung, resounded in his ears.

"We may have a problem here, Ing."

"What sort of problem?"

"Our moles inside the DEA have confirmed that the Americans are planning to strike at the house tonight. We also believe that the Rajero woman is leading the attack, and…" The man's voice dropped off. Obviously, he was reticent to give the Scarlet Dragon leader this next piece of news.

"I don't have time for guessing games, Yin," Kaochu said impatiently.

"We believe she may be working with Belasko on this one. We think he may plan to assist them with the raid."

Ing Kaochu only chuckled. "Well, I can assure you, my friend, that if she's working with Belasko, then her immediate superiors don't know about it. He is presently considered a fugitive of the DEA, and I know that both the Mexicans and Colombians would like nothing better than to slit his throat if they could get their hands on him."

"That's the other part of my news. It seems that Jose Carillo is dead. We just got the word that Belasko wiped out his entire personal security force before killing Carillo himself.''

This was fantastic news. Just as Kaochu had predicted, Belasko was doing much of their job for him. He had tried to convince Shui before that keeping Belasko alive was probably in their best interests for now. This turn of events was proving him right, and before long Belasko would finish their work for them. Then they could destroy Sapèdas and end the war between the Kung Lok and the Carillo-Nievas alliance. That would leave just the Colombians to worry about—or at least the FARC—and Kaochu realized that was no problem.

''What about Colonel Nievas and his men?''

''We don't know where he is,'' Kung replied. ''Some of our intelligence sources believe he's fleeing for his life, rather than report their failure to his superiors. Now that General Jikwan has choked off the arms pipeline to the Colombians, it is only a matter of time before someone will have to take the blame.''

''And Nievas is the natural choice,'' Kaochu said, casting a quick look in Hoffner's direction. The shifty-eyed bastard was watching him intently, seeming to hang on to every word. After all, it was Hoffner who had really masterminded the entire operation from the beginning. Kaochu had to give the American that much. He was connected, resourceful and intelligent; that made him extremely dangerous in the eyes of the Scarlet Dragons. But for some reason, Lau-Ming Shui trusted him— Kaochu just hadn't figured out why.

''All right,'' Kaochu finally said. ''Just keep your eyes open and be prepared. If Nievas wasn't wiped out along with Carillo, that could mean he's planning an attack on our operations there in Las Vegas. They took a tremendous amount of loss when Belasko destroyed their shipments. They'll need some way of recouping those losses.''

"You think Nievas would actually attack us here? We would have him at a terrible disadvantage. We are prepared and heavily armed.''

"Whatever you do, do not underestimate the enemy. It would be our undoing.''

"I understand. Buddha keep you, Ing.''

"And you, my friend.''

Kaochu hung up and then stared intently at Hoffner. The guy didn't seem intimidated by him. Probably because he knew Kaochu was under orders to keep him alive and treat him decently at any costs. Hoffner knew if anything happened to him that it wouldn't set well with Lau-Ming Shui. Kaochu had already experienced enough lapses in judgment and committed enough errors that he wasn't going to add Hoffner to the list of them. Beside, Kaochu had met Hoffner's kind before, and he knew well that eventually the American would do something or say something to prove he'd outlived his usefulness. Shui would eventually see this, and then Kaochu would be given the okay to eliminate the DEA leader.

"I can't tell if that call was good news or bad news,'' Hoffner said, seemingly unconcerned about Kaochu's stare. "You always wear such a flat expression, Kaochu. You should learn to relax more…like me. Learn to enjoy life, man.''

"There are many things that demand my concern, American. I do not think it is honorable to simply toss aside my responsibilities and commitments so casually.''

"Oh,'' Hoffner said, smiling, "that almost sounded like a comparison. I hope you're not suggesting that I handle my commitments in such a manner.''

"Did I say that?'' Kaochu replied, raising his eyebrows. "I was simply stating a fact. We Chinese are not so inscrutable as you pretend, Hoffner. That is an old stereotype. It is a cliché of the Asians adopted by your people and predicated on what I may never understand. So you see, I do not know how you handle your own obligations, nor do I care. It is my job to deliver you alive to my master, and I will do this. After that, I have little interest in your schemes."

"After I managed to get you and your prize out of El Paso alive, you should be quite familiar with how I handle my responsibilities."

"You did this only to save your own neck."

"No, I did it because Shui and I had a deal. That's right, I actually honor my word. I don't expect you to understand me any more than I understand you, Kaochu. I don't even expect you to like me. But you see, after I talked with Lau-Ming Shui, he saw the wisdom of what I told him. The only way the Chinese will ever control the criminal activities in America is through guys like me. Even the mobsters of the sixties saw the truth of that fact. That's why they bribed judges, politicians and law officers—they knew that was the secret to controlling crime."

Kaochu raised his eyebrows and with a taunting smile said, "So you view yourself as an idealist?"

"Not hardly," Hoffner said with a snort.

"Then a visionary, perhaps."

"I prefer to think of myself as an entrepreneur of opportunity," Hoffner replied, flashing Kaochu one of his golden smiles. "After all, America is a land of opportunity."

"Yes, but you have sold out on America. You realize that you will never be able to show your face in your own country again."

"Somehow, I think I'll get over that. I never liked America all that much when I did work for her." Hoffner looked up thoughtfully at the ceiling of the cabin as he said, "Perhaps I will become a British citizen. I hear that London is beautiful this time of year."

Kaochu just shook his head and looked out the window. He could feel the plane descending and he knew they were close to Toronto. Of course, he'd known quite some time in advance that Carillo and Nievas might try to take Vegas back. He'd finally convinced his master to return to Toronto where it was safe. After all, there was little Shui could do about Las Vegas. The Scarlet Dragons had established a large foothold in the city, as well as L.A. and Houston. They also controlled most of the street and border action in Calexico, Nogales, El Paso and Brownsville.

These days, the traffic up into California from the Baja wasn't substantial enough to worry about controlling that part. There were many places where small-time outfits moved cocaine and marijuana across the border, but most of the crystalline powders and the 3-4 MDMA used to make Ecstasy were manufactured in the States after the raw products were smuggled across the U.S.-Mexican border. To attempt to send the finished product across wasn't good business. That meant as long as they controlled the storage and distribution of the majority of the stuff in the Southwest, the smaller dealers and runners played no real part in threatening the overall cash flow. It would be business as usual, and the Scarlet Dragons would deal with any up-and-coming competitors as required, rather than trying to take every little bit of the action for themselves.

Beside, Kaochu mused, that was America and there

was nothing wrong with a little "friendly" competition now and again.

The plane landed and Lau-Ming Shui's personal driver was there to greet them. They were immediately rushed away from the airport and taken to Shui's gigantic estate on the outskirts of Toronto. It was a beautiful place, and when they had passed beyond the gates and rode along the driveway lined with huge trees and decorated with Chinese gardens, Hoffner remarked how much nicer the place was compared to Carillo's hacienda and flowered gardens.

"Way nicer place," Hoffner added to his remarks.

Kaochu pretended he hadn't heard the American's comments. He wished that Hoffner were more like Sapèdas, who had kept his mouth shut the entire trip. As a matter of fact, the former Border Patrol chief hadn't really said anything since they'd retrieved him from the El Paso Intelligence Center—he'd asked for a drink of water aboard the plane, which Kaochu granted since the guy was cooperative. But other than that, he hadn't bitched about his treatment or whined he was hungry, or any of the other shit. Hoffner, on the other hand, had become increasingly talkative throughout the trip and now he wouldn't shut up.

"Is Lau-Ming here?"

"He is here," Kaochu replied.

The driver stopped the car in front of the house, and the four weary men climbed from the car. The one Dragon who had survived with Kaochu whispered a request to usher Sapèdas away to an isolated room, which the Dragon leader granted. Kaochu then showed Hoffner to the library and instructed him to have a seat and wait.

Once that was accomplished, Kaochu went to his master's study and found Shui anxiously awaiting his arrival.

The older man stood and greeted Kaochu with a cere-
monious bow, then he grabbed the young Scarlet Dragon
and embraced him.

"I cannot tell you how glad I am to see you survived
your mission against the Americans. You have brought
both honor and respect to our name. And you managed
to discover who the American was that first approached
me. It was a truly glorious mission for our cause, Ing,
and you shall be rewarded."

"The fact you have honored me with your gratitude
is enough reward, Lau-Ming."

"The honor is mine. Now, sit and tell me of our
guests."

"We have sequestered Sapèdas until you are ready to
speak with him. This Liam Hoffner is waiting for you
in the library."

"Let him wait. Have there been any new developments?"

"I received a call from Yin Kung in Las Vegas. He
tells me that the Americans are planning an assault
against Danny Tang's place."

"What will they find?"

"Nothing. After you left, I ordered them to abandon
the place. The house is empty. We wiped it clean. There
will be no trace of our presence or that we ever existed
there. It will be a futile effort. However, there is another
piece that concerns me greatly."

"And that is?"

"Our moles recently acquired some intelligence regarding Jose Carillo. They tell us that Carillo is dead,
and that it was Mike Belasko who killed him. They have
also informed us that the Rajero woman is still alive,
despite our attempts to destroy her in El Paso. It's believed that she and Belasko are working together again,

and that she will lead her government's assault against our people."

"How do you plan to deal with these new developments?"

Kaochu shrugged. "I am not overly concerned about it. If they strike at our former headquarters, as the intelligence suggests, it is unlikely they'll be able to go further. They might hit a few of our smaller operations, but this won't be enough to cripple us in any way. The U.S. police forces are the least of our concern. I think we have a greater worry."

"And what is that?"

"Kung told me that Nievas is still alive, and it is not believed he fled to Colombia."

"He did not die when the American hit Carillo?"

"No."

Lau-Ming Shui sighed. "I see. Well, I guess that means we have to be concerned about Colonel Nievas. He might wish to seek revenge for Dim Mai's betrayal of Colombian confidences in the arms deals."

"Yes, but he would have no reason to connect that directly with us."

"Of course he would. In either case, we must stand prepared for an attack."

"And how do you propose to do that, master? Certainly we outnumber his force, but they are trained and they have the advantage of surprise. There is always a chance they could seize considerable control of our assets in Las Vegas before we had prepared an adequate defense."

"Then there is only one thing I can do," Shui replied, picking up the telephone. "It is time to call Deng. We will need his help."

CHAPTER TEN

Las Vegas, Nevada

"Okay, people, stay sharp out there," Rajero's voice crackled through the static in Bolan's headset.

The Executioner smiled. If Lisa Rajero was anything, she was damn gutsy. Bolan had met many women during his career, but those like Rajero came few and far between. He regretted being so hard on her earlier, but he had to do it to shake her up and get her thinking clearly. Obviously, she was still suffering some posttraumatic stress from her ordeal with Kaochu, and watching her friends die at the hands of the Kung Lok. Not everyone could handle the burden of vendetta.

Bolan had learned long ago that revenge was a dangerous motive—he'd learned to deal with it in his own way. A walk through the hellgrounds had taught the Executioner that there was a time and place. He called it "tactical retaliation," and he'd learned to exact retribution out of duty. Others, like Rajero, were less experienced with the taste vengeance left in the mouth, and a deeper understanding would only come with time and experience.

Thoughts of vengeance occupied another part of Bolan's mind, as he turned to thoughts of Catalina Milaña.

Although he felt—in some strange way—that he probably owed his life to the woman, there was still something about her story that just didn't fit. Milaña had definitely suffered a loss—of that he was certain—but the story about her husband being a part of the FARC and suddenly relinquishing his allegiance to Nievas just sounded unconvincing. Either way, it didn't matter. He'd only accomplished part of his mission in the assault on Carillo's estate—he still had to find Nievas and bring him down. In a way, he knew he was doing some of Lau-Ming Shui's dirty work, but it didn't matter. He couldn't risk the FARC and Scarlet Dragons facing off in a full-scale conflict on the streets of Las Vegas. It was his job to stop that before it could happen. When that part of his mission was completed, he would then turn his attentions on Shui, Kaochu and the Scarlet Dragons.

The war was still in its infancy—he had a long way to go.

"All units check in," Rajero said, jarring Bolan from his contemplations.

The Executioner looked at her and nodded with assurance as each observation team called in and confirmed all was quiet. When the last team had signaled, Rajero switched to the internal VOX frequency of the chopper and studied Bolan's resolute gaze as she spoke.

"Why are you staring?"

The Executioner grinned. "Hard not to."

"Don't flirt," Rajero replied, but she winked at him. "You'll break my concentration."

Bolan shrugged.

Rajero continued, "You still haven't told me where you got all of this intelligence on Carillo's operations."

"All I can say is that my connections are need-to-know, and unfortunately you don't qualify for the title, even with your clearances.''

"I've kept bigger secrets."

Bolan only smiled. "Not like these. Look, it isn't as important where I got it as that it's reliable. You can be sure of that. Beside, it's the only thing that makes sense. When I hit Carillo's place in Juárez, I didn't encounter any of Nievas's troops. I don't think Nievas would risk going back to Juárez empty-handed."

"You mean the guns?"

"Yeah." Bolan looked out the window of the chopper as he added, "I recently found out that the entire weapons deal was nothing more than a ruse by the triads to divert Nievas's attentions. There was no way Carillo and Nievas would have put it together before the Kung Lok took over their operations in most of the Southwest. Shui knows the secret to controlling the drug trade is controlling the borders."

"And Carillo knew it, too."

"Yeah, but the difference is that Carillo wasn't counting on that kind of resistance, and neither was Nievas. Tactically speaking, their plan might have worked if I hadn't been involved."

Rajero shook her head, her lovely face contorted with an expression of puzzlement. "We knew about the Kung Lok's involvement very early in this game. What I've never understood is why Carillo didn't figure it out sooner. The guy was well connected."

"I have an answer."

"Which is?"

"It has to do with the 'high-up' in the government who's been pulling the strings. Somebody cut a deal with ranking members in the Chinese political arena."

"How do you know that?"

"Because a well-known Chinese military commander somehow plays into all this. You ever heard of General Deng Jikwan?"

Rajero appeared to think about it a moment and then shook her head.

"I'm not surprised, since I don't think he's the standard subject of interest in DEA textbooks. Jikwan's never been into drug running. He's strictly a military-arms-and-tactics broker, and one of the chief sources of transportation for a guy named Dim Mai."

"Now that name I've heard," Rajero said. "Mai is one of the largest arms dealers in all of Southeast Asia."

"Correction...he *is* the largest. Mai is also head of the eastern Kung Lok triad, and it's no secret he's had his eye on controlling the West for some time now. He'd probably already be in charge by now if Shui hadn't established such a foothold in Canada. His operations in Toronto will be my final targets after we've finished shutting down the Scarlet Dragons here in Vegas."

Rajero shook her head. "Sounds like it's getting more and more complicated."

"No argument there."

An excited voice broke through the headsets. "Attention, Skywatch One. We have a sighting at Area Three."

Before Rajero switched to open frequency, Bolan said, "See if they can tell us how many."

Rajero nodded as she replied, "Acknowledged, Team Three. Can you give us any kind of head count?"

There was a long silence as they waited for a reply. It became apparent to Bolan that Rajero was starting to panic when the team leader finally reported, "Estimate nine or ten, Skywatch One. Do you copy?"

"We copy."

Cooper's voice now resounded in their ears. "Skywatch Two to Skywatch One. You want us to proceed toward that area?''

Rajero looked at Bolan and he shook his head. This would be something he'd have to handle. Area Three was on the very edge of the city—an abandoned bowling alley with an interior converted into a brothel and head shop. The place was usually packed on the weekends, and it had survived only because of its remote location. It was a major area, but it would probably be crowded tonight.

Bolan cut out his receiver and shouted to her, ''Tell him to stand by, and we'll take this first one. I want to try to get inside on a soft probe first, and that means me alone. We'll need them for the centralized areas. Also advise Team Three to sit tight, and under no circumstances engage.''

Rajero began instructing her men as Bolan crossed the open area of the chopper and tapped Grimaldi on the shoulder. The pilot turned and Bolan made a swinging gesture with his finger. Stony Man's ace pilot nodded, tossed the Executioner a thumbs-up, then maneuvered the chopper to line up for touchdown just outside Area Three.

Bolan returned to the back and double-checked his weapons and equipment. The Beretta 93-R rested in its usual place under his left arm, and the .44 Magnum Desert Eagle rode in a leather military holster on his hip. Bolan had cleaned and inspected the FNC, and had it locked and loaded. Military webbing held six more 30-round box magazines, along with the Colt Combat Knife and six M-26 fragmentation grenades. The Executioner's concealed pockets housed additional clips for the Beretta and Desert Eagle.

"One minute, Mike," Grimaldi said through the VOX.

Bolan acknowledged the pilot's warning, and then chambered a round in the FNC. He could feel his stomach roll from the adrenaline surge coupled with the sudden drop in altitude. Grimaldi had managed to acquire a Sikorsky S-70 chopper, a commercial variant of the Army's UH-60 Black Hawk series. As a civilian version, it wasn't equipped with external armament, but it was just as fast, and Stony Man had managed to arrange equipping it with some extras in anticipation of Bolan's activities in Las Vegas.

Grimaldi set the bird down in an open parking lot approximately two blocks from the target. The landing gear never actually touched the ground, but Grimaldi brought it within a yard of the ground and was climbing from the spot as soon as Bolan's feet hit the pavement. He would maintain radio contact with the Executioner and be ready for any eventuality, including rapid extraction if it got too hot.

Bolan could hear the echo of his boots on the pavement as he jogged toward the target area. He knew the approximate positions of the two INS agents who had been watching the place, so he was aware of his firing limits. He hoped the pair would obey orders and not engage or try to help. Bolan wasn't trying to cut the men from their duties; he understood they just wanted to lend a hand and get a taste of the action. But the fact remained they weren't experienced enough or equipped well enough to butt heads with combat-hardened FARC troops.

This was the Executioner's area of expertise, and they needed to leave him to it.

Bolan crouched at the corner of a sporting goods store

across the street from the bowling-alley-turned-house-of-ill-repute and watched the building exterior. He could make out the shadows of the FARC troops as they leap-frogged in two fire teams of five men each, using the scattered vehicles strewed across the parking lot for cover and concealment. It looked as if he'd arrived just in time. The Executioner decided to wait, knowing that they would have to get inside before making his move, and simultaneously hoping the INS agents didn't become too restless and decide to jump the gun. It would turn into a disaster if they moved on Nievas's team now.

Bolan decided to break radio silence. "Team Three from Skywatch One. I'm on top of you. I see them. Hold your positions and do not engage. I'm going to wait until they're inside."

"Acknowledged," the team leader replied.

Bolan watched and waited patiently. The two fire teams reached the door in less than a minute, and then the first team moved inside with the fluidity of well-oiled gears. The second five-man team followed a moment later, one of them taking up a covering position outside the front door as the rest moved inside. The Executioner waited, staying in the shadows of the building, but the guy didn't move. He was going to hold an outside covering position. Bolan cursed himself for underestimating their savvy.

The Executioner decided to get closer. He figured he could close the gap to fifty yards before he had to take the sentry.

Bolan left his cover and kept low, running in the shadows of the sporting goods store. At the far end he broke into a full sprint and crossed the street, drawing the Beretta and thumbing the selector switch to 3-round bursts on the run. He got within thirty yards before the sentry spotted him, but the soldier already had target acquisition. He squeezed the trigger twice on the run. The guy managed to evade the first salvo, but all three rounds from the second burst hit home. Two 9 mm Parabellum slugs slammed through the guy's head, one tearing away his right cheek and the second shattering his jaw. The impact spun the sentry, but it was the third round that proved fatal, cracking his skull at the temple.

Bolan was on top of the FARC soldier seconds after his body hit the ground. The Executioner knelt and turned the guy over. Yeah, he was definitely dressed like a FARC trooper, complete with camouflage fatigues, bandoliers and an assault rifle.

The soldier was about to report the ID to Rajero and the other units when another team called in with a new sighting on the other side of the city. He heard Rajero acknowledge and then order Cooper and his men to take that one. Bolan was upset, but he quickly put it from his mind. He couldn't be everywhere at once. If he'd just looked further ahead, all of the unnecessary loss of life might be avoided. Still, the others were doing their duty just like he was, and he admired every last damn one of them.

The Executioner rose, turned and entered a doorway he knew might lead him straight to hell.

RAJERO COULD FEEL her heart beating in her chest as she watched the man she knew only as Jack pilot the Sikorsky S-70 with the confidence of a veteran airman. As he circled the city, Rajero tried to convince the pilot to take her to assist Cooper or touch down so she could bail out and help Belasko—anything but sit in this damn chopper. But she knew this was where she really needed to be; someone had to coordinate all of the action, and since she was in charge it was basically up to her to make sure things went as smoothly as possible and there was a minimal loss of life.

Rajero was still skeptical about Belasko's entire plan, although she would never have admitted it to the man. There was something commanding about the guy—almost arrogant—and he always seemed so self-assured and confident. It was as if he was in charge all the damn time, never letting loose or showing any emotion. It was something…something she just couldn't put her finger on. Yes, Mike Belasko was an intriguing man.

"Heads up, Rajero." Jack's voice snapped her from her reverie.

"What's up?"

"They've got a third sighting at Area Seven."

Rajero thought a moment and then nodded to the pilot, even though he couldn't see her. "That's another major target Mike identified. Damn. We only have three or four on that site, correct?"

"Four, as I recall."

"We need to move in there and assist," Rajero said, chewing her lower lip as she thought furiously about their situation.

"No dice, Rajero," Jack replied. "Belasko said you needed to coordinate this business from the air."

"Belasko's not in charge of this operation, Jack, I am. Now take me down there so I can help my people."

The pilot did as instructed. Rajero hated to pull rank, but she didn't work for Belasko and he didn't work for her. She did things the best way she knew how, and she didn't need anyone second-guessing her—least of all Belasko, since he wasn't even with her at the moment. There was no easy way to do this. Nievas just had too many men, and Rajero's people couldn't be in twenty places at once. That meant she had to be ready to support them whenever and wherever they needed support, and to hell with the plan.

Before she knew it, the chopper was hovering a yard off the ground, and Jack was telling her, "You're in the show, lady."

"Thanks, Jack."

"No problem. I'll try to maintain close air contact if you need me, but I know Mike is going to need extraction."

"It's going to have to be first come first served. I understand that. Listen, if this doesn't work out, you tell Belasko I'm sorry but I did what I had to do."

"Understood. Live large, lady."

"You too, Jack." And Rajero was out the door of the chopper and running across an open softball field.

The target was a double-wide manufactured home in a quiet park on the north side of the city. The area was underdeveloped, but that didn't make much difference. What had Rajero most concerned was that the trailer park in which the home sat was predominantly a retirement community. That meant a lot of innocent elderly people might get hurt. She would have to be damn careful.

Rajero was cognizant of the sound of the Sikorsky's rotors and droning engine as it lifted away, but she had a sense of oppression that washed through her body as a chill and sent all sorts of alert signals to her brain. Rajero wasn't feeling good about the situation; her stomach was upset and she could almost taste her fear. They had only four men, plus Rajero if she arrived in time, and there was no way of telling how many they were up against.

Rajero felt even less confident when she met the first

of the resistance in the form of tracer rounds as she reached the eight-foot-high chain-link fence that separated the field from the trailer park. She went up and over the fence in one fluid motion, dropped to the other side and went prone.

She found her first target standing on the roof of the house where Belasko's intelligence told her the Kung Lok would be. The muzzle-flash from the shooter's rifle illuminated him. He was aiming well over Rajero's head, which told the DEA agent that her target couldn't really see her. She aligned the sights of her MP-5 on the guy and squeezed the trigger. The impact of 9 mm Parabellum rounds flipped the gunner over the roof cap, and his body skidded from view.

Rajero sighted on another FARC soldier who was firing from the cover of a support post attached to a large deck outside the double-wide home. The first 3-round burst missed entirely, chopping splinters of wood from the two-by-four decking, but the second and third bursts hit dead-on. The six rounds slammed into the man's chest, neck and head, taking him permanently out of play.

She was about to take on a third FARC trooper using the far side of the deck for cover when the front door opened and a half-dozen Kung Lok soldiers poured through the opening. Rajero could immediately tell they were Scarlet Dragon soldiers, probably assigned to protect the place from just this kind of assault. None of them could see Rajero, but she continued to hug the ground as the Kung Lok soldiers turned on their FARC invaders.

One Scarlet Dragon raised his Jatimatic machine pistol and sent a salvo through the roof of the covered porch. The rounds didn't strike any human targets, but Rajero saw the two remaining FARC soldiers stop short of advancing toward the porch to help their comrades. It was apparent to them that the lone, armed female—despite her ferocity and tenacity—was no longer the chief threat.

Rajero immediately seized advantage of the situation and decided to utilize the MP-5 to snipe her opponents, since it made little difference which side went down first. Both the Kung Lok and FARC were her enemies, and if she could work them against each other, so much the better. Ultimately, she planned to wipe out both sides. There wouldn't be any prisoners—the rules of the game had changed. Rajero knew it would probably be the end of her career, but Belasko had been right.

This was war.

She keyed up her radio and confirmed that the three members of the team were still alive. Two of three answered, which meant that the third man was either dead, too frightened to answer or unable to hear his radio due to damage or his proximity to the thunderous reports of assault rifles and machine pistols. She ordered her men to follow her example and risk only single shots against viable targets.

Rajero aligned the sight post of her MP-5 on a Scarlet Dragon who was hiding at the foot of the deck stairs. He had his back to her, and Rajero knew the opportunity was too good to pass up. She took a breath to calm herself and stroked the trigger. The 9 mm round smashed through the guy's back and left lung. The impact tossed him against the side of the double-wide home's vinyl skirting.

The DEA agent couldn't see a lot of details in the dark, and aside from the lighting that spilled from the edges of the blinds, the porch light cast the only other real illumination on the hot zone. Rajero managed to drop one of the FARC soldiers on the roof who had hesitated before stray rounds blew out the porch light. The immediate area was now covered by darkness, and Rajero could just make out images and muzzle-flashes.

The sounds of battle were rapidly receding, and Rajero could hear the first sounds of police sirens echo through the night air. The DEA agent knew that L.V.'s finest would be no match for a fully armed conflict against the Kung Lok and FARC, especially not before SWAT units arrived. Rajero keyed up the microphone, ordered her men to get into the game and then switched frequencies and advised Jack of her intention.

Rajero got to her feet and sprinted toward the house, the other pair on her team following her lead and approaching from different directions. As she drew closer to the porch, Rajero sprayed the area, the hail of 9 mm Parabellum rounds spitting from her weapon and punching through Kung Lok Dragons and FARC soldiers alike. The combatants were obviously taken by surprise at the ferocity of their new arrivals, and neither side was certain whose side these people were on.

But Rajero and her men quickly made it apparent that they weren't on either side. Rajero took out three more, and a total of five additional gunners fell under the assault of her men. A lone FARC soldier hiding behind a car gunned down one of the DEA pair approaching from the other side. The guy shouted in surprise, dropping his MP-5 even as a half-dozen rounds ripped through his body. He danced in place for a moment, coughed blood, then fell to his knees before collapsing.

Rajero produced a scream of fury before raising her MP-5 to shoulder level and returning the favor. The 9 mm chattered as Rajero depressed the trigger and held it. She could feel the hot sparks from the smoking shells as she drilled the FARC soldier with a dozen rounds or more. The bolt finally locked back on an empty chamber, and the sounds of the autofire died her ears.

The woman was breathing hard, and she spun on her heel even as she ejected the spent magazine and inserted another. The sounds of the sirens were drawing closer by the moment, and she knew there was no time to waste. She blinked back tears of stress as she realized they had overcome the odds and beaten the Kung Lok and FARC at their own game.

Rajero could scarcely find her voice as she asked her only surviving agent, "What's your name?"

"Carey," the agent replied. "Joe Carey."

"All right, Carey, let's get inside and search for evidence. We're looking for anything we can get our hands on. Drugs, weapons, whatever they have is now ours."

"Understood, ma'am," Carey replied.

Rajero knew he was one of the agents attached to the Las Vegas DEA office, but she hadn't known his name. It bothered her that two other good men now lay dead, the dry desert ground soaking up their blood, and she didn't know their names, either. Still, she would make it her personal mission to insure they received burials fitting of heroes. They had given their lives to protect their fellow officers and American citizens—nobody could ask for more than that.

Rajero covered Carey as he cautiously advanced on the front door to the mobile home. Rajero was watchful, sweeping the muzzle of the MP-5 in every direction, focusing on every possible threat, fighting distraction as the first of an army of Las Vegas police vehicles entered the park. She knew she couldn't afford even a moment's loss of attention on their mission, or it could spell doom for both her and the man she was covering.

Once Carey had entered the house, Rajero moved in immediately behind him. She keyed up her microphone and advised Jack and the rest of the units that they were inside the house. She also asked Jack to contact LVPD and let them know that two armed DEA agents were inside the house. He confirmed the message and then she switched off.

Rajero turned and watched as Carey crossed the room. They rendered hand signals to each other during their sweep of the interior. They searched one room after another, but soon they were giving each other the all-clear sign. Finally, Rajero returned to the main living area, where she saw large quantities of crystalline powder were spilled from bags strewed haphazardly across a large table. Some of the glass bottles and beakers belonging to what looked like nothing more than an eighth-grade chemistry set were smashed or steaming from the boiling liquids inside of them.

Carey shook his head as he approached her. "Can you believe it? They were using this place for a processing lab."

Rajero nodded slowly, then thought of something. She said, "This doesn't make any sense."

"What do you mean?"

"Well, I was under the impression that Carillo did all of the processing in his labs in Brownsville and San Felipe. There was nothing to indicate they were doing local processing."

"Maybe they weren't. Maybe this was something the Chinese started."

"Okay, but—"

Rajero stopped, taking in a sudden sharp breath as she heard the noise for the first time. "Do you hear that?"

"What?"

"That beeping sound."

"Shit, ma'am," Carey said, "my ears are so fried from all the shooting, I couldn't hear a drunk fart in a—"

"Get out of here!"

Rajero grabbed Carey and pushing him toward the front door, nearly knocking the guy over in her haste to escape from the chemical death trap. Lisa Rajero felt her feet leave the ground as she shoved Carey through the doorway....

CHAPTER ELEVEN

The Executioner was prepared for his encounter with the enemy.

The same couldn't be said for the two FARC soldiers maintaining rear security. Their expressions registered surprise at seeing the ghostly wraith that entered the narrow hallway.

Bolan didn't hesitate to let his enemies know he was on a search-and-destroy mission. He raised the FNC and triggered two short bursts. A volley of 5.56 mm NATO rounds spit from the muzzle, taking the first man in the face before he could bring his weapon to bear. His head exploded under the high-velocity impact, spraying the wall and floor behind him with blood and skull fragments. His partner tried to take cover, but the door leading from the hallway was locked, and the sheet-metal trim of the doorjamb was no match for the heavy-caliber ammunition. Two rounds sent shards of razor-sharp metal and shell fragments into the FARC terrorist's face, and a third slammed through his chest. He staggered away from the doorway before toppling onto his dead cohort.

Three down, seven to go.

Bolan never broke stride as he moved up the hallway. He couldn't hear anything over the heavy-metal music blasting from unseen speakers. It echoed up and down the hallway, and the Executioner could only thank fate that it was probably masking much of the sounds of battle. On the other hand, it made it difficult for him to detect opposing movements. He would have to rely on sight and instinct to stay one step ahead of the enemy.

The soldier hugged the wall and knelt as a door opened. Another pair of FARC troopers emerged from the room, wisps of smoke issuing from the muzzles of their Beretta AR-70s. They had obviously terminated whoever was inside the room, but now it was their turn. The Executioner depressed the trigger of the FNC and fired a sustained burst. The NATO rounds punched through the stomachs and chests of the pair, and Bolan swept the muzzle of his weapon in a corkscrew pattern. Large chunks of flesh erupted from the gaping holes left in their backs, and one man left a gory smear on the wall as he slid to the floor.

That brought the count to five, but those weren't the real numbers ticking in the Executioner's head. He was more concerned about the level of resistance he could expect from the Kung Lok. Bolan knew where the logical strike zones were, and he could fairly guess Nievas's plans. Still, he was fighting dual enemies, each just as eager to destroy him as the other, and a two-front war was never easy to predict.

Bolan advanced another few feet down the hallway before the new enemy appeared. About half a dozen Asian men tore around the corner, obviously hell-bent on getting away from something. Some of them were armed with pistols, and all wore street clothes; the only sign of their allegiance was evident in the scarlet bandannas draped around their necks. They stopped short, skidding to a halt on the slippery linoleum of the hallway at the sight of Bolan.

The Executioner already had an M-26 primed and readied. He tossed the grenade underhand as he moved toward a doorway. The spoon popped away as Bolan slammed his foot against a door, dislodging its hinges. He could hear the shouts of confusion and the few stray rounds of their pistols as he took cover inside the room. There was a tremendous blast and Bolan noticed the hallway take on an odd tint. The ignited TNT seemed to shake the very foundation of the building, sending chunks of debris in every direction and clouding the hallway with thick, acrid smoke.

Bolan used the clouding for concealment as he emerged from the hallway and continued his progress. He kept low, watching for signs of movement. He could barely make out the bodies littering the hallway, and it took considerable skill for him not to lose his balance on those areas of the floor settled by puddles of blood. The smoke stung his nostrils, coupled with the odor of death.

The Executioner reached the end of the hallway and encountered three more FARC troopers as they were gunning down one of the Kung Lok survivors. Bolan decided to keep the enemy off balance. He pulled a second M-26 from his web harness, yanked the pin and tossed the bomb into their midst. Bolan receded behind the wall of the adjoining hall and could hear them shouting and scrambling to escape as the first crew had, but the sounds were again drowned by the HE blast. A new cloud of smoke and dust whooshed down the hallway, covering the lights and casting the entire corridor into darkness.

Bolan immediately moved up the hall of the collapsing structure, doing his best to avoid the dust and charred remnants of ceiling that dropped randomly. One flaming piece of roofing crashed across his back, but the flames weren't intense enough to ignite his blacksuit. Bolan contemplated how his enemies were probably reacting to his acts of violence and destruction. It gave him a distinct psychological advantage, not to mention the tactical benefits. There were only two FARC soldiers left alive, and they might have decided it was better to find an alternate exit and live to fight another day.

No such luck.

He encountered a door at the far end of the hallway, but a careful attempt to turn the handle confirmed it was locked. His opponents were either hiding behind the door, waiting for Bolan to make a fatal mistake or they were secure behind one of the other doors scattered along the labyrinthine hallways. In any case, he didn't have time to worry about them. They would show themselves when they thought they had the advantage. The soldier wasn't about to fret over two FARC soldiers.

What *did* have Bolan concerned was the total lack of resistance from the Kung Lok. He knew there had to be more than the six or so he'd already brought down, and the fact they hadn't put up some sort of effective defense served to heighten his senses. Something just wasn't right—he couldn't put his finger on what exactly, but it didn't feel right. Every sense in his mind was screaming at him to get out of there.

The Executioner took a deep breath and crept in the direction from which he'd come. The blaring heavy metal had ceased abruptly and now the area was deathly silent. Bolan moved quietly, willing himself to remain calm and alert.

The reason for the silence suddenly came to light. A

group of eight Scarlet Dragons emerged from a dissipating cloud at the far end of the hallway, attired in full battle dress. They wore black fatigues and combat boots, and were heavily armed with a variety of Jatimatic machine pistols and submachine guns. Still, they weren't ready for a direct encounter with the Executioner, and while their reaction at seeing him was admirable, it wasn't all that effective.

Bolan triggered the FNC, dropping two of the Dragons before they could secure adequate cover. Four dropped to the ground and hastily sprayed the hallway with high-velocity ammunition. The soldier barely evaded the deadly fire. He jumped to the side of the hallway and fired a fresh salvo as he tried a door handle. This one was unlocked, and Bolan moved through it, keeping low. He swept the dimly lit room with the muzzle of his FNC as he closed the door with his shoulder. The room was empty except for a large table stacked three levels high with square packages wrapped in brown butcher paper.

It was a gold mine of processed junk. The Executioner was immediately concerned at first, because he didn't see another way out, but then the dark outline of a door across the room caught his attention. Pulling an M-26 from his harness, he armed the grenade, and then stuffed it beneath the packages, leaving the spoon intact. Bolan crossed to the door and checked it. Locked. He took to backward paces as he drew his Beretta and aimed it at the lock. A 3-round burst made short work of the handle.

Bolan pushed the door open, dropping to one knee, and peered into the adjoining room. It was very large—probably the main part of the bowling alley—now remodeled and partitioned into work-space cubicles. This was the part of building that was supposed to look like a legitimate business office. It was dark, the air musty and stagnant, and it probably hadn't been used since the Kung Lok confiscated it from Carillo's people.

The Executioner stayed in place on one knee, waiting and watching both sides for trouble. He didn't have to wait long. The hallway door burst open and the Kung Lok gunners moved into the room in pairs. They didn't see Bolan at first, but he wasn't concerned. He aimed the FNC at the dope spread across the table and squeezed the trigger. The Kung Lok looked surprised at first, since the Executioner's shots weren't even coming close. White powder erupted from the table, and the grenade dislodged, as the exploding bags no longer contained its weight. The Executioner launched himself from the doorway and sprinted along the inside wall. The blast came a moment later, the orange ball of flame coming through the doorway and illuminating the office area. Bolan stopped to catch his breath, the screams of the dying and injured reaching his ears as the reverberation from the blast diminished.

The building fell silent. Bolan waited a few minutes, but there was no further resistance. It was possible that the two missing FARC soldiers had found another way out, perhaps even the way he'd discovered, but he couldn't take that chance. As long as any of Nievas's or Shui's men were still alive, then his mission at this fire zone was incomplete. He wouldn't exit the battleground until every last one of them was eliminated.

The FARC troopers burst through another doorway at the far end of the office area. Bolan crouched against one of the thin dividers and held his breath, listening for their footfalls. He was confident they hadn't seen him, and he knew that they would be easy to take if he waited until they were almost on top of him before showing his hand. Seconds ticked by, turned into a minute, then two minutes. The Executioner could hear occasional scraping movements and once caught the sound of whispering voices, but it was still too difficult to pinpoint the FARC pair's position.

A newer and much louder noise suddenly called for Bolan's attention. The two members of Team Three, which had been assigned to watch the target area, came crashing through a side entrance with about five local police officers. The Executioner shook his head and swore beneath his breath. Now he not only had his own hide to worry about, but the hides of seven law officers, as well. He couldn't hesitate when the moment of opportunity presented itself, which came immediately after their entrance.

The two FARC soldiers stood and began firing Beretta AR-70 rifles, sending a hail of autofire in the general direction of the cops. Bolan used the opportunity to flank them. He got within pistol range before rising and drawing the .44 Magnum Desert Eagle. The Executioner popped off two rounds, both head shots. The 280-grain boattails from the Israeli-made pistol did unspeakable damage, nearly decapitating the FARC soldiers. The men disappeared from view before the echo of the Eagle's reports died away.

The Executioner's headset buzzed for attention, and he engaged the VOX interface that linked him with Grimaldi.

"Skywatch One to Striker, what's your status, over?"

"All's secure," Bolan said. "What's up?"

"I'm headed for your position now for rapid pickup. We've got trouble."

"What is it?"

"It's Lisa," Grimaldi announced. "I think she's dead."

Mack Bolan felt his heart sink into his stomach.

"ARE YOU SURE?" Bolan asked from the back of the chopper as Grimaldi lifted off.

"Additional info just came through," Grimaldi replied. "It's been confirmed. I'm sorry, Sarge."

The Executioner could hardly believe his ears. Damn! He'd told Rajero to stay on the chopper and coordinate efforts. He didn't actually expect she'd disregard his instructions. Then again, she was in command of the operation from the DEA's side of it. Bolan shook his head and whispered a heartfelt farewell to the brave lady. He was saddened by the loss—as deeply saddened as he would have been for any fallen comrade. America had lost a good cop that night, and most of its citizens would never even know her name.

"How did it happen?"

"From what I can tell on the PD channels, the firefight was over by the time the locals got there. Rajero reported they were secure, and in turn asked we advise LVPD that there were undercover agents inside the house. Apparently, the place blew right after they arrived. One of the DEA agents with her said that she pushed him out before the blast got her. She was pronounced DOA by ER doctors just a few minutes ago."

You went out with style, Rajero, the Executioner thought. He asked, "What's the status on the rest of the teams?"

"That Cooper made short work of the few they ran into at Area Seven. From initial reports, it sounds like they did a hell of a job."

"Do they have a body count on the enemy's side yet?"

"Negative, but estimates are around a dozen and some change."

"That brings the count to roughly thirty, maybe forty at most," Bolan replied, "and that's counting some of the Kung Lok. There's something we're missing. I hope to hell the Bear's intel was accurate."

"He doesn't usually screw up intelligence. When the chips are down, I'd trust Aaron's guesses before I'd trust other people's facts."

"Ditto," Bolan said, although he knew his voice lacked conviction even as he said it.

Grimaldi flashed him a quick glance. "But?"

"But it's not the predictable that worries me. It's the unpredictable."

Another report was coming through, this one based on one team that was constantly monitoring local police channels. Bolan listened intently and as the report came through he and Grimaldi looked at each other with the same horrific expression. Approximately twenty armed men dressed in jungle camouflage were reported entering a hotel along the Strip. As soon as the Executioner heard the name of the hotel, he realized his miscalculation.

Grimaldi read the grim expression in the warrior's visage. "What is it?"

"I know what Nievas has planned now. The first time I tracked the Kung Lok to Las Vegas, they had a hit team operating at that hotel."

"Okay, but that doesn't explain how Nievas would know they were there."

"I have a feeling the answer to that lies with our mysterious government traitor."

"Makes sense."

"Yeah. The guy seems to figure into everything else. Get me there, Jack. It's time to end Nievas's operation once and for all."

Toronto, Canada

LIAM HOFFNER HAD BEEN SITTING there for nearly an hour, and getting damn bored, when Shui suddenly entered the room and greeted him. He couldn't understand why the Kung Lok's western underboss was treating him like this. He held the key to Shui's fortunes and control in America. He was incensed that Shui seemed to look on him as some lackey. If he weren't careful, Hoffner would offer a better deal to Jikwan and Dim Mai. Perhaps he would anyway—it might earn him the respect he deserved.

"Mr. Hoffner, welcome to my home."

Hoffner rose and shook Shui's hand. The Chinese mobster had a limp handshake—as limp as the first time they had met in Florida. Here was Shui, one of the richest and most powerful crime lords in North America, and he had the grip of a girl. Still, Hoffner knew that Lau-Ming Shui was to be feared and respected. He could have Hoffner's life snuffed in a heartbeat. In some strange way, the fortunes had reversed. Mostly it was due to the ineptitude of Carillo, Nievas and all of their respective lackeys. But that was ancient history, and what Hoffner had to focus on now was convincing Shui that he was still a useful ally.

"I'm sorry you had to wait, but I was unavoidably detained."

Hoffner shook his head. "Forget it. I'm just happy that you accepted my offer. I trust that the outcome has met with your satisfaction."

"I wish I could say that were true," Shui replied, "but then I would be lying. I'm not completely happy with the situation as it stands."

Hoffner shrugged, a little uncomfortable with Shui's forthright remark. "In what way? I thought everything went just as planned. I did as I promised I would, Lau-Ming. I trust you aren't planning to renege on our deal."

Shui's smile was anything but friendly. "I would never think of going back on our deal, Mr. Hoffner. However, I will not meet my end of our agreement until this little problem in Las Vegas is resolved."

"I'm sorry, but I'm afraid I don't understand. What little problem are you having in Las Vegas?"

"The American, Belasko, and all of his comrades," Shui said. "He's proved quite resourceful in the past. At first, I assumed he would be an unwitting ally as he destroyed Carillo's operations, thus eliminating our competition. Unfortunately, I was wrong. It appears that this Belasko cares little for sides. He is simply out to destroy anything in his path. I cannot have that, Mr. Hoffner."

"I don't know what to tell you. It sounds to me like this guy is strictly your problem."

"Perhaps in the strictest sense you speak the truth," Shui replied. "But do not forget that eventually this man's perseverance will lead him here."

"Then why not shut him down in Vegas?"

Shui chuckled. "You almost make it sound easy."

"It isn't?"

Shui went to a nearby hutch and opened the thin doors to reveal a swing-out bar. The shelves were lined with everything from some of the finest wines and champagnes in the world to a large assortment of hard liquors. Shui pulled a small bottle from the cabinet and poured himself a drink in a ceramic container not much larger than a thimble.

"May I interest you in some Yangshao, Mr. Hoffner?"

Hoffner simply shook his head.

"Anything at all? A beer? I know that you Americans are very fond of beer. Particularly the Dutch and Mexican imports."

"No, I'm fine. What I want to know is what you plan to do about Belasko?"

"I have left that in the hands of a mutual friend of ours."

"I wasn't aware we had any mutual friends."

"Of course we do," Shui replied. He turned and clapped twice. A few seconds elapsed before General Deng Jikwan entered the room, accompanied by one of the most beautiful women Hoffner had ever seen. He could barely believe his eyes when he saw Jikwan. He knew that the military man was always looking for new ways to further his own personal ambitions, but he would never have imagined Jikwan conspiring with the likes of Lau-Ming Shui.

"A pleasure to see you again, Hoffner," Jikwan said.

"Yeah, it's been a while."

"Actually, it has not," Jikwan said with a wave, "but we shall dispense with the pleasantries and get directly to business."

"What business is that?"

Lau-Ming Shui cleared his throat. "I think General Jikwan is talking about the deal you made with him and Dim Mai."

Hoffner was suddenly feeling less confident. So that was how they were going to play it—they were sticking together. The bastards were actually talking to each other now, whereas a week ago they were participating in secret meetings in a hotel room, each looking for a way to gain the advantage on the other. Hoffner could do little more than shake his head with disbelief.

"So it seems you *are* reneging on our deal," he told Shui.

"In my country, Mr. Hoffner, it is not customary to insult your host. I was gracious enough to listen to you in West Palm Beach, so I'm sure the least you can do is sit down and be civil."

Hoffner nodded slowly, realizing it wasn't a request. He took a seat and decided to hear them out. He knew that it was the smartest thing to do. He wanted to curse himself for believing the Chinese were people of their word, but apparently he'd misjudged their foresight. He could almost figure where the whole thing would go, but since he seemed to be fresh out of leverage, he would just have to play turd for Shui and Jikwan.

At least until another opportunity presented itself.

"I am realistic enough to know that you have neither the resources nor the wherewithal to go up against Belasko," Shui said. "It is only by the generosity and friendship of General Jikwan that we shall survive this little…incident."

"You're kidding, right?" Hoffner asked. "I've heard the stories about Belasko, and he's damn well overrated. Get him within fifty feet of me and I'll kill him myself."

It was Jikwan who snorted as he took a cup of Yangshao liquor from Shui. He tossed it back and offered the cup for a refill before turning his attention on Hoffner. The expression in Jikwan's eyes told Hoffner that the Chinese soldier would have liked nothing better than to kill him right there, but for some reason he was holding back. Perhaps he did still hold some leverage.

"Don't be a fool, Hoffner," Jikwan said. "Particularly not a fool with false bravery. I understand Belasko too well."

"As do I," said the dark-haired beauty who had entered the room with Jikwan. "He single-handedly destroyed Jose Carillo's empire, and even as we speak he is in Las Vegas and destroying the last of Colonel Amado Nievas and his FARC mercenaries."

"This is Catalina Milaña," Jikwan said, waving in her general direction as he downed a third glass of Yang-shao. Hoffner could tell he was quickly becoming intoxicated.

"Miss Milaña helped us dupe Belasko into destroying Carillo and Nievas."

"And even though you thought you were controlling the situation," Jikwan said, "we were actually controlling you. So don't pretend to be intelligent. My military intelligence agents profiled you very early in this, Hoffner. They said you would be easy to fool, and they were correct."

"So you put one over on me," Hoffner said. "So what? You think I'm afraid to die?"

"You are afraid to die," Shui said, "but that really is not the point. The point is that you have a tremendous amount of knowledge regarding the activities of your government and the various law-enforcement agencies. I'm sure that a considerable hunt is under way for you right now."

"Are you insane?" Hoffner said. "I couldn't go back and show my face now. If you want me to do that, you might as well just kill me because I'd be virtually dead anyway."

"We have no intention of sending you back," Jikwan said. "You're going to accompany us to Hong Kong and

work with our people. You will become our greatest asset against the law-enforcement agencies of your government.''

"Of course, first things first," Shui said with a laugh.
"We must now make our plans for Belasko's arrival."

"You actually think he's going to come here?" Hoffner asked.

"I know he will come," Shui replied.

CHAPTER TWELVE

Las Vegas, Nevada

As Jack Grimaldi flew the Sikorsky over the Windfall Hotel and Casino, Bolan could see the logjam of squad cars and other police vehicles blocking the street in front of the hotel. It would have been impractical to put the chopper down in the street, and there hadn't been time to get to the hotel by ground vehicle. Grimaldi was going to put the Executioner down on the hotel roof.

"Give me fifteen minutes before pickup, Jack," Bolan said. "I'll have to search floor by floor. I'm sure Nievas is with them."

"How will you get back topside if they cut you off?" Grimaldi asked.

"I'll manage," the Executioner replied. "If that doesn't work, then I'll hook up with Cooper's people and slip out when the time's right. Rendezvous A here, rendezvous B at the airport."

"Understood," the pilot said as he swung the chopper into position a few yards above the hotel roof. The plan seemed good to him. Cooper had radioed to say he and his team were on their way to the hotel.

Bolan left the Sikorsky and moved toward the roof access door. A quick inspection revealed the thing was constructed from heavy steel. The Executioner knew explosives were his only option. He retrieved an M-26, primed it and placed it against the door before racing to cover behind a large ventilation pipe. The M-26 made short work of the door, blowing it from its hinges with a fiery blast.

The Executioner quickly moved through the smoking hole, careful not to brush against the molten metal left behind. As he descended the stairs, Bolan considered the layout. The hotel had fifteen floors. Since his original encounter with the Kung Lok had taken place on the ninth floor, he decided that one of the top five or six floors most likely housed the Kung Lok. It was a place to start.

Bolan reached the fifteenth-floor landing in less than a minute and moved into the hallway. The Windfall wasn't as large as the majority of hotel casinos along the Strip, which was something for which he could be grateful.

The warrior found it difficult not to think of Rajero as he advanced down the hallway in search of Nievas and his men. He didn't regret knowing her—would never regret that—but he regretted having brought her into his war against the Kung Lok. Still, she'd gone out fighting for what she believed in, and she'd done it willingly. There wasn't anything more gutsy or honorable than that, so Bolan couldn't find fault with Rajero. He'd always made it his practice to work alone, and he knew he should have stuck to that policy.

That was why the Executioner had done his best to keep Stony Man out of his war against the Kung Lok and the Nievas-Carillo alliance. It wasn't that Brognola and the teams weren't capable—it was the risk they stood of exposure and involvement battling the FARC and Kung Lok triad on American streets. Mack Bolan was one man, and he could keep on the move and disappear into the crowd more quickly than Able Team or Phoenix Force. Plus, he didn't have to operate with the same stealth.

And that was his advantage.

Although stealth did him little good as he encountered the first of Nievas's FARC commandos. Bolan could hear the sounds of movement coming in his direction. He moved to the edge of the adjoining hallway and peered around the corner. Four men in jungle camous and toting assault rifles were spread across the wide, central hallway of the hotel. Bolan was standing in one of the corridors that terminated one end of the hallway. The hotel was I-shaped, with a grand walkway lined with smaller rooms, while the terminal ends served as wings for the master suites.

The Executioner knelt, extended the folding stock of the FNC, then raised the weapon to his shoulder and braced it against the corner. He moved the selector switch to single shot and squeezed the trigger. The high-velocity NATO slug punched through the forehead of the pointman, blowing out the back of his head and showering his comrades in gore. The remaining trio of FARC troops responded admirably, diving in every direction. They set up prone firing positions and immediately lined up for shots down the hallway, but Bolan already had a second one targeted before they could open fire.

He stroked the trigger again, and this time the round caught one of the soldiers in the left cheekbone. The angle of trajectory wound up ripping half of the guy's face away, but it didn't turn out to be lethal. It was enough of a shock to cause him to forget his rifle. He screamed in agony and began writhing on the floor. The other two soldiers hesitated to open fire, obviously torn between saving their comrade or themselves. They had to have realized that discretion was the better part of valor because they chose the latter and opened fire.

Bolan ducked behind the wall in time to avoid a swarm of 5.56 mm NATO rounds. They rocketed from the FARC troops' Beretta AR-70s at a cyclic rate of 650 rounds per minute, chewing up the walls and floor and raising a cloud of glass, wood, plaster and debris. Bolan simply let the violent reaction play out, waiting for the eventual lull he knew would happen—the lull that occurred when they stopped to reload their weapons. It came a moment later, and the Executioner seized the advantage by swinging his weapon around the corner and shooting a third FARC soldier with a sustained burst. The rounds ripped apart his chest and face before he could get a fresh magazine fully seated in the rifle.

The last soldier jumped to his feet and hightailed it down the hallway. The Executioner was about to shoot his retreating form when two security guards emerged from the other end of the hallway. Bolan held his fire and shouted a warning. They tried to take cover, but the FARC soldier didn't give them a chance. He sprayed the area with rounds. Bolan launched himself down the hallway in a flat run. He could see one of the guards go down, his arm bleeding profusely, but the other had miraculously survived without getting hit.

The Executioner bent over the wounded guard. He watched as the FARC trooper entered a stairway at the far end, but he decided not to pursue him. The guy in front of him needed his immediate attention, and Mack Bolan wasn't about to leave a wounded man behind without at least insuring he would be okay. Bolan yanked packing from the small medical pouch attached to his web harness. He slapped the compress on the security guard's arm.

The other officer was getting on his feet and reaching for his gun, but Bolan held up his hand. "Don't draw down on friendlies, guy."

The security guard's hand fell on the butt of his revolver, but he didn't draw it. Something told Bolan the guy could read the sincere expression in his face. Not to mention that the very fact the soldier had stopped to help his comrade indicated they were on the same side. The enemy wouldn't have stopped to help in this manner, and the guard damn well knew that. Still, he was being cautious.

"Who the hell are you?"

"Not important," Bolan replied. "What's important is that you get your man here to a doctor and everyone else out of this hotel quick."

"Who died and left you in charge, pal?"

"Listen, the fact of the matter is I could have shot you both dead," Bolan said. "I didn't. Now, you think about that and decide right now whose side I'm on."

Bolan could see the wheels turning behind the young man's eyes. He still looked like a kid—maybe in college. Had to be at least twenty-one to work security in a casino, but there was definitely no question he was green to the job. The Executioner understood how traumatic something like this could be for raw men.

"I told you to decide now," Bolan repeated.

The kid moved his hand away from the gun and bent to help his friend control the bleeding.

Bolan tried to give him a reassuring grin. "It's just a bite. Keep pressure on the wound and he'll be okay until you get him a doctor. Meanwhile, get on that radio and let your people know this place is crawling with armed terrorists. Get everyone out of here.''

''How?'' the guard stammered.

''You'll think of something,'' Bolan replied, and then he took off in search of his prey.

CAPTAIN ROD COOPER and Commander Wesley Haggis entered the Windfall Hotel and Casino with a group of well-armed DEA and BATF agents on their heels.

Cooper barked orders at them and they immediately obeyed, grouping in trios or quartets and moving in different directions. They moved precisely and kept together, each pointman carrying a shield while others followed behind with MP-5s held at the ready. They were the cream of the crop, some of the best special-tactics agents in the country, and Cooper couldn't help but feel proud of them this night.

Although he and Haggis had only worked with Lisa Rajero a short time before her death, they'd come to respect her tenacity and dedication to duty. Now she was dead, and Colonel Nievas was planning on wreaking havoc and putting the lives of innocent civilians in jeopardy. And what had the two lawmen most upset was that between these battling factions was Mike Belasko, a one-man army who planned to wage a private little war against the FARC and Kung Lok, and he didn't give a damn about the costs.

''Did you see that out there?'' Cooper asked Haggis, jerking his thumb in the direction of the street.

Haggis nodded as he studied the main area of the casino. ''They're going to start eating each other pretty soon.''

Cooper knew the DEA commander was being wise, but he also believed there was some truth to what Haggis was saying. The LVPD was trying to keep angry patrons at bay—patrons who were either in the middle of losing or winning a fortune, albeit mostly losing with the exception of maybe a slot junkie or two. Meanwhile, the mayor was now screaming for the governor to call in the National Guard because there were armed terrorists running through a hotel in *his* city, and Cooper and Haggis were trying to keep the survivors of the teams organized as they converged on the Windfall.

"I wonder where Belasko is?" Haggis asked.

"I don't know and I don't give a damn," Cooper snapped. "He hasn't called in, and his supposed pilot hasn't responded to any of our calls."

As they continued walking through the casino and looking for the security chief, Cooper added, "As far as I'm concerned, he can rot in hell."

BOLAN ENCOUNTERED a team of six Kung Lok ambushers who were waiting for Nievas's men to come off the elevators. The Executioner figured their plan held merit, since he couldn't see the FARC using the stairs—particularly not in a fifteen-story hotel. Nievas was on a strict search-and-destroy mission, and if he was half the tactician Bolan thought he was, the Colombian terrorist would want it done quickly and efficiently.

Bolan knelt, retrieved his last M-26 and primed it; he'd have to make this one count. He let the spoon fly and waited two seconds before tossing it in the direction of the waiting troops. The Kung Lok turned to the sound of the grenade hitting the ground in their midst with a thud. The men looked at the grenade, but the Executioner never saw their reaction as he ducked behind the cover of the wall.

The area surrounding the elevator bank shook with the

explosion. Bolan heard the screams of dying men over
the cacophony of whistling metal and flaming debris that
crashed against the walls and rained from the ceiling.
Bolan risked a glance at the damage left in the wake of
the HE and did a body count—not a single Kung Lok
gunner had escaped. The Executioner nodded with satisfaction and moved back toward the stairwell and the
next floor even as residents rushed from their rooms to
investigate.

Bolan found no resistance on the thirteenth or twelfth
floors, but a few Scarlet Dragons met him descending
the stairs to floor eleven. Bolan dodged out of view on
the stairwell in time to avoid the rounds that issued from
three chattering Jatimatics. Shell fragments whizzed past
Bolan's head from ricochets off the polished concrete
walls, and one nicked his face. The Executioner was
about to retreat to the twelfth floor and find another route
when the sound of assault rifles rang in his ears.

The hail of bullets stopped and Bolan guessed at the
reason even though he couldn't see it. FARC troops had
flanked the Kung Lok and engaged them to the rear. He
used the moment to open up on them, as well. With no
place to go, the trio of Kung Lok enforcers fell under
the deadly cross fire.

Bolan moved up the stairwell and reentered the
twelfth floor, confident the FARC was in hot pursuit.
The soldier needed some combat stretch to stay one step
ahead of them. As he sprinted down the central hallway,
he also considered the possibility that Cooper and Haggis had arrived with reinforcements. They would have
their hands tied awhile on the lower floors, especially
since they had no idea where Bolan was—or the enemy
troops for that matter.

The Executioner reached the opposite side of the hotel

and ascended quickly, bypassing the remaining floors and heading for ground zero. It would make little difference to search the remaining floors. Bolan estimated there weren't enough Kung Lok or FARC gunners left to be any real threat, and hotel security had evacuated the public areas. The Scarlet Dragons weren't likely to hide behind closed doors, and it wasn't advantageous for Nievas to have his men kick down every door in the place in the hopes he'd find a few Kung Lok stragglers.

Mack Bolan knew they were mostly gone. It had been fairly obvious from the get-go that this whole sordid mess was a setup, and he thought he was pretty sure who had instigated the entire thing. Now it was just a matter of waiting for the FARC and Kung Lok to fight their way past the SWAT and task force teams now circling the building. From his earlier visit, the Executioner knew there were only three ways out of the Windfall, and both ground exits were undoubtedly sealed tight.

That left the roof and Bolan knew he'd have to provide Grimaldi a secure LZ.

Bolan reached the fifteenth floor, then exited into the hallway and headed for the separate stairwell to the roof access. The sound of footfalls approaching took him by surprise. He moved into the shadows of an alcove of pay phones along the central hallway and crouched. The enemy appeared a moment later, true to his predictions. Four soldiers moved along the hallway, rifles at the ready. A fifth man took center point between them, and Bolan immediately recognized him as Colonel Amado Nievas.

The Executioner raised the FNC and triggered his first 3-round salvo.

"I DON'T CARE if you haven't found anything yet," Cooper replied to the radio call. "Keep looking, Lieutenant.

I want every one of those bastards either dead or in custody. And that includes Belasko!"

Haggis and Cooper were positioned at their temporary command post behind a circular counter in the main lobby. The Las Vegas police department's SWAT team had signaled minutes earlier that the entire block was now sealed off. Nobody could go in or out without coming through them, and the commander of the SWAT team had assured them the roof was being covered by a police chopper.

"I hope they don't get trigger-happy on Belasko," Haggis remarked. "I know you don't think much of him, Cooper, but he is on our side."

Cooper drew his lips back to expose gritted teeth and snorted. "You've got to be kidding me. I think Belasko is our mysterious commando from last week's fiasco at Tang's place. He damn near killed a bunch of the LVPD."

"That's not the way I heard it," Haggis said. "I heard he saved their asses."

Cooper looked at Haggis with a surprised expression, and while the DEA commander was Cooper's superior, he shrunk under the baleful stare. "Tell that to Rajero, Wes."

Haggis concocted a biting retort but held his tongue. He had to admit that it was Belasko's idea to handle the FARC in the matter they had, but the guy had probably saved a lot more than he'd killed. Reports of the action at Area Three were already coming through, and the team who'd stormed the place attested to the fact that Belasko had eradicated the enemy single-handedly. The body count was rising, and Haggis couldn't ignore the fact that with the exception of three from the task force, all the casualties had been on the enemy's side.

So it didn't really make a damn to him what Cooper thought. Cooper had an attitude anyway, and had for as long as Haggis had known him. He was entitled to his opinions, but that was all they were. Haggis would remember that. And he'd remember just how damn many people were going to live today because of the courage of a guy who even now, even against unbelievable odds, was somewhere above them and putting it all on the line. And Haggis could only respect someone like that.

THE MUZZLE of the FNC smoked as the echo of its reports died.

Four men lay sprawled around Colonel Amado Nievas, victims of the Executioner's deadly marksmanship. Their leader now stood and studied their bodies with only a cursory expression. Bolan could see the defeat in the FARC terrorist's face, the fact he knew it was over written all over his features. Over the past week, he'd lost nearly one hundred men to either a gang of Chinese thugs or the combat skills of a single man.

The colonel made a show of keeping his hands clear of his pistol belt. He rendered a smile for Bolan, and there was something in his eyes that signaled respect. The warrior studied him with impassivity, the FNC never wavering.

"You are quite a man, *señor,*" Nievas finally said. "I would have given most all I own to have just one like you on my side."

"It would never happen, Nievas. In this life or the next."

Nievas shrugged. "Perhaps not. But I believe in fate.

I think we agree on this, no? Or you would not be here now.''

"I believe in only one thing," Bolan said.

"What?"

"Justice." The Executioner stepped forward and relieved Nievas of his side arm. He stepped back, dropped the magazine, then quickly and expertly cleared the chamber before dropping the weapon to the floor.

Then he turned and headed for the roof.

"Where are you going?" Nievas called.

Bolan stopped and turned to face him. "Looks like I'm leaving."

"You allow me to live?"

The Executioner smiled—a cold smile. "Killing you serves no purpose. I'd rather take comfort knowing you'll have to take your chances with the Kung Lok."

"Some of my men survive."

"But they won't get past the police. There's no way out of here, Nievas. If the Kung Lok don't get you, my government will. In either case, it's over for you and your partner. The Carillo-Nievas alliance is dead. As I'm sure you'll be within the hour."

Bolan turned and continued for the roof, shaking his head as Nievas stood in the hallway and continued to scream at him. The man was venting with obscenities, but his voice faded from the Executioner's consciousness. The echo of his screams diminished as Bolan climbed the steps, and by the time he'd reached the roof, he could no longer hear the FARC leader at all.

"UNIT THREE to Command," Cooper's lieutenant called over the radio.

"Go," Cooper replied.

"We encountered some of the FARC troops. They

surrendered without incident. Another team is still sweeping the area. We've also found dead Asians in two separate areas. They look Chinese, so we're assuming they're triad.''

"Affirmative," Cooper replied with a nod of victory at Haggis.

Haggis got on the communications unit and asked, "Any sign of Belasko?"

"Not yet, sir, but we're still searching."

Cooper slammed his fist in his palm. He wanted that son of a bitch alive, and he didn't hesitate to let his people know it in those terms before signing off. It irked him that they had trusted him at all.

Haggis said, "You know what, Cooper? You're an asshole.''

"What?"

Haggis turned and walked toward the front entrance.

"He's not on our side, Wes. He goes around blowing shit up and thinks he's not accountable for it. I don't like hot dogs. I want people to do things by the book. And I'm sure Washington would agree with me. The guy's a menace.''

"So are you, Cooper," Haggis said as he left.

A moment later, the SWAT commander advised that a chopper had flown low over the top of the building. Cooper immediately started chewing the man out, wanting to know why the police chopper hadn't spotted them. He couldn't believe his ears when the SWAT commander reported that the chopper had been pulled off for a traffic accident. Cooper felt the anger rise within him when the SWAT commander described the chopper. Mike Belasko had slipped through his fingers.

But it wasn't over yet.

CHAPTER THIRTEEN

Stony Man Farm, Virginia

The first thing Hal Brognola did when he saw Bolan was call the team doctor out to give him a thorough checkup.

Brognola knew the Executioner didn't like to be mothered, but it didn't much matter. The guy looked as if he was about to draw his last, and with his upcoming mission to Toronto, he needed medical attention and rest. And he needed support, which Brognola planned to give him no matter what the President said. Bolan had been fighting his war for a week now, and it was far from over. The very idea that the Executioner could utterly lay waste within a few days to what governments could not seem to topple in a few years simply amazed the Stony Man chief.

Even as long as he'd known the man reverently called the Executioner.

"You look like hell," Brognola said as Bolan slumped into a chair in the War Room.

"Good to see you, too, Hal," the warrior managed to say with a wry smile.

"I'm glad you're all right."

"We're all glad," Barbara Price added.

She had joined them along with Aaron Kurtzman and

they were patched into a conference call with Carl Lyons. Brognola had received the go-ahead to dispatch Able Team to investigate the activities at the El Paso Intelligence Center, and they had gleaned a considerable amount of information since their arrival. Bolan was glad to see his friends. A part of Stony Man Farm would always be home to the soldier, no matter where he laid his head.

"I heard you've had a rough go of it, Striker," Lyons said.

"I'll make it."

"Well, I *know* that."

Brognola cleared his throat to signal for attention. "What do you have for us, Ironman?"

"Well, other than a hot-ass motel room and an itch for some action, we got dick," Lyons reported in his usual no-frills manner. "Four Chinese hardcases busted into the El Paso Intelligence Center and started cutting people down without warning. They killed seven law officers and injured three or four civilian workers. Not to mention that they found Conrado Diaz shot in the director's office."

"Diaz," Bolan said with a nod. "Carillo's right-hand man."

"Well, now he's pushing daisies," Ironman continued. "Plus the fact, they managed to get away with Ramon Sapèdas *and* the director of the center, Liam Hoffner."

Brognola shook his head and sighed. He could hardly believe what he was hearing. In a way, he couldn't help but blame himself for it. It was easy to say he'd been following the President's orders, or honoring the Executioner's wishes, by not involving the Stony Man team sooner, but he considered himself beyond such pettiness.

He was the head of the most elite antiterrorist organization in the world, and he'd sat on his hands while his people—even his friends—were out there putting it on the line.

It frustrated Brognola, but it was an occupational hazard he'd come to live with. The head Fed had never considered himself a worrywart, but he was probably one of the world's last greatest pessimists and he was a damn bit closer to manic when it came to their operations. Were it not for the calm assuredness of people like Barbara Price and Aaron Kurtzman at his side, Brognola didn't at all doubt he'd probably be locked in some padded room by now, wearing a straitjacket and being slipped food and water through a slot in a door three times a day.

"All right, Ironman. Anything else important that comes to mind?"

"Nothing really. I'm just sorry we weren't here in time to stop it."

"Don't sweat it, guy," Bolan said. "I'm not done with the Kung Lok."

"I hear ya. If that's all you need, I'm going to go see what kind of trouble Pol and Gadgets are getting into."

"Funny, but they're usually the ones keeping you out of trouble," Brognola quipped.

"Right. Stay hard, Striker."

"You, too," Bolan replied.

Lyons broke the connection.

"Well, that was interesting," Price said with a smile.

Brognola nodded. "Looks like the Kung Lok don't hesitate to wreak havoc wherever they go."

"That's to be expected from the triads," Bolan interjected. "Something just doesn't ring true with me, though."

"What's that, Striker?"

"This little operation at the intelligence center. Seems like they put a lot at risk to grab Sapèdas. I think they initially hit the place to kill Lisa Rajero, but this second operation was unexpected. I don't see how Sapèdas is of any use to them."

"Not to mention the ease of their escape," Price added.

"That's what I was thinking," Brognola said.

"You're talking about them taking this Hoffner as a hostage?" Bolan asked.

Brognola nodded.

"We've known for some time now that somebody inside the government has been manipulating the Kung Lok against Nievas and Carillo. My money's on Hoffner." Bolan turned to Kurtzman. "What can you tell me about this guy?"

Kurtzman turned to a computer terminal and typed an entry with lightning speed. Only a moment passed before the system returned information from the DEA's files. He glanced through the output on the display and grunted with satisfaction. The system still hummed as additional information poured into the permanent record, which, like the records for every government employee, was available to Stony Man at the push of a button.

"Liam George Hoffner, age fifty-two, present position DEA liaison and operations director for the El Paso Intelligence Center, where he's been for the past ten years. Formerly served as a deep-cover agent with the DEA in various drug centers of South and Central Americas, as well as operations in the Middle East and Southeast Asian theaters. Before that, he worked stateside in Miami, Boston, Los Angeles and Seattle. He even did a two-year stint in Wonderland as a consultant for the Senate subcommittee on East Coast narcotics trafficking during the Clinton administration.''

Kurtzman turned from the console and shook his head. "Says he was also a highly decorated veteran and undercover agent.''

"Any investigations?" Bolan asked.

Kurtzman tabbed through a few pages before replying, "Under investigation for drug use during an undercover operation in Bogotá. Spent three months in a private drug treatment facility, bought and paid for courtesy of the DEA. Been clean since.''

"So he's had his finger in a lot of different pies," Brognola said.

Bolan nodded. "Sounds like our most likely candidate. I suspect he saw an opportunity to get out with the Scarlet Dragons and he took it.''

"Well, there aren't any further reports of solid leads since his disappearance, and there haven't been any ransom demands.''

"And there won't be any ransom demands, whether he's working for them or not," Bolan replied. "Hostage negotiation is hardly the Kung Lok's style. He's either hiding or dead.''

A long silence followed before Brognola finally said, "Do you suppose it's possible the Kung Lok snatched Sapèdas to shut him up?"

"Why?" Bolan said, shrugging. "If they wanted to keep him quiet, they could have killed him as opposed to risking a kidnapping.''

"Good point.''

"No, something tells me this goes deeper than that," Bolan continued. "In either case, it doesn't matter. What I need to do is get to Toronto and find Shui. If Hoffner's flipped to the Chinese, I'm sure I'll find him there. Along with Sapèdas.''

''Are you willing to let us help on this one, Striker? I know you could use our support, and the President has green-lighted any operations required to assist you.''

It was the first time Brognola had seen his friend smile since he arrived, and it warmed his heart. Through all the death and horror, the Executioner somehow managed to maintain his sometimes dry sense of humor. The big guy had a lot of ghosts on his conscience. He bore a burden nobody else would bear—or could bear if they wanted to.

''I think we've got a problem,'' Kurtzman said.

Brognola stood and moved over to the terminal screen, which the Bear was now studying intently. ''What is it?''

''Seems that the DEA has put out an all-points bulletin on Striker.''

The Executioner nodded with an expression that betrayed his acceptance of the report. He'd obviously known this was coming, although that didn't really explain how he knew. It was Kurtzman's habit to maintain a flag on any computer links that utilized the names or pseudonyms of every Stony Man team member, including the Executioner.

Brognola leaned over Kurtzman's shoulder to peer at the output and then turned to Bolan. ''Request was submitted by a Captain Rodney Cooper.''

''He's a tactical officer for the DEA in Las Vegas. He was part of Rajero's task force.''

''All right, Bear, delete all references to Striker and I'll make a phone call to his superior. We sure as hell don't need someone from the DEA snooping around.''

Kurtzman nodded even as he hacked into the system

to delete the files directly. In a few minutes, there wouldn't be any such name or person as Mike Belasko, now or in the past—at least not in any database that allowed public access. To the world outside of Stony Man—for the time being—it would be as if Mike Belasko never existed.

"Now that we've taken care of that," Brognola said, returning his attention to the Executioner, "what's your next move?"

"I'm going to need weapons support and all of the current intelligence you can give me on Shui's activities in Canada, particularly in Toronto and surrounding areas. I'll want everything, Hal, including anything the Company might have on him."

The Stony Man chief nodded. "Done. I'll have Bear get right on it."

"Also, I'll need a fresh supply of weaponry."

"Anything in the armory is yours, as always, Striker," Brognola said. "And if we don't have it, let me know and we'll get it posthaste."

"How can I help?" Price asked.

Brognola wasn't surprised at her question. Despite his own initial feelings of hopefulness, he couldn't imagine what Price might have been thinking through this period. She wasn't much about voicing her feelings to begin with, and she'd been even less talkative over the past week. While it wasn't Barbara Price's style to sit at the Farm and pine for the warrior, it didn't mean she wasn't concerned. As the mission controller, she was concerned for every member of the team when they were operating in the field, but she held a particularly special place in her heart and mind for her occasional companion.

"I've got something special I need you to do for me," Bolan said. "Reach out to your contacts at the NSA and get everything you can on General Deng Jikwan and his relationship to the Hong Kong triads. I want to know where he's been and who he's been talking to.''

"You're thinking he has some sort of connection with Shui?"

"We know he attended the meeting in Florida, which leads to that possibility. It's no secret he's a strong supporter of the Kung Lok," Bolan replied.

"Not to mention his connections with Dim Mai."

"Yeah, that's another thing. I'm not sure how Mai figures into all of this, either. Whoever arranged the arms sales between Mai and the Colombians had to know about the partnership between Nievas and Carillo. The Kung Lok's involvement at such a critical time for the Colombians was no coincidence."

"Shui and Mai are fierce competitors, as well," Kurtzman interjected as he continued typing.

It never ceased to amaze the members of Stony Man that Bear's steel-trap mind could simultaneously focus on so many tasks. While some people couldn't walk and chew gum at the same time, Aaron Kurtzman was like a machine, able to process information while carrying on a conversation about practically anything at all if it interested him.

Brognola nodded in agreement. "He's right. There's no love lost between Mai and Shui."

"In either case, we're running out of time," Bolan said. "I'm going to catch a couple hours of shut-eye. Have somebody wake me when you have what I need. I'm going to need Jack, too, Hal, and I can't say right now for how long."

"He's yours," Brognola said, waving goodbye. "Now nighty-night."

Hong Kong, China

NYENSHI FUNG WATCHED Dim Mai pace the room like a nervous cat.

She hated to see her husband acting this way, but she also knew he had a lot on his mind. She didn't have all the details—it wasn't really her place to know them. But she *did* know that the arms deal Jikwan had arranged between Dim and Nievas was now ancient history. She was angry with Jikwan for betraying her husband, but she was even angrier at the thought Lau-Ming could have betrayed her confidence.

What Fung didn't want to admit—especially as she listened to Dim's ravings—was that she still felt something for Lau-Ming Shui. She was certain he still had feelings for her, as well, and that troubled her greatly. She knew this was a world of men, controlled by domineering power brokers and financed by greedy politicians.

Fung had once been quite active in politics; many years ago she'd shared that passion with Shui. But now she was a servant, married for convenience and condemned to a life of boredom and drudgery. Fung wasn't like most Chinese women and was the first to admit it. Many of her friends and acquaintances were considerably happy in their positions, and those who held the same status would most readily have welcomed the opportunity to live her glamorous life.

Yet dinner parties and formal engagements with the elite in political and social circles could only carry a person so far, particularly a woman of Fung's curious nature. Still, she supposed it was wiser to be contented in her life and the things that Dim Mai gave to her. She wished more for his attention and respect, and less for material things, but she drew comfort from the knowledge that he loved her.

At the moment, however, he was having considerable trouble showing her that.

"Why don't you sit down, Dim," she chided him.

"I cannot rest," Mai responded. "Not until I know why Deng Jikwan has betrayed my trust and taken refuge with my competitors."

"Deng is a soldier and a statesman," Fung said, trying to be respectful while acting as a voice of reason.

She knew her husband had a terrible temper, and she didn't want him to take out his frustrations on any of the expensive vases or other trinkets that decorated their penthouse of Hong Kong's tallest apartment building.

"I cannot believe he would consciously betray you," Fung added.

Mai stopped pacing and appraised her, red-faced and short of breath. "Are you siding with him?"

"Of course not." She averted her eyes and bowed her head.

Some of the arrogance left Dim Mai, but she could tell his anger was far from satiated. Her worst fears would be realized if he chose to express his anger in a more practical way. Fung knew that he was capable of considerable wrath. It would do little good for her to instigate him into considering a more *permanent* solution to his problem. When Dim Mai sent some of his personal enforcers to exact his vengeance, people always died.

Mai stepped forward and lifted her chin in his meaty palm. "You are not to blame, and you have nothing for which to be sorry." He turned from her and resumed his pacing. "Of course it could be as you say, and the good general is simply a victim of circumstance. But it does not change the fact that he chose to hide in Canada instead of owning up to his failures.''

''Perhaps it is not his failure. Perhaps someone failed *him*.''

''Impossible. I have know Deng Jikwan since we were schoolchildren, and I have never seen him hold an underling accountable for something he was charged with overseeing.''

''If that is true, then the man you are describing is one of loyalty. Loyal men don't usually betray others, particularly not those they call their friends.''

Dim Mai stopped pacing and studied her for a long moment before nodding. She knew her words held soothing truth, and there was no way Mai could deny the logic in them. At times, she could sway her husband when he hadn't already made up his mind. But he was strong willed and stubborn, and very difficult to turn once convinced of what he perceived as the truth.

''I will agree to defer this for now. But I am hurt that he would not come to me first.''

''Perhaps he will.''

Mai nodded and kissed his wife's hand before leaving her alone. She waited several minutes, insuring he'd left for good, before rising and going to the phone. She needed to speak with Shui right away. She had to take the initiative to at least warn him of a possible retaliation, lest he be surprised by an unwarranted attack by Dim Mai's contacts in Toronto. Despite her husband's agreement to control his anger, there might be advisers who persuaded him to attempt a coup against Shui.

She picked up the phone and dialed his private line.

LAU-MING SHUI LISTENED to Nyenshi Fung's words with considerable interest. After they ended the conversation, he left his office and proceeded to private quarters in the attached guest house he'd arranged for Jikwan's stay. Sapèdas was being held in a special area of the cellar designed for prisoners, and Hoffner and Milaña had rooms in the main part of the three-story mansion. It was just as well. He wanted to talk to Jikwan in privacy.

Shui found the general engrossed with a Russian porno movie while soaking in a hot bath. He had a glass of brandy and a cigar in his massive fist. His beefy arms were spread across the tile of the tub and the room stank of cigar smoke mixed with whatever perfumed concoctions Jikwan had poured into the bathwater.

"Lau-Ming!" His words were slurred, his face reddened by the liquor. "Would you like a cigar? They're Cuban. A gift from Colonel Nievas. Ha!"

"I do not smoke," Shui replied.

"Of course. I knew this."

Shui shook his head and said, "I just received an interesting call from Nyenshi."

"Ah, the beautiful Nyenshi Fung," Jikwan replied, rolling his head lazily on a bulging neck. "And how is she?"

"She is not happy. She told me that Dim Mai is concerned about your loyalty to him and his cause. He is apparently convinced that you betrayed him in the deal with the Colombians. I think he feels cheated."

"Cheated?" The booze-induced reddening in Jikwan's face took on a darker hue now. "I did not cheat him. I saved him from his own arrogance. Do you honestly think that the Colombians would have come through on their end of the bargain? As soon as they found out about the Kung Lok's plans to acquire Carillo's operations in America, they would have turned on us."

"We both know this," Shui replied. "And I also know it was your intention to sabotage the deal from the beginning. But I was under the distinct impression that Dim Mai knew this. You never told me you were keeping it from him."

Jikwan set his glass calmly on the edge of the tub and then rose from the water with surprising grace, given his size and present condition. He quickly grabbed a towel from a nearby rack, tied it at his midsection and stepped from the tub. He didn't appear the least concerned that Shui was there. Military personnel learned immodesty rather quickly, sharing close quarters with others of the same sex. What seemed rude, almost vulgar, to Shui was perfectly normal to Deng Jikwan.

"I wasn't aware you needed to know, Lau-Ming," Jikwan said quietly. "I think you forget that I do not work for you. I support you because I respect your shrewdness and your business sense, and because I know your family is committed to China. But I think it fitting to remind you that I answer only to the premier and supreme commander of military forces."

Shui knew that Jikwan spoke the truth, but he didn't like it. He'd always felt that despite the general's support in previous campaigns, Jikwan was ultimately concerned only with himself and his political masters. Of course, Shui also realized that this was the way it had to be. Jikwan could never serve money and power, and he'd chosen power, which he wielded formidably against those he considered enemies. Shui didn't trust Jikwan now, but he wasn't going to tell him that, and despite his stature and his friends in China, it wouldn't have been wise to make himself an enemy.

Deng Jikwan was too well known and highly respected in many elite circles. He commanded a military force to be reckoned with, and he could easily make Shui's life miserable. No, Shui was quite prepared to placate the military man indefinitely, as it would be better for him and his plans. Their losses to the FARC and Carillo were minimal. Even Belasko hadn't hurt them enough in Las Vegas to have Shui concerned. And Shui had that confidence only because he knew Jikwan could come to his aid with considerable forces if it became necessary.

"I never intended to suggest you reported to me," Shui replied. "Our respect has always been mutual. I consider you an equal, and in some ways a superior man to me."

Jikwan's expression softened and after staring at Shui for a while, he smiled. "I can't imagine how difficult it must have been for you to say that, Lau-Ming."

"It's never difficult for me to speak the truth," Shui replied.

"Quite."

Jikwan picked up his drink and moved into an adjoining dressing area.

Shui ceased conversing while Jikwan toweled himself dry and dressed. He stared into the darkness through one open window of the bath enclosure. A stiff breeze cooled the sweat on his forehead and chilled him. He shivered in response and turned from the window as Jikwan emerged wearing tailored slacks and a black silk shirt.

"Don't concern yourself with Dim Mai," Jikwan said as if it had been the topic of the conversation all along. "I will take care of him. Perhaps when this is over you may have Nyenshi Fung for yourself."

"I am faithful to my wife, Deng," Shui replied in a formal tone.

Jikwan laughed. "You might be loyal to her in body,

Lau-Ming, but I know you are not totally loyal in mind and spirit. I know all about your former relationship with Nyenshi. I saw the way you looked at her in West Palm Beach. I believe she feels the same way about you."

"My personal relationships are not the issue." Shui stood erect and smoothed his shirt. "I will leave Dim Mai to you. However, I want to know how you're planning to deal with Belasko. He's coming and I am sure we all agree on this point."

"I thought you wanted to let Ing handle Belasko."

"I'm not sure how effective the Dragons can be in this situation."

"Well, they are charged with your personal security. If Belasko comes here, I will deal with him. I will call for one of my special security teams. They were assigned for my personal use. A gift from the premier."

"Then I will leave this in your capable hands, General." Shui turned and left the quarters quickly, not so much because his business was concluded as because he simply wanted to escape Deng Jikwan's malevolent presence.

CHAPTER FOURTEEN

Stony Man Farm, Virginia

Mack Bolan managed to get six hours of deep sleep before his internal clock woke him.

He rose quickly, showered and then went to the armory, where he found John "Cowboy" Kissinger waiting for him. The resident weaponsmith was hunkered over a table, retooling an H&K MSG-90 sniping rifle, and totally engrossed in the project. He looked up when the Executioner came in. A broad grin split his features, and he rose to shake the Executioner's hand.

"Barb came and talked to me about what's happening. I got concerned when I didn't hear from you after your little jaunt in L.A. She thought maybe I could lend some insight."

Bolan nodded. "Sharp as usual, that one. I'd forgotten you worked with the DEA."

"Well, it was a long time ago, but as soon as she mentioned Hoffner's name, it all came back like yesterday."

"In what way?"

Kissinger returned to his seat and reached down to pull a couple of beers from a miniature refrigerator he kept near the workbench. He offered one to Bolan, who accepted, and then took a long pull from the bottle before setting it on his workbench and wiping the residual foam from his lips with the back of his hand.

"I worked with Hoffner during my stint in Nogales. He was my immediate supervisor for nearly six months. Hell of a guy, but it wouldn't surprise me in the least if he's flipped on us."

"What makes you think he's our traitor?" Bolan asked, genuinely interested.

"Hoffner was all right, but he was cocky as hell. Always running off at the mouth about how one day he'd make it big, so forth and so on, blah, blah, blah."

"You ever know him to have connections with the Chinese?"

Kissinger shook his head, but he obviously couldn't resist smiling over the tip of the beer bottle. "Barb asked me that, too. She's got you pegged, Striker."

"That wouldn't surprise me," Bolan quipped.

Kissinger laughed before continuing his narrative. "Anyway, I first suspected him when I heard he was director of the El Paso Intelligence Center. It came together when I heard about those weapons disappearing from the U.S. Border Patrol office down there. And when I heard who was in charge, I figured Hoffner had to be involved."

"You're talking about Sapèdas."

"If it's the same guy I knew."

"You knew Ramon Sapèdas?"

"Hell, I worked side by side with him. The guy was a weasel then, and it sounds like he's a bigger one now. He was just starting with the Border Patrol. Small potatoes on a big farm, but it didn't stop him from sucking up to Hoffner every chance he got."

"So Hoffner knew Sapèdas," Bolan said.

Now it all made sense to the Executioner. Hoffner had probably come into a sweet deal with Jose Carillo's predecessors, and he'd probably used Sapèdas to keep things running when he left. So Hoffner skimmed profits while Sapèdas and his boys did all the work. Sapèdas snatched a few runners here, a few guns and drugs there, hung them out to dry and moved up quickly. By the time Hoffner arranged the glorious return to Texas ten years later, Sapèdas had a sweet deal of his own and Carillo had his claws into the Border Patrol chief.

When Hoffner learned he was playing second fiddle, he got angry and started pushing Kung Lok buttons. Sure, he used his intelligence connections and the vast resources of U.S. law-enforcement agencies to find holes in Carillo's operations. Then he cut a deal with his Colombian contacts by convincing Nievas he couldn't do without Carillo's help, even while he knew that Nievas had a deal to get weapons from the Chinese.

What Hoffner hadn't counted on was the Executioner getting involved. His initial attack on the truckload of 3-4 MDMA that crossed the border in Brownsville had actually originated with some secondary information he'd received through his own contacts. If the Scarlet Dragons hadn't attacked him in Juárez while he was trailing Sapèdas, Bolan might never had made the connection between the Kung Lok and Carillo's operations across the Southwest.

"I wouldn't have given Hoffner that much credit," Bolan said quietly. "But what you just told me is the missing piece to the puzzle, Cowboy."

Kissinger tipped his hat back and raised his bottle to toast the soldier. "My pleasure, partner."

Bolan inclined his head in the direction of the sniper rifle. "How soon before that might be ready for use?"

"How soon do you need it?"

"I'd like to take it with me, if that's possible."

"Anything's possible, Striker."

"I figured you'd say that."

"I'll make sure it gets on the plane, along with everything else Hal told me you'd need."

"That will save me some time. I appreciate it, Cowboy."

"Good luck, Mack."

Bolan shook his hand and left the armory. He crossed the compound and found Barbara Price in the War Room sorting through a stack of documents. She smiled sweetly at him and the Executioner returned it.

"Sleep well?"

"Yeah, thanks." He nodded in the direction of the papers. "My intelligence?"

"Yes, and I think you'll find it very interesting." Price tried to appear as if she was busy with the stuff, but Bolan could immediately sense something was wrong. Under normal circumstances, he probably wouldn't have pried. Their relationship was built on mutual trust, and they kept their feelings out of it as much as possible. It worked better that way—for her and him.

"Something on your mind?" he asked.

She stopped, turned and put her hands on her hips with an expression that told him she was seriously considering the question before deciding how to answer. Finally she replied, "You haven't mentioned Lisa Rajero since you got here. At least not in anything other than an official capacity, and I thought that was strange."

"Why?"

"Because I know you respected her. I just wondered how you're handling her death."

"I'm handling it."

Price nodded and then returned to her work.

Well, that was that. Bolan realized that maybe he was being a bit too cold, and he also knew Price didn't deserve it, but he couldn't give up more than he was willing. The damning thing of it was that Price was much the same way in many respects, and they were almost too much alike when it came to things like this. Nonetheless, he appreciated the fact she'd asked him. It told him that she still cared.

IT DIDN'T TAKE LONG for the Executioner to get his weapons and equipment gathered, and to secure all of the information he could on Kung Lok activities.

Within the hour, Bolan was aboard one of Stony Man's several RC-35 Learjets, Grimaldi at the stick, and headed for Toronto. Bolan's primary focus would center on two major operations in the heart of Toronto. The first was a major studio that belonged to the Shui Films & Arts Corporation, a front where their smut films were actually produced.

The second was a large drug-manufacturing warehouse on the outskirts of the nearby town of Caledon. Bolan also had a raid planned on Shui's estate, but that would come last in the game. First he needed to put down those operations that poured billions of dollars into Shui's pockets while it corrupted men, women and children alike. Bolan wasn't as concerned about the porn as he was the drugs, but both vices still angered him because innocent people were usually exploited somewhere along the process.

If it wasn't slaving twelve-year-olds for kiddie porn, then it was finding down-on-their-luck citizens—Canadians and Americans alike—to smuggle drugs over the borders. That was the thing most people didn't understand. While Shui didn't control a large part of the drug trade, he controlled enough to create a problem. Based on the intelligence Bolan studied, Lau-Ming Shui and his Scarlet Dragons were responsible for almost half of the dope that found its way onto the streets of Toronto and New York City. Not to mention the fact that the dope then got moved out of there to reach kids in suburbia.

As for the pornography, who couldn't walk into the back room of just about any store selling pornography in America and not see children being filmed to commit sexual obscenities of every imaginable kind. It took considerable willpower for Bolan not to become angry and lash out. It was enough to make any decent human being's blood boil, and the Executioner was going to do something about it.

The occasionally disheartening thing was the thought that it didn't make any difference if he took out Lau-Ming Shui and his operations. He couldn't very well destroy the entire KLCT organization, which meant that it wouldn't be enough to take down Shui's operations, and even Shui himself. He'd have to go after the higher-ups; that meant Hong Kong, possibly even Beijing.

"I'll tell you what, Jack," Bolan said as he perused the documents provided by Price and Kurtzman.

"What's that?"

"I think the powers that be in Hong Kong have their claws deep into Shui, Dim Mai and every other triad underboss."

"I'm not surprised," Grimaldi said. "And it wouldn't be the first time that government officials had ties to members of the underworld."

"You're talking about the Mafia?"

Grimaldi nodded. "When I worked for them, they

were connected to a lot of well-known politicians. I don't know how they managed to keep it quiet as long as they did sometimes.''

"I learned quite a bit about that during my wars against the Mob," Bolan replied. "There were even rumors that Murder, Inc. was little more than a front for the Company. It was said that members of the organization were actually professional assassins and employees of the CIA, hired to target major OC bosses who had direct ties to the government and presented security risks.''

"I don't know if I buy that theory," Grimaldi said. "But I do know that there were members of federal and state governments who were associated with members of the Mob. Some were even related.''

"History repeats itself.''

"Amen to that.''

The men rode in silence until Grimaldi indicated they were about a half hour from the Infield Cargo Facilities buildings of Toronto's Lester B. Pearson International Airport. The Executioner acknowledged the pilot's report, and then took the opportunity to move to the back of the jet and check his equipment. There wouldn't be another chance, and Bolan wanted to make sure he was packed and prepared for every eventuality. The past week he'd been flying by the seat of his pants, really, with no clear plans outlined. It wasn't customary for him to operate like that, and he didn't want a repeat of the situation.

A large part of his troubles had stemmed from trying to fight his war against Carillo, Nievas *and* the Kung Lok on multiple fronts. With Carillo and the FARC neutralized, he could now completely focus his attentions on the Kung Lok and forgo a defensive posture, putting

Shui and his cronies on the run. And there was a small part of him that would find some way to avenge the death of Rajero.

He planned to start with the drug-manufacturing plant.

Bolan stripped from his civilian clothes and donned black tactical fatigues and combat boots. He pulled a special fanny-pack-style satchel from a compartment beneath one of the jump seats and then opened the munitions bench built into one wall of the cabin. He smiled when he saw that Kissinger had stocked the thing to the rim with everything he would need, including a dozen Diehl DM-51 grenades. The Executioner had become quite fond of the Diehl DM-51, because of its offensive and defensive capabilities. The DM-51 weighed less than a pound and contained PETN high explosive. The grenade was designed as an offensive weapon, but could be converted to defensive with the addition of a plastic sleeve containing thousands of steel balls that fit over the body of the grenade. Upon detonation, the steel balls had a range exceeding twenty-five square meters, and were quite effective for an antipersonnel weapon.

However, the Executioner wouldn't need them for this part of his mission—he had a more effective deterrent in mind for Shui's drug factory. Bolan stuffed the satchel with twenty one-pound sticks of C-4 plastique and then secured the trunk. That would do the trick on the factory.

As far as small arms, Bolan didn't know what kind of security or resistance he would encounter. The satellite photographs did indicate the possibility of electronic surveillance, but that concerned the Executioner much less than the human factor. Bolan went to the weapons locker and withdrew an M-16 A-2/M-203. He also stuffed eight 30-round clips of SS-109 NATO ammunition and four M-383 40 mm HE grenades into the satchel before closing the weapons locker.

He then sat in one of the seats and studied a layout of the factory. It wouldn't be easy to penetrate the place quietly. He'd wanted to hit it at night, since it was entirely possible there were innocents inside—possibly staff workers who didn't have any idea what was going on. The Executioner didn't want to just start indiscriminately blowing things up where there was a chance bystanders could end up in the line of fire. That meant he'd have to sweep and clear the interior before bringing down the house.

Well, he'd done it with Carillo's place outside the airport in Los Angeles. He could surely pull it off now. Bolan suddenly realized he was hungry, so he pulled a military-type MRE from a supplies locker and ate mechanically as he continued to study the factory plans. Within a few hours, he'd be sending his first message to Shui and announcing his arrival to the purveyors of death.

Yeah, the blitz was on.

MACK BOLAN LAY ATOP a ridge and scanned the factory exterior through binoculars.

The place was a bigger hardsite than he'd figured. At either end of the factory were two guard towers, disguised to look like smokestacks, which were equipped with what looked like H&K 21-E machine guns. The H&K 21-E was considered one of Heckler & Koch's best heavy-defense weapons. Bolan also counted four armed men, one pair per tower, armed with light assault rifles. He was going to have to watch his step during penetration.

Which brought him to another problem: the considerable amount of heavy equipment in the area. There were several semitrailers backed against a long dock, which looked as if it would be the easiest way to gain access. However, drivers occupied those trucks, and the dock was like a busy beehive with all of the loading activities of workers moving materials onto the trucks.

Materials that most likely contained drugs, the Executioner reminded himself.

Still, Bolan knew he had a responsibility to the people there, and he refused to start wasting just anybody. There had always been a reason for Bolan's killing, and he wasn't about to change his ideals now. Whether or not it was convenient, there were people down there who quite likely were just trying to make an honest living, and didn't have the faintest idea they were working for a slime-sucker like Shui.

Well, the Executioner was about to educate them.

Bolan moved backward from the rise before standing and heading down the slope. Grimaldi had landed at the airport, and the soldier immediately secured a van for transport through Toronto, courtesy of Stony Man's ties with the CIA. The van was marked with some blue-and-red company logo of a well-known courier service, and Bolan had all of the proper credentials awaiting him in the glove compartment. The Executioner stowed the binoculars beneath the seat and then stepped into the courier jumpsuit and zipped it up to his neck.

The suit fit tightly over his combat fatigues, but it was only a temporary measure. Once the Executioner was inside, he'd shed the garment and get down to business. He started the van and drove slowly across the rugged terrain until he reached a side road that led to the main highway. There was a single utility road from a highway exit that led right to the factory. Another road branched off this one and circled the area, probably to provide a patrol route for security.

Bolan drove straight up to the factory and rolled down his window. An Asian guard stepped from the gate shack and Bolan smiled at him. The guard's face remained impassive as he held out his hand and Bolan surrendered his identification card. Apparently, this was a regular drill, which would actually prove to the Executioner's advantage if the guards were used to seeing these trucks all the time.

"You have a package to deliver?"

Bolan nodded and then showed him the doctored manifest. Kurtzman had managed to break into their computer records and secure the names of several administration records, then crosscheck that with the name most commonly signing for deliveries. The recipient was usually the dock manager and his secretary always signed, which was what led Bolan to the decision that he'd make entry through the dock.

The guard put the identification card in the shack and then signaled for Bolan to exit the vehicle. Another guard remained inside the shack, his hands out of view. Bolan knew the guy was probably holding a firearm at the ready, just in case trouble presented itself. The soldier had no intention of giving them that impression.

Once the guard had completed his search, he ordered Bolan to open the back of the van. The Executioner complied, ready for it to go south right there, at which point he'd have to put in his alternative battle plan. The guard made only a cursory inspection before nodding his satisfaction to Bolan.

"You know where to go?" the guard asked the Executioner.

Actually, Bolan didn't have the faintest idea but he

nodded as he closed the back doors of the van. He'd manage to find the place once he got past the gate—he knew the layout pretty well. It would be a lot easier to pass scrutiny if he acted as if he'd been there before. The guards would probably be less suspicious. As the guard moved into the shack, Bolan was about to ask for the return of his ID card but then thought better of it. He figured it was probably SOP to keep it until he left the grounds.

Bolan climbed into the van and slowly accelerated through the open gate. He drove straight along the road until it became crushed gravel and proceeded directly to the dock, passing the line of loaded semis. He reached the opposite side of the dock and found a parking space next to some other private vehicles, and then went EVA. Bolan moved to the back of the van and retrieved the package he'd prepared for his mission.

Bolan walked up the ramp and moved past the dock-workers. Only a couple even bothered to look at him, the rest seemingly engrossed in their respective operations. The soldier managed to get directions from one of them to the office, and soon found the front-office gal who probably signed for most packages.

The blond woman showed him a nice smile. "Hi! How's it goin'?"

"Busy today. Didn't even stop for a break."

The woman tsked in commiseration, taking the package from him and then signing the doctored manifest. The Executioner nodded and bid her good day, then turned and went back to the van. Instead of closing the doors, he retrieved the M-16 A-2/M-203 and satchel, then walked calmly up the ramp and onto the dock for a second time. He'd slung the satchel over his shoulder and held the weapon down against his hip, the majority of it concealed behind his right leg.

The dockworkers didn't notice him this time, which wasn't surprising since delivery drivers were probably a common sight, and once he had established his presence he wasn't anything more they chose to concern themselves about. Bolan simply breezed past them nonchalantly and a minute later he was back in the dock office.

Weapon still concealed behind him, Bolan said to the surprised woman, "Listen to me very carefully. I want you to clear everybody out of here. Do it quickly and quietly, and don't do anything to alert security. Understood?"

The woman inclined her head with a quizzical expression. "Excuse me?"

Bolan produced the M-16 A-2/M-203 and added, "Do it now."

She nodded slowly, rose and immediately left the office to warn her coworkers. Bolan got out of the jumpsuit and retrieved the package, then left the dock office and moved deeper into the bowels of the factory. As he'd suspected, a majority of the large old building was unused. There were unkempt punch presses and other machining equipment in one large part of the factory—but they probably hadn't been used in twenty-five years or better.

Bolan moved through the labyrinthine rows of heavy equipment until he found what he was searching for in the center of the main factory floor. Two old, large generators hummed away behind a large chain-link fence cage with a door. Bolan aimed carefully at the lock and fired a single shot. The SS-109 bullet made short work of the flimsy security lock. After all, who in his right mind would have planned to sabotage a generator? Shui

probably figured most people didn't even know about
the place, so there was little reason to maintain heavier
security. That would have just alerted law-enforcement
authorities to the fact he had something to hide.

Bolan stepped into the cage and left the package near
the generators. He trotted from the area before reaching
into the satchel and removing an electronic detonator.
He opened the switch cover, activated the detonator and
then pushed the button to send the radio signal. A hor-
rendous blast shook that part of the factory as the entire
factory went dark, all power now cut to the place.

The Executioner put the over-and-under assault rifle
combo into battery with a yank of the charging handle
and the loading of a grenade. It was time for the sweep
operation. He skirted the machine area and continued to
the other side of the factory, shuffling along the wide,
darkened aisles on the perimeter of the main factory
floor. Bolan swept the area with the M-16 A-2/M-203
as he quickly and quietly moved into another area of the
factory. It was quiet here, too, the place open and airy
with old office machines stockpiled on a table against
one wall.

Bolan went to the table and primed a couple of sticks
from the satchel with blasting caps. He set the frequency
for his remote detonator and headed in the direction he'd
come after completing his task. Now it was a bit too quiet,
and Bolan wondered if the woman at the dock office had
followed instructions or run to get security. He was hoping
she was wise enough to follow his advice, if for no other
reason than a sense of self-preservation.

The soldier was wrong, and he barely avoided the
sudden gunfire that erupted in his direction. The Executioner dived to the floor beneath an open workbench,

narrowly escaping the vicious attack launched by two Chinese security guards. The reports were loud as the area above Bolan's head was suddenly filled with 9 mm pistol fire. The Executioner moved under the cover of the noise to a flanking position, and waited until there was a lull in the firing before he exposed himself.

Bolan raised the M-16 A-2/M-203 to his shoulder and squeezed the trigger. The first high-velocity 5.56 mm round slammed through the face of the closer guard, ripping flesh and bone from his skull before the impact dumped him on the ground in a heap. The second guard was no more fortunate, as Bolan's unerring fire caught him in the throat. Cartilage erupted out the side of the guard's neck, the scream dying in his throat as blood began to spurt from both carotid arteries.

The Executioner continued through the factory floor, heading for the docks. He managed to get through the door that separated the two areas of the factory before his sixth sense began tingling. He dropped and rolled as he heard the heavy boom of a shotgun followed by the unmistakable sound of a thousand pellets striking the wall above his head. Bolan got to one knee and held his breath, listening and watching for a target to present itself.

The guard appeared a moment later, coming around a far corner in an attempt to flank Bolan. The Executioner was ready for him, rolling away as the guard dispatched a hurried shot. He was in midejection of the shell when Bolan took a prone firing position, aimed, set the selector to 3-round bursts and squeezed the trigger. A trio of SS-109 hardball rounds punched through the guy's chest. Blood and pink, frothy sputum erupted from the guard's mouth as he crashed against the wall and slid to the ground.

The Executioner got to his feet and pressed onward in his objective, the over-and-under assault rifle combo held at the ready.

CHAPTER FIFTEEN

Bolan reached the dock to find the place had been abandoned.

The truck trailers were still there with the doors wide open, but there wasn't even a hint of movement. The Executioner didn't hear any sirens and he knew he probably wouldn't. That was okay—he didn't need an encounter with Canadian police to complicate matters. What did bother him, though, was that he hadn't found the processing lab yet, and he'd only brought enough explosives to have an effect when using the processing chemicals as an accelerant.

Bolan moved across the dock, sweeping the area and waiting for any enemy troops to show themselves. He heard the first wave before he saw them. The screeching of brakes and sound of tires skidding to a halt on gravel were the prelude to the attack. Bolan sought cover behind a large crate and waited for his enemy to show themselves.

The Executioner rested his arms on the crate, the M-16 A-2/M-203 primed and ready, and waited patiently for them. He'd wait it out as long as he could without compromising his own position. When they first appeared, clutching assault rifles and leapfrogging up the ramp, he did a quick count and noted at least twelve.

And God knew how many other troops had yet to arrive. What puzzled Bolan most about these ''security guards'' were their movements. They didn't operate like a standard security force; rather, they moved like trained military troops. They didn't even act like Scarlet Dragons, and they weren't wearing the symbols. *All* Dragons wore the scarlet-colored kerchief around their necks. Bolan couldn't put his finger on the techniques employed by this group, but they seemed damn familiar.

Either way, it wouldn't make any difference. They would die the same way as the FARC—the Executioner wasn't about to be picky. These men were in the service of a criminal who had perverted the lives, the very existence even, of government officials and innocent bystanders alike. That meant they had sworn their allegiance to the enemy, and that made them Mack Bolan's enemies. He didn't hesitate to tell them how he felt about that as he opened fire on them.

The pointmen went down first, one taking two rounds in the chest while the other collapsed from a shattered hip and leg bones. Bolan didn't hesitate to acquire his next target even as the first two fell. The Executioner triggered a single round that bored through the guard's skull, blowing out the back of his head. The man's body did a strange pirouette before collapsing to the concrete dock. The rest of the gunners realized they were under fire and dived to the ground to avoid being the next target.

Bolan yanked a Diehl DM-51 from his belt, quickly slid a fragmentation sleeve into place and then tossed the bomb overhand before ducking behind the crate. There were shouts of surprise just before the defensive weapon exploded. Six thousand 2 mm balls of super-heated metal whistled across the dock, melting clothing and searing the skin of those closest to the blast, and shredding flesh from the bones of those not so close.

The soldier could immediately smell the pungent odors of burned human skin and hear the sickening screams of the dying. These were sights and sounds that had become almost too familiar for him. The Executioner rose and began to target the wounded with mercy rounds. One man had managed to escape the force of the blast. Some shrapnel had caught him, but he hadn't suffered the terrible wounds of his comrades. He rose to one knee and aimed his AK-74 in Bolan's direction. The warrior shoulder rolled in time to avoid ventilation by a stream of 5.45 mm Soviet rounds. He came out of the roll, snap-aimed the M-16 A-2/M-203 at hip level and squeezed the trigger. The high-velocity rounds pummeled Bolan's would-be killer, staggering him before he finally fell under the attack.

Bolan decided it was time to find another way out as he heard two more vehicles grind to a halt. However, he decided to leave a little surprise for his enemies. He crossed the dock to an area of cover and released the safety on the M-203. He raised his weapon to stomach level and triggered the first shell into the nearest truck. A shower of sparks and a fantastic ball of flame erupted from the truck as the 40 mm M-383 grenade did its work. The Executioner could feel the heat rush past his arm, even behind the cover of a thick wall separating another part of the factory from the dock. Bolan had used this type of HE grenade before, and while it was powerful he knew it didn't pack that kind of wallop.

Bolan grinned as he realized he'd found his drugs— a lucky encounter.

The Executioner primed the M-203, and the launcher projected the grenade with a plunk, blowing another semitrailer into oblivion. Bolan knew he was destroying the product, but that didn't take care of destroying the production line. He had to find out where they were making the stuff, and wire the place. He repeated his attacks on the truck trailers with the next two in line to keep down the heads of his enemies, and when he felt he'd made enough of an impression, he pressed deeper into the factory.

Bolan couldn't understand it. He'd covered nearly every part of the building, and he still hadn't found what he was looking for. It wasn't often that Stony Man's information was wrong, but it happened now and again—that was just the nature of intelligence work. Of course, it happened with considerable frequency to the other intelligence agencies operating in and outside of America. Price and Kurtzman were wrong now and again, but those times were the exception and not the rule. He wondered for a moment if Shui had somehow predicted Bolan would come for him, and decided to move his operation, but he just as quickly dismissed the idea. Shui would have considered himself at greater risk than his operations. He wouldn't have likely counted on Bolan hitting him where it hurt the most before coming after him personally—the Executioner had done it to keep him off balance and guessing.

So Bolan continued trotting through one darkened area after another in search of the booty. His persistence eventually paid off. In the last possible area to search, a small room of the factory—maybe six hundred square feet—Bolan found the manufacturing area. It had been wiped clean as far as the drugs were concerned, but the equipment and chemicals were still there. The Executioner didn't waste any time wiring the table with several blocks of C-4, and then he made his way from the room.

As he continued toward the docks, Bolan placed charges here and there along his path, leaving a single stick or two of the C-4 with a detonator like a trail of breadcrumbs. The Executioner had devised a plan and he was going to need the cooperation of his enemy to see it through. He was going to kill two birds with one stone, and the security forces allied against him were going to help.

Bolan was near the docks when the first enemy gunner appeared. The soldier raised his weapon and began to trigger wild bursts, merely to keep their heads down more than to try for an actual kill. He kept firing, moving a few feet along the path he'd lined with charges, bringing more into the fold in his game of fire-and-cover, fire-and-cover. Every step he took closer to the drug room brought more trouble into the fray. He figured that at least twenty or more troopers were hot on his trail, looking to avenge the mess he'd left them, the bodies of their comrades strewed across the dock, wading sole deep in the blood of the fallen.

Bolan could imagine how that would anger him to the point of seeking vengeance on the offenders. But that was the effect he'd wanted to leave them with. Now they were bloodthirsty in their pursuit, each one hoping he would be the one to bring down the infiltrator. Well, it wasn't going to happen this day. The Executioner waited until he was inside the room and then locked the door. He stepped away in time to avoid the deadly shards of splintered wood as the first bullets began to shred the flimsy door.

Bolan didn't hesitate to make a hasty departure. He fired at the tinted casement windows of the factory, shattering them under a hail of 5.56 mm fire. He then slung his weapon and sprinted across the room, leaping onto the windowsill. The Executioner was a fearsome sight, silhouetted in the window as the sun now streamed through the shattered opening, steam rolling off his body as the sweat was exposed to the bleak midmorning cold. The wooden door flew inward even as the Executioner raised the detonator, flipped the switch and jumped from the window.

He hit the cold, dry ground outside and covered his ears as the first explosion ripped through the room. There was a strange silence just before every window in the room blew outward. Bolan covered his head with his forearms as debris rained on him. The explosion had barely subsided when the alternate explosions reached his ears, nearly drowned out in the aftermath of the main blast. The Executioner could imagine the expressions on the security forces trapped inside that building, watching the equipment along the path of their quarry erupt into flames.

Explosion after explosion rocked the factory as intense heat and flame contacted the remnants of oil in the machines, or detonated the explosive chemicals in the vats running along the center of the building. The Executioner waited another minute before rising and heading toward the van. Bolan was nearly to his vehicle when the *rat-tat-tat* of a heavy-caliber machine gun echoed in the air, and dust rose around him as 7.62 mm NATO rounds chewed up the ground.

The soldier dived to the ground and rolled beneath one of the semitrailers, seeking cover between its charred remains. The smoke from the burning shells was thick enough to conceal his movements. The Executioner cursed himself for not remembering the guards in the towers and the H&K 21-Es they manned. He needed to find a way to neutralize them. The Executioner thought furiously, realizing the M-203 was probably his best option, but he'd have to get close enough to make the shots count, and there was no adequate cover that would put him in range.

That left the van as his only way out alive. It would be difficult enough for the enemy just to hit a target at that range, particularly one that was moving. Yeah, it was his best bet. Bolan began to crawl beneath the smoking hulks of burning trucks. The machine-gun fire had stopped, and he knew that the gunners were just waiting for another opportunity to shoot him dead. The destruction and havoc he'd wreaked on the semitrailers was now paying off in more ways than one. The Executioner actually considered it ironic that the same trucks he'd destroyed to save the lives of others would now, in the wake of their destruction, save his life.

Bolan reached the van and climbed inside. He fired up the engine, put the gearshift in reverse and tromped the accelerator. The van lurched backward, tires smoking and displacing gravel in every direction. He dropped the selector into drive and put pedal to the metal. The van rocketed from the docks.

The van wouldn't be hard to see with its white paint and colorful red, white, and blue logo, but Bolan wasn't concerned with that. He would still be difficult to hit, even given the H&K 21-E's unerring accuracy and cyclic rate of fire. Even 850 rpm wasn't necessarily effective when trying to hit a speeding van from fifty yards or better.

Bolan also kept as close to the perimeter line of the towers as possible, making it more difficult to aim at him. He couldn't hear the guns firing over the roar of the engine, but he knew damn well his enemies were shooting. He continued toward the front gate, preparing his M-16 A-2/M-203 as he neared the gate. When he was within about thirty yards of the guard shack, he could hear the tink-tink of rounds as they hit the back of the van. The rear windows shattered a moment later under the assault, but Bolan didn't slow.

The Executioner aimed his weapon at the windshield and pulled the trigger. The 5.56 mm rounds splintered the glass but didn't blow it out. He then shoved the weapon against the outside seal, clearing enough away so that he could see the road ahead. He stuck his arm through the opening, finger now poised on the trigger of the M-203, and carefully aimed at the guard shack. The two guards he'd encountered earlier had taken up firing positions on either side of the gate.

Bolan squeezed the trigger and managed to hold on to the bucking weapon even though he held it with one hand. The M-383 grenade hit a spot just in front of the guard shack and the HE blast shook the area, the concussion dismembering the closest guard while the fiery blast ignited the clothing and hair of the second. The guy now awash in flames screamed and danced in place. Bolan fisted his Beretta and fired a 3-round burst as he passed, putting the human torch out of his misery.

The last remnants of machine-gun fire dissipated as he rounded a bend in the private road and continued toward the highway. This mission hadn't gone exactly as planned, but that was okay. His next stop would require a little bit more finesse, and he'd have to play his cards right. It was time for a bit more role camouflage, and this particular role would put him deep in the heart of Shui Films & Arts Corporation.

And Mack Bolan would literally be playing the role of his lifetime.

"DESTROYED!"

Lau-Ming Shui tossed a sheaf of papers across the room, scattering them in every direction. The impact knocked an empty cup from a burnished antique table in his office. Several of the army of house staff Shui kept on hand at all times rushed to clean up the mess, but the Kung Lok underboss yelled at them to leave the papers where they were and to get the hell out.

Ing Kaochu stood quietly and respectfully near his master's desk. He raised his eyebrows and looked questioningly at General Jikwan, who was sitting calmly in a chair and reading a Beijing newspaper. The military man's eyes flicked up to meet Kaochu's expectant gaze, but he quickly returned his attention to the paper and let out a deep sigh.

Shui whirled to face Jikwan, his face reddening. "You promised me security, Deng. I cannot believe you would allow this to happen. That little stunt Belasko pulled ruined a major processing operation. Not to mention the millions of dollars' worth of product he destroyed!"

Jikwan lowered his paper and looked at Kaochu before turning to face Shui and raising his eyebrows.

Shui looked at Kaochu, and then waved in his direction. "Ing is my most trusted ally, and one day the person I hope to succeed me. Whatever you want to say to me you can say in front of him."

Jikwan nodded, and then replied, "My dear Lau-Ming, you surprise me. It isn't as if you weren't expecting this to happen."

"I wasn't 'expecting this to happen,'" he replied. He knew he was mocking Jikwan, and probably the general knew this, but he didn't give a damn. As a matter of fact, he hoped Jikwan did know Shui was mocking him. "He destroyed all of the product meant to replace what was lost in Las Vegas. Not to mention the fact that this will cost me millions of dollars.''

''Millions of dollars?'' Jikwan chuckled and rose from his chair. He walked across the room and poured himself a drink, then turned and raised his glass in Shui's direction. ''Out of the billions you now possess? Come, Lau-Ming, it sounds like a very small loss to me.''

Shui had to suppress the urge to rush across the room, wrap his hands around Jikwan's throat and choke the life from him. He could almost visualize the military officer's eyes bugging out of his head. Had Jikwan not held the current position of prominence he did with the premier—had he been an underling rather than an equal—Shui would have ordered Kaochu to kill him there and then for such insolence. Instead, he had to hold his tongue and keep his temper in check.

Through clenched teeth Shui said, ''The money has nothing to do with it. Of course I can replace this. What angers me is the fact that you are not holding up your end of the bargain.''

''In what way?''

''You promised me protection.''

''Yes, I promised you protection,'' Jikwan said, downing his drink and pouring a fresh one before adding, ''And you shall have it. But there has been no direct attack on you here. You are perfectly safe.''

Shui's eyes narrowed as he replied, ''Perhaps Dim Mai is correct about you, General Jikwan. Perhaps you can't be trusted with an agreement after all.''

Jikwan looked up from the crystal tumbler, and his face took on an almost scarlet color. Shui could see his words had stung the man, and he couldn't say he regretted it. He also wouldn't take them back, even if Jikwan demanded it, and to hell with caution. He was tired of playing these games. He was the most powerful Chinese crime leader in the Western hemisphere. He commanded an army of nearly a thousand Scarlet Dragons, and had his finger on the pulse of political supporters everywhere.

Lau-Ming Shui had nothing to fear from Deng Jikwan.

"Be careful, Lau-Ming," Jikwan said, his voice a bare whisper. He pointed at Shui, adding, "You have enjoyed my support up to this point. I both respect you and like you personally, but I will not tolerate such blasphemies against me or against any of my allies. You don't want me as an enemy."

"No, General," Shui replied. "It is you who do not want *me* as an enemy."

Jikwan stared at Shui a moment longer and then smiled. Shui couldn't tell if the smile was genuine or simply a way for Jikwan to relieve the pressure, but he would remain suspicious just the same. He certainly wanted Jikwan's support, but he wasn't willing to beg or grovel for it. He was a powerful man, after all—as powerful as Jikwan if not excelling to the degree in some cases—and he demanded the respect of any associate. Why he would let Jikwan walk over him was a mystery.

"My dear Lau-Ming Shui," Jikwan said, walking forward and awkwardly hugging the man. He pushed him away and looked him in the eye. "Why should we fight with each other? We are friends. No...no, you are like a brother to me. I cannot stand it when we fight."

"How touching," a female voice interjected.

All eyes turned to see a curvaceous figure silhouetted in the doorway of the office. All three men held their breaths as Catalina Milaña entered the room. Shui looked in Jikwan's direction and noticed an expression on his face that betrayed his lustful interests. Shui could see the want in Jikwan's expression—he'd seen the look before on other men. He imagined that same look probably crossed his face when he looked at Nyenshi Fung.

"Good evening, Catalina," Jikwan said.

He turned to Shui. "Did you know that Catalina is part Russian?"

Shui shook his head. "I did not. I'm actually fond of Russians. For some strange reason, they are always loyal to their friends and associates. You never have to worry about trusting one."

The comment seemed awkward and off-handed, but Shui intended it to be that way. He knew that if there was any weapon he might wield effectively against Jikwan, it now stood before him. Jikwan had been married six times previously, but after a certain amount of time, all of his wives mysteriously disappeared. Jikwan would always given some half-convincing story, telling his trusted friends and colleagues that each woman had left him and went into hiding, afraid he might do something. Shui was convinced that most of them were now saltwater skeletons, chained to a heavy object at the bottom of the South China Sea.

Shui wondered if Catalina Milaña would end up the seventh in the long line of Jikwan women to live under, and eventually die by, the hand of the good general. Not that it was any of his business—what Jikwan did was his own affair. Although that didn't mean that Shui agreed with it, or even had to like the lifestyle, for that matter. He'd also noticed Jikwan drinking much more lately; he wondered just what Jikwan was celebrating. With Belasko still alive, it was a bit early for celebrations.

"I'm sure you can understand the reasons for my concern,'' Shui said to Milaña as she crossed the room and took the seat Jikwan had occupied earlier.

The half Russian, half Colombian beauty crossed one shapely leg over another and put her finger to her forehead. She cocked her face to one side and smiled as she looked at the men in the room in turn for a few minutes. Finally, after spending a long time staring at the now seemingly entranced Jikwan, she turned her full attention to Shui and her smile grew wider.

"Of course I can understand your concern, *señor*," she said. "That does not mean I agree with it. I do not think you understand how to handle a man like Belasko. You must know your enemy well in order to predict their next move."

Shui was interested now. He had to admit that Milaña had been the only one present in the room to successfully seduce Belasko, deceive him and ultimately convince him that she wanted the same thing he did—the death of Colonel Amado Nievas. And she had done it without a great deal of trouble. She could become a powerful ally, perhaps a suitable replacement for Deng Jikwan. Certainly she was a more attractive and amusing partner. But she was a woman, and women could be dangerous. Shui thought even more so when she smiled at him.

"Do you know why you're having so much trouble stopping this man?" Milaña asked.

All the men in the room shook their heads in unison.

"It is because you have not taken the time to understand him. You do not know what it is that motivates him. And that is too bad, because if you understood this, then you would know what he was going to do next and you could predict his moves."

Milaña rose and poured herself a glass of wine. Every

eye was on her, their attentions now commanded as much by her words as by her beauty. Shui found himself quite intrigued with what she had to say. This was the part of the feminine wiles that could be dangerous. Shui couldn't even understand Milaña's motivations in this. She was dangerous, this one, a kitten who could instantaneously transform into a lioness protecting her cubs. She was sly, ingenious, and cunning—all traits Shui tried to emulate. He knew that probably the only more dangerous person in the room was Ing Kaochu, and only because of how deadly he was in battle.

"What are you going to do, my pet?" Jikwan demanded. He slammed his tumbler on a table, sloshing his drink. "Are you planning on keeping us in suspense all night? Or should we guess?"

Milaña continued studying her glass a minute before replying, "There's only one thing I know of that motivates Mike Belasko. It is his compassion." She looked up with an icy smile, and added, "He cares about everything and everyone. Think about it, gentleman. He could have been selfish, simply gone directly after Carillo or Nievas. He could have even hit your operations directly."

"He did."

Milaña clucked her tongue and replied, "Aha, but not the predictable manner you thought he would. He doesn't risk any innocent lives. Haven't you ever noticed how selective he is about his targets? Even against your Dragons in Las Vegas, he was selective. His operations are almost...surgical. He even chose not to kill Nievas. It seemed more important to him that somebody remain alive to take responsibility."

"What makes you an expert on this man?" Ing Kaochu finally snarled. "You simply played a whore to get what you wanted."

If Milaña was affected by Kaochu's vicious reply, she didn't show it. "Do you think I was always just the wife of a FARC soldier? Do you think that's all I did in Colombia?"

Kaochu shut his mouth, and Shui nodded his agreement that this was probably the wisest course of action for the moment. The woman was right—whether he wanted to admit it was another matter—and he couldn't ignore the logic in her argument. Belasko had always seemed much like a crusader, flitting from place to place like some bothersome insect, and wreaking havoc wherever he turned. He'd been the single greatest thorn in Shui's side since the start of the operation. Shui was interested in hearing how to remove that thorn.

"So what do you suggest?" Shui asked.

"I would guess that Belasko doesn't intend to stop with your factory. He will most likely turn his attention to your other major businesses before coming here for you personally. Remember, he is not here out of revenge. He is here to do what he sees as his duty. Otherwise, he would not have risked so much to come here."

"So you think he will go after my production studios."

She nodded.

"And what do you want in return?"

"I want to be the one to kill him," she replied. "I want him captured alive so that I can kill him for failing to destroy Nievas. That is all I ask."

"But no man has ever lived through an encounter with this Belasko," Kaochu said. "What makes you think you will?"

"As you have already pointed out, no 'man' has ever lived through an encounter with him. And as you can see, I am not a man."

CHAPTER SIXTEEN

The Shui Films & Arts Corporation was headquartered in the heart of Toronto's urban sprawl. The metal-and-glass structure towered above many of the buildings that surrounded it, painting an intimidating and formidable image to all who entered—although it wasn't that intimidating to the Executioner.

Bolan pushed through the front doors and proceeded directly to a directory of the offices housed within the thirty-floor structure. Shui owned many businesses that were mere sidelines to the main productions. In addition to Alternative Films, Ltd., the entertainment company that produced "legitimate" adult films, Shui Films & Arts was the parent company to Ming Textile Designs, China Doll Imports and Exports, Green Tea Foods, Shang-Tzu Pottery and Asian Consultants, LLC. And those were only the major ones.

Basically, Shui had his hands into everything. Many businesses were legit, on the whole, but a small number served as nothing more than fronts for Shui's criminal activities. It wasn't so much that the various sovereign countries throughout the world approved of Shui's activities; it was more because the governments allowed him to operate due to the increased revenue and taxes he paid. It was peculiar and all at once insensible to

Bolan that legitimate political parties allowed a man like Shui to practice business within their borders. Everybody knew what kind of man he was—that wasn't the problem. The problem was that those roaming the halls of power were apathetic to those things they either couldn't see or chose not to see, as long as they got their little cut of the action.

The Executioner had a larger stake in this game. He was in Toronto to make sure that Shui's operations got shut down once and for all. And he was going to start with Alternative Films, Ltd., which he located on the twelfth floor.

Bolan was dressed for the part. He straightened the tie beneath his three-piece black pinstripe. Patent leather shoes and a pastel silk shirt completed the ensemble. A scarlet handkerchief was stuffed in the suit coat jacket, which was the trademark for non-Asians who were on official business for the Scarlet Dragons. The Executioner had the name of the Scarlet Dragon leader, and he planned to use that name to his advantage.

Bolan exited the elevator and proceeded straight down the hallway until he located the manager's office. When he stepped through the doorway leading into the suite, a beautiful Asian woman whose lithe form was practically dwarfed by her huge glass-top desk greeted him. She was busily typing at a computer terminal but she stopped immediately when she saw the Executioner and smiled.

"Good afternoon," the woman said.

Bolan nodded. "I'm here to see your boss."

"Do you have an appointment."

"Tell him that I'm here on business for Mr. Kaochu. Important business."

"I see," she said, her expression becoming flat as the

smile faded. She reached to the phone on her desk and stabbed the flash button, not taking her eyes from his towering form as she waited for her boss to answer. She immediately engaged in a hushed conversation, but Bolan could hear her mention Kaochu's name. She nodded after listening a moment, then hung up the phone. "He'll be with you in a moment."

Bolan nodded and took a seat nearby. He kept his hand close to the Beretta that was snuggled in shoulder leather beneath the tailored jacket. Stony Man had arranged for the tailoring prior to his arrival through some Canadian contacts. Price had insured the coat was tight enough to look clean at the waist and shoulders, but bulky enough at the chest to conceal any hardware.

About five minutes passed before the manager poked his head out from his office doorway. He was short and wiry, obviously Chinese, with gelled hair that was closely cropped and stood straight off his scalp. His smile was as pearly white and perfect as that of his assistant, but he projected an aura of distrust and subterfuge. It was obvious the guy had something to hide, but Bolan couldn't tell if that was by nature or because of his surprise at a sudden visit from a Caucasian claiming he was a representative of Ing Kaochu.

"Hello," the man greeted Bolan with a heavy Asian accent. "Please come in, sir."

Bolan entered the office and took a seat without being asked or waiting for his host to be seated. If he was going to look the part, he had to act the part, as well. The Scarlet Dragons were the chief enforcers, messengers and whatever else Shui or Kaochu appointed them to be. All in the employ of the Kung Lok respected them, and it was probably rare for the Dragons to send a Caucasian to do their bidding.

The manager didn't make any secret of his immediate dislike of Bolan's presence. "My secretary indicated you were sent here by Ing Kaochu."

Bolan nodded curtly.

"In some cases, it is considered in poor taste for such an important man to send a non-Asian to do his bidding."

"I don't really give a damn," Bolan replied.

The manager cleared his throat and showed the Executioner a half smile. It was obvious he didn't want to insult Bolan, but it was also apparent he wasn't totally buying Bolan's story. "I do hope you're not going to insult my intelligence by trying to tell me you are actually a member of Mr. Kaochu's organization."

Bolan smiled and shook his head. He couldn't believe this shyster was actually stupid enough to think he hadn't done his homework. "You know better than that. If you're not Chinese, you can't belong to that club. I'm here strictly to deliver a message and do some inspections. I hope I can report back to him that I had your full cooperation."

Now the guy was looking uncomfortable, which was just the way Bolan wanted him. "I see. I suppose that Mr. Kaochu has his reasons. And what is this message that you were to pass along?"

"It would seem that Mr. Shui is unhappy with your, ah, let's say output. Would that give us an understanding?"

The man only nodded, still staring suspiciously at Bolan. It was hard to tell if he was scrutinizing the Executioner or simply being politely attentive. In either case, he wasn't reaching for the phone to verify the story, so Bolan figured he still held the upper hand at the moment.

"This is the position of Lau-Ming Shui?"

"Yeah. He also wanted you to know that he's willing to overlook this, given that other, more important matters require his attention, but he doesn't want it to continue. He wants you step up production."

"To what degree?" the man asked.

"Double it."

"What?" The guy stood now, incredulous at the news and obviously incensed with the very suggestion. "I don't have the staff to do that. I would have to hire two more crews. We're working full-time now."

"Look, pal, I'm just the messenger. Now Mr. Kaochu has told me in confidence that maybe they're being a little hard on you. Fact still remains, though, that you need to increase production."

"But surely Mr. Shui realizes that I'm doing the best that I can." The guy shifted in his chair, the tone in his voice cool and level.

Bolan resisted the urge to smile. His plan was working, and now he was going to go for the jugular. "Of course he does, which is why Mr. Kaochu sent me. I'm going to be your best friend for the next twenty-four hours. I'm going to inspect your various studios, and see where the motivation is required. Then I'll make a few suggestions and go back with a good report to the boss."

"*You're* going to inspect my operations?"

Bolan shrugged and rendered his best expression of indifference. "No, I don't have to be the one to do it. Mr. Kaochu said to tell you that if you preferred, he could come personally with some of his own people. He thought maybe he'd save you the stress. Plus the fact I've been in contact with some of my fellow Americans. It seems white men dig Asian chicks. They want to see more of it, and they're ready to pay. Now, you can both cooperate and profit by this, or I can walk away and let you make your own decisions. Which way is it going to be?''

The guy rose and stuck his hands in his pockets. Bolan sat and let him stew for a minute, watching the wheels as they turned. He knew that even if the guy took the bait, he'd probably call Kaochu and tell him how much he disliked the idea. Then Kaochu would realize something was very wrong and he'd send his people to investigate. While they were tied up with one operation, Bolan would tackle another. He'd play cat-and-mouse with them as long as he could, gathering the Scarlet Dragons into an arena that got smaller, tightening the reins as he dished out his own unique brand of justice. Then he'd nail the coffin shut.

''Supposing that I do cooperate,'' the manager finally said, shrugging. ''Then what's in it for me?''

Bolan showed him a frosty smile. ''Then you get to keep living.''

''I see.'' He shook his head and snickered. ''I suppose I don't have much of a choice, then.''

''You don't have any choice.''

''Fine. Where would you like to start, uh... I don't even know your name.''

''You can call me Mike.''

''Okay, Mike, so where would you like to start?''

''I'm new in town,'' the Executioner replied. ''Give me my options.''

A FEW HOURS LATER, Mack Bolan studied his first option through binoculars.

It was late afternoon, but the day had already turned to twilight as a bank of storm clouds moved across the horizon and obscured the setting sun. Bolan had positioned himself at the corner of a building roof and watched the two-story house from across the street. The interior was actually a multiroom filming studio, where Chinese women of all ages were exploited and forced to defile themselves in every way imaginable. Bolan fought to quell the sense of rage bubbling away on his insides.

The manager, whose name he eventually learned was Nutao Mung, told him that the women were kept crammed in the cellar. They only had half the number of beds for the women, since one half slept or ate while the other half worked. The girls were inoculated for disease, and inspected regularly by physicians so they didn't pass any of the nasty social ills onto their partners. Chinese woman weren't hard to come by, especially those who sought asylum into Canada. It was much easier to get them into the British districts, particularly due to the close ties between Britain and China.

Smuggling them from Canada into the United States was even easier. Once they had gotten their use of the women, they shipped them across the border where they were killed. Those lucky enough—or unlucky enough— to be spared were sold into a miserable existence as mail-order brides, high-priced prostitutes or drug mules. In either case, their existence was short-lived, and if they didn't end up dead in a short time from the lifestyle, they sought an easier exit by simply killing themselves.

The fact this was going on didn't surprise the Executioner in the least. He wouldn't have been able to convince anyone he wasn't knowledgeable about such activities. What bothered him was that the governments of Canada and his own country knew it was going on, and yet they chose to ignore it. It was just another example of that good old political apathy, and it made the Executioner want to vomit. The slave trade had always been good for business, especially for the heads of organized crime, but it was an even bigger cash cow for the lob-byists and conservatives who appropriated millions of dollars for rehabilitation programs. Border guards inter-cepted maybe a hundred of the thousands of women who passed between the borders every year. About a third were deported as ethnically undesirable, and the rest either wound up in jail for drug running or got thrown back to the sharks of society that had birthed them.

The foulest beast on the planet wasn't deserving of that kind of inhumane existence, and Bolan couldn't help feel some empathy for them. They came from China as an oppressed people with a new hope based on nothing more than grand promises spouted by some fork-tongued diplomat, and then they were brutalized and scorned by their own countrymen. Meanwhile, men like Lau-Ming Shui and Ing Kaochu got richer off their labor, and in return they were demoralized beyond rehabilitation.

But Bolan had something for the brutes—something they wouldn't soon forget.

He lowered the binoculars and then checked the actions on the Beretta and Desert Eagle before turning his attention to his rifle. He donned a pair of thin leather gloves and moved behind the Heckler & Koch MSG-90 sniping rifle he'd braced against the corner of the parapet. A cheaper variant of its predecessor, the PSG-1, the MSG-90 was no less effective for that fact. Bolan appreciated the weapon both for its precision and lighter weight. The trigger was factory set for a pull of 1.5 kg, but Kissinger had retooled the weapon for .85 kg. It was mounted with a 6×45 scope with an infrared night-vision feature and illuminated reticule. The rifle was chambered for 7.62 mm NATO ammunition in a 20-round magazine.

Bolan braced the weapon against the parapet and focused the scope on the front door to the house. He had a plan, but he knew that now it was just a waiting game. Eventually, the Scarlet Dragons would show, and he didn't want to show his cards too early. He needed to put down Shui's operations here, and he'd follow his mission to completion, yeah, but he also wanted to send a clear message to Shui. He wanted to shake him up, get him on the defensive. Plain and simple, he wanted to scare him because scared men made mistakes.

The Executioner waited patiently. A half hour ticked by, an hour and then two hours. The sun had descended, the only illumination now a corner streetlight. The rest of the street was dark, and he knew that would provide additional cover.

A black van rolled to a stop at the curb, and four Scarlet Dragons exited. They kept their hands close to the openings in their leather jackets as they walked toward the front door.

Bolan brought the high-powered range finder scope to his eye and adjusted the illumination for infrared. The head of the first Chinese gang member filled the scope. Bolan took a deep breath as he locked the butt against his shoulder, made a slight adjustment in the sight picture for drop trajectory and then squeezed the trigger. The NATO round left the rifle with a muzzle velocity of 820 meters per second. The slug plowed through the back of the guy's neck, cracking his spine and severing the better part of his head from his body.

The soldier already had his next target before any of the men could react. He squeezed the trigger again, this round taking the target in the chin as he turned to locate the shooter. The bodies of both men were hitting the ground as Bolan took a third Dragon, catching this one in the center of the chest. The high-velocity round ripped through the aorta and continued out the man's back. The impact lifted him off his feet, and his head split open on impact with the front porch steps.

The last gunner was now on the stoop with his back to the door and firing wildly in every direction. Bolan was a bit surprised at the reaction, considering the training of the Scarlet Dragons, but he knew that part of the success in sniper actions revolved around the psychological impact. There was logic at work in such operations. The Executioner aligned the sight picture once more and squeezed the trigger. The round was intended for the forehead, but someone opened the door a millisecond before it connected, and the impact ripped out the Scarlet Dragon's jaw. Bolan could see the blood spray even at that distance.

The hood's body toppled into the man who had opened the door. The surprised doorman caught the body and immediately disappeared from Bolan's view. The Executioner nodded with satisfaction. He reached into a fatigue pocket and withdrew a thin, high-tensile nylon rope with a titanium grappling claw. Bolan wrapped the claw around a steel standpipe, secured it with a quit knot and then vaulted over the parapet and descended to the pavement.

The soldier sprinted across the street. He approached the house, Beretta out and tracking the area as he kept his eye on the door. The man was still struggling with the body, trying to get it out of the doorway so he could secure the house while another man out of view was screaming at him. Bolan reached the stoop as the doorman spotted him and clawed at shoulder leather. The Executioner thumbed the selector to single shot and squeezed the trigger. The 156-grain subsonic 9 mm Parabellum round punched a hole between the man's eyes.

The doorman's body stiffened and he collapsed in the doorway, creating an even larger obstacle.

A new enemy trooper appeared and met the same fate, two rounds from the Beretta knocking him off his feet and depositing him on the ground in a crumpled heap. Bolan ascended the steps and leaped over the corpses cluttering the doorway. He moved inside, keeping low, every sense on alert. Either side of the hall opened onto wide living areas that were sparsely decorated. Both were empty, and the Executioner turned his attention to the sounds of footfalls coming from somewhere below. A moment later, he discovered the source as a door at the end of the hallway opened and two men burst through it toting pistols.

Bolan was ready, moving against the wall for cover as he flicked the selector switch to 3-round bursts and switched the Beretta to his left hand. He took the closer of the pair high in the chest, spinning the man into his comrade. The Executioner followed with a second burst, two of the rounds hitting the surviving gunner in the thigh, the third ripping through his abdomen. Blood poured from the exit wounds as the guy screamed in agony.

Bolan heard the shot as a round buzzed close past his head. He turned to see another house guard standing in the living area on his left. His legs were spread in a weaver's stance, both hands wrapped around a semiautomatic pistol. Bolan crouched, quick-drawing the Desert Eagle from his hip holster and firing it from a spot beneath his outstretched arm. The Eagle's report thundered in the confines of the hallway as a 280-grain .44 Magnum slug blew open a hole in the gunner's chest. The force of the bullet drove the man into a fireplace in the far wall, his body smashing through the glass doors.

The house fell silent, but Bolan suspected it wasn't empty. He quickly holstered the Desert Eagle, then moved through the first floor of the house before ascending the stairs to screen the second. Many of the doors on this floor were open, which spared him the possibility of any further nasty surprises. He quietly opened one closed door and found it was a bathroom. Another closed door on the second floor, which was actually designed as a master bedroom suite, contained a king-size bed with satin sheets, and little else beside lighting and camera equipment. It was a filming room. Bolan quickly primed one of the few sticks of C-4 he had left, planting it on a mounted camera for maximum effect before leaving the room.

The rest of the second floor was clear. The Executioner descended the stairs, continued down the hallway and stepped over the two dead men who had earlier come from the basement. He moved through the doorway leading from the hall and had to duck to avoid an overhang.

The sights, sounds and smells of the downstairs nearly overcame his keen senses. The basement was unfinished, with cobwebs in every corner. Several rickety beds were bolted to the floor, and Chinese females ranging in age from ten to sixteen occupied some of them. Bolan instantly knew that the expressions on every one of those battered faces would haunt him. The girls were manacled to their flimsy bunks at hands and feet. Some were in various stages of dress, including torn silk nightgowns or revealing undergarments.

One girl of about twelve appeared to be nude, her body covered only by a cheap wool blanket. Her skin was reddened, her lips cracked with a visibly swollen, dry tongue hanging half out of her mouth. Bolan couldn't understand why Shui's people would have chosen to treat them like this. They needed to present a sexual aura on screen, and not a single one could have produced such an appearance even with a decent makeup job. Bolan could only conclude that these were still part of the "breaking in" period he knew was sometimes required.

The Executioner could tell that all of them had already lost hope. He raised his hands and very slowly asked, "Do any of you speak English?"

There was a long pause as they silently watched him. Finally, the little girl raised her hand. Bolan nodded and walked over to her. He knelt and reached for her face, but she shrank from him. There was pure fear in her eyes and her breath visibly quickened. Bolan retracted his hand and tried to give the girl a reassuring smile.

"Listen to me carefully," Bolan said. "I'm not here to hurt you. Okay? I'm here to help you. Will you tell the rest of them that I'm here to help?"

She started to shake her head, but then something unknown—perhaps something in Bolan's manner or expression—caused her to change her mind. She continued to keep an eye on him, but she started speaking in her native language. Bolan turned to watch their reactions. Most of them looked skeptical, and the soldier couldn't say he blamed them. They had probably heard similar promises before from the devils assigned as their caretakers, right before they were raped and beaten, and God knew what else.

When the girl finished speaking, Bolan said, "I'm going to get you out of here. Nobody else is going to hurt you. I promise. I won't let anyone else hurt you, no matter who they are. You understand?"

The girl nodded, and her expression brightened just

enough to melt some of the icy lumps that stabbed at his chest. He started to rise but the little girl reached up and threw her arms around his neck, whimpering and repeatedly asking him not to go away.

"I won't leave you. I'm telling you, I won't leave. I have to find the keys." He disentangled her arms from his neck as gently as he could manage, and she finally released her hold. Bolan went up the stairs and searched both bodies of the deceased pair lying at the top before finding the keys. He quickly returned to the filthy den and released the little girl first, then freed the others in turn. There turned out to be a total of eight.

Bolan led them up the stairs, leading with the Beretta as he continued to glance behind him and insure they were following. When he got to the top of the stairs, he turned to the little girl, who was now holding his hand, and put the muzzle of his pistol to his lips as a signal she should remain quiet. She in turn passed it onto the rest of the girls.

He emerged onto the first-floor landing and panned both ways down the hallway before indicating for the girls to follow. They had almost reached the front door when a house guard suddenly burst through the front door and kicked the gun from Bolan's grasp. The hood charged at the Executioner, trying to get his hands around the soldier's throat.

Bolan sidestepped the attack, willing himself to ignore the sudden, high-pitched screams coming from the girls. He deflected both arms away in an entrapment motion and fired a rabbit punch to his opponent's kidney. He grabbed the wrist and continued the forward motion while sweeping the man's legs backward. The hood hit the ground face first, and Bolan ended the fight by dropping a knee onto the back of his attacker's neck. A popping sound echoed in the hall as the soldier's move snapped the cervical spine like a twig.

The girls were still screaming as the Executioner rose and retrieved his pistol. He shushed them and told them to keep together as he exited the house. The street was quiet, and Bolan didn't hear any sirens. He had a dilemma on his hands. He couldn't leave the girls—he'd promised he wouldn't leave. At least he couldn't leave them until he knew they would be safe.

Then he noticed the van that had brought the Scarlet Dragons, and he smiled.

CHAPTER SEVENTEEN

Mack Bolan's plan to deliver the eight frightened girls to the Canadian police went off without a hitch. He parked the van outside of a local precinct office and told the twelve-year-old to keep her friends calm. He then collected his gear and a clothing bag and walked across the street to a pay phone to place a call to the police station. Within a minute of hanging up, Bolan entered a small bistro and watched as an army of officers came out and found the girls in the van. At last, they were in capable hands and had been liberated from their living hell.

The Executioner disappeared in the confusion, and soon he was in his rental sedan and traveling to the next hardsite. Thus far, things were going as planned. Bolan was confident that if all continued as it should, he would have eradicated all of Shui's major holdings by morning. Mung had disclosed nearly a dozen separate locations, but the Executioner decided he would leave the smaller sites in the capable hands of the Toronto police. His mission called for a hit against Shui's operations where it hurt the most—he planned to stick with that mission.

In some ways, Bolan knew that Ing Kaochu was the real figurehead in Alternative Films, Ltd. As Shui's chief enforcer, it was Kaochu's responsibility to keep things operating smoothly. That also meant that when things went sour for the Kung Lok, Shui had a whipping boy, somebody to blame when something got broken or when profits were down and operations fell apart.

That didn't negate the fact Shui was the real brains behind most of it, and Bolan knew the Kung Lok underboss wasn't to be underestimated. A soldier usually got killed when he refused to render a certain degree of respect for his enemies.

Bolan stopped a few blocks from the next target and used a nearby alley and the cover of darkness to dress out of his fatigues and into the three-piece suit he'd stowed in the garment bag. Once he'd knotted his tie and donned a navy-blue wool overcoat, he ditched the bag and then continued down the street until he arrived at the house. Bolan knew this one would be filled with Kaochu's Scarlet Dragons. Blasting his way into the place wasn't his plan.

It was time for more role camouflage.

Bolan rang the doorbell, and only a few moments passed before a Chinese man opened the door just enough to poke his head out. "May I help you?"

"The name's Mike," Bolan replied. He pulled one of Nutao Mung's business cards from the half dozen he'd snagged off the guy's desk, and added, "He sent me here to look things over."

"I know nothing about this," the Dragon replied.

"He didn't call you?"

"No."

"It figures. I knew he'd forget to call you."

"What do you want?" the hood asked, visibly impatient.

"I told you, I'm here on behalf of Ing Kaochu. I've

been ordered to look this place over for Mr. Shui, and report back on what I see.''

''Well, you no come in here without okay from the big boss.''

''I have okay from the big boss,'' Bolan said, changing to a more threatening tone. ''I can always get him to come out himself if you'd like. Although I don't think he'd like that.''

''No, you need clearance from house boss. Hold on.'' The guy closed the door in the Executioner's face.

Bolan wasn't sure about his next move. They either were buying his story, or the doorman was putting together a dozen guns, and any moment they'd ventilate him through the door they were hiding behind. Then again, he could play it cool and wait to see what happened. A moment later, he got his answer as a different man, this one white, opened the door and stepped out onto the porch.

''Who are you?''

''Name's Mike, and I've got orders from the man himself to come down here and give the place a look-see.''

The guy studied Mung's business card, which Bolan had proffered, and then nodded. He stuffed it in his pocket—probably evidence for later if the visitor wasn't who he claimed to be.

''Mung never called ahead. He always calls ahead.''

Bolan splayed his hands, acting just as surprised as the house boss. ''I can't argue with you about that. I just do what I'm told.''

''Well, what kind of look are you supposed to be doing? Is this an inspection? If this is an inspection, I'm not going to be happy about it. I don't like being spied on, you know what I mean? I do my job and nothing more, nothing less. I do not do any takey-takey on the side, I do not play with the girls.''

"Hey, hold on a sec," Bolan said. "I never said I was here on that kind of a look. I'm here to see what you need. Mr. Shui wants to step up the output. We lost a lot of cash with the recent problems in Vegas.''

The guy looked suspicious now. "What problems in Vegas? I know nothing about this. I run a clean place here.''

"And I'll tell you once more, nobody said you didn't. I'm trying to help you out. That's what I do, okay? You don't like that? Fine. I walk and you can deal directly with Kaochu.''

Bolan turned and started to leave, but the guy grabbed his coat sleeve. The Executioner turned and threw him an icy stare, looking first at the man, then the hand on him, and then the man again. The house boss realized he shouldn't be touching one of Ing Kaochu's representatives in any sort of aggressive manner, and immediately released his hold. At five foot three and maybe 140 pounds soaking wet, the guy didn't look as if he could have taken a troop of Girl Scouts, and it was obvious to the Executioner that working around so many professional guns already had him nervous.

"Sorry," the man said with a genuine smile. "Listen, you don't have to involve Mr. Kaochu. I will be happy to let you look around. If he wants us to increase our production, there are some things I'll need anyway. Perhaps you help me. Perhaps we can help each other.''

Bolan put on his best show of congeniality, shrugging and then indicating for the guy to follow. So he'd smoothed things over and it got him inside. Now all he had to do was find what he was looking for. But even

as Mack Bolan entered the house, he knew that somebody was watching him.

And the Executioner smelled a trap.

ING KAOCHU WAITED in the shadows of the alley and
watched with interest as Mike Belasko talked his way
inside the house. He couldn't get over the resourceful-
ness of his enemy. It seemed that no matter what Belasko did, he did it with the cool precision of a veteran.
He was an experienced combatant, and a professional in
every sense of the word. Of course, the phone call from
Nutao Mung had helped.

It was now obvious that Belasko was planning to hit
them where he thought it would have the most effect.
As a matter of fact, it had gone just as Catalina Milaña
had said it would. The plan had come together, and as
soon as they had the signal from the Colombian vixen,
they would move on the house and take him.

BOLAN COULD FEEL the comfortable weight of the FNC
beneath his overcoat, and he was a little surprised when
none of the Scarlet Dragons moved to frisk him. It only
served to reinforce the Executioner's suspicions that he
was walking into a trap. Still, he couldn't worry about
that now. There were more important considerations—
such as whether or not the enemy had another group of
girls sequestered in the basement, chained to their beds
and sleeping next to buckets full of their own excrement.

The Executioner quickly put the thought from his
mind. He was inside now, and he'd just have to take the
mission as it came. The Canadian introduced himself as
René Poulain, and he was just as squeamish introducing
Bolan to the various Dragon members scattered around
a table playing some kind of Chinese board game. Most

of the names he couldn't pronounce, neither did he care nor did it appear that they cared. Their silence was only customary before they turned their attention back to the game.

If security was that lax, the Executioner figured it would be a cakewalk. He wondered how they would have reacted if he'd tossed a Diehl DM-51 into the center of the table, but he resisted the urge. Not that he couldn't have, since he had one in each pocket of the overcoat.

Bolan turned to Poulain. "Now that we've had our introductions, why don't you show me what you've got set up."

"Sure thing," Poulain replied, clapping his hands together and rubbing them. "Come with me. I had the whole upstairs renovated for shooting. The guards come and go in shifts. Mr. Kaochu loves my work, so he put money out of his own pocket to fix the place up."

"Is that what he told you?"

"What do you mean?"

"Never mind." Bolan gestured toward the stairs. "After you."

Poulain led the Executioner to the second floor, which opened onto a long, wide hallway with three doors. One door was open, providing access to a bathroom. The other two faced each other at opposite ends of the hallway, and the man led Bolan through the one to their left. The scents of fresh paint and wood validated Poulain's reference regarding the recent remodeling he had done. This suite had two beds against opposite walls. One was decorated with satin sheets and pieces of Chinese art and pottery. The other was more grotesque, covered with black sheets and a variety of whips, chains and other bondage devices.

Bolan was sickened by the sight, but he kept his reactions in check. He didn't want to give Poulain any reason to doubt his story about being experienced in the business. Stony Man intelligence had indicated that Shui's film company catered to a large clientele with varying degrees of taste. Alternative Films, Ltd. possessed a huge market base in both Canada and the U.S. Profits drove the entertainment business—particularly the kind in which Shui participated—and while the films his people produced weren't exactly breaking box-office records, it was a decent profit margin considering the expense of porn films.

"I've got top-of-the-line equipment," Poulain told the Executioner, encompassing the room in a sweeping gesture of his arms.

"Where are the cameras?"

Poulain gestured toward the other door. "We've got a job going right now. You want to watch?"

The Executioner gave the room another cursory inspection and then nodded. Poulain seemed obliging enough, a grin splitting his face as he motioned for Bolan to follow him. They left the room and crossed the hallway to the other door. Poulain put a finger to his lips. He opened the door quietly, stuck his head in first and then moved inside.

Bolan followed him. His sixth sense went on full alert, and he wasn't sure if it was simply the aftereffect of knowing somebody had watched him upon his arrival to the house, or if his combat instincts were trying to alert him to a danger on the other side of that door. In either case, he knew he was committed now and he'd have to improvise if it came down to it.

As he stepped into the room, he first noticed a pair of Scarlet Dragons standing on either side of the door. He marked their stances and distance, and then focused his attention to the scene ahead. Beyond the cameras, bright lights and boom microphone, two women were sprawled across a bed. One was moaning with what Bolan wasn't sure was pleasure or pain. The woman was young, maybe eighteen, with straight black hair and almond-shaped eyes. Her gaze caught his, but the Executioner remained stone-faced. Her head bobbed back and forth as her white, male partner ramrodded her from the rear.

The second woman was instantly recognizable. The Executioner had seen those firm lines and curves before; that enticing shape was recognizable because it had tried to seduce him once. She seemed distracted, but when her eyes met the Executioner's he felt as if someone had stabbed him through the heart with an ice pick. Catalina Milaña let out a startled gasp and the reaction had obviously been noticed, because every head in the room turned in his direction.

Bolan knew the gig was up and sprang into action. He opened his overcoat and produced the FNC with blinding speed, pointing it at the nearest Scarlet Dragon and squeezing the trigger. The weapon chattered as a 3-round burst stitched a bloody pattern in the hood's chest. The second Dragon clawed for his pistol, but he was a split second too late as Bolan turned the FNC on him and triggered a second salvo, blowing his head off.

Poulain started to shout and reach for Bolan, but the muzzle of the FNC in his gut stopped him short. Bolan pulled the trigger, sending three 5.56 mm NATO rounds through his stomach and out his back, taking part of his entrails and spine with them. Bolan grabbed Poulain's body and shoved in the direction of the surprised cameraman and director. The gaffer dropped the boom and tried to get away, but Bolan shot him through the back, the impact carrying him into a wall.

The Executioner stepped forward and swung the stock of the FNC to catch the nude male in the teeth. His jaw cracked under the impact and his head snapped back as the force of the blow drove him off the bed. The man hit the side of his head on the floor and lay still. The Executioner looked at the girl and commanded her to get dressed and get out. She scrambled to follow his orders, although Bolan wasn't sure if it was because she understood his words or the tone in his voice. In either case, she got the message.

The Executioner turned his attention to Milaña. "You want to explain this?"

"I don't think this is the time, Belasko," she replied.

The soldier had to admit there was some logic to her answer as he heard the footfalls of the Scarlet Dragons on the stairs. They were about to have company, and Bolan didn't plan to wait around for them.

"You have some clothes?"

She shook her head.

Bolan slung the FNC, retrieved the two Diehl DM-51 grenades and then shed the overcoat and tossed it in her direction. She shrugged into it as Bolan returned to the door, yanked the pin on the DM-51 and rolled the bomb down the hallway. He closed the door, locked it, then moved away as the grenade blew. The walls rocked with the explosion, and Bolan could hear screams as the grenade did its work.

He then looked around the room for a window. There wasn't one, and the Executioner wondered for a moment if maybe he'd trapped them inside. He noticed a door on the opposite side of the room and crossed the gap to open it. It led to a bathroom with a full-size window

against one wall, its panes blackened by plastic. Bolan
snapped the release catch and slid it upward. He looked
out and noticed it led onto the sloping roof and the back-
yard. The Executioner returned to the bedroom, and Milaña was now in the overcoat but gesturing to the man-
acle around her leg.

"Turn your eyes away," he said.

She complied and then Bolan pulled the Desert Eagle,
set the muzzle a few inches from the chain and squeezed
the trigger. The heavy-caliber bullet made short work of
the restraint. Bolan grabbed Milaña before she could offer any protest and dragged her into the bathroom. He
kept the Desert Eagle trained on the door while gesturing
for her to climb through the window. She followed his
orders and he came out after her. She had her bare feet
braced on the shingles with her butt against the roof.

"The fall would be worse than getting shot," the Executioner told her.

She looked at him a moment and then nodded before
crab-walking face first down the roof. Bolan kept pace
with her, keeping his center of gravity low while risking
glances back at the window. He had to get them off the
roof and fast, since they were vulnerable as long they
were in such a precarious position.

When he reached the lip of the gutter, Bolan vaulted
over the side and dropped the five yards or so to the
ground. He tracked the area around him with the Desert
Eagle before holstering the weapon and turning his attention to Milaña, who had now reached the edge, her
legs dangling over the side.

"Jump," he whispered hoarsely, trying not to give
away his position to the enemy.

Milaña hesitated.

"Do it now," Bolan said.

The woman took a deep breath and did as she was told. As she got close to the ground, Bolan snatched her in midair, encircling her waist with muscular arms, and dropped to one knee to absorb the impact. Milaña's feet touched the ground with little force, and the Executioner rose to face her. She looked at him and Bolan could see the grateful look in her eyes. He grabbed her hand and led her away from the house, keeping to the shadows cast by trees in the moonlight. Bolan got his bearings and led her in the direction of his sedan.

A few minutes later, they reached it without incident and before long, Bolan had powered away from the neighborhood and was driving in the direction of the downtown area. He didn't say anything as he drove, but in his peripheral vision he could see Milaña was staring at him. Bolan didn't have anything to say to her at that moment, choosing to concentrate on the road ahead and watching his rearview mirror for tails. His senses were still on full alert, and his gut was telling him that something wasn't right. Finding Milaña had seemed too convenient, too easy. The Executioner didn't believe in coincidence.

Believing in coincidence could get a soldier killed.

Las Vegas, Nevada

AT FIRST SHE THOUGHT that she'd gone to some sterile version of heaven. Eventually, Lisa Rajero realized she was still alive, and had awakened in the intensive-care unit of a downtown hospital. The ICU nurse caring for her was so surprised to suddenly see the woman awake and staring at her, that she dropped her syringe and ran out of the room calling hysterically for a doctor.

While she waited for the unending flock of attending

doctors to arrive, Rajero studied the room around her as she ran her tongue across the pasty film covering her teeth. The DEA agent was meticulous in her oral hygiene, and she couldn't wait to get to a toothbrush and some dental floss. For the time being, she lay in the bed and took allowed her surroundings to become focused. Habit and years of training forced her to immediately take stock of her physical condition. She wiggled her fingers and toes, felt her ribs and hips for any significant damage, and then slowly moved her legs.

There was pain in her back but it wasn't intolerable. With a deep breath, she managed to pull the covers from her body and swing her legs off the bed, using her left arm to assist getting her body into a sitting position. The room spun for a moment, but a few more deep breaths dispelled the dizziness and nausea. Rajero got to her feet and went to the bathroom, toting the IV stand along with her.

Two doctors and three nurses returned just as she was coming out of the john, and Rajero smiled at them. "Good morning."

"Actually, it's evening," one of the doctors replied. He had dark eyes and a bronze complexion, which left Rajero to conclude he was probably East Indian, maybe Pakistani or Arab. "You're lucky to be alive, Agent Rajero."

Rajero rubbed the small of her aching back and said, "Maybe not. What happened?"

The doctor looked at his colleague, who nodded, and then returned his attention to her. "Well, it's kind of a long story. You were brought to the ER late last night with injuries from an explosion. The receiving doctor was an intern, and he pronounced you DOA."

Rajero shook her head. "I don't feel dead."

"It was an error," the doctor replied. He jerked a thumb in his colleague's direction and continued, "This is Dr. Radnish. He's an orthopedic surgeon. My name is Dr. Singh, and I was the chief resident on duty. We knew immediately that you were comatose, with a very slow heartbeat and respiratory rate, which was causing a hypoxic condition."

"You want to give me that again in English?" Rajero said matter-of-factly, putting her hands on her hips.

"The intern thought you were dead because the oxygen content of your blood was so low," Radnish interjected. "What we found out was that this was a secondary response to the shock your brain experienced due to the concussion of the explosion."

"So my brain was in shock from the blast," Rajero replied, "and my body followed suit."

"Yes," Singh said with a nod.

"Well, I feel pretty good now. If you'll just get me my clothes, I'll get out of your hair."

There was a long, uncomfortable silence as Singh and Radnish exchanged frantic looks while their nurses stood in the wings and muttered their disbelief. Rajero could understand the reaction, but she planned to hold firm. She didn't know the current status of the mission, but she knew it wasn't completed yet. And now she'd lost nearly twenty-four hours, which meant that her people might still be out there, or they might all be dead.

"Agent Rajero, I wouldn't advise that. You may feel okay, but you've suffered a considerable head injury. Now, we can move you off the ICU ward and allow visitors, but we'd like to keep you here at least a couple more days for observation."

"No way," Rajero said.

"Lisa, be reasonable," Radnish added, trying a more personalized and less official approach.

"I'm sorry, but I can't stay," Rajero said. "And I'm smart enough to know that you can't hold me here against my will as long as I'm oriented to myself and my surroundings. Not to mention the fact, I don't think you want to take the responsibility of forcefully restraining a federal officer against her will. So, if you'll just get me all of the proper forms, and my clothes and weapons, I'll be on my way."

"Your weapons were signed over to personnel from your organization early this morning," one of the nurses said. "They were surprised to hear you were still alive."

"Then my clothes…?"

The nurse looked at Singh, who cast another concerned glance at her before nodding his consent to the nurse. He advised her to make sure the release forms were clear that he wouldn't take responsibility if Rajero dropped dead outside the hospital entrance. Rajero could see he didn't like the decision one bit, but they both knew there wasn't a damn thing any of them could do about it.

"The federal government appreciates your cooperation in this," Rajero told Singh. "As I'm sure will the Drug Enforcement Administration."

"What you're going to attempt is absolute suicide, Agent Rajero," Singh said, jabbing his finger at her. "And I don't think that anyone in your organization would appreciate the fact you're taking your life into your own hands. I'm sure you're more valuable to them alive than dead. You could still have an aneurysm that might burst, or some other cerebral malady that could result in instantaneous death."

"I do appreciate your concern, Doctor," Rajero replied. She looked at Radnish and added, ''Both of you. But I have people out there who could be in trouble, and they're going to need my help. There's a lot more at stake here than my pride.''

Rajero wasn't bullshitting them one bit, and their expressions told her they knew it. She didn't know what had become of her task force or Belasko. Really, Belasko had passed beyond the status of a stranger. The guy was much larger than that—he was becoming a very real and large part of her world. She wasn't going to let him just go it alone; she didn't give a damn if that's the way he wanted it. It wasn't the way she wanted it. So there was a lot at stake, yes, but there was something else even more important.

Rajero was most concerned with the life of the man with whom she had fallen in love.

CHAPTER EIGHTEEN

"I'm ready for my explanation," Bolan said to Milaña.

They were now secure in a two-room suite of a downtown hotel that Bolan and Grimaldi were using for a base of operations. There was a mobile communications center set up on a table nearby, which Grimaldi was constantly monitoring for the Executioner. Courtesy of some sophisticated equipment built by Gadgets Schwarz and programmed by Kurtzman, Grimaldi heard every one of Nutao Mung's conversations through the bug Bolan had planted in the smut manager's office before leaving. The communications system had also facilitated two-way contact with the Executioner during his blitzing missions.

"There's nothing to explain," Milaña said as she dried her hair with a towel. She wore nothing more than a cream-colored terry-cloth robe that shone starkly against her dark skin, still wet from her shower. The bright, exotic eyes stared at him with an intensity he wasn't sure originated from her equally intense personality or something more intimate.

"I think there is," Bolan replied with a cool smile. "Finding you was just a little too easy, Catalina. It wasn't a coincidence."

She stopped drying her hair, lowering the towel to her

side as she sighed and stared daggers. "I have to hand it to you, Mike. You're not easily fooled. And you're right…it wasn't a coincidence."

"Just like I said. The Kung Lok wouldn't benefit by snatching you. They didn't know anything about you. Come to think of it, I didn't even know you existed before a few days ago. So one more time, I'm going to ask what you're doing here."

"I went after Nievas on my own," she said quickly. "I didn't think you would follow through on your promise. When I went after Nievas, the Kung Lok kidnapped me and brought me to Toronto. They forced me to…" She paused, seemingly unable to finish as tears began to roll down her cheeks.

Bolan studied her a moment and then shook his head as he withdrew the Beretta and pointed it at her. "I've got to admit, you're pretty good at what you do."

An expression of terror spread across Milaña's face. "What are you doing?"

"Deciding whether I'm better off reducing the liability you pose to my mission against the Kung Lok."

"You think I'm someone other than I claim to be?"

"I know you are," Bolan replied. "I didn't buy your story back when we met, and I think even less of it now. So start explaining, or I kill you here and now."

"I work for the Colombian government!" she said.

"What?" Grimaldi interjected, looking up from the communications console with surprise. He looked at Bolan and said, "That's crazy. Please don't tell me you actually believe her."

"I'm listening," Bolan said, nodding at her and gesturing to Grimaldi that they should at least listen to what she had to say before making a snap judgment.

"I was instructed by my superiors to make contact

with Deng Jikwan. Jikwan was arranging a major arms sale with the FARC, and my government ordered me to stop it.''

"So what does that have to do with me?" Bolan asked.

"It was never about you, Belasko. I care little for you or the United States. Yes, I used you, and I'm sorry about that, but this mission was my priority just as your mission was yours.''

"Duty I understand," Bolan said in a grim tone. "But you still haven't explained why you're in Toronto.''

"When I found out Jikwan was coming here to meet Lau-Ming Shui, I managed to convince him to let me tag along. I had reliable sources tell me that Colonel Nievas was buying guns from the Kung Lok, but I didn't know who was supplying them for Jikwan. He wouldn't tell me.''

The Executioner nodded. It was all beginning to make sense to him. "So when you heard about Shui, and saw an opportunity to get inside, you thought maybe they would reveal it.''

"And they did.''

"So who's behind the arms sales?" Grimaldi asked.

She looked in Grimaldi's direction and quickly replied, "Dim Mai.''

"That makes sense," Grimaldi said, looking at Bolan with a grim expression. "We knew he was involved in this. Now we know why.''

Bolan cocked his head and studied Milaña a moment longer before lowering his pistol. He had decided she was being truthful, although he didn't totally trust her. She had lied to him once, and managed to play a Chinese military officer for a fool to boot; Milaña was one of the most dangerous women he'd ever encountered. She wasn't dangerous in the sense he'd originally thought of her—she was a cool tactician who knew how to play her feminine wiles on the male ego with rare skill. Bolan had met a few like her, but they were few and far between. Some had been on his side and some hadn't, and the Executioner didn't yet know where Milaña fell. He wanted to trust her, but there was still something about her that his senses couldn't quite overcome. He would have to watch her carefully if he planned to stay alive long enough to destroy Shui.

"So it was Jikwan who arranged the arms sale between Mai and the FARC," Bolan said.

Milaña nodded as she dropped the wet towel on the bed and went into the bathroom to brush her hair.

Bolan turned to Grimaldi and asked quietly, "Do you believe her?"

Grimaldi looked in Milaña's direction a moment and then nodded.

"Ditto," Bolan said. "It would definitely fit all the pieces of the puzzle. Shui decides he wants to pick up the drug action in the States. Jikwan figures out that's Carillo's territory, so he convinces Carillo that the only way to control the drug trade is to control the borders."

"And the only way he can do that is with plenty of men," Grimaldi interjected.

Bolan nodded and continued, "So he arranges for an alliance between Carillo and the FARC, funnels the arms to Shui's people through Sapèdas instead and then tries to convince Shui that it's Dim Mai's gesture of support."

"In the meantime," Milaña cut in as she emerged from the bathroom, "Jikwan conveniently arranges for a meeting between Hoffner, Shui and his political masters in Beijing and Hong Kong to angle for a better espionage network in the United States.''

''That would increase the Chinese military's position in this country, and not only make him one of the most powerful men in the world, but also put him in the financial position required to fund and maintain the Scarlet Dragons as the single largest espionage network that ever existed.''

''My God,'' Grimaldi whispered. ''It's absolutely brilliant.''

Bolan nodded. ''And it almost worked. Jikwan managed to get me to destroy Carillo and the FARC.''

''Which leaves only the Kung Lok. Once Shui is dead, Jikwan will be in total control with no witnesses,'' Milaña said.

''I can't let that happen,'' Bolan replied.

''You're going to hit Shui's place now?'' Grimaldi asked.

''And hard.'' Bolan looked at Milaña. ''You said Jikwan was at Shui's mansion?''

''Yes.''

''Then now's the time.''

The door to the hotel room opened and two Scarlet Dragons clutching Jatimatic machine pistols burst through the doorway. Milaña, who was closest to the door, shouted in surprise as they shoved her out of their way and trained their weapons on her male companions.

Bolan executed a back roll across the bed and sought cover behind the mattress, the Beretta still in his hand and coming up to track on the first target. Grimaldi snatched his readied Ingram Model 11 from the nearby window ledge and dived beneath the table. The Jatimatics roared in the confines of hotel room as the Dragons filled the air with 9 mm slugs.

The Executioner took the first target high with a single shot. The subsonic bullet ripped through the Dragon's throat and lifted him off his feet. He collapsed to the floor, his weapon slammed from his grip and rolling to within inches of Milaña's nose. Grimaldi got the second Dragon hitter, stitching him from groin to sternum with a sustained burst of 9 mm shorts. The hood almost looked as if he were dancing as he staggered backward and fell into the doorway.

Three more Dragons entered the room through the hotel doorway and two more crashed through the sliding glass doors. Grimaldi took that pair while Bolan and the now-armed Milaña opened up on the storming trio. Milaña got the two closest to her, as they didn't immediately notice her given she was so close and low to the ground. The Jatimatic rocked in her small hands as she depressed the trigger and held it. The chattering weapon spit 9 mm Parabellum rounds at a cyclic rate of 650 rounds per minute, and literally ripped the flesh from two of three attackers. Bolan got the third with a head shot that cracked the man's skull wide open and blew his brains against the wall behind him.

Grimaldi surprised the pair who had busted through the balcony doors. He triggered the Ingram with two short bursts, the first catching the closer man in the ribs while the other dropped from multiple rounds in the thighs and knees. Bolan whirled in time to put a mercy round between the wounded hood's eyes.

The threesome waited a moment longer for another attack before Bolan ordered Milaña to put on some clothes while they watched the doors and windows. The Executioner was now confident that he was right in sensing he'd been followed to the house, and subsequently to their hotel room. Not that it mattered. They had used it as a base of operations long enough, and it was time to move out.

"Jack, is the comm equipment okay?"

Grimaldi quickly inspected it, then looked up and replied, "It's going to need some new components, but I've got spares in the plane."

"All right. Take Milaña with you and get back to the jet. Contact the Bear and let him know our situation, then wait for me."

"You're going after Shui?"

The Executioner nodded and said grimly, "Yeah. It's time to end this."

LISA RAJERO'S FLIGHT touched down at the Lester B. Pearson International Airport at about 2200 hours. She hit the ground running, collecting her baggage and immediately proceeding to the rental-car area, where she had arranged transportation. Nobody knew what it was she was planning—she hadn't even told Charlie Metzger. The DEA agent was intent on helping Belasko, and she was willing to break any rules to that end, including risking her career.

It had occurred to Rajero during her flight that Mike Belasko was a loner, and it was possible he didn't feel the same way for her that she did for him. But that thought did nothing to dissuade her, because she felt how she felt, and the way Rajero saw it, she still had a score to settle with the Kung Lok for the deaths of her friends and colleagues. She only hoped her presence in Toronto wouldn't result in some international incident. She sure as hell didn't need that on her conscience.

Within an hour of touchdown, Rajero was in her car and negotiating the sixteen-mile drive to Toronto's downtown section. Rajero had never been to the Greater

Toronto Area before, but she knew from information she'd gleaned out of a travel brochure during her flight that it was split into numerous regions. What had her most interested were the in-flight news reports that indicated an outbreak of gun battles and explosions, which authorities were initially calling gang-related activity.

Rajero smiled at the thought. She knew damn good and well that it wasn't gangs battling it out for control. It was Belasko doing what he did best: kicking ass and taking names. Rajero considered for a moment that the fight might be over well before she could join it, but she was undaunted in her mission. She wasn't even sure where to start looking for Belasko, since the trouble had not only broken out in Toronto, but also apparently in a warehouse off the highway near the neighboring town of Caledon.

Through a laptop she'd secured from her possessions in Las Vegas, Rajero researched the company that owned the warehouse. The company was Ming Textile Designs, and its president and CEO was none other than Lau-Ming Shui. That was no coincidence, and it actually surprised Rajero that the Canadian authorities weren't digging a bit deeper knowing that piece of information.

As a matter of fact, she couldn't understand why Shui had been allowed to go on with his activities as long as he had, given the fact everyone within the international law-enforcement community knew he was a gangster. Rajero could be sympathetic, however, in one respect, because she understood the bureaucracies and red tape that those in the field fought every day. It had taken her just as long to put down Jose Carillo, and even the DEA hadn't ultimately been responsible for his demise.

So in one sense she understood how difficult it was to bring down a criminal as shrewd and intelligent as

Lau-Ming Shui. In another sense, she'd come to realize that those like Carillo and Shui wouldn't be brought to justice through any standard or legal means. That's why the tactics of men like Mike Belasko worked, because he didn't follow any of the rules. The criminals didn't have to play by rules, and it wasn't fair to Rajero that law enforcement had to when the facts were so clear. She'd accepted that reasoning for far too long—it was time to change her thinking.

Rajero quickly located a cheap motel and was settled in her room within the hour. Her first step was to make a call to the Canadian police, posing as a journalist. She managed to pull some information from their PR officer, albeit none of what he told her was really helpful, and most had already been released to the press. She couldn't tell them her real capacity, since that would then raise red flags.

One interesting tidbit she got from the guy centered on a group of twelve-to-sixteen-year-old girls who had obviously been sexually and physically abused. The PR officer wouldn't say more, other than to tell her they had made the discovery after an anonymous caller phoned in and said the girls were in a van outside one of the sub-stations. And, of course, they were all going to live despite the abuse they had suffered.

Rajero knew immediately she was on the right track when she heard that bit of news. That sounded like Belasko's work, no doubts there, which meant she wasn't too far behind him. Rajero was about to grab a quick shower when she heard a late-breaking news report over the radio. A firefight had taken place between unknown parties a few hours earlier at a hotel in York Region on the outskirts of Toronto. Witnesses were certain they had seen at least two men and one woman involved, but there was no other information available, and it appeared the suspects had fled the scene before the Toronto police could apprehend them.

Rajero knew it was too much of a coincidence. Belasko *was* in town, and it sounded as if he was lighting up the Kung Lok operations and good. Rajero knew her first order of business was to get cleaned up and then make a contact that could help her. If she alerted her people, they would most likely ask a lot of uncomfortable questions. That meant her only real friend was Belasko, and she wasn't sure he'd be that easy to find.

Rajero took her shower, dressed in woolen slacks and a thick burgundy sweater, then went through the various pockets of her suitcase until she'd secured all the pieces of her Glock 19. It didn't surprise her in the least that she'd managed to smuggle the case with disassembled weapons parts across international boundaries. Security still wasn't what it could have been; even after repeated terrorist attacks in the United States, people were still lax. She couldn't understand that—she would never understand that attitude of apathy that seemed so prevalent among her people.

Once she'd assembled and loaded the Glock and secured it in a high-riding holster beneath her bulky sweater, Rajero left the hotel and drove to York Region, north of Toronto. She specifically avoided the few blocks surrounding the hotel where Belasko had most likely had some kind of encounter, drove through the surrounding areas watching the streets for any sign of him or Jack. She didn't find anything, and that didn't surprise her.

Suddenly, she got an idea and immediately increased speed, heading toward the airport. It suddenly occurred to her that if the two men seen by witnesses were Belasko and his pilot, then they had probably flown into the country via private means. It seemed that Jack was able to get his hands on aircraft at a moment's notice, just as he had in Vegas, so it only made sense that the pair might have come in via a private flight or charter of some kind.

Rajero headed toward the smaller hangars owned by the various airlines or the City of Toronto, and were usually rented to the smaller craft. It took her almost three hours to search each area, and while the mechanics and security were cooperative, nobody remembered any charters with two men coming from Las Vegas, or anywhere in the United States for that matter.

Rajero then proceeded to the Infield Cargo Facilities, which appeared to be under construction in some areas. She checked with the customs people, and none really remembered anything like that except...well, yeah, there had been a Learjet that came in with two Americans, but they were only there for a couple of days to inspect a delivery services company. To his knowledge, they hadn't declared a thing coming in, and it was pretty usual, so he didn't think anything of it.

"Is the plane still here?" Rajero asked.

The customs guy nodded and pointed to a very small hangar directly across from theirs. "Yeah, that's it. It's usually empty most of the time, but apparently they use it now and again. Don't see them much, but when we do they are usually in and out within a day or two."

"And they never declare anything?"

"Naw, I think they're mostly executives. We search their luggage and all, but we've come to expect we won't find anything. Seems like most of the people they send are friendly enough."

"Do you mind if I check it out?"

The customs officer shook his head. "Go ahead. I can't unlock the hangar, since I don't have a key, but you're most certainly welcome to see if someone happens to be there. I doubt it, though…at least not at this hour."

Rajero nodded, thanked the customs officer, then left the building and walked across the tarmac to the nondescript hangar. As she approached, she studied the exterior emblems. She smiled as she thought that it was probably just the type of cover Belasko might use. A very popular delivery company, an executive jet, people in and out—it all made sense to her. There was little doubt that Belasko worked for the U.S. government in some capacity. Maybe he wasn't officially employed, as he'd claimed, but he was definitely connected with some important people.

Rajero tried the hangar's entrance door and found it was locked. She proceeded along the length of the hangar until she reached the main doors and, to her surprise, found them parted just enough that she could squeeze inside. The inside of the hangar was sheltered from the bitter night wind, and the interior of the hangar was relatively warm.

Rajero looked around and was about to give up when she noticed a small light spilling through the crack of an open door on the far side of the hangar. The DEA agent moved quietly along the outside walls of the hangar, careful to stay far from the small Learjet, and as she neared the door, she drew her pistol. Something didn't feel right to her. She continued along the wall and was about to reach for the door when she heard the unmistakable sound of a hammer being cocked on a pistol. A moment after that, she felt the cold barrel of that pistol pressed to the back of her head.

"You so much as even twitch," the familiar voice told her, "I'll kill you where you stand."

Rajero raised her hands and left the Glock 19 dangling on her finger by the trigger guard. This wasn't the time to get cute, even though she was almost certain she knew her captor. The man took the weapon from her and then brought the pistol away from her head and ordered her to face him. She turned slowly, and the face of Jack Grimaldi twisted into an expression of shocked surprise.

"Holy shit," he whispered.

Rajero smiled. "You look like you've seen a ghost, Jack."

"I think I have."

Rajero shook her head, giggled and then found herself moving forward and hugging him, although she couldn't explain why. The awkward moment didn't last as Grimaldi pushed her away gently and looked her in the eyes. Even after physically touching her and talking to her, she could tell that he still didn't believe his own eyes.

"We thought you were dead."

"So did a very young and inexperienced medical intern," Rajero replied, which she knew was all the explanation the sharp pilot would require.

"Well, all I can say is that I'm damn glad you're not. But what are you doing here? And how the hell did you find us?"

"I'm a police officer, remember? It's my job to investigate!" She punched him playfully in the arm and he blocked it only half-heartedly.

"Yeah, I guess."

The pilot then surrendered her pistol, and she immediately holstered it. He secured his own weapon, and then led her through the door and into a wide back room that was sparsely furnished with gray metal chairs with vinyl padding on the seat and back. There was a couch and a shapely form was spread along it, sleeping soundly. Rajero recognized Catalina Milaña immediately, and she turned to Jack with a searching expression.

He gestured to her and quietly said, "Mike found her at one of the Kung Lok's porn operations."

Rajero just stared at him with a look that said she didn't understand.

"She's a narcotics agent for the Colombian government. She was hired to stop Nievas from buying guns supplied by Dim Mai. Somehow, she got dragged into this bigger problem with the FARC's alliance with Carillo, and it got out of control. So she managed to convince Shui that she would act as bait and trap Mike, but once he showed up she saw her opportunity to get out of a bad situation and she helped him escape."

Rajero stared daggers at the sleeping woman as she replied, "Sounds more like he got her out of the scrape."

"Isn't that the way it usually goes?" the pilot said, doing nothing to hide his smile. He then shrugged and asked, "You want some coffee? It's fresh."

"That'd be great, thanks."

He poured them both a cup, then gestured for her to take a seat at the table. She held the steaming cup close to her face, letting it warm her nose and cheeks still cold from her walk across the tarmac.

"So why are you here?"

"I came to help you guys," she replied. "Where's Belasko?"

"He went to finish his business with Shui and Kaochu. Catalina told us that Deng Jikwan's involved with this. You know him?"

She shook her head. "No, but Belasko mentioned his name to me back in Vegas. He's some sort of military man?"

The pilot nodded. "Chinese army. He's not only part of the chiefs of staff in command of the PLA's infantry forces, but he's apparently head of a program that developed crack special force troops employing military-style tactics to enforce secret political aims. Their job is to gather intelligence and then act on that intelligence on the whims of Jikwan and *only* Jikwan. Basically, they go wherever he tells them to go and do whatever he tells them to do."

"How do they get their information?"

"The Scarlet Dragons."

Suddenly the horror of it occurred to her—and the genius. The Chinese government turned its back on the activities of the Kung Lok because their chief enforcement group, the Scarlet Dragons, provided a spy network for this Jikwan's special military team. So the Chinese didn't stand to lose either way. They could implement both their political and military goals, and gain a foothold in the nations of their enemies by looking the other way when it came to criminal activities.

"It's…it's…unthinkable," Rajero whispered.

Jack nodded. "Now you know why it was so important for Mike to come here and put this thing down before it got out of control."

"Who is he, Jack?" Rajero said. "I mean, you guys work for the government. Don't you? You can tell me…I swear I won't ever repeat it."

He shook his head. "I can't tell you, Lisa, I'm sorry. I can say that, yes, I work for the government. Belasko doesn't work for anyone but himself."

"I don't even know if Mike Belasko is his real

name," Rajero said. "But I do know that I've fallen in love with him, Jack. Do you think he feels the same way?"

He sat back in his chair and sighed, then shook his head and rubbed his temples. "I don't know. But I do know this much. You've fallen in love with the wrong man."

But Lisa Rajero didn't want to believe it. She couldn't believe it.

CHAPTER NINETEEN

Situated northeast of Toronto, the grounds of Lau-Ming Shui's estate were massive. The mansion and grounds were fortified by a large wall with one main gate, and surrounded by four hundred hectares of prime woodland. There was only one road leading to and from the house, and Bolan had hiked through several miles of dense forestry in the cold and dark, relying on only a compass and his wits to reach the estate.

The grounds were larger and more magnificent than Carillo's homestead, but much easier to penetrate since Stony Man's intelligence had it there was no electronic security. Shui probably considered himself quite well protected, since no one individual was ambitious enough to launch a full-scale operation through thick woods at night, and especially not in the dead middle of a Canadian winter.

Mack Bolan was the exception to that rule.

The Executioner announced his arrival to the Kung Lok in the form of a 40 mm HE grenade through the first-floor window of Shui's mansion. The grenade exploded on impact, blowing razor-sharp fragments of glass, wood and metal in every direction as Bolan advanced on the house. He wore a restocked satchel pack, which contained plastique and M-383s. The Desert Eagle dangled from his hip holster, and the Beretta was also in place. Two guards appeared around a corner of the mansion, sprinting toward the blaze and totally blind to the tall, lithe form approaching their position.

Bolan waited until he was within range before raising the M-16 A-2/M-203 to his shoulder and triggering the weapon on the run. The SS-109 NATO ball ammunition struck the first guard in the side of the head, splitting his skull in two and blowing his brains against the wall of the house. His partner stopped and turned, dropping for cover and immediately spraying the area with autofire from an Uzi machine pistol. His panicked shots went high and wide as the Executioner dropped to one knee, acquired the target and took him with a double tap to the head.

Bolan rose and continued forward, loading another 40 mm shell into the breech as he moved. He reached the house and kept his back to the wall as he knelt. Holding his weapon in a ready position, he reached into his satchel and withdrew a block of C-4, which was actually four one-pound sticks he'd lashed together with some det cord and an electronic blasting cap snuggled beneath the blocks.

Bolan duck-walked between fern bushes that filled the space around the recessed area where he'd blown out the window. He reached quickly through the jagged and charred remnants of the window frame and slapped the sticky side of the C-4 to the exterior supporting wall. The Executioner grunted with satisfaction and then moved away from the alcove.

He continued onward in his mission, watching for targets as he circumvented the exterior walls of the house. He rounded the first corner and nearly bumped into another pair of Shui's security team as they rushed toward the front of the mansion. Bolan swung the butt of his assault rifle upward, catching the closer of the two on the chin and knocking him to the ground unconscious. The second guard raised a semiautomatic pistol to shoot Bolan, but the Executioner already had his Beretta out and tracking. He squeezed the trigger, catching his enemy in the chest with a 3-round burst of 9 mm Parabellum slugs that ripped through the man's lungs and heart, and exited his back. The man's body went erect as his brain told the rest of his body he was dead, then he sagged to the ground.

Bolan pressed onward, cursing himself for almost being taken off guard. He needed to pace himself—he was trying to rush the job. It was the final stretch, and he needed to remain focused on the tasks at hand. Allowing himself to be sidetracked with the urgency of his job would ultimately get him killed.

The Executioner found a side entrance that was unlocked and moved into the darkened interior of the mansion. He had seven more explosive charges that required strategic placement. He intended to level Shui's house in one fell swoop, hopefully destroying the Chinese crime lord and his cronies in a single action. He considered the possibility Shui wasn't even on the grounds, but he couldn't worry about that now. Shui wasn't the kind of guy to run or hide—he'd stay and fight to the bitter end. And that was something on which the Executioner was counting.

GENERAL DENG JIKWAN paraded his crack assault team with satisfaction in the dim lights of the small underground bunker located in a hillside opposite Shui's estate. He could hear the sounds of battle were now joined. Belasko was definitely getting the show off with a bang, but Jikwan wasn't concerned about that. He was confident in the expertise of his men; these were the finest combatants in all of the People's Liberation Army. Each had a particular area of expertise for special operations, and all were united and loyal to Jikwan and the Chinese people to the point of death.

Jikwan had handpicked each member of his elite fighting force, which now numbered almost two hundred strong. The majority of his men were out on various operations, or back at a training camp outside of Beijing. They were supplied with the finest equipment and facilities Jikwan's political allies could afford, and well armed with weapons from Dim Mai's gunrunning empire. And they answered only to Deng Jikwan.

"This is our moment of victory," Jikwan told the ten men, pacing a line in front of them while Shui and Kaochu looked on. "Once you have eliminated Belasko, you have your instructions for getting out of the country. I am going ahead of you to prepare your victory celebration. I will see you in Hong Kong in three days. Understood?"

The men nodded, the leader of the team saluted, then Jikwan nodded to them. "You have your orders. Move out."

The team would approach the house in two fire teams. Stealth would be their greatest ally, and Jikwan figured it improbable that Belasko knew anything about this minibunker area, as it was well away from the house and concealed from both ground and air observation. While they made their attack, Jikwan, Shui and their remaining Dragons would take a circuitous route through the woods to a clearing where a chopper awaited.

"I do not like the idea of running away," Shui told Jikwan once the fighting team had departed.

"I understand."

"Do you really, Deng? This is my home, and I should stay behind to defend it. I am hardly afraid of Belasko. I would kill him myself, if Ing would allow me close enough. I would strangle him with my bare hands. I would choke the life from this American for his infernal and ceaseless interference in the affairs of the Kung Lok."

Jikwan chuckled. "I admire your spirit, my friend, but I am forced to agree with Ing Kaochu. You are not a fighter. You are too intelligent to lower yourself to such barbarity. Leave that to Kaochu or my men. They are the trained combatants here. Beside the fact, I need you much more now than ever. I need you to smooth out the differences between Dim Mai and me."

It was Shui's turn to laugh. "You actually think that Dim Mai would listen to me?"

"Yes, because I happen to think he respects you."

"Ha! You are truly insane if you think that Dim has anything but loathing for me. It's no secret that he's wanted control of my Western faction since the time I began building it."

"Perhaps that is true," Jikwan conceded. "But let us not forget that he also respects and fears your authority. He knows that you command the highest regards of our leaders in Hong Kong, as well as the premier's office in Beijing."

"That is strange," Shui said. "I thought I had rather fallen out of favor with the premier and his people."

"On the contrary I have kept your spirit alive with my most influential circle of friends. These are people well respected in our country, and they command the ears of some of the premier's closest advisers. He is anxious to see you upon your return to China. I see no better time than now."

Shui nodded thoughtfully, then turned to look at Kaochu, who had sat quietly and respectfully as the two leaders spoke. "Ing, what do you think?"

"I believe that you are wise enough to make your own decision in regard to this matter, my master," Kaochu replied with a bow of his head. "If you wish to stay and fight, I will immediately gather the remainder of my people and destroy Belasko once and for all. However, my first duty has and always will be to protect you, and if General Jikwan thinks it is better that you reestablish your political alliances in China, then you should go immediately. The way I see it, there is only one real way for me to protect you, and that is to destroy the threat. I could not go with you in good conscience while I know that there's a chance Belasko lives. I must stay and finish this."

"As always, you have spoken wisely, Ing."

He turned to Jikwan and said, "I will go with you, but I believe that Ing wishes to stay behind."

Jikwan looked at the Scarlet Dragon leader, who quickly nodded his affirmation. It was obvious that, despite Jikwan's assurances his team could do the job, Kaochu felt he had a personal score to settle with Belasko. He understood the Dragon leader's sense of duty. Kaochu had proved himself a faithful ally and protector to Lau-Ming Shui for many years. He was fearless in the face of danger—a fierce and competent warrior who deserved nothing less than the opportunity to defend that which he considered his own.

"You are a brave and able man, Ing Kaochu," Shui finally said. He put his hand on the Scarlet Dragon's shoulder and his voice wavered. "Much braver than that sniveling Hoffner, who chose to stay here and hide in Canada instead of going with us. I wish you success in your mission, and bid you to come home when you have destroyed the American.''

''I will fight with honor for you, Lau-Ming Shui,'' Kaochu said with a bow. ''I thank you for your understanding.''

''My men will give you every cooperation,'' Jikwan assured him. He shook hands with Kaochu, and then the Scarlet Dragon leader left the bunker.

''Come, Lau-Ming,'' Jikwan said to Shui, who was watching the bunker door through which his longtime friend had exited. ''It is time to go.''

THE FIRST THING Mack Bolan noticed about the house was that it appeared empty. He'd met resistance on the outside, but nothing as he'd foreseen. It now seemed unlikely to him that Shui was on the grounds. In fact, the Executioner suspected that he might have walked into a trap—that somehow Shui had foreseen he would come and had formed some sort of alternate plan to escape. Still, Bolan had known the risks of hitting Shui's operations before hitting Shui himself.

Bolan would give the Kung Lok underboss no quarter. If he didn't get him now, he would hunt him down like an animal. The warrior would chase him across the globe, if that's what it took, but before he took his last breath Bolan would make sure that he destroyed Shui. And he wouldn't do it out of vengeance or some inflated sense of morality—he would do it because it was his duty to do it.

The soldier continued through the house, planting the charges and sweeping the area with the M-16 A-2/M-203. He didn't want to become distracted by being overly cautious, since he had to place the charges with precision if the building was to come down as planned. He was planting the last charge when a whisper of sound attracted his attention.

Somebody had entered the room, and the Executioner could hear the intruder moving slowly. The shadowy form took shape as Bolan's eyes adjusted to the gloom. As the figure drew nearer, the soldier slowly reached to his shoulder holster and slowly withdrew the Beretta 93-R. He could sense only one presence, but if this one had any cover, Bolan didn't want to betray his position with the loud noise or flash of the FNC.

The form was short and lithe, and it moved with the fluidity of a trained professional. When it was within a few yards of him, Bolan raised the Beretta and squeezed the trigger. For the first moment after he'd fired, the soldier thought maybe he had missed because the shadowy form didn't move. Another moment elapsed before the Executioner realized he'd hit his opponent dead in the center of the chest, but the man was only wheezing.

Bolan jumped to his feet and moved in for the kill, the combat knife rasping from the sheath as drew the knife, stepped in and drove the blade through the side of the man's neck. He slashed sideways, cutting through both carotid arteries and jugular veins in the process. The man could only gurgle in response to what had started as a scream. He slumped to the ground as the hot blood spurted from his severed vessels.

The Executioner sheathed the knife, finished setting the last charge, then checked the corpse for equipment. As he frisked the body, he felt the body armor, which provided an explanation for why the chest shot hadn't dropped him. Bolan didn't find anything in the man's pockets, just as he had expected he wouldn't. He rose and left the room, moving with stealth, but efficiency. Bolan didn't plan to leave the same way he'd come. There were plenty of vehicles parked in an outbuilding, and he planned to hot-wire one of them for his escape, thanks to a trusty little device he'd brought along courtesy of Hermann Schwarz.

However, the arrival of four new hostiles was obviously going to cause him some delay. They were moving up the wide, main hallway of the house—two on either side—weapons held at the ready. Bolan's suspicions were finally realized in that moment. It had been a trap! This team had obviously been sent to kill him, and Bolan knew he'd probably just killed their pointman.

The Executioner went prone, bringing the M-203 into action as he went to his knees, then elbows. At that range, he knew he risked injury or even death, but there wasn't a choice. He triggered the M-203 and then rolled into an adjoining hall as rounds from his weapons filled the space he'd just occupied. A violent explosion rocked the area a moment later, the heat and flames searing his forearm and left shoulder from the HE grenade impacting the ceiling above and behind the enemy troops.

The flaming plaster and debris, and the ignited explosive that lit up the entire hallway in a single, orange flash drowned the screams of the troops. Body parts sailed down the hallway a moment later, including the head of one unfortunate. Bolan panted with the exertion, his lungs burning from the intense heat. He looked down to see the heat had incinerated the left sleeve of his blacksuit, and blisters were forming on the second-degree burn on his forearm.

He'd been damn lucky.

Bolan got to his feet, still winded, and checked the hallway again to make sure nobody had managed to sur-

vive the blast. No one had. As he continued up the dec-
imated hallway, the soldier couldn't tell where one body
ended and another began. Naturally, the M-203 wasn't
a short-range weapon, and the damage a 40 mm HE
grenade could do was renowned in military circles. Bolan had seen that kind of carnage many times before,
and he could never dismiss it casually.

The soldier managed to reach the exit to the house.
He knelt in the relative safety of the doorway and
watched the immediate area with concern. Whoever he'd
encountered inside the house had probably only been
part of the welcoming committee. Shui was clever. He
wouldn't leave just a handful of troops behind. Not to
mention the fact that his attackers had been attired in
combat fatigues, wearing Kevlar and toting AK-74 assault rifles. They hadn't been regular house guards or
Dragons—those had been specialized military troops.

That meant Jikwan had probably left them behind.
And there were undoubtedly more. Milaña had warned
him that Jikwan was planning to bring them in, but she
didn't know how many, or any of the details. She could
only tell him how he'd incessantly bragged about them
to Shui and Kaochu.

Bolan waited another full minute, then turned and entered the house once more. He climbed the steps to the
second floor and quickly located a room that provided a
view of the entire rear grounds. The Executioner also
found an unexpectedly grisly sight: the body of Ramon
Sapèdas. He'd been shot through the head with a low-
caliber pistol, probably a .22 short, judging by the size
of the wound. Bolan wasn't surprised to find him dead.
He'd already expected that they'd killed the Border Patrol chief, and this simply confirmed his suspicions.

Bolan moved to the window, reached into the hip

pocket of his blacksuit and retrieved the night-vision scope he'd detached from the MSG-90 sniping rifle. Bolan activated the small electronic switch that powered the device and then peered through it, sweeping the entire area. Finally, he spotted what he was looking for. Along a low flagstone patio wall, he noticed another one of the special commandos moving quietly through the darkness. The man knelt, obviously unaware that Bolan was watching him, and turned to signal to his fire team that it was clear. The enemy had made a fatal mistake.

The Executioner mounted the scope to the carrying handle of the M-16 A-2 by the attached clamps. He raised the scope to his eye again, turned the rifle's selector switch to single shot and then brought the pointman into acquisition. Once he was certain he could take him accurately, Bolan changed the sighting to the soldier who was on rear guard. He steadied his breathing and then squeezed the trigger without much hesitation. He was a skilled marksman, and the range was one from which he could hardly miss. The SS-109 hardball round punched through the side of the rear guard's head, flipping him onto his side. Bolan could see his body twitching a moment before he moved to the next one in line and fired again. The remaining trio—having now watched two of their people go down in less just over one second—threw themselves flat behind the patio wall.

Bolan managed to graze one of them who wasn't totally hidden from view. The bullet ripped through the man's calf. Bolan could hear the scream and shout of surprise as a hand appeared and dragged the wounded leg from the sight picture. The Executioner lowered his weapon, nodded with satisfaction, then headed for the ground floor while he detached the scope on the move.

Bolan figured he would have to take the rest of the

enemy in close quarters, but at the same time the numbers were ticking off and he realized that he'd already spent too much time clearing an escape path. That realization became even more obvious to him as he reached the bottom of the stairs and found himself staring in the face of a young Chinese man. He was dressed in the standard attire of the Dragons, the black fatigues and scarlet kerchief visible even in the dark interior of the house. But there was something else on the kerchief—an embroidery of a golden dragon with jade eyes. That was the sign of ultimate authority in the Scarlet Dragons, and Bolan figured the odds were pretty good he was looking at none other than Ing Kaochu.

"I've been waiting for you, Belasko," Kaochu said in a tight whisper.

"Have you?" Bolan asked, looking for a weapon and not seeing one.

"You have brought shame to the Scarlet Dragons and to my master. I am going to teach you an important lesson regarding this. You should not have come here. You should have tended to your own business."

"Putting those like the Kung Lok and Scarlet Dragons out of commission is my business, mister," Bolan replied. "And I think it's you who's going to learn a lesson tonight."

The movement was so fast that the Executioner barely managed to get out of the way in time to avoid having his brains smashed inside his skull. It seemed as if his enemy had almost floated off the ground as he executed a jumping side-kick. Bolan moved away from the attack but wasn't quite as prepared for the follow-up. Kaochu caught him in the diaphragm with a spin-heel kick. Air exploded from Bolan's lungs as the kick drove his back into the wall.

Kaochu tried to finish the job quickly with a smashing hammer-fist to the top of Bolan's head, but the Executioner took it in the shoulder while firing a punch to Kaochu's midsection. Avoiding the punch significantly lessened the killing blow Kaochu had executed, but the pain still jarred Bolan as the shock ran down his shoulder into his burned forearm. Kaochu recovered much more quickly than his adversary, and he nearly knocked the Executioner unconscious with an inside crescent kick to Bolan's jaw, the blow nearly breaking his chin.

The soldier thought he was going to pass out, and he figured the moment was finished, but as the impact of the kick rolled him away his senses and instinct took over. He felt one of the Diehl DM-51 grenades attached to his chest. It was primed for a defensive yield, with the sleeve already intact. As Bolan's chin scraped the floor, he gritted his teeth and—despite the pain—managed to dislodge the grenade from his harness.

He sensed Kaochu stepping forward to stomp his head, and Bolan rolled away and pulled the pin. He got onto his back and Kaochu was immediately on him, swinging his fists at Bolan's face with blinding speed and trying to pummel him into submission.

The Executioner managed to grab the lapel of Kaochu's fatigues and get a cocked leg between them. He executed a judo circle throw and dropped the grenade inside Kaochu's shirt as he vaulted him over and through a closed door. The door gave way under Kaochu's weight, and he landed on his back on the hard kitchen floor. As Bolan rolled away from the door and sought cover behind the wall, he could hear Kaochu let out a mixed cry of horror and surprise.

And then the Diehl exploded.

The whoosh of hot air and thunderous blast was dead-

ened only by the fact Bolan had covered his ears and
leaned away from the blast. As the debris and concussion
subsided, the Executioner slowly climbed to his feet and
walked toward the door. He didn't look back—there
wouldn't have been much left to see of Ing Kaochu anyway.

Once he got outside the house, Bolan waited in a darkened area of the perimeter where he could watch the
entrance. It wasn't long before he spotted the remaining
pair of Jikwan's special forces access the house through
the side entrance. They obviously thought he was still
inside, and they had no idea they were entering what
would literally end up as their tomb.

Bolan left his cover and moved toward the garage. He
hoped that there was a decent vehicle available to get
him off the grounds and away as quickly as possible. He
was injured and tired, and he didn't really feel like fighting his way through the woods back to the van.

The Executioner tried the door of the outbuilding that
housed six separate parking spots for vehicles, and made
his entry without a sound. He was a bit surprised to find
it open. Every instinct suddenly went on high alert, and
Bolan immediately drew the Desert Eagle. He wasn't
alone in the building. He could hear noises coming from
the garage bays, and hear somebody swearing under his
breath.

Bolan moved deeper into the shadows cast by the light
coming from the garage, which hadn't been visible from
the outside since there were no windows in the outbuilding. He looked through the partially open interior door
that led from a well-stocked workshop and saw the
source of the noise. A man was hunkered over the wheel
of the closest vehicle, a Hurricane 4×4, and Bolan immediately recognized his face from pictures he'd studied

carefully during his trip to Toronto. Stony Man had provided the dossiers and information on all parties involved in this war for control, and one subject was Liam Hoffner.

The Executioner stepped forward, opened the door and nonchalantly stuck the barrel of the Desert Eagle inches from Hoffner's temple.

"Can I help you with that?" he asked.

Hoffner turned a surprised glance in the Executioner's direction.

"Hands up, and do it slowly."

Hoffner complied as he said, "You've got it all wrong, mister. I'm on your side."

Bolan shook his head and chuckled. "No, it's you who got it wrong, Hoffner."

"You know my name?"

"Yeah, and I know what you're up to." Hoffner went to open his mouth in explanation but Bolan didn't give him the chance. "Don't bother lying to me. I'm not buying it. I've already talked to Milaña, and know exactly what you're about."

Now Hoffner's expression went dull and lifeless. He simply replied, "That bitch."

"Yeah, you didn't know she was on our side. She's a narcotics agent for the Colombian government. Thanks to her, you're one less thing America has to worry about. Now shut up and slide over here."

Hoffner did as he was told and Bolan secured him to the door frame with a pair of riot cuffs. He then closed the door and went around to the driver's side. He retrieved the small box provided by Stony Man from a hidden pocket in his blacksuit, inserted the contents of the device into the ignition, then jiggled it back and forth until it freed the ignition lock. A flip of the switch on the box and a full turn of the ignition, and the engine roared to life.

Bolan opened the garage door via the remote, and keeping his lights off, he pulled out of the garage and headed up the road toward the main gate. Hoffner watched with interest as the Executioner then withdrew the remote detonator from his satchel. Bolan flashed a wicked grin at Hoffner as he opened the switch guard, flipped the switch on the remote, waited until all lights went green, then pushed the button. The interior of the vehicle lit up with the flashes of sequential explosions. The loud pops were followed by balls of fire emerging through the roof as the building erupted into flames.

Hoffner turned to watch the view Bolan caught in the rearview mirror as Lau-Ming Shui's mansion crumbled to the ground. The Executioner nodded with satisfaction. He had finally brought an end to the Kung Lok empire in Toronto.

Bolan now turned his attention to Hoffner. "Now, let's talk about where Shui and Jikwan have gone."

CHAPTER TWENTY

Not one of those who had kept vigil at the small air hangar did anything to conceal his or her relief when they saw Mack Bolan come through the door with Liam Hoffner in tow. Grimaldi and Rajero immediately stood, and Milaña—obviously sensing a new presence in the room—twisted her sultry form on the couch and opened her eyes. It was obvious she was surprised to see Hoffner, but the surprise turned to genuine happiness when she saw the Executioner was alive and well.

Bolan shoved Hoffner into a chair, the man's hands now manacled behind him with a set of riot cuffs. "Keep quiet and don't move."

Hoffner scowled at Bolan, but the soldier wasn't affected by the look. He would have liked to put a bullet right between the traitor's eyes, but he wasn't a murderer and it wasn't his practice to shoot a man in cold blood. It would be a better form of justice for the former EPIC operations director to stand trial in a U.S. court and be forced to publicly answer for his crimes against the American people.

Rajero rushed forward and unceremoniously threw her arms around Bolan. He was a bit taken aback by the gesture but he let the moment go, more for her sake than his own, and then gently detached her arms from his neck. She stood back and looked at him, and he was immediately surprised to see tears form at the corners of her eyes.

"I'm glad to see you, Belasko," she said.

"I guess you're not dead," he replied, smiling at her.

She smiled back, then punched him playfully in the chest. The banter was short-lived when she cocked her head and noticed the bruising and swelling around his jaw. He reached up self-consciously and realized that in the adrenaline-charged moments following his battle at Shui's estate, he hadn't really taken time to assess his pain-racked body. But now, noticing the almost horrific look on Rajero's face, Bolan was beginning to settle down and feel the effects of his war.

"A little present from Ing Kaochu."

"Is he dead?" she asked, a slight tremor evident in her voice.

"Very," Bolan replied. He turned to see Grimaldi produce a lopsided grin.

"You going to be okay, Mike?"

"I'll make it. But thanks for asking."

Grimaldi nodded, and then jerked his thumb in Hoffner's direction and asked, "Who's your friend?"

Rajero answered, "Liam Hoffner. The director and DEA liaison with the El Paso Intelligence Center." Her eyes narrowed as she studied the trembling man. "I suppose you have a good explanation for why Belasko has brought you here in handcuffs. Don't you?"

"There's been a mistake," he said. "Lisa, you know me. I helped you, remember?"

"I remember you helped me almost get killed!" she snarled, before hauling off and landing a punch on his nose. The sounds of cartilage breaking echoed through the office, and Grimaldi had to reach out and hold Rajero back. Her face was flushed and she was biting her lip, pulling against Grimaldi's bear hug and trying to deal out some additional good old-fashioned street justice on the man.

"Whoa, lady," Bolan said, interposing himself between her and Hoffner. He reached out and nodded for Grimaldi to release her. The Executioner kept one hand on her shoulder, gentle enough not to hurt but firm enough to restrain. "I have no love for the guy, either, but I want him to go back to America alive and I'm expecting you to take him. So get it in control."

Rajero's breathing was still ragged as she pointed at him and said, "But he—"

"I know what he did," Bolan said. "And it will be up to you to make sure that Washington knows what he did. But killing him won't change what's already happened, and we need to be able to show our elected officials just what kind of stuff is going on in the government so that they can do something about it."

"You think they're actually going to do something to this guy?" Rajero said with derision. "Come on, Mike! He'll get some slick-tongued lawyer to talk him out of a jail sentence, and he'll be right back in the DEA before they're done booking him!"

"Listen to me, Lisa," Bolan said, trying to keep his voice quiet and gentle. "You're not thinking clearly right now. You're a cop and you have a cop mentality. You've worked hard all of your life but you're afraid the system doesn't work. And maybe sometimes it doesn't. But I guarantee you that it's better than anywhere else in the world, and if we don't have a little faith in our own people to do what's right, then all those who sacrificed themselves to make America a little bit safer place to live in have done so in vain."

"What are you talking about?"

"I'm talking about duty, lady," Bolan said. "Everything I do, I do out of duty and out of love for my country. None of us is perfect, and the American system isn't perfect, but it's what we have and I think most Americans try to be decent people. It's the rotten handful like Hoffner and Sapèdas whose actions cause us to digress into something we're not...something we were never meant to be."

Bolan stepped aside and released his hold on Rajero's shoulder. He withdrew the Beretta 93-R, released the safety catch and shoved it into Rajero's hand. "I'll tell you what. If you want to execute Hoffner, I'm not going to stand in your way."

She looked at him, surprised and uncertain, but the Executioner simply shook his head and then gestured in Hoffner's direction. Out of his peripheral vision he could see the guy moving around, trying to break free of his bonds and protesting in a squeaky voice, but the soldier ignored his outbursts.

"Go ahead—I mean it. Put a bullet right in his brain if it makes you feel better. You can believe me when I say I understand revenge. But as you're pulling the trigger, bear something in mind for me. You're making a statement that you don't believe in your own country. You're saying you don't believe in all the things that people like Willy and Noreen Zahn died for."

Rajero had raised the barrel of the gun as Bolan talked to her, but her hand was now quivering and her lip trembled. Yeah, she was thinking damn hard about what he said, and he could tell it was getting to her. Rajero was a passionate woman who loved her country—he had no doubt of that. But she wasn't the experienced combatant the Executioner was, and she didn't fully understand the situation the way he did.

"Not so easy, is it?" Bolan finally asked. "I know, because I've already been in this situation. More than once, I've been there, and I've had the exact same thing go through my mind I imagine is going through yours."

Finally, Rajero lowered the pistol and the Executioner could hear a sigh of relief from everyone in the room.

She turned to look at Bolan, the tears now streaming down her face. "But you've killed so many. We've killed hundreds of them. I don't see any difference."

"Yes, you do," Bolan said, taking the Beretta and securing it in his holster. He stepped closer and put his hands on her arms. "You're sharp enough to know there's a big difference. Maybe you don't yet know what it is, but you certainly took a large step closer to figuring it out. And it's not up to me or anyone else to explain it. You have to do that for yourself."

"And when you do finally understand," Grimaldi added, nodding at Bolan, "you'll understand why Belasko does what he does."

She lowered her head, unable to watch those piercing blue eyes, but Bolan cupped her soft face in his rough hands and studied her with a cool glance. Her beautiful brown eyes blinked back more tears, and the Executioner knew he'd finally gotten through to her. He thought he knew why she'd come to Canada—he'd sensed her affection for him ever since stealing her from the torture machinations of Kaochu and the Scarlet Dragons.

"I'm sorry," she said.

"Nothing to be sorry for," Bolan told her.

"Hey," Hoffner finally said, blood pouring from his nostrils. He was holding his head back and trying not to choke on the equal amount running down the back of his throat. "Could somebody maybe help me here?"

"I'll get some ice from the cooler," Milaña said, rising from the couch and heading to the refrigerator-freezer.

Bolan released his hold on Rajero's face and then turned to Grimaldi. The awkward moment had passed, and now that he was confident the DEA woman would deliver Hoffner to U.S. authorities in one piece, it was time to get down to business.

"Jack, is the jet fueled?"

Grimaldi nodded. "Yeppers, and ready for action. Frankly, I'm a bit restless myself. This sitting-around stuff really gets to me after a while."

"I hear you. But be careful what you wish for. I think we're about to get more action than we're planning. I need you to get in touch with our friends and tell them we'll need all the support they can give us at our next destination. Shui and Jikwan managed to split before I could put them down."

"Do you know where we're going?"

Bolan nodded. "Hong Kong."

Hong Kong, China

LAU-MING SHUI HAD no doubt Dim Mai was anything but happy to see them when they arrived at the arms broker's penthouse suite in the center of Hong Kong's urban sprawl. He was cordial—almost polite—upon their arrival, but Shui sensed immediately that it was just as Nyenshi Fung had told him over the phone.

"Welcome," Mai said, raising his arms and bowing twice ceremoniously. "Welcome to my home, my friends."

"We're honored by your graciousness," Shui replied, returning the bow in ceremonial fashion.

After further and less formal greetings were exchanged between Mai's counsel and Nyenshi Fung, Shui, Mai and Jikwan settled down for a drink in Dim Mai's private office—unaccompanied by Fung, much to Shui's dismay. He hadn't been able to take his eyes off her for long during their entrance and while he was unhappy that she wasn't sticking close, he understood her reasons for being discreet. After all, the affairs they needed to discuss were the business of men; it was a business in which she had no place and she knew that.

"So, my friends," Mai said, once they had been served and the staff were out of the room, "you've had quite a trip from what I've been told. You must be tired."

"Infuriated is more like it," Shui snapped.

Mai cocked his head and studied Shui. He was frowning, but the Kung Lok's western underboss was quite aware that the beast was probably smiling ear to ear in his heart. Shui had never cared all that much for Mai to begin with, and he cared even less for him now. He'd suffered a terrible tragedy, and significant losses—losses from which he had already considered the fact he might never recover. His plan had been to increase the profits and power of the Kung Lok's presence in America, and instead he had lost nearly everything.

"I am sorry to hear that your home was destroyed," Mai told Shui.

"Thank you."

"Is there anything I can do to help?"

"Well," Shui began, looking in Jikwan's direction before continuing, "I am not yet sure, Dim. General Jikwan seems to feel that his special commandos will be successful against this infernal American, this…butcher. I am not so sure. Even the Scarlet Dragons were unsuccessful in bringing him to his knees, and I am now deeply concerned for Ing, as I still have had no word from him.''

Mai nodded with a contemplative expression, and then suddenly turned his attention to Jikwan. ''What of your men, General? There has been no word from them, either?''

Jikwan shook his head and then did something that took Shui completely by surprise. He lowered his eyes, a sign of humility and respect. It was a gesture Shui had never seen Jikwan do before, not even in the company of his political masters, and he wondered if the gesture were genuine or merely Jikwan's more subtle methods of playing whatever role suited the moment. Over the past few years, the military officer had become more and more unpredictable, both in his behavior and his movements through the various political circles and countries of the world.

In short, he wasn't a man to be trusted, and Shui was sorry he'd ever agreed to come here just so Mai could shame him in person.

''This is not good,'' Mai said in response to Jikwan. He looked at Shui and added, ''Who is this man?''

''I'm not sure exactly who he is,'' Shui replied. ''We do know he's an American, most probably working for his government, and that he is well trained in arts of war. He seems to possess an uncanny skill for escaping death, even against unbelievable odds, and he is persistent.''

''I see.'' Mai was quiet for a time, and Shui decided not to offer any more information than was absolutely necessary.

"And what of you, General?" Mai asked. "What is your assessment of this man?"

Jikwan raised his eyes and said, "There are moments I believe he must be empowered by the demons of an ethereal existence."

Mai nearly choked on his drink, and as he set the tumbler down and dabbed his mouth with a napkin he replied, "You can't be serious."

"I am most serious. This man is a skilled soldier. In this there is no question. His tactics are effective and his methods unorthodox. He fights with the expertise of a veteran, and he seems driven to any length to accomplish his mission. The man has personally killed more than two hundred men since our first encounter with the Mexicans and Colombians. He has destroyed nearly all of the original operations in the United States, the ones that we seized from the Mexicans, and managed to eradicate three of Lau-Ming's major business concerns in Canada."

"He sounds like quite a man," Dim Mai replied.

"He is a menace," Shui said, "and he must be stopped!"

Mai smiled—barely. "Are you asking for my intervention?"

"We've come to you for asylum," Shui said. "At least I have, and I'm begging you to help me, both for concern of the Kung Lok and our people. If this man survived against Jikwan's elite force, he will most certainly come here to finish what he's started. This has me worried."

"You have no reason to be worried, my friend," Mai said, rising and walking toward his desk. He let out a chuckle. "I can assure you that we are quite safe from this...this... What did you say his name was?"

"Mike Belasko," Jikwan replied.

"Probably a cover name or pseudonym if he is working for the Americans."

"Obviously," Shui said.

"And even if he isn't officially employed by his government, say if he is working as a mercenary for one of our other enemies, perhaps the Europeans or a competitor, he most certainly isn't invincible."

Mai picked up the phone and after waiting a few seconds spoke into it in a voice low enough that Shui couldn't make out what he was saying. After concluding the call, Mai returned to his seat and took his drink in hand once more. He sipped the Chinese rice wine with a contemplative expression, and then looked at the two men in turn.

"I am confident of one thing," Mai said. "A man like Belasko, one who is so compulsive and seems to be acting out of some misguided sense of patriotism or duty, will most likely harbor some passion. That passion will be his weakness, and that is what we shall exploit."

"What do you mean?" Shui said.

"I know what he means," Jikwan interrupted. He looked at Mai and continued, "I know what this man's concern is."

"And that is what?" Mai asked.

"The innocent people. He seems particularly careful in picking his targets. He evacuated both the hotel in Las Vegas and the textile factory where Shui's people were packaging drugs."

"Ah, you see, my friend?" Mai said, turning to Shui. "Every man has a weakness, and thanks to the good general here we now know what that is. I will put my men out on the airports. I will need this Belasko's description, and any other information about him you might think useful. We will be ready for him when he arrives. In the meantime, I have a surprise for you this evening, so I would suggest that you get some rest.''

Shui could only nod, seething on the fact that he'd been cornered into this absurd plan conjured by Jikwan and Mai. Both men were as insane as Belasko, but Shui knew it was in his best interest to play along and wait for them to concoct whatever scheme they could to prepare for Belasko's arrival. And it was a crazy scheme. Mai was suggesting some sort of social event for the evening! In the midst of all that was going on, the arms dealer wanted to throw a party! Well, all Shui could do was accept his plan; after all, with the exception of the two bodyguards Kaochu had ordered to accompany Shui to China, he was alone. He'd sent his wife to Beijing to stay with her family until the hostilities ended, both for her protection as much as his own peace of mind. So the best he could do was to find other things to occupy his time.

And Nyenshi Fung was the first thing that came to his mind.

IT WAS LATE AFTERNOON in China by the time Grimaldi and the Executioner's flight touched down and taxied to one of the cargo facility terminals at Hong Kong International Airport. For the sake of expediency, they had opted to hop aboard a Cathay Pacific cargo hauler out of Toronto. Getting inside the country with weapons on short notice, especially considering the heightened security of customs and Chinese intelligence in recent years, seemed more trouble than it was worth, so Stony Man had arranged to supply Bolan with whatever he needed upon his arrival.

Actually, the Executioner was less concerned about

equipment than where he was going to start his search. Intelligence on Dim Mai was sketchy—even from what Price and Kurtzman could dredge out of some rather sophisticated computers. Mai was a gunrunner and known criminal, and celebrated as a hero only in his own country, so he didn't travel much. Within Hong Kong it was said he kept twelve different residences, some inside the city and some in immediate outlying regions, and it was unknown which one he occupied at any given time. When he did travel, he was well guarded to deter assassination attempts, and because of his political affiliations he usually traveled under the umbrella of diplomatic immunity.

However, the activities of the Kung Lok entity in Hong Kong were less of a mystery, so Bolan knew once he'd hit a nerve center or two, the enemy would most likely come to him. Either that, or someone would eventually talk and Bolan would have the information he needed to track down Mai. The Executioner was playing a hunch that this was where Shui and Jikwan would seek to hide. For the most part, Jikwan's people were in Beijing, as were Shui's; only Dim Mai had a significant presence here in Hong Kong. Thus, it seemed likely—especially given his understanding from Milaña that Jikwan had engineered the entire deal between the FARC and Dim Mai—that they would hide like rats under Mai's benevolent protection.

It wouldn't do them any good. Bolan had come to Hong Kong for one purpose, and that was to eradicate the Kung Lok influence in the West once and for all. The Executioner was enough of a realist to know that he couldn't destroy the entire organization in a single campaign. Such a mission would take many months, perhaps even years, and Bolan didn't have that kind of time.

Still, he could blitz their operations in Hong Kong, and by shaking the tree he would see who fell out.

Then he would crush them underfoot.

Once Grimaldi and Bolan had cleared customs, the pilot headed to a nearby airfield to prepare the chopper arranged by Stony Man while Bolan took a taxi to the red-light district. Even at the late hour, the streets were packed with cars and people. Hong Kong was just as Bolan had remembered it. He'd come to the great city dozens of times in previous missions, and he was familiar with the culture and the environment. He'd even learned enough of the language to get by, and he was familiar enough with Chinese customs to pass as a resident alien.

Bolan had the cab drop him three blocks from the rendezvous, and as he stepped out of the vehicle he immediately sensed someone was watching him. He hadn't noticed a tail, but once they had entered the downtown section, the congestion on the streets had slowed the cab enough that a tail could have followed on foot at any point.

The Executioner put his hands in his pockets and strolled along the crowded street, deliberately stopping now and again to look in a window at something. As he walked, he whistled like someone without a care in the world, and his sixth sense began to warn him increasingly of danger. He knew that they—whoever "they" were—wouldn't make their move on a crowded street. Sudden outbreaks of violence weren't uncommon in Hong Kong, particularly against foreigners, but there would be no sense in the Kung Lok making a move like that.

No, they would wait for their opportunity, and the

Executioner had no qualms about offering it to them on a silver platter.

By the time he reached the street where he was scheduled to meet the weapons supplier, Bolan had counted three who were undoubtedly tails, and possibly a fourth. They weren't skilled watchers—that much was obvious—and they looked more like inexperienced and overzealous youths than skilled assassins. Bolan considered for a moment that it was possible he'd drawn the attention of nothing more than a group of street punks, but he quickly dismissed the idea.

The soldier didn't see his contact, and since it didn't seem his tails were planning to make a move, he decided to entice them by entering a small bar. The place was dark, smoky and unoccupied. It was possible they might stay outside and simply watch the place, in which case the Executioner would miss his meet, but they posed the greater risk at this point, as well as the priority.

The Executioner moved over to the bar, leaped over it and in less than a minute he found what he was looking for. It was a lead pipe—about two feet long and encased in a thick, heavy rubber material, but it would do. The bartender emerged from a back room and immediately noticed him, but when the Executioner tossed him a wad of Chinese currency that exceeded a hundred dollars, the barkeep shrugged and went back to his own business. He looked half Chinese and half something, but Bolan couldn't tell what and he didn't care. His attentions were focused on the door as he found a dark corner near it and waited for his quarry.

A minute ticked by and then two. Bolan glanced at his watch and realized he had less than five minutes before rendezvous time. Well, if he'd numbered his tails correctly, he figured it wouldn't be difficult to take three or even four within a few moments. In fact, he was hoping to nab one of them alive. He needed more intelligence on Mai's operations.

And then his opportunity walked through the doorway.

CHAPTER TWENTY-ONE

The Executioner waited until all three men were inside the bar before he stepped from the shadows and made his move.

The bartender, who had gone to the back room and then reemerged once more, had their attention and it was just the distraction Bolan needed. He took the rear guy first, grabbing him by the back of his collar and clubbing him at the knees. The impact of Bolan's weight behind the blow took the guy off his feet, and he landed hard on the barroom floor.

The hood in front of him turned, and Bolan could see he wasn't more than twenty. He definitely wasn't professional, and it was unlikely he was in the Kung Lok, even as a member of the Scarlet Dragons, since he didn't move as if he had any training at all. Bolan caught him clean across the jaw, the rubber-wrapped lead bouncing off his head several times before he hit the ground.

Bolan's weapon, similar to the nightsticks carried by police officers in Germany, worked well. It was strong enough to deflect another object, including those like it along with crowbars, tire irons and baseball bats. The layer of rubber wasn't wrapped tightly against the lead, but rather loose enough to provide an air gap. The net result was when the object struck yielding flesh, the vibrations caused a repeated hammering that was murder to the human body, which made it a crude but highly effective weapon.

The last one managed to clear a Type 59 semiautomatic pistol from beneath his leather jacket, but the one 9 mm shot the hood got off went wide as Bolan stepped inside and cracked the wrist bone of the shooter's gun hand. The pistol flew from his grip, and Bolan immediately worked the advantage. The guy yelped in pain as the Executioner grabbed his arm and drove the point of the pipe into his stomach. Bolan then twisted his enemy's arm with very little effort, and drove him to his knees.

"Who sent you?" the Executioner asked.

The man began to speak in Chinese, but Bolan tapped him on top of the head lightly with the pipe to remind him of what would happen if he didn't start getting some straight and fast answers.

"Try again," Bolan commanded. "I know you speak English, because it's a mandatory second language in China. So quit stalling and start answering."

The one Bolan had caught in the back of the legs started to rise and reach for the pistol, but the Executioner saw him in his peripheral vision. He stepped forward, twisting in such as a way as to force the man he was questioning to accompany him to his knees as he stomped on his would-be assassin's hand. The guy looked up in surprise, and Bolan struck him behind the ear with the pipe. His body slumped to the ground.

Bolan turned his attention back to the leader. "I'm listening."

"W-we work for Dim Mai," the youth replied. "You do—do not know who you-you're dealing with."

"Yes, I do, and that's the problem. Where's Mai now?"

"I do not know." Bolan tightened his grip on the young man's wrist, but he quickly added, "I swear to you, American. We do not get our orders directly from Dim Mai. We work for his assistant."

"And who is that?"

"I cannot tell you his name," the kid said with an expression that betrayed his horror at Bolan's suggestion. "He will kill us."

"If you don't tell me," Bolan replied quietly, "I'll kill you using only this pipe."

It was an empty threat, but the Executioner knew this kind. More than likely he was a coward.

"Okay, I will say," the man said. "But I will never be able to return to this country. You give me asylum in America?"

"Fat chance," Bolan said, shaking him by the back of the collar. "Now cough it up."

"His name is Ran Chikwang."

"Where do I find him?"

"I do not know," the guy said, groaning with the exertion of fighting the pain in his wrist. "He contacts us by phone for our jobs, pays us up front. We always meet him near the Shao Mung Temple."

"What were your instructions?"

"To watch for your arrival in our country."

"You were at the airport?"

The man nodded, and Bolan felt a cold knot settle in the pit of his stomach.

That explained a few bothersome tidbits. For one thing, it confirmed beyond any doubt that Shui and Jik-wan had come to Hong Kong to seek out Dim Mai. It also meant they were onto him—knew everything about him. It didn't matter where Bolan was now, or what he was doing. He wouldn't be able to rest until he took down the Kung Lok once and for all.

It also meant, because Jikwan was involved, that the threesome was working very closely with Hong Kong's politicians. The spy network they had in the Scarlet Dragons was a significant investment. This alliance between high-ranking members of China's leading politicians and the Kung Lok Chinese triad posed more than a distinct security risk to America—it was a direct threat to every American citizen.

As various street gang cells throughout the country, the Scarlet Dragons didn't pose much of a threat. But as a tightly guarded secret in China's espionage activities against the United States, backed by the money and authority of officials within the Chinese government, the Dragons—and their masters in the Kung Lok—were every bit a threat to America's national security.

And Mack Bolan fully intended to get to the heart of the matter concerning the Kung Lok by driving a spear straight through it.

THE CITY LIGHTS TWINKLED and shimmered in the darkness; it was a breathtaking view from the balcony of Dim Mai's penthouse suite. The crown prince of guns actually owned the entire building, but the penthouse was separate from the rest, accessible by only two elevators—one private and one accessible by security and maintenance through key operation—from the main bank. The towering spire of living quarters was occupied by some of the most famous—and infamous—people in China.

The penthouse had also been built well after the building upon which it was founded, and was reinforced with steel and concrete. It didn't occupy the entire space of the building top, allowing room for a private helipad. The areas surrounding the living space and helipad were enclosed by a decorative wrought-iron fencing, and a heavy wire-mesh fence encompassed the outermost periphery, anchored into the top of the parapet by thin, iron poles tightly wound with heavy-gauge wire.

Nyenshi Fung, dressed in a strapless afternoon dress and thin silk robe of deep purple with gold-thread embroidery, looked out on the city that served as the pseudoempire of her husband. But she could only think of Lau-Ming Shui, and she was ashamed of that fact. He'd arrived earlier that evening with the expression and pallor of a beaten man, to be sure, but looking handsome and competent all the same.

Fung couldn't help her feelings for Shui. They had been lovers for a long time in their youth, and that passion wasn't something easily dismissed. In some sense, she was still resentful that Shui had opted to take a more ambitious path, and his plans didn't include her, but she understood the man's passions as much as she loved him. It had become increasingly difficult, since seeing him again in America—however briefly—to think of almost anything else. They had spoken nearly every day, although most of the time Fung had gone out to a public phone. She knew it was possible that her husband monitored the phones, although she had no proof. He hadn't made any mention of her cryptic call to Lau-Ming Shui to warn him of possible retaliation by Dim Mai.

Frankly, she now had to admit how wrong she'd been. It appeared her husband had other plans, peaceful plans. His acceptance of Shui and General Jikwan into his home was only part of the surprise. Now he was actually taking an active role in bringing down the American who had been destroying their operations. Even the thought of the American intrigued her, and she was beginning to wonder when he would come. She knew he *would* come. Eventually, one of Mai's people would make a tactical error, and the American would find out where they were hiding, and he would come and destroy everything, if his past actions were any indication.

Of course, by that time, she would be...

"Good evening."

Fung turned abruptly at the interruption, although she knew who it was. There was no mistaking that smooth, cultured voice—a voice that her whispered her name repeatedly during their intimate moments of the past. Fung smiled and inclined her head toward Shui, something she would only have dared do for no man other than her husband under normal circumstances. She could tell from Shui's expression that the gesture wasn't lost on him.

"Did I startle you?"

Fung returned her attention to the breathtaking vistas of Hong Kong's nightlife and replied, "A little."

Shui sidled up next to her and placed his hands on the wooden balcony railing. He didn't say anything else for a long time, and Fung wasn't exactly sure how to take his silence. She knew what he was thinking; at least, she thought she knew what he was thinking. He was trying to find some way of revealing how he felt about her, and she wanted to pour out her own emotions on him, but she also realized he had important matters on his mind. She didn't want to distract him from making sound decisions—he'd lost everything in Toronto and after all of his hard work he had returned to Hong Kong empty-handed. He was no longer the favorite son.

"It is truly beautiful here," Shui finally said. "I have missed China."

"Yes."

Quietly, Shui added without missing a beat, "And I have missed you."

Fung turned and looked at him, knowing that her surprise was probably evident. He hadn't literally come right out and said he loved her, but it was obvious this was his way of doing it. Shui had revealed his true feelings in his own way, and she couldn't believe he was making these known to her so soon after his arrival.

"I have missed you too, Lau-Ming," Fung replied. "I have missed you so much that it made my heart ache."

Shui appeared to let out a sigh of relief. "So you do feel the same."

"Of course. And I think that you knew it. I did or said nothing to hide my feelings."

"I know," Shui replied. "But I could not... There was not an opportunity to tell you that I felt the same. Until now." He moved closer to her and took her hand. "And now I'm afraid our feelings will betray us. Dim Mai has offered his friendship, and somehow I feel that I'm betraying his kindness."

"You never have to feel beholden to Dim. He wants to help you and honor you. I think I finally realize that now. In fact, he's planning a party tonight in your honor. He's inviting some of his most influential friends in the political parties. You have always loved politics, Lau-Ming, and I'm sure you will enjoy it. I know that perhaps it is hard for you to accept this, but he has always respected you."

Shui chuckled. "You mean, in his own unique way?"

"I suppose that's one way of saying it," she said with a smile, her heart leaping into her throat as Shui's hands

enclosed hers. She looked down at his hands and continued, "He coveted everything you gained. He saw how
successful you were in the West, and he knew he could
never have equaled that success. So he built his own
success in China and across all of the Southeast Pacific.
And then, when he saw how all you had earned was
destroyed in a single week, he realized how blessed he
was. He understood how much you had suffered, and he
asked himself what you would have done if the situa-
tions were reversed. So he decided to lay aside his ambitions and jealousies, and bring you into his own success. He means to protect you."

Shui tried to stand straighter, lifting his chin when he
heard that, and replied, " I don't need protection."

"Of course not," Fung replied quickly. "That wasn't
what I was saying. Not exactly. I was merely suggesting
that he is trying to protect your feelings. Dim is actually
a good and sensitive man. I know that may be difficult
for you to believe. He wants to be successful, and to be
recognized for his accomplishments. But mostly, he
wants the friendship of men like you and General Jikwan. He wants your respect."

"I have nothing but respect for Dim Mai," Shui said,
moving his hands away from hers and taking a deep
breath. Without meeting her gaze, he added, "Which is
why I cannot betray his trust. No matter how I feel about
you, I need Dim's friendship and trust more than ever
right now. I will do nothing, *nothing,* to betray that
trust."

Fung realized the impact of his stinging words, but
simultaneously she understood his reasons. He had to
protect himself and his family first—that was his first
duty and she understood it. She could have only hoped
for that kind of loyalty from Dim Mai. Her husband

would have certainly protected her, given her anything that she asked, but it didn't mean that those things that had brought him to his own greatness wouldn't ultimately take precedence had Mai ever had to choose between her and them.

She knew the decision wouldn't have been difficult for her husband. The Chinese society in general still took a medieval, almost feudal, perspective on the roles of women in society. While Dim Mai thought the world of her—and was rather demonstrative in this fact—she knew he considered her as his property. Therefore, were he forced to choose, he would choose his lifestyle and consider he could always find another like her somewhere. Shui knew this, as well, and despite this he chose to protect his family. It was these admirable qualities about him that made Fung love Shui, and she was sorry that they had parted ways. Still, she knew it was futile to belabor the issue. She had other plans, anyway; they were important plans.

"I understand your dedication to Dim," Fung finally said. "And I respect you for it. I guess it's one of things I love most about you. I always have and I always will."

And then the two of them turned to watch the city in silence.

BOLAN MADE THE MEET with the weapons supplier provided by Stony Man, and after a brief phone conversation with Grimaldi he headed toward the Shao Mung Temple. He had convinced the men sent to tail him that it was in their best interest to contact this Ran Chikwang and arrange a meet at the temple under the story that they had information regarding the American they were assigned to watch for. Bolan had let them go after the leader made the call, which he knew was probably a mistake. They couldn't afford to have their master think they had set him up, and probably called back and told the story of how they had arranged the meet under duress.

Still, it would work to the Executioner's advantage because he knew they would probably act as if they had no idea he was planning to ambush them, and they would, in turn, set up their own ambush. The Executioner was just a little smarter than that. As a matter of fact, he was counting on this move from his enemy, because whoever ambushed him would be doing so under the direct orders of Dim Mai. And Bolan fully intended for them to lead him straight to the head of the Eastern Kung Lok powers.

He now toted a bag that, from an exterior inspection, looked like any normal gym bag, but its contents told an entirely different story. The bag contained an unusual variant to the Executioner's normal choices for armament. His contact had provided him with a pair of Heckler & Koch MP-5 Ks, which were special short versions of the MP-5. This particular version, the A-5, also allowed 3-round burst capability, and iron or telescopic sights, but Bolan had asked for laser sights. The contact was more than happy to reply. Bolan also received six loaded 15-round clips along with two hundred additional rounds of ammo.

Additionally, the trusted Beretta 93-R rode in its customary place beneath his left arm, and the bag also contained four Russian-made RGN offensive hand grenades, which had a wax-RDX filling and an effective range of eight to ten yards. The Executioner was prepared for a blitzing offensive, and he'd wanted to travel light, so his choice of armament was exactly right for his mission.

Bolan arrived at his destination twenty minutes after

he'd hung up with Grimaldi. He took up a position in an alleyway where he could watch the entrance to the Shao Mung Temple unseen by passersby, and still cover himself from assaults in any direction. The Executioner didn't believe he was invincible—he was hardly infallible and definitely not bulletproof. Still, he was a brilliant tactician, a skill that had saved his hide more than a few times.

Grimaldi wasn't enthused about not being able to help the Executioner immediately. It wasn't the Stony Man pilot's wish to be sitting around on his thumbs, waiting for something to happen, but he also realized that when Bolan needed him he'd utilize him. Jack Grimaldi understood all too well that Bolan had to call the shots, and fight the War Everlasting on *his* terms and nobody else's. That was the way Bolan operated, and Grimaldi had grown quite accustomed to it. Still, while Grimaldi didn't thirst for action like David McCarter, he still wanted to feel that he was helping.

"You want to help," the Executioner had told him, "you just be ready to put that chopper in the air on a moment's notice, Jack. Because I still don't have a clue where this is going to go."

"You can count on me, Sarge," Grimaldi had told him.

And Bolan knew it was the unadulterated truth.

The Executioner stood in the shadows nearly forty minutes before something attracted his attention. A vehicle pulled to the curb in front of the temple, and three men got out. Two were definitely security types. They looked small and agile, and were dressed in loose-fitting coats to hide the hardware Bolan knew they were wearing only because of the way they carried themselves. The third man was also Chinese, a little taller, though, with slick black hair.

All three of the men wore sunglasses, even though it was now dark outside. It was obvious that these were Scarlet Dragons, evident by the kerchiefs protruding from the breast pockets of their suit coats. It never ceased to amaze Bolan that these men wore such clear and identifying marks, and yet the Hong Kong police were never seen detaining or arresting them for questioning. As a matter of fact, it was almost as if they avoided members of the Scarlet Dragons. Bolan knew it had nothing to do with ignorance. While those markings might have meant little to most citizens on the streets of America, it was a clear reference in Hong Kong, even to bystanders.

Bolan watched patiently as they walked through the temple entrance. He waited a few minutes, and then knelt to the bag at his feet and withdrew the two MP-5 Ks. He made sure both were in battery, then shed his heavy overcoat to reveal his blacksuit, and slung them along either shoulder by their the cross straps. He then attached the RGNs to retaining hooks on his military webbing, then donned the overcoat once more. He stowed the bag in a garbage container before walking across the street.

A man suddenly emerged from the driver's seat, obviously noticing Bolan was headed for the temple entrance. The sight of an American intent on entering a Chinese Taoist sanctuary was unusual, to be sure, but probably especially so during such a time of heightened alert. The guy called to Bolan, but the Executioner ignored him, acting as if he didn't hear the man above the sounds of beeping horns and sudden rush of traffic.

The driver-sentry started to reach beneath his coat,

and Bolan was certain he knew what the guy was reaching for—but he couldn't actually take the chance of risking the lives of bystanders unless he knew for sure. He readied himself by nonchalantly reaching beneath the coat and wrapping his hand around the cold handle of the Beretta 93-R. He turned to look in the man's direction, waiting until he caught his first sight of the pistol as his enemy cleared the weapon from shoulder leather. Bolan turned his body in such a way that he presented a narrower target while at the same time drawing the Beretta from his shoulder holster without actually bringing it into view.

Bolan squeezed the trigger, and suddenly three small holes appeared in the side of the overcoat just milliseconds before three red blotches appeared in the driver's midsection. The subsonic cartridges hardly caused a report, and to observers it looked as if the driver had suddenly reached for his chest before keeling over. Several onlookers immediately rushed to the man and, in the confusion of it all, Bolan holstered the Beretta and calmly walked through the front door of the temple unnoticed.

The interior was dimly lit. Bolan shed the overcoat to reveal the twin H&K machine pistols, and scanned the darkness with every sense attuned. He didn't hear anything, but Bolan could sense that the enemy was lying in wait.

As the warrior passed beyond the vestibule and entered the temple proper, he immediately noticed the place appeared empty. There were no Taoist monks at the altars, and none standing against the highly decorative walls, painted with the brilliant reds, blacks and golds so prevalent in great Chinese art.

But then, following a minute of silence, the enemy

appeared. Bolan turned to his left to catch two Scarlet
Dragons with a short burst from one of the MP-5 Ks,
spraying a volley that ripped open their chests and bel-
lies. The temple echoed with the report of autofire as the
two men danced under the impact before crashing to the
ground in a tangled heap of arms and legs.

Bolan whirled and dropped to one knee as another two
Dragons took up firing positions and burned the air
above his head with pistol fire. The Executioner triggered both MP-5 Ks, peppering his enemy with 9 mm
slugs. One took a majority of the bullets in his chest and
coughed blood before he sank to the hardwood floor, his
blood flowing freely and staining the thick, red carpet
that covered the center area. The second died an iden-
tically gruesome death, many of the shots hitting him in
nonvital areas before a fatal round severed his spine. The
Dragon's body stiffened before he fell face first against
a pillar and then slid to the ground.

Six more Dragons jumped from the cover of a large
brass gong brandishing a variety of pistols, machine pistols and submachine guns. The Executioner sent a furious volley of 9 mm rounds from one of the MP-5 Ks to
keep their heads down as he yanked an RGN from his
belt. He pressed the pin to the floor beneath his boot to
anchor it so he could prime the explosive. As the chamber of the machine pistol clacked backward on an empty
magazine, Bolan tossed the grenade and then threw himself to the floor.

The hand bomb exploded on impact, the sound of the
gong dislodging from its swinging mount and crashing
to the ground reverberating as the sounds of the explosion died. Several of the Dragons were killed immediately, while the others managed to survive with few or
no injuries. Bolan stepped forward and quickly dis-

patched them with controlled 3-round bursts from the other MP-5 K.

After Bolan took down the last of his enemy, he dropped behind the cover of a pillar and reloaded both weapons. Then he heard a noise above him and in the darkness he could barely make out a shadow that was running across some kind of narrow catwalk that bordered the temple. Bolan aimed his weapons in that direction to counter the threat, but it looked as if the shadowy figure was intent on fleeing, not attacking.

The soldier moved away from the pillar, watching his surroundings for ambushers on the off chance the fleeing form was simply trying to draw him into the open rather than attempting to escape. Bolan continued along the wall, following the same path and tracking his quarry by sound. Then the running abruptly ceased, and Bolan stopped and crouched, watching the area above for any sign of a threat. He waited nearly a minute before hearing a commotion at the front entrance.

The Executioner rushed for the doorway that led back to the temple entrance, and he nearly walked into the wall of autofire sprayed in his direction by the pair of bodyguards he'd first observed out front. He shoulder rolled and got to one knee, triggering his MP-5 Ks and hammering his enemy with a fusillade of 9 mm Parabellum rounds. The bullets punched holes through hearts, lungs and stomachs, spraying the walls and door behind the pair with gore.

Bolan leaped over the fallen bodies, emerging onto the street in time to watch the man he assumed was Chikwang jump behind the wheel of the white Mercedes and lurch away from the curb, tires smoking and squealing in protest. A few angry drivers leaned on their horns as this madman nearly ran into their vehicles trying to merge with the solid line of speeding traffic. Onlookers studied Bolan with mixed looks of fear and puzzlement, and when he realized it, he quickly pulled the overcoat around him to conceal the guns.

Bolan then jogged a few blocks to a pay phone and called Grimaldi.

"What's up, Sarge?"

"Saddle up, Jack. You're looking for a white Mercedes." Bolan gave him the road and general direction in which it was headed. "Traffic is heavy tonight, and there aren't a lot of white Mercedes in Hong Kong, so I don't think you'll have trouble locating it. I need you to find this thing and track it."

"Consider it done."

"When you find it, meet me back at the airport and pick me up."

"Roger that."

Bolan hung up and then hailed a taxi to take him back to the cargo facilities at Hong Kong International. He had a score to settle with the Kung Lok.

And the numbers were running down.

CHAPTER TWENTY-TWO

"You're serious?" Bolan asked Hal Brognola as Grimaldi lifted the chopper off the helipad and ascended into Hong Kong's night sky.

Grimaldi had received the excited call from Stony Man as he was landing, and the head Fed had demanded to speak with Bolan immediately. The soldier's face was filled with grim determination as he listened to what Brognola told him over the secured satellite linkup created by Aaron Kurtzman, which allowed two-way communications almost anywhere in the world at any given time.

"I'm dead serious, Striker," Brognola replied. "The organized-crime unit of the Hong Kong police department have been waiting for this opportunity for years. They claim to have an agent buried very deep and very close to Dim Mai, and they claim there's a party tonight that Mai's apparently holding in honor of the arrival of Shui and Jikwan."

"Do we know where?"

"Haven't been able to get that information yet. Apparently, the operation to raid the party and arrest key targets is being kept confidential until just before the raid goes down. We don't where yet, but we do know it's scheduled for 2300 hours."

Bolan looked at his watch. That was less than two hours. "What kind of party is this?" Bolan asked.

"The kind where lots of important people rub elbows with lots of other important people. Some major political hitters are involved with Dim Mai. The faces there will be many of the same faces that met at the hotel in West Palm Beach about a week ago."

"The one that included Shui, Mai and Jikwan," Bolan concluded.

"Exactly."

"Well, that washes with what Milaña told us. It does look like the Chinese diplomats who've been touting peace are actually in bed with the largest triad in the world."

"And I think Mai's planning to solidify the relationship between the Eastern and Western factions tonight," Brognola replied.

"You could be more right than you know. Mai's people were on to me as soon as we got in-country. I think the Kung Lok is a lot bigger here than I originally thought. I figure if I'm going to stop this thing, I'm going to have to go to the heart of their operation. I think that's Dim Mai."

"Well, I trust your judgment. We'll give you whatever support you need on this end, up to and including sending in Phoenix Force to help if that's what it takes."

"I'll keep it in mind. By the way, who came by this information on Mai's party?"

"Barbara got it through one of her NSA contacts who's connected with a heavy hitter in the Hong Kong police department. The guy's actually an American liaison agent who works with the organized-crime division to coordinate efforts against smuggling operations from Hong Kong to the American West Coast. We've tried to keep the law-enforcement ties open between our two countries. We work on preventing smuggling Chinese artworks, which are particularly priceless on the black market, into our country. In return, the Chinese help us keep out guns, drugs and slave labor."

"Based on everything I saw of Shui's operations," Bolan said gruffly, "it doesn't look like they're doing a very good job."

"I couldn't agree more. But it does give us a presence in Hong Kong, and that's vital to our intelligence networks."

"Well, at least it gives me something to go on. Jack managed to trace one of Mai's cronies to a small warehouse at some seaside docks. We're headed there now to take care of business. I'm hoping that this doesn't turn out to be a dead end."

"Well, watch your back, Striker."

"Always."

"And as soon as we know anything, we'll be in touch. I know you've got a job to do, but I felt it was important to let you know about this. I know it's your policy never to drop the hammer on a cop, and I figured it was prudent to let you know that if you hit Mai where he lives and breeds, it's possible you'll have friendlies to watch out for, as well."

"I appreciate the heads-up," Bolan replied. "Out here."

"What's up?" Grimaldi asked after Bolan broke the connection and switched back to the VOX frequency.

"It looks like I've got my work cut out for me," Bolan said. "Hal thinks that when and if I find out where Mai's at, I'm going to have to watch out for a police raiding party."

"Great."

"Yeah, that's not what I needed to hear right now," Bolan said.

The Executioner wasn't really complaining about Brognola's news, but he didn't like the idea that he'd have to watch for cops now. The key would be to shut down Mai's base of operations before the Hong Kong PD raiding party got to him first. There was no question in Bolan's mind that Mai wouldn't go down without a fight, and if Mai was forewarned of the attack, it would be a bloodbath for the HKPD.

That meant Bolan would have to get to them first. He didn't have a choice. But for the moment, he needed to concentrate on the task at hand and see if he couldn't get the information on where to find Mai. And he would have to start with the warehouse where he knew Mai's people were operating.

It took only ten minutes for Grimaldi to get to the site, and he put the helicopter down inches above the warehouse roof. Bolan came off the Kiowa chopper, the MP-5 Ks ready for action. He'd shed the overcoat, and now he was attired in just his blacksuit, his face smeared with combat cosmetics. He advanced across the roof like a specter of swift justice and retribution. Bolan reached the roof edge of the warehouse and risked a glance over the side. Two Scarlet Dragons, dressed in fatigues and combat boots, stood outside a door clutching Jatimatic machine pistols. Their eyes were turned skyward, searching for the source of the noise of the helicopter. Grimaldi passed directly over the Executioner a moment later to draw their attention.

They pointed at the chopper, shouting at each other and then raised their weapons to fire. Bolan already had an RGN out and primed for action. He released the grenade, the spoon flipping away from it as the heavy hand bomb dropped into the midst of the two Dragons who were now concentrating on blowing Grimaldi out of the sky. The grenade exploded, the RDX filling instantly incinerating the two men, the concussion ripping the door they were guarding from its hinges.

Bolan waited for the debris to settle before climbing over the side and dropping to the very narrow ledge outside one of the factory's windows. The Executioner immediately pressed his body to the glass, enough to keep his muscular form balanced precariously on the ledge. He looked through the glass and noticed a small army of Scarlet Dragons rushing across the first floor of the warehouse, headed in the general direction of the explosion. Bolan could see that the second floor actually comprised a large, metal walkway that wound its way through crates stacked from floor to the ceiling.

The Executioner tried the window and found it was unsecured. He lifted it and jumped inside, watching for his enemy to notice him. The majority of the Dragons rushing to help their fallen comrades were so intently focused on the destruction that they didn't notice Bolan. He decided to use this to his advantage and let them know he was there in a more spectacular fashion.

Bolan found an area on the second-floor catwalks that provided an excellent view of the first-floor activity while affording him some decent cover. He leaned over the nearest railing and opened fire. The machine pistols shook, spitting flame from their muzzles as Bolan poured the wrath of autofire onto the enemy troops. Some went down immediately under the assault of 9 mm Parabellum rounds, while others stopped short and looked up with complete surprise, trying to determine from where the destruction was coming.

A few managed to think on their feet and go for the

cover of crates as soon as Bolan opened up on them. The Executioner was quick but selective, trying to conserve ammunition for shots that made sense. His assault was intended to deliver the most amount of destruction with the least amount of sacrifice, and he was doing just that. The Scarlet Dragons had been taken completely unawares, and they were now finding out firsthand why their American counterparts had failed so miserably against this one-man army.

Bolan dropped the magazines, reloaded and then advanced to another position for some fresh targets. He opened up again, shooting a few straight through the top of the head, first taking out the targets that were immediately below him since they had the ability to potentially shoot him through the catwalk where he couldn't really see them or return fire effectively. About a dozen of the Dragons got smart, moving into cover and heading for stairwells that would provide them access to the second floor.

Bolan had already factored this into his plan. He switched positions once more, loading his last two 15-round magazines and blasting away at any Dragons who moved, foolishly trying to gain an advantage by going for any area they thought would provide them cover and a chance to take out the Executioner. One Dragon managed to get lucky and found himself in a position for a shot. The bullet ricocheted off the catwalk railing, however, and then it was Bolan's turn. The soldier went prone, snap-aimed one of the MP-5 Ks and squeezed the trigger, shooting the man through the head. The Dragon's skull exploded under the close-range impact of the 9 mm, and his body convulsed before falling to the ground.

Bolan switched positions in the shadows and pulled

another RGN from his belt. As he yanked the pin, he watched with interest as the Dragons below leapfrogged among the crates, desperately searching for him. He could tell by the expressions on their faces that they had no idea where he was, so most of them concentrated on covering their comrades, who had now managed to access the catwalk that comprised the upper level of the warehouse.

Bolan remained completely still, gripping the grenade and waiting for the correct opportunity. The Executioner had a good plan, but it would take split-second timing and unbelievable restraint. Too early and he'd blow his cover—too late and he'd blow himself to kingdom come. Bolan secured the MP-5 Ks so they wouldn't make noise when he decided to act.

The Executioner lay absolutely still, marking his targets and watching carefully as two fire teams of Dragons now moved in and out of the shadows of the catwalks. He watched and waited, measuring his respirations and breathing slowly and evenly. The two fire teams drew closer and closer until they were now on the same section of the catwalk but on opposite sides and closing on his position. In the darkness, and given that Bolan's face was blackened by cosmetics, they still didn't see him.

When the two teams were within about fifteen yards, Bolan set the grenade next to him and then rolled beneath the catwalk railing and dropped to the ground below. As he entered the light, the two fire teams advanced on his position, neither cognizant that they were headed right for destruction. Bolan sought quick cover behind a crate and the fire teams actually got off a few rounds before the grenade exploded.

A ball of flame engulfed the immediate area under and around the eight men, propelling superheated fragments of wood, metal and glass in every direction. Sparks popped from the warehouse lights—not all of which were on—as the fixtures were separated from their mounting boxes. There were pops and sizzles as flames erupted from the broken electrical connections and began to slowly spread across the ceiling, fueled by the heat from the explosion.

Bolan was on his feet and moving before all of the debris had settled. Two attackers emerged from cover on the left, but the Executioner was ready for them. He triggered the MP-5 K under his left shoulder, which still held ammo, and cut one across the midsection and the second with a 3-round burst that shattered the gunner's hip and thigh. The Executioner didn't lose a stride as he continued toward the gaping exit he'd created at the beginning of his assault.

The soldier continued through the warehouse, avoiding the Dragons where he could and eliminating those he couldn't. He kept his eyes open for the man he assumed was Chikwang. One trio of Dragons nearly surprised the Executioner, but he shoulder rolled in time to avoid being ventilated by a swarm of 9 mm autofire. He rolled to one knee and triggered his weapon, emptying the last of the machine pistol's clip on two of the three. One took a 3-round burst in the face, which splattered the man behind him with flesh and gray matter. The second fell in midcharge, the low-velocity hollowpoint slugs ripping flesh from his stomach and groin.

The remaining Dragon charged Bolan with a bloodcurdling scream, now apparently out of ammo, his weapon held over his head like a club. The Executioner whipped the Beretta from the holster and shot the man point-blank. The bullet passed clean through his liver and out his right kidney, but the Dragon continued forward, carried now by sheer weight. The soldier barely moved out of the way in time to avoid a full collision, and the man crashed to the ground face first.

There was another shout as a man leaped from a crate immediately above Bolan and dropped onto his back, knocking the Beretta from his grip. The impact drove the air from Bolan's lungs, but the soldier quickly recovered from the attack. He drove an elbow backward and managed to catch his assailant in the stomach. The man grunted with the impact, but it didn't seem to weaken his grip. He'd managed, in the moment of surprise, to get a forearm wrapped around Bolan's throat and he was cutting off the flow of oxygenated blood.

Stars popped in front of Bolan's eyes, and he could already feeling himself sink into unconsciousness. He knew that the sleeper hold was capable of rendering a full-grown man unconscious in less than a minute, and although the attacker was only two-thirds Bolan's size, he was strong and agile. Bolan tried to drive the back of his head into the guy's face, but the assailant had his head turned in such a position as to protect himself from the tactic.

Bolan wheezed for air but immediately realized the mistake as the momentary lapse afforded the man a tighter grip on his neck. The Executioner was becoming desperate, but he quelled any panic and let his senses relax even though they were screaming at him to get free. His best weapon at this point was his mind, and the only way he would take down his opponent was through his wits. It was obvious that his attacker didn't understand the same concept, because he suddenly relaxed his hold some, obviously convinced Bolan was succumbing to the pressure.

It wasn't much of a release—but it was enough.

Bolan's lungs burned with relief as he sucked in two quick breaths. His opponent suddenly realized that his adversary wasn't as subdued as he'd originally thought, and he tried to regain the advantage.

It didn't work.

Bolan, with renewed energy, reached around to the small of his back and managed to grab the Dragon by the groin. He squeezed with enough force to cause his enemy to release his grip and scream with pain. The man never completed his exclamation as Bolan spun and delivered an elbow strike that cracked his upper jaw. The man's teeth caught on the soft tissue of his lip, and blood spurted onto the sleeve of Bolan's blacksuit. The Executioner continued his spin, releasing his hold on the man's groin as he crouched and executed a leg sweep. The move knocked the Dragon off his feet, and he landed on his back, his head smacking the concrete. Bolan finished the attack with a stomp kick to the man's throat. His opponent choked on his own blood and crushed cartilage.

The Executioner quickly retrieved his Beretta and continued for the exit. He'd arranged an extraction time with Grimaldi, and the drawn-out fight with the Dragon had cost him precious minutes. And there was still no sign of Chikwang. The fire he'd started was spreading so rapidly across the timber ceiling of the dilapidated warehouse that the Dragons now seemed more intent on escaping the destruction than paying him any concern.

Bolan moved through the cover of smoke and darkness unmolested. He had just emerged through the gaping exit left by the grenade he'd used to take out the sentries when he saw Chikwang headed for a distant outbuilding. There were two Dragons accompanying him, and it looked as if he kept turning to shout orders at them.

The *whup-whup* of the chopper blades was closing on his position rapidly, and Bolan waited until he was in Grimaldi's sight before he waved in the direction of the fleeing trio. It took the Stony Man flier only a second to realize what Bolan was trying to say. Grimaldi whipped the chopper into a sharp turn and flew over the running men as Bolan sprinted after them on foot. The pilot waited until he was about fifty yards ahead and then dropped down in their path, landing the chopper with the blinding speed and control indicative of a veteran flier.

The men slowed, then came to a stop and started to change directions. The Executioner's long strides now got him within shooting range of his quarry. A couple of quick, well-aimed shots dumped one of Chikwang's Dragon escorts into the water, and dropped the other in his tracks, leaving Chikwang to stand alone. The guy started to reach inside his jacket but Bolan shook his head.

"Don't do it!" As he got closer, the Executioner added, "You won't make it."

"Don't shoot!" the man replied in accented but clear English, slowly drawing a wallet from his coat and letting it fold open. "I'm a policeman!"

HIS REAL NAME WAS Nang Bailun, and he was indeed a cop with the Asian police force in Hong Kong that specialized in organized crime. His accent was actually more British than Chinese, which didn't come as a big surprise to either of them. Bailun wasn't the first Chinese man surrounded by the British influence, and he certainly wouldn't be the last.

"How long have you had someone inside?" Bolan asked Bailun.

The Executioner was seated across from the man in the booth of a small, run-down eatery. Grimaldi sat next to the guy where he could easily cover him with the pistol beneath his coat, and Bolan could watch both of their backs by keeping his eye on the door. Bailun had suggested the place because it was in a quiet, small, out-of-the-way part of town where they could be assured of some privacy. The Executioner had agreed to put off his activities briefly and hear the cop out, but not until Bailun agreed not to try to contact his department first, and only under those conditions.

Bailun took a sip of the strong tea and then replied, "About two years."

"How close is this person?"

"She's close. She's *real* close."

The Executioner raised his eyebrows. "She?"

"Yeah," Bailun replied with a curt nod. "Her name is Nyenshi Fung. She's Dim Mai's wife, and she's been feeding me and my people information on his activities."

"Can you trust her?" Grimaldi interjected.

Bailun stared at the pilot a moment, acting as if he really had to think it through. His expression set off an alarm in the Executioner's psyche. It was quite possible that Bailun didn't trust her, and that meant she wasn't reliable. And if Fung wasn't reliable, it was all too possible her information wasn't reliable, either. In fact, it meant she might have been feeding the cops bad intelligence from the start. It was the oldest trick in the book. Her reliability was now predicated on the answer to Bolan's next question.

"Did she come to you?"

"No, we approached her," Bailun replied immediately.

"You didn't answer my question," Grimaldi said. "Do you trust her?"

"Yes, we trust her. The reason I didn't answer you right away was because I'm not entirely sure I trust you yet."

"Fair enough," Bolan interjected, intent on getting the conversation back in control and steering Bailun in the direction he needed. "But I give my personal assurance that we're on your side."

"Are you?" Bailun asked.

"Yeah. But I know you're planning to bring down Dim Mai soon, and I can't have you getting in the way."

"We wouldn't have been in the way. I was expecting you."

"How?"

Bailun shrugged with an expression that said the answer was already obvious. "Nyenshi told us. Mai's been expecting you for some time now, a fact of which I'm sure you are already aware."

"The thought crossed my mind," Bolan said.

"Unfortunately, you got onto me faster than I had intended."

"It was you I saw leaving that Buddhist temple," Bolan remarked. "Care to explain why you set me up for an ambush?"

"I didn't. After I got the call from those punks you talked into setting me up, I knew they would report the information to their superiors. They would have to explain how one American could have dishonored them. The street gangs in China have something of an honor system."

"I know about the street gangs in China," Bolan said. "Go on with your story."

"I was trying to get there in time to avoid the trap I knew they would set for you. I had no idea you were so...well, talented."

"Yes," Grimaldi chimed in with a beaming expression, "we're quite proud of him for that."

The joke wasn't lost on Bailun, who laughed under his breath.

The Executioner couldn't refrain from smiling, either. There were moments when Grimaldi's slapstick sense of humor was a welcome relief. The stress of the past few days had left Bolan exhausted, and only by keeping up his sense of humor did he find some form of relief.

"Well," the Executioner finally said, "I don't know when you're planning on hitting Dim Mai, but there won't be much to hit."

"You mean you still intend to go through with your plans?"

Bolan nodded. "I don't have any choice. My people won't be able to rest as long as the Kung Lok have any real power. The only way to put them down is by cutting out the heart."

"That is our intent, as well," Bailun said with some consternation. "Although we would like to take Mai alive and see that he stands trial. Can't you cooperate with us on this?"

"Look," Bolan said quietly but firmly, "you and I both know there won't be any cooperation between me and officials within your department. We do things differently. They would like to avoid a scene. I intend to make one, because it's the only statement animals like Mai and Shui understand. I'm not in this for glory or gain. I do what I do out of necessity. Maybe my tactics won't completely disassemble the Kung Lok organization, but they will certainly think twice before trying to start another turf war in America.''

''In what way?''

''In the ashes of their leaders. Now, I can promise you that I'll get this Fung out alive. And if I can manage it, I'll keep Mai alive so your people can have a piece out of him. But Deng Jikwan and Lau-Ming Shui are finished. Deal?''

Bailun studied the Executioner for a moment, then extended his hand with a smile and replied, ''Deal.''

CHAPTER TWENTY-THREE

Lau-Ming Shui watched with interest as Dim Mai and Nyenshi Fung stood in the reception area of Mai's posh luxury penthouse and greeted their honored guests.

Even Shui had to admit that the party list was quite impressive. Many of the arrivals were either wealthy businesspeople or influential in a multitude of political circles. There were members of the city cabinet ministry present, along with the mayor of Hong Kong, and some dignitaries visiting from a province in northern Mongolia, where—if memory served Shui correctly—there were some hidden Chinese missile sites holding nuclear ICBMs.

In addition to Mai's friends, a few of Jikwan's contacts were also present. One of the assistant ministers of defense for the South China Sea region was there, along with members of the Chinese admiralty, and even one protectorate attaché with the premier's office. And throughout the room, dressed in tuxedos and obviously not part of the elite crowd, were Scarlet Dragons acting as security.

Mai had told Shui earlier that evening that he wasn't expecting Belasko to show up, since the American had no idea where they were, but he wanted to be ready just the same. Shui was skeptical either way. Thus far, even

Jikwan's elite military troops hadn't been able to bring down Belasko, let alone a half-dozen or so Dragons in formal dress. However, Shui was the first to remember that looks were deceiving, and that—aside from the fact Mai was a cunning individual—the penthouse was quite secure from any sort of official or unofficial ground raid. The added reinforcement would also contain any stray gunfire, if it came to that.

Still, in spite of himself, Shui was feeling pretty comfortable. It was time to start mingling with some of Shui's and Jikwan's friends, and reestablishing some of his acquaintances. After his miserable failures in Canada and America, Shui could only hope he had not entirely lost his credibility with the elite class.

He had turned to observe the room, looking for any familiar face watching him, or at least with an expression that they were willing to lend a sympathetic ear, when he suddenly felt a hand slip through his arm. He turned a surprised glance to Fung. He looked wildly in Mai's direction, but the arms dealer wasn't even paying attention. Obviously, Fung had managed to slip away unnoticed, while her husband puffed his chest at people and acted the role of a gregarious host.

"You're neglecting your guests?" he asked her.

Fung smiled. "Not really. They are in capable hands." She leaned up to his ear and whispered, "As you know, Dim is quite the diplomat."

He didn't say anything, just nodding and grinning as she gently steered him away from the reception area. She maneuvered their way through the crowd, all the while tugging on his arm while somehow managing to make it look as if he were actually the one doing the leading. Her grace and poise was as fantastic as her beauty, and Shui wondered how he could have ever let his own ambitions get in the way of experiencing such a consummate woman.

Yet, he couldn't escape the truth of his vow, and he wouldn't violate his loyalties to either Dim Mai or his wife. He wanted to; he wanted to give her every part of his mind and body. But he was a man of honor and allegiance, and he knew she understood this. She had never treated him unfairly since their first reunion after so many years had passed, and while he'd told her how he felt, she hadn't acted upon it. It would have been easy to give in and to surrender everything to her, but then he would have been compromising more than his conscience would ever allow. That compromise wasn't worth the few hours of bliss, even in the arms of a woman like Nyenshi Fung.

Shui then saw, as they reached a break in the crowd, the object of Fung's attention. It was the attaché to the premier's office. He was a tall, graying man with gentle brown eyes. He seemed in good shape, standing there talking with a couple of other dignitaries that he'd obviously deemed worthy of his notice. Most everyone else in the room, with the exception of the Mongolians and the staffers from the Chinese defense ministry, were either city officials or known criminals. This man wouldn't have been caught dead mingling with either; he would have considered them common riffraff.

The attaché stopped talking and turned to look at Shui. A moment later, the two men simultaneously recognized each other, and they bowed in concert.

"Lau-Ming Shui," the man said, shaking Shui's hand.

Shui could hardly believe his eyes as he stared into the face of none other than Ji-Zhi Wul. Wul had served as Shui's former mentor and his chief instructor at the political school that, at that time, had been sponsored by high-ranking Soviet diplomats hoping to increase the sphere of Red Chinese influence throughout the Asian Pacific. Shui had always respected Wul, not only for the man's insight into Chinese politics, but also for his strength and guidance in the face of adversity. In many ways, Wul had brought focus to Shui's life, and he'd never forgotten the man for it.

"It is a pleasure to see you again, master," Shui said, bowing once more.

"Please, we may dispense with such formalities," Wul said. "It has been many years. I do not think it is any longer necessary to address me by such an honorific. You have earned your place in society as a man, and a very fine man, as I understand it."

"I am glad I have not lost favor with you."

Wul chuckled, his laugh almost like the cackle of a hen. He'd once had a strong, vivacious laugh, but the years hadn't been kind to him. Shui estimated he had to be in his early seventies now. It had been more than thirty years, but Shui was remembering his former teacher and mentor as if it were yesterday. Only the puffiness around the eyes and the age spots on his wrinkled hands betrayed his age.

"You could never lose favor with me, Lau-Ming." He excused himself of the present company and pulled Shui aside, adding, "Do not be discouraged. I am aware of your recent losses. Your wife's father called me as soon as she had arrived. We understand perfectly, and we will see to it that those responsible are punished. No American will dare to dishonor the People's Republic of China and live to tell about it."

"I am honored by your grace," Shui said with another bow. "And most certainly undeserving."

"Come now," Wul said, cackling some more. "You

must realize that we all suffer setbacks. You are quite respected in the eyes of our political office. We are sorry to see you suffer such losses, but I am simultaneously hopeful you will consider an offer to come live in Beijing and serve on my staff.''

''Serve with the premier's staff?'' Shui could hardly believe his fortune. ''I would be honored.''

''Good.'' Wul nodded with satisfaction.

Then abruptly, the entire room seemed to suddenly swell with a massive vibration, and simultaneously everybody stopped talking. It was as if everyone stood frozen in place for a single heartbeat, trying to determine the source of the heavy reverberations pulsing in their ears. A moment later, the source of the noise became evident when a man crashed through an upper window of the penthouse on a wire. The thrumming became much clearer now, the sounds of the chopper blades unimpeded by the heavy glass of Mai's penthouse. The man landed on his feet, no longer connected to the wire that disappeared from the view of the window.

He was an ominous sight, attired in black from head to toe, with black cosmetics on his face. He held a machine pistol in each hand, and grenades dangled from a military harness. He also wore a pistol in shoulder holster. Even from his position on the first floor, looking up at the balcony that looked down upon the main entertainment area, Shui could see the icy blue of the man's eyes. They were cold and hard in the glint of the bright penthouse lights, and they burned with an ominous fervor.

WHEN BOLAN SWUNG through the window on a cable suspended from the chopper, he knew he'd have only a few seconds for a threat assessment. Mostly, he simply counted on surprise and confusion amid the party guests to provide him enough cover and present enough confusion for the Scarlet Dragons that he'd have time to determine the enemy's location and numbers.

His plan worked beautifully. As he slapped the quick disconnect on the cable hook-up and landed catlike on his feet, the women and men on the upper balcony ran into one another in the hopes of escape. Some women were screaming, and even a few men, at the malevolent sight. The Executioner had produced the desired effect, and he quickly scanned the upper level to count four Dragon toughs. Two were on the opposite of the balcony, trying to clear the weapons but having trouble due to the crowd of people rushing for the only stairwell to the lower level. The remaining two were to his left and right.

The one to Bolan's left acted with admirable speed and vigor, but he was hardly ready for the Executioner. Bolan swung the MP-5 K in his left hand and triggered the weapon, shooting a 3-round burst that pierced the Dragon's hand as he was reaching for his weapon, then continued through his chest and heart. The Dragon soldier did a strange pirouette before collapsing to the ground.

The second threat came in the form of the Dragon on his immediate right, who charged Bolan with a knife in each hand. He tried a slashing move, but the soldier managed to step in and drop to one knee. The guy went straight over the Executioner's back, and Bolan helped him to the first floor by rising and turning so the man's body went airborne over the railing. His body crashed to the ground twenty feet below, head first, in a grotesque heap.

The remaining two had gotten clear of the crowd and

now managed to clear their weapons and line of fire. The Executioner rolled away from the shots, got to one knee and stuck the muzzles of both MP-5 Ks through the gratelike safety railing of the balcony. He triggered the weapons simultaneously as a few of the rounds ricocheted off his almost ineffective cover. The bodies of both Dragons twitched and danced under the impact of multiple 9 mm Parabellum slugs, and turned to run into each other before falling.

Bolan got to his feet. As he continued to move around the circular balcony, heading toward the stairs leading to the lower main level, he looked over the railing and watched for his enemies. It took only a moment to spot Jikwan and Shui. He still didn't see anything of Mai, but he did notice that Shui looked as if he were trying to protect a woman. A second look and Bolan immediately realized the face looking up at him belonged to Nyenshi Fung.

The Executioner had promised Bailun he'd get her out alive, and he meant to keep that promise.

"WHAT ARE YOU WAITING for?" Jikwan screamed into a small transmitter. Lau-Ming Shui couldn't tell if his rubicund pallor was the result of liquor or rage, but the military officer was obviously infuriated. "He's shooting the place up! Do it now!"

It came as some surprise to Shui when several closet doors, as well some doors leading to the various bedrooms, burst open. The rooms seemed to vomit men dressed in black combat fatigues and berets. They didn't wear the symbol of the Scarlet Dragons, and Shui could immediately tell they were more of Jikwan's special forces, simply by the way they moved.

The room became a cacophonous chamber of noise,

the autofire and sounds of broken glass, plastic and wood rumbling through the air as every one of Jikwan's soldiers opened up on Belasko. Flame and hot sparks spit from the muzzles of their Type 85 SMGs as they hammered the upper level with 7.62 mm Soviet rounds. A variant of the gas-operated Type 79, the Type 85 used a blow-back design. Shui knew it was the preferred weapon of Chinese special forces, and now seeing one in action he could understand why.

Shui didn't risk an upward look for fear of losing an eye or being hit in the face by flying debris. The smell of burned gunpowder and dust from the assault burned his nostrils, and he hugged Fung tightly to him, keeping his body over hers to shelter her from falling plaster, wood and glass. His ears rang with the vicious blasts issuing from the Type 85s, and a part of him almost regretted he'd even come here. Still, he wasn't going to be in nearly as bad a shape as Belasko, and that thought brought a smile to his lips.

THE EXECUTIONER HAD BEEN expecting resistance, but not to the degree he'd met so far. As he reached the stairwell, a group of at least twenty of Jikwan's special forces appeared below and began to flood the upper floor, the rounds from the Chinese-made submachine guns ventilating everything around him. Bolan barely managed to escape the onslaught, drawing back as bullets whined past his head and crashed into the ceiling. He reached up to his harness for a grenade but then thought better of it. There were innocent people down there, as well, and he was intent on making sure they didn't get hurt.

A quick glance to his right gave Bolan his idea. It was a large wooden chest made of almost paper-thin cedar.

Enough to contain a blast to a very confined area, but not so much as to risk the lives of those in the periphery. He snatched two of the RGN grenades from his harness, yanked the pins, then quickly opened the drawer of the waist-high chest and tossed them inside. He closed the drawer and then, insuring to keep it tilted back, he picked it up and tossed it over the railing, barely escaping a new hail of gunfire.

Bolan couldn't see what was happening from his point of cover, but he could imagine the results. He could hear the chest hit the floor, and it was enough to cause a lull in the firing of the troopers attempting to keep him pinned down. They were obviously surprised to see this enemy, whom they had probably heard so much about, an enemy who was allegedly well trained in the art of soldiering, had resorted to battling them with small pieces of furniture.

But that wasn't nearly as surprising as when the fragile chest exploded just as it hit the ground. The twin blasts rocked the upper floor, shattering a couple more of the windows that had already spiderwebbed from the automatic weapons' fire. Women began to scream again, but Bolan could tell they were screams of surprise and not pain. The firing had ceased. He risked another glance over the railing and saw the results of the devastation. Bodies were heaped together, piled on one another in the center of the floor, the clothing of a few smoldering from the heat of the blast. Other special-forces troops were nearby, sitting on the ground, some cradling useless weapons, injured limbs or both.

Bolan quickly advanced down the stairway, alert for danger. A few of Jikwan's soldiers had managed to fully escape the effects of the grenade. Two burst from a room and opened up on Bolan, but the Executioner was ready.

He leaped over the stair railing and landed behind the natural barrier created by the framed stairwell positioned as it was against one of the finished support stringers of the upper level.

The rounds passed harmlessly over his head, or slapped into the side of the stairs. Bolan rolled through his landing and came up in a new position that provided excellent cover while giving him an advantage over the two soldiers, who were still looking at where he'd been and not where he was. Bolan caught the first one with a shot through the head, while the second soldier took a 3-round burst through the head. The impact split open his skull and dowsed the people around him with blood and brain matter.

The other survivor charged the Executioner from behind, foolishly convinced he could overpower Bolan. The soldier caught him with a back kick to the midsection that knocked the wind from him, then finished the fight with a rock-hard uppercut that lifted the smaller man off his feet. He landed on his back and sighed once before going unconscious.

The Executioner quickly entered the main area and kicked weapons away from the reach of Jikwan's wounded. As he performed the task quickly and efficiently, the dignitaries and politicians watched him with frightened expressions. When he'd completed the task, Bolan looked into their faces and realized that nobody there really had the first clue what was going on. Sure, some of them supported the Scarlet Dragons and the Kung Lok, but they were apathetic observers, not murderers or professional soldiers in the direct employ of the Chinese triads. Killing them served no purpose.

Bolan checked to see that Jikwan, Shui and Nyenshi Fung hadn't moved, then his eyes scanned the room for the fourth target. He found him after a minute of searching; the guy was hiding behind one surviving Scarlet Dragon, who appeared unarmed. Bolan walked across the room to where the Dragon was trying to conceal Dim Mai. He cocked the two MP-5 Ks and put the twin muzzles inches from the Dragon's face.

"Him or you?" the Executioner asked.

The man didn't even have to think about it. He stepped aside and nodded for Bolan to do as he saw fit. The Executioner grabbed Mai by the back collar of his tuxedo jacket and hauled him across the room, dragging him through the injured and dead for everyone to see. He knew that disgracing the man was the worst thing he could have done. Once he'd put Mai with the other three, he turned to the crowd, staring at each of them as he scanned the variety of fearful expressions.

"My fight is not with you." He gestured toward Shui, Mai and Jikwan and added, "It's with these men. So get out of here."

Nobody moved.

Bolan shook his head and added, *"Now!"*

The people then started scrambling for the exit, wasting no time. Some of the men were in such a haste that they left their women trailing behind them. These were diplomats and high-society types, and they had probably never seen such death and destruction in their lives, other than on television or at the movies. And now, having seen the rewards that criminal activity could reap, they would probably find other pursuits. Bolan could only hope that they would anyway. Perhaps they would put their money to meaningful use, instead of wasting it on scum like Dim Mai.

Once the room was vacant, Bolan turned to the foursome. He pinned Jikwan with a hardened stare, but the general seemed unaffected.

He smiled, and said, "So, Belasko, we finally meet face-to-face. It has been a pleasure knowing you. We are much alike, you and I. I will regret not seeing you in the afterlife."

"We're nothing alike," Bolan said.

"Perhaps you are right," the general snarled, clawing for what Bolan assumed was a concealed weapon. The Executioner drew his Beretta in one fluid motion and shot Jikwan through the forehead. He then turned the weapon on Lau-Ming Shui. He could see the fear mixed with resentment in Shui's expression, but there was something else there. It was almost defiance, or perhaps simply resignation; it was obvious that Shui had accepted the fact he was going to die this day.

"It looks like you have won, Belasko," Shui said quietly.

"Nobody won, Shui," Bolan said. "There are a lot of people who have lost this past week. Lots of innocent people lost their lives in your dirty little war against my country."

Shui chuckled. "You see, American, this is exactly what proves such ignorance in your thinking. It was never about starting a war in your country. It was about taking something from it. I am an artist. I provide a service that is readily sought. All people, Americans or otherwise, seek to escape. They use vices such as sex and drugs as means of providing that escape. So you see, I am only meeting a need. Whether you like it or not, Belasko, that is the way of things. I provide a service, and there is nothing, *nothing*, you can do to stop that."

"Yes, there is," Bolan said, and he squeezed the trigger.

Shui died instantly, his body stiffening before his corpse landed on top of Jikwan's corpse.

Bolan then turned to Nyenshi Fung and said, "I promised to bring you out of here alive." He turned to Mai and added, "You, too. The Hong Kong police are quite interested in hearing all about your activities, Mai. I'm planning to make sure that none of your guns ever get into the hands of the Scarlet Dragons again. Especially those in my country."

Mai smiled with an expression that left Bolan feeling as if he were staring at only the shell of a man. It was that eerie kind of feeling that was left by looking at the almost permanent, sickly smile of a skeleton. Some had once referred to it as a death's-head smile.

"I'm afraid that will be quite impossible," Mai said. "You will not be able to take me alive, nor my wife. We are all going to die in less than two minutes."

"What are you talking about?"

"You see, the good General Jikwan was kind enough to make sure that even if you managed, through some miracle, to overpower our forces that you would not escape. His special forces wired this entire floor with heavy explosives, and I have already activated the timer." Mai looked at his watch and added, "You have less than ninety seconds."

Bolan slapped the link hookup on his belt and said, "We're hot, Eagle One. Bring it in now!"

The Executioner grabbed Nyenshi Fung and shoved her toward the stairwell, even as Mai began to laugh and taunt him with flippant comments. Fung was screaming for Bolan to save her husband, as well, but the Executioner wasn't listening. He knew that he couldn't waste the precious seconds afforded him by fighting with the man, but he also had to keep his deal with Bailun. So Bolan did the only thing he could. He used the Beretta to knock the arms dealer unconscious.

The Executioner hauled Mai over his shoulder, thankful the guy was small and light. He sprinted toward the stairs, yelling at Fung to keep ahead of him. She followed instructions, turning back to watch and insure that Bolan was right behind her. They reached the door, but it was locked, and Fung was beginning to beat on it and yell with panic.

When Bolan reached the door, he ordered her out of the way. After she was clear, Bolan kicked the safety bar of the door, warping the latch and nearly knocking the entire thing from its hinges. The door flew open and he nodded for Fung to go as he followed behind.

Bolan watched the chopper come down just as they reached the helipad. As usual, the Stony Man flier's timing was impeccable. Fung looked at Bolan uncertainly, but the Executioner shoved her roughly through the open door, tossed her husband's body on the floor, then leaped into the chopper. Grimaldi was watching the area behind him, and as soon as Bolan tossed him the thumbs-up, the pilot lifted away from the helipad.

The numbers ticked down in Bolan's head. They had escaped with only ten seconds to spare. The penthouse then erupted in a massive explosion, the concussion of which threatened to vibrate the rivets from the chopper. The Executioner wiped away the sweat from his forehead, leaving the cosmetics smeared on his face. He turned to insure that Fung was secure in a seat and Mai was still unconscious before donning the headset.

"You saved my bacon once more, Jack. Thanks."

"Any time, Sarge," Grimaldi replied. "Any time."

EPILOGUE

Brownsville, Texas

DEA Special Agent Lisa Rajero left her office and headed home for the day. It had been several weeks now since she'd heard from Mike Belasko, and it had put her in some weird melancholy state—almost a state of depression. At least, that's what the organization's psychologist had told her. But Rajero didn't buy any of that crap anyway. She just wanted to do her job the best she knew how on a professional level.

And a personal level? Well, she wanted to find comfort and security in the arms of Mike Belasko. Rajero turned the key in the back door of her home, and as she stepped inside, she immediately sensed something wasn't right. Rajero reached beneath her pantsuit jacket and produced a Glock 19. She scanned the darkness, and while she didn't see anything, she could sense a presence.

"I know someone's in here," she said. "You might as well show yourself."

Mack Bolan emerged from the shadows of the hallway. "Still as sharp as ever."

Rajero rushed forward and threw her arms around him. She kissed him forcefully but passionately on the lips. Bolan returned the kiss and then gently pushed her away and looked into those dark brown eyes. It was hard for him not to want to spend more time looking into those eyes. Yet, he knew it wasn't meant to be.

"You look good," he told her.

"Thanks," she said with a shrug. "I'm stuck on a desk until Hoffner's trial. Guess Metzger wants to keep me out of the field and in the office where it's safe, since I'm really the only witness against Hoffner. Still, he confessed everything."

Bolan nodded and then said, "Listen, I've come to tell you something, so let me say it, and then I have to go."

"Uh-oh," she replied quietly, stepping away from him as she holstered her pistol and looked the big guy in the eyes. "I don't think I'm going to like this."

"You're not. Look, Lisa, I can't be what you want me to be for you. Or anybody, for that matter. I lost somebody once...somebody that was important to me. Important to me like you want to be important. I won't go through that again. So I'm asking you to understand that what I do, I do because somebody has to. That's the hand destiny has dealt me, so I'll take it for better or worse. But that means if I'm going to do it, I have to do it with all of me. That's just the way it is. And unfortunately, that doesn't leave any room for something personal and intimate. I couldn't do that to you. I couldn't do that to any human being and still say I cared about them."

"So this is goodbye," she whispered, "isn't it?"

"Yes."

The tears rolled down her cheeks, but Rajero stood tall and proud. Bolan could see her anguish as she battled over whether or not to grab him and kiss him and never let go of him. But he knew that would have only made it harder for both of them. That was his signal that it was time to go.

"I'll never forget you, Mike," Rajero said before bringing her hand to her mouth.

"Nor I you," he replied.

And after kissing her on the forehead, Bolan left without looking back.

Live large, lady, the Executioner thought.

DEATH LANDS®

Bloodfire

*Available in December 2003
at your favorite retail outlet.*

Hearing a rumor that The Trader, his old teacher and friend, is still alive, Ryan and his warrior group struggle across the Texas desert to find the truth. But an enemy with a score to settle is in hot pursuit—and so is the elusive Trader. And so the stage is set for a showdown between mortal enemies, where the scales of revenge and death will be balanced with brutal finality.